THE VOICE OF MELODY

A NOVEL

THE VOICE OF MELODY

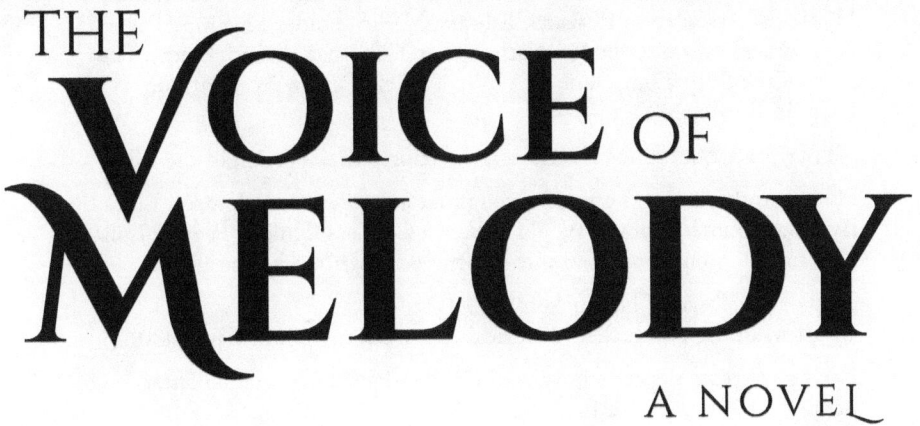

A NOVEL

KAYLENE POWELL

Raymond
Shop Press

Omaha, Nebraska

Quotations from original letter in Chapter 3:
From photocopy of original document (location unknown) in Nantucket Historical Association Research Library, MS 15, Folder 51, Ships' Papers: "Ship *Essex*," as transcribed in Nathaniel and Thomas Philbrick, eds., The Loss of the Ship *Essex*, Sunk by a Whale: First-Person Accounts, pp. 4–5, Penguin Books, 2000.

All Scripture quotations taken from the King James Version of the Bible.

Hymns and folk songs quoted throughout are now public domain. Lines by Byron are quoted from "I Would I Were a Careless Child." "Peggy's Lullaby," "Owen's Sea Song," and "Gardner's Poem" were written by the author.

Map of the Town of Nantucket, 1858
Courtesy of the Nantucket Historical Association, MS1000-rolled30

Early glass plate negative images of Captain Paddack's original letter, penned 15 February 1821
Courtesy of the Nantucket Historical Association, GPN3253

Inquiries can be directed to the publisher:
Raymond Shop Press
c/o Concierge Marketing Inc.
4822 South 133rd Street
Omaha, NE 68137
raymondshop@conciergemarketing.com

Library of Congress Control Number: 2018939436

Cataloging in Publication Data on file with Publisher.

Paperback ISBN: 978-1-7321633-1-7
Kindle ISBN: 978-1-7321633-2-4
EPUB ISBN: 978-1-7321633-3-1

Author photo by Pat Mingarelli.

Design and production by Concierge Marketing Inc.

Printed in the United States of America

10 9 8 7 6 5 4 3 2

for Jodi:
loyal daughter, sister, wife, and mother—
sheltered in the cleft of the Rock, you are
stronger than you know

and

for Becky
who believed in "Phebe Ann's story"
from the very beginning

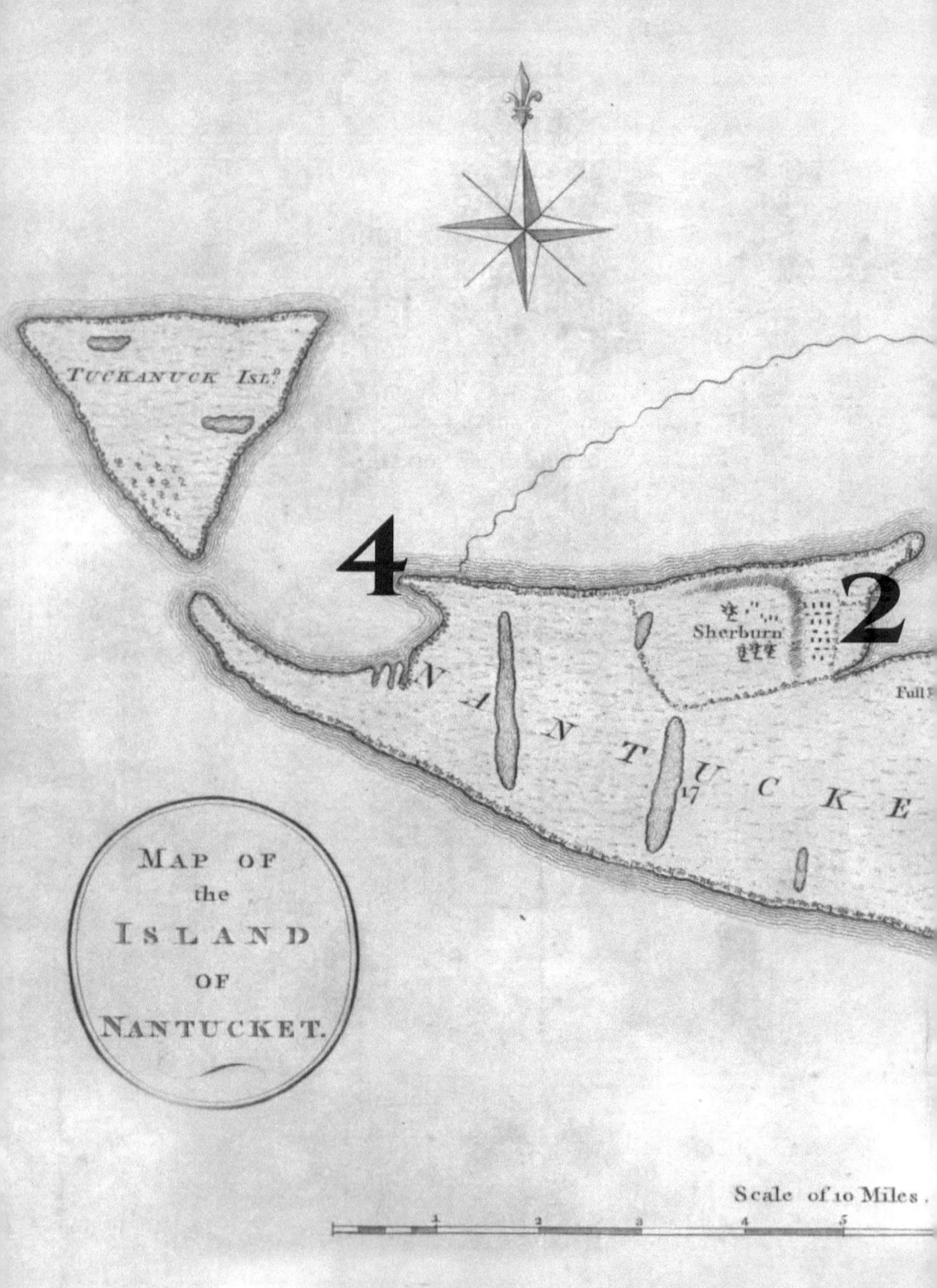

TUCKANUCK ISL.ᴰ

Sherburn

N A N T U C K E

17

Full

4

2

MAP OF
the
ISLAND
OF
NANTUCKET.

Scale of 10 Miles.

1   2   3   4   5

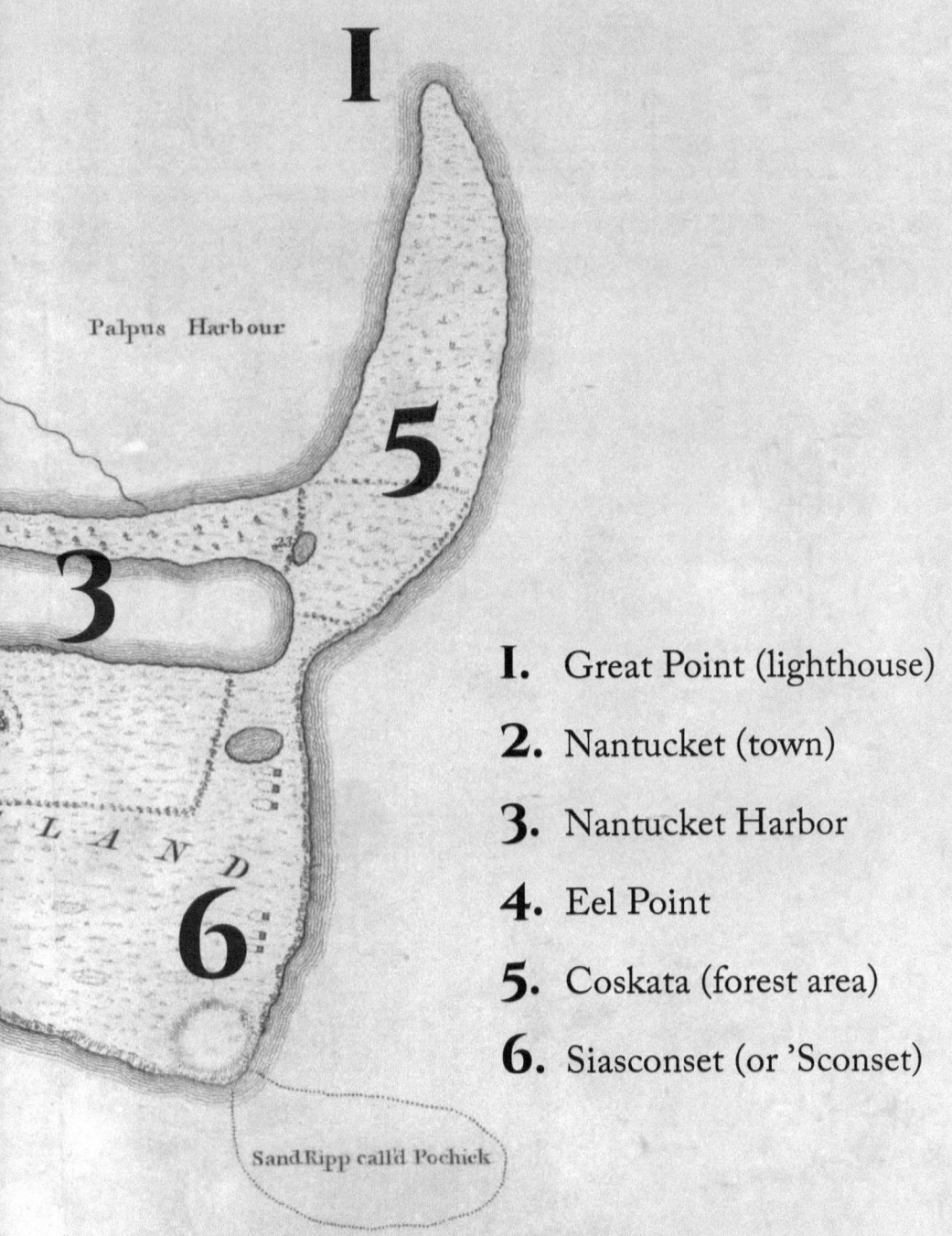

I
Palpus Harbour
5
23
3
L A N D
6
Sand Ripp call'd Pochick
10

1. Great Point (lighthouse)

2. Nantucket (town)

3. Nantucket Harbor

4. Eel Point

5. Coskata (forest area)

6. Siasconset (or 'Sconset)

PRELUDE

The men of Nantucket, a small island off the coast of Massachusetts, led the way in the hunt for whales. In a time before the discovery of petroleum, those men had the grit and determination to go after the largest animals in the world, bringing back products that would illuminate homes, streets, and businesses, lubricate the machines of the industrial revolution, and increase the potency of perfumes.

Facing highly depleted whale populations, however, sailors had to leave their families behind for increasingly longer periods. During the golden age of the industry, it was common for one voyage to last up to three years or more. While some crews did very well, a ship would often return home with a less-than-respectable haul in her hold.

Women and children carried on with daily tasks and held out hope that their men would come home alive and whole. Some men went on to have long and fulfilling careers at sea. Yet, many returned injured or ill—and some did not return at all. Drawing from historical figures and details, this tale illuminates the experience of one such family, the family of Captain Owen Chase.

PART 1
PEGGY

APRIL 16, 1820

"A woman knows the face of the man she loves as a sailor knows the open sea."

~ Honore de Balzac
French novelist, 1799–1850

CHAPTER
ONE

"Call her Phebe."

The words somehow find their way from my lips though this tongue seems thick as my winter quilts, still as the air in the room, heavy as the blood draining from my body. Yet, Martha hears and understands. I suspect 'tis all the years of her fulfilling such a primary vocation as this that makes her able to translate the whispers and croaks from the parched throats of exhausted laborers into sensible, meaningful language.

"A fine name that, Peggy. A Bible name and a family name," Martha says. In her sigh I hear she's as tired as I.

And why should she not be? She who has been here alternately prodding and comforting me these past fourteen hours or more, she who is old enough to be my grandmother, she who has delivered at least a third of the people recently born on the Island. Her now-aged hands once cleaned the birthing from my face, just as she has done the same for my tiny daughter this Fourth Month evening.

"Yes, to honor my mother-in-law." I gasp as I shift against the pillows while my body sharply protests the motion. When the wave of fresh pain recedes, a thought flashes through my mind. Perhaps it is a vision of who my daughter will be. I must speak further. "But I know she will be her own person. Her name should reflect that in some way."

"What's it to be, dear? A different spelling?" Martha bends her snow-crowned head near and settles the swaddled mite in the crook of my waiting arm. Then she turns to pull out her small notebook and pencil, awaiting my reply before she records details of this birthing day.

"No. A second name," I say with certainty when I behold the babe's searching eyes. "Ann. That is her own. Simple, small, and pure."

She speaks aloud as she writes. "Phebe Ann. I've entered it here, and I'll tell the record keeper when I can next go to report."

With great effort, I lift my eyes to glimpse the top of the high window above me—a sea of darkness broken only by starlight. The diminished blaze on the hearth provides an accurate measure of the hours lost to my labor. And Martha may well be called to another bedside this very night, needing to sleep tomorrow's day away. This is her life as a bringer of life.

I close my eyes and allow myself the bittersweet luxury of imagining him viewing a similar sky from the ship's deck. His strong neck muscles flex when his head falls back to observe the stars shining "like polished diamonds scattered across black silk." He's reaching back to rub that neck, taut and tired after covering the night's first watch. I recall the quiet delight of massaging his tension away and feeling the muscles begin to relax under my fingertips. And I wish I could reach out and do the same for him again, tonight.

But he is away, far out upon the sea, at a spot we must estimate given the last report posted in town. Word from their crew has been sparse these many months—only a dent in the years their voyage might stretch. I've had less time for writing with caring for our plot and preparing for this little one's arrival, and there's no way of yet knowing if my short missives have reached him. Even in those messages I have never mentioned my condition, afraid that our child would not arrive healthy and whole.

Now I open my eyes and gaze on her once more. She looks upward while her tiny lips move in silent, instinctive pleading. Martha also observes it. She helps move us further back upon the bed. Then, without my asking, she deftly demonstrates the easiest way to begin the feeding process.

Gratitude and embarrassment over my ignorance battle deep inside. My vision blurs. "I cannot pay you any amount great enough to reflect what your services—and your presence—have meant to me this long day," I whisper around a small sob. "Truly, I thank you." She long ago gave up plain speech outside the Meeting House, and so I address her without a thee or thy, though she is so many years my senior. In fact, the only times I have used those words since the day I married are when attending First Day gatherings or speaking to my parents. Owen and I decided from the start that we would not be bound by such conventions at home—though use of the numbered names for months and days has remained our habit.

She squeezes my shoulder and presses a worn handkerchief into my free hand before instructing me while I wipe my cheeks to the rhythm of my daughter's suckling. "I'm leaving the chamber pot here, at the foot of the bed, and I've moved the sleeping box you prepared a little closer. I'll add fuel to the fire to keep you warm through night's end. There's a cup of tea—you should drink it soon. I'll ask Patience Foster to bring Sadie out at first light. And I'll send word to your parents and your husband's family. They will certainly want to visit and assist you."

I listen and do not contradict her, but I wonder at her assumption, at how they will receive this news and what their responses will be. Bright lantern in hand to pierce through the thick mist, Martha shuts the wooden door of our humble house behind her. And before I fall asleep, I make a silent vow. When I am strong enough to put the words on paper, I will surely write again to tell of Phebe's safe arrival. My husband is a father, and he has every right to rejoice in it.

* * *

Shortly after dawn, I awaken to renewed pain. I grit my teeth and breathe deeply. The baby stirs and searches for her voice. Tilting my head, I observe her in the sleeping box Martha carefully placed on a small table beside the bed. I am so tired I can't recall tucking my little one in. At the sight of her pale cheeks, pink lips, and tiny grasping fingers, my heart skips and the pain recedes.

"You were worth it," I whisper in the cool, gray-lit room. "Every moment of pain. I'd experience it all again to have you here with me."

At the sound of my voice, she shifts to look vaguely in my direction.

My smile turns to a grimace when I sit up and arrange the pillows behind me before reaching out to lift her.

She lets out a noise that's something between a squawk and a melodic tone. When I laugh in delight, she does it again. I loosen my neckline and attempt to nurse her—a challenge without Martha's guiding hand. "Phebe Ann is a lovely name, and I've no regrets in choosing it. But you are sweetness sewn up in skin. I want to call you by another name, something dearer."

She finally latches on, and her eyelids flutter when she pauses to snatch a deep breath.

"To me you shall be Annie." Stroking her downy hair with my other hand, I test the sound of it. "Annie. I love you."

She pushes a hand up into the air and stretches her fingers wide before bringing them down to rest near her mouth.

"What's that? You love me too?" I smile before tears prick my eyes. "I will do everything in my power to protect you and make you feel cherished. With the help of Providence, I pledge it."

After a soft but persistent knocking, the door opens, and an aged voice rolls in. "Hello, Mizzus Chase. Miz Martha sent us." An elderly woman hobbles through the bedroom doorway, her knobby hand grasping an equally rough cane. Wisps of dark gray and white hair peek out of her red kerchief. And her weathered, wrinkled skin reminds me of walnut hulls. "I'm Patience Foster. I brung your helper out, her not knowing the way and being pretty new here."

"That's good of you, Mrs. Foster. I hope it wasn't a great burden for you to come all this way." I study her, sensing something familiar.

"No burden at all. My grandson, Victor, got a mule and cart. Waiting outside to take me back after I make introductions."

Watching her face, the memory floods my mind. My first recallable trip into town when I was seven. This woman being the first black person I'd ever encountered up close. My staring at her curiously. And her meeting my gaze, directly but kindly, before Father pulled me away.

Now I again glimpse her heart and soul in her beautiful, deep eyes.

She calls back over her shoulder, "Come on in, child." Then she turns back to me. "Her full name be Sadie Peterson."

A girl steps completely into the bedroom but presses her back to the wall and looks at the floor. On the cusp of womanhood, she is tall, willowy, and showing the first hint of curves. Her dark, flawless complexion looks like fine brown linen. Her eyes are evenly set and rich in tone like chestnut shells—from what

I can see of them. Her hair is woven in a series of short, thick braids. Emerging sunshine seeps through the window, casting her in a warm glow.

Immediately, I am drawn to that warmth. "I'm pleased to make your acquaintance, Sadie."

She stands still and silent.

"Go on," Patience says, setting a hand on Sadie's arm. "Like I told you."

She fidgets and then gives a small curtsy. "Pleased to meet you, Miz Peggy." The tone of her voice is like a mourning dove cooing as evening approaches.

"There now." Patience's mouth turns up. "I think everything gonna be fine."

Patience exchanges a few more words with me. When Sadie follows her out to the entryway, I hear Patience's low parting words. "Remember what I said. Things be different here, not like where you come from. Miz Martha says Miz Peggy be extra nice. I trust it, and you can trust it too. Be polite, but don't be afraid to speak your thoughts, or ask a question if need."

Sadie returns alone and resumes her earlier stance.

I search for a way to break the silence. "Your voice is lovely, Sadie. Where are you from?"

She moves to stoke the fire. "We come up from Kentucky. First to New York, arriving there a year ago. Then on over here 'bout six weeks ago. Daddy heard we'd find a better life." Her voice drops to a whisper. "People here—y'all talk funny."

I lift Annie to my shoulder. "I've heard we have a special way of speaking, but I've never thought it strange. I've spent my whole life here."

She spins around, and her gaze flies up. "You mean you never been off the Island? Not even to the Cape?" She bites her lip, drops her gaze again, and grips her skirt with both hands.

"Never. I'm an only child of a light-keeping couple, you see. That is a lonely and often isolated life, especially here. Last year, I married the son of a farmer who's been working his way up the ranks on whaling ships." I sigh. I've traded one type of lonely life for another. "He's a first mate at present, and until now he's had little money to his name."

She asks with some hesitation, "Which ship's he on?"

"The *Essex*. It departed eight months ago—"

"I know. My daddy's uncle's on that ship!" she cries before her eyes widen and she throws both hands over her mouth. She flinches and turns her face away.

My own eyes widen at her fear. "Really?" I lean toward her. "Tell me about him."

She simply drops her hands. And when I look closely, I notice her shaking.

How can I set her at ease? "Sadie," I coax in my kindest tone, "please don't be afraid. I am indeed happy for your company. You can speak freely with me." At her doubtful glance, I whisper, "Truly you can."

Though she still trembles and her voice drops so low I can barely make out her words, at least she finally answers me. "Name's Richard Peterson. He's a sailor from New York, though he had to come here this time to get a ship. It's his third voyage, and he told us it done gonna be his last. Says he getting too old for it. But he needed to do something to make money and provide for Auntie Grace."

She fidgets, her eyes trained on Annie. "Want me to help you?" she offers a bit louder.

I nod and thank her. "You said you went to New York. Did you spend time with your uncle there?"

She lifts Annie back over to the sleeping box, tucking her in with a tender, sure hand. "We stayed with them. They was so nice to us—Uncle Richard got a faith as big as the heavens. But my daddy said we was a burden to them, and we all felt like we was suffocating in that big city, so we had to move on."

"How many are in your family?"

Sadie moves to straighten the room for a few moments before answering me. Again the soft, low tone and the guarded expression. "My daddy, Solomon, and my two brothers. My twin brother, Joshua, and me—we twelve. And Isaiah—he six. We live in the place y'all call 'New Guinea.' But then, you surely know that."

"Martha said you were coming, but she didn't say…"

She stills and bows her head. Now it's her voice that shakes. "That I be black? She told me not to worry. Said it wouldn't matter to you."

"She was right," I say without hesitation. "I've had few opportunities to meet black people in the past. But I should like to know you better."

"Really?" Her eyebrows lift, but she still won't look at me fully.

"Yes. Why?"

She starts to dust the shelves and furniture with a nearby cloth. "Well, we heard we could find a good life here with freedom and acceptance 'cause of what those 'Friends' believe. But it ain't always so. You," she eyes me sharply for a split second, "one of them?"

"Yes. I am. What do you mean that it's not always so? Have you been harmed by any Islanders since you arrived?"

She looks away over my head. "It ain't like that, thank the Lord. But we ain't exactly been embraced either."

"But Martha's accepted you."

"From what I can tell, Miz Martha's loved by most everybody. And them that don't love her, well she be too old to worry about making them happy anyway!" Again she clamps a hand over her mouth and turns her head to the side.

I smile. "Why, yes. I think you've observed correctly."

She resumes dusting with increased vigor. "Mama said I got to learn when to say what I'm thinking and when to be silent," she mutters.

I laugh. She jumps at the sound so I pause before speaking. "You are forthright, to be sure. But I think it's refreshing, delightful."

"And I think you one of the most beautiful ladies I seen since we come here. I mean, I hope you don't mind if I keep on speaking plainly?" Her wide eyes plead for a moment and then seek the floor.

My reply flows, light and warm. "Be yourself with me."

She continues to look away while her voice drops again. "The ladies I saw in Kentucky and some of them in New York got all fancy with curling rods and painting their faces. But when my mistress went to bed at night, her washed face looked so pale. Like when we helped clean off them cosmetics, we washed the life away. The ladies here be different and plain." A note of awe seeps in. "But you be beautiful with your corn-silk hair and them eyes like spring grass. A light inside glows from your face."

I smile, flattered by her words. "And I was thinking the same of you when you walked in."

She gasps and twists the cloth. "You ain't just being nice?"

"I mean it. I think your parents must be very proud to have such a beautiful daughter."

Annie has started to fuss, and Sadie steps over to lift her across to the bed and change her diaper. I watch her movements and make silent mental notes concerning her efficient method. "Mama used to say beauty's a curse sometimes. That's one of the reasons Daddy wanted to take us north. To get Mama and me away from the master."

I hear the wobble in her voice. My heart cinches with dread. "But you're so young—were even younger then. Surely no decent man would think of…" I grip the quilt and hold my breath.

She lifts a hand from her pinning and swipes at her cheeks.

"Sadie?" Heartache echoes in my whisper.

Her reply finally comes. Flat. "Master did a whole lot more than think. With Mama and others. Then with me." Her hands ball to fists and press down in the blankets on either side of Annie. She grinds out between clinched teeth, "Ain't nothing decent about all that."

I shiver and let out a ragged breath of my own. "I'm indeed sorry that you were owned by such a man. No person should suffer like that."

She seems to gain control of her emotions and lifts Annie, rocking her while looking up at the window.

I must change the subject for both our sakes. "You're good with her. Is that why Martha is training you?"

She sits in the rocking chair by the fire. "I don't know much about birthing babies, but I do know lots about caring for them. Miz Martha says that be a good place to start. A few days after we got here, our neighbor was having a terrible time with her labor. And somebody ran and found Miz Martha. I stayed and helped her. Later she said I'd be good for training. To give us a new midwife after somebody named Esther passed on last summer."

"In her wisdom, Martha sees much potential."

She stares at the low blaze. "I ain't had much schooling except a little readin' and writin' the mistress taught me. Rev'run Johnson says they want to build a Meeting House where the colored children can come and get lessons. But not for at least a couple more years. By that time, I think I'll be too old for schooling. So guess this is a way to help support my family."

"Here on the Island, we believe that women should be industrious and enterprising. It would be wonderful if you could provide your family with some income and provide your community with a midwife as well."

She glances in my general direction. "What can I help you with, ma'am? I can stay a few days, if Miz Martha don't send for me earlier."

"I can't tell you how much I appreciate it. I am a little hungry, and I long to feel clean. But drawing a bath is a great deal of work."

Finally, she looks me full in the face with a gaze both firm and earnest. "Miz Peggy, you best know that serving 'cause you wanna be a whole lot different than slaving 'cause you gotta." Annie has fallen asleep. Sadie lays her carefully back in her box. "She should rest for a good while now. Let's see to her mama."

* * *

Sadie heats water over the fire and then adds it to the upright tub, which she has situated near the hearth. "You good at readin' and writin'? I wish I could read better, but where I gonna go to learn? You one of the friendliest people I ever met. Do you think…" She takes a deep breath, her next words tumbling out. "If I help with your baby sometimes, could you give me lessons? I want, more than anything, to write a letter to Uncle Richard all by myself." Her voice fills with quiet wonder. "Don't you think he'd be surprised when he gets it on that ship clear around the world?"

"Yes, I think I could manage to help you. And it would be nice to have a hand with Annie from time to time. I'll need to finish spring planting soon, and there are many other things to take care of—oh dear! The cow hasn't been milked since early yesterday morning. And the chickens need to be fed."

"Don't fret. I'll go out and see to them and then make breakfast. Water be just right now. Let it soothe you."

I take my first shaky steps away from the bed as she sees herself out. Once covered by the warm water, my tense muscles immediately begin to loosen. Heavenly. At some point in my soaking and washing, I hear her come back in and start to work in the kitchen, singing a song about riding a chariot upon the clouds in a voice like melted wax.

My mouth waters as the aromas of hot oatmeal and fried eggs fill the air. I dry off and slip into a clean nightgown. My limbs are heavy and my steps shaky. I think of walking to the kitchen and sigh.

As if reading my mind, Sadie calls, "Get warm and comfy again. I'll bring the food to you."

I spread a fresh sheet over the mattress and crawl back under the quilts. Sadie carries in a shallow bowl and a cup of milk.

The dish warms my hands. "You must be hungry after all this hard work."

She takes a step back, "I gotta clean up. Then maybe I'll eat a bite. In the kitchen."

"I miss having someone to eat with." I fiddle with the spoon handle. "Everything will keep. Please. Won't you join me for a few minutes?"

Her discomfort clear, she finally gives a small nod. After she gathers another serving, she sets her cup on the side table and sits on the far corner of the bed, her profile to me.

I scoop up a spoonful. "This is wonderful, Sadie. You know how to cook as well?"

"Auntie Grace taught me. It's the fresh butter that gives them such good flavor. She said I's gotta be a good cook, now that I had three men to cook for all by myself."

"Your mother," I set down my dish and spoon. "If I may ask…"

Sadie swallows hard. The hand grasping her spoon stills. "Master sold Daddy years ago. Mama said the rest of us staying together so long be a true miracle. Turns out Daddy just sold a couple counties east. He got the chance to run and come back for us."

"He sounds like a good, brave man."

She stares at the edge of her dish. "Truly. But Mama said he be foolish too, cause a lone man running be real different than a man with a woman and children besides." She nods. "Our getting away be such a fearful time, with Master hunting us hard. Mama got sick, and all that runnin' took too much out of her. We buried her somewhere in Maryland, I think."

"That must have been terribly hard for your family."

"Nearly broke Daddy's heart, he loved her so much. At first, I think he just kept going for us." Her voice takes on a peaceful note. "He be better now. But we all miss her."

"Mothers are very important. They nurture and love us and train us in the right way to go. At least, those are the things they're meant to do." I look over at Annie who still sleeps deeply, and my heart squeezes.

Sadie starts to nibble at her food again. "Your mama coming, ma'am?"

"Martha sent word to her, but I don't expect her before tomorrow. They live out east and then a little north, toward Great Point, and she sometimes helps my father keep the light at night."

"Don't you worry about a thing. I'll care for you and the babe till then."

Pleasantly full and completely weary, I slip into a deep, contented slumber to the sound of dishes being cleaned.

Through the rest of the day and evening, Sadie cooks and helps to care for Annie. I sleep in stages, getting the extra rest while I can. Sometime in the night, between Annie's pleas for milk and dry diapers, I open my eyes to see Sadie curled up on the far side of the bed. She has apparently collapsed there. Now I see the tiredness clearly written across her face.

I ease forward and pull one of the quilts on my side to cover her. Then, I let my fingertips brush the tops of her thick braids. *Thank Thee for sending Sadie to us. Fill me with extra Light to bless her. Give her rest, and help her to know she can trust me.*

I lie back against my pillow and focus on the dim glow of the fire. In that moment, my heart overflows with love for the baby to my right—and for the girl on my left.

* * *

By the next morning, I am strong enough to get up and care for Annie myself.

"You supposed to be resting," Sadie murmurs when she brings in the milk pail.

"You shouldn't have to do everything. And I'll be here alone again before long," I offer quietly. I can't afford to be spoiled and grow lazy.

A little before noon, a knock sounds at the door. "Hello," Mother's low, even voice calls.

Blessedly, Sadie is out in back, hanging the laundry she's washed.

Mother deposits a basket at the foot of the bed and draws near to kiss me fleetingly on the forehead. "Martha sent a man out from town to inform us. And young Caleb Cushman is staying with thy father in case I can't make it back by nightfall."

She has already shifted her attention to Annie who is awake and actively reaching for the ceiling. "Hello," Mother sighs as she pats Annie's belly. "A daughter?"

"Yes. I've named her Phebe Ann. The labor was very difficult, yet she is healthy."

"But quite small. Like thou wert. Has she cried much? Is her breathing strong?"

"She has a surprisingly robust cry. Though small in form, I believe she will have a powerful voice."

Mother frowns. "Then thou will have a challenging job— raising her to control it."

"Of course, Mother." I stare down at the quilt. "I'm glad thee could come to meet her."

"It's a great duty to be a good mother. And a good grandmother. I will certainly do what I can to assist thee, though thy father does need my help more and more with each passing year. How hast thou gotten along on thine own?"

"I haven't been by myself—except for a few hours." I swallow, striving to keep my tone bright. "Martha sent someone to keep us company for a few days. A wonderful young woman. She's hanging the wash to dry now. I'm sure she'll be in soon."

"Well, that was very good of Martha."

"She took the greatest care of me."

Mother nods. "She's always done her job well."

"How is Father? Is his rheumatism worse, then?"

"A little worse than when thou left us. He's suffered a great deal because of the recent rains."

"Please tell him I'm sorry to hear it. And that I'll pray for his increased strength."

"Thou well knows if thou had accepted Ephraim's suit and married him instead—"

"Mother, please—"

"—thou would now be snug in his house not quite so far from us. I could have attended thee during the birthing, and thou would have a husband who stays near thee when thou bears his child—"

"Mother—"

"—instead of an overly-ambitious young man who abandoned thee three and a half months after he wed thee to go to the ends of the earth, leaving thee to fend for thyself and his child in this tiny house outside of town, apart from close neighbors."

"Thou must recall he didn't know about the baby."

Mother lifts an eyebrow. "I doubt he would have stayed if he had known. If only he had followed in his father's footsteps. Farming is not the most profitable vocation, especially here, but it is honest work. It roots one to the earth."

The years have hardened the core of her, as a rod of iron. So I am not surprised that she now pours out all the mounting grievances she has certainly been holding inside for the past year. Nor am I shocked that she delivers all those words with a stoicism that George Fox could have described in some prototype from his revered writings. Her expression barely changes, her volume never rises, and her tone remains oddly congenial. It is only through the words she chooses that I sense an undertow of bitterness which could pull anyone caught in it toward some abyss.

Phrases flood my mind: words to explain why I could never have married Ephraim, words to defend my husband's character, words to beg her for a shred of the tenderness and compassion she showed me as a young girl. "I have no regrets with the choices I've made." Only a deep longing for my husband's solid presence at this moment.

"Aye, but thou well may when he doesn't return for years—or he doesn't return at all and leaves this little one fatherless. I know it has become a way of life for so many of our people. I only hoped thee might be spared this fate."

As she speaks, Sadie steps silently into the doorway, her downturned eyes and clenched hands on the edge of the empty laundry basket testifying to how much she has heard.

Mother sees that my attention has shifted. She turns around and pulls back slightly, throwing an arm across Annie's basket and raising her other hand to her heart.

"Mother, this is Sadie Peterson, the young woman who's been assisting me. Martha wants to train her in the profession. Sadie, this is my mother, Judith Gardner."

"Mizzus Gardner." Sadie gives a slight curtsey.

Mother's words stumble forth. "I—thank thee—for thy service. To my daughter and granddaughter." The hints of a smile touch the corners of her mouth but there is only iciness in her eyes. "Thou must have worked hard. Perhaps—thou should stop. Rest for a moment."

Sadie seems reluctant to do so, but at my slight nod she moves to lean against the wall a modest distance from us. She hides her hands in the folds of her apron and stares at the bedpost. Mother asks her several stilted questions—an interrogation cloaked in polite phrases. Sadie keeps her responses soft and short while maintaining a guarded expression.

I marvel at my mother's earlier cutting words to me compared with her feigned interest in Sadie, and I choke down a laughter-filled sob. It's ironic that my mother has just berated me for marrying a man who's now a first mate—one who has been said to be a sure spitfire on board but who was generally full of kind words and loving caresses for me.

When Sadie goes to collect fresh water, Mother turns on me again. "Could Martha not have found someone else? Though it sounds like this girl can clean and cook well enough, it would be better if someone from thy Meeting were also here."

Better, she means, if there were someone here to protect Annie and me from any worldly evil a poor, uneducated black girl might bring into our lives. Then I recall my first conversation with Sadie and am struck by the truest challenges she faces here. Some folks will see past her skin tone. But how many will overlook her off-Island roots? Or her failure to join the Friends?

My desire to befriend—and now defend—her only increases. "Sadie has helped me a great deal, Mother, and she is very good with Annie. Martha was wise to send her."

"Take care," she says while running her hand over Annie's downy hair. "In the future, it is best if thee avoid her. Associating with her too closely will only carry thee away from the Light. She must stay where she belongs."

"And where is that?" I cannot help but ask, though it comes out in a whisper.

"With her people. They are different. Therefore, we should remain separate."

I turn my face toward the wall. Silence stands between us— the only form of protest to which she must listen.

And I bite my lip when I realize that the sight of Annie in my mother's arms presently could never set my heart at ease like the image of Sadie rocking her.

Over the course of the afternoon, pressure to cry builds up until it gives me quite a headache. Sadie steps outside to gather the dry laundry, and Mother goes along—to supervise her efforts, no doubt. I hold Annie close and trace my finger over her perfect, tiny features as my tears fall. My heart steps briefly into the past—eight years ago, months before a blaze devoured our home.

KAYLENE POWELL

My hands expressed my mind's creativity as my sewing needle, filled with the most brightly colored thread I could find, pulled forth bold stitches in fanciful designs all along the hem of my new skirt. All the while, my voice hummed out a beautiful song I heard coming from the North Church when we were in town a few months earlier. The humming turned to joyful singing where I could still remember snatches of the words.

'Tis Sovereign Mercy finds us Food
And we are clothed with Love:
While Grace stands pointing out the Road
That leads our Souls above.

I looked up to see Mother standing in the doorway, hair windswept-wild after making the journey out to the tower and back. Her eyes blazed like I'd never seen before when she took in my activities. The song died on my lips.

She stepped across the room and jerked the cloth from my hands. "What kind of daughter am I raising? Where hast thou learned such horrid traits? When did thou leave behind thy steadfast and quiet obedience to unleash these signs of rebellion?" When my tongue froze in my mouth at her malicious tone, my silence seemed to further kindle her anger. She smacked me hard—first across one cheek and then the other.

After that, I practiced imaginative stitching and the singing of hymns and my own made-up tunes while taking solitary walks on the beach or in the vibrant woods of Coskata. And at home I toed the perfectly-straight line she had measured for me.

She never hit me again.

It is a great relief when, shortly after returning inside, Mother declares she will leave us. "Though I hate to part from this sweet child," she says as she leans over to kiss Annie, "I would rest easier tonight knowing I am nearer to thy father should he need me. Just now, I looked up and saw Jonathan Marshall coming down the path in his calash. He's agreed to take me home and says we should be there by dark if we leave now."

I don my dressing gown and walk slowly to the entry as she climbs up to the seat of the rig. I call a greeting to Jonathan, a respectable fisherman who lives with his family to the south of my parents, closer to Siasconset. He replies with warm congratulations on a healthy delivery.

"Please tell Father that I'll bring Annie out to see him when I can."

"I will. Take good care of her and make sure she cries a little before picking her up. Don't spoil or coddle her." She turns her face forward, sitting with her head and back straight as a rod—just like her life. Jonathan nods to me and flicks the reins. They take off, fairly flying down the sandy road.

* * *

I give Sadie credit for not voicing the many questions she must have about my family's relationships directly after my mother departs. When she's seen to the animals, I've fed the baby, and we've had our supper, she sits in the rocker with Annie while I settle in the wing chair and do some mending by candlelight.

"Miz Peggy?"

"Hmmm?"

"How'd you meet your husband?"

I lift my head and close my eyes, summoning the vision of him as last I saw him: striding down to the wharf, looking back over his shoulder one final time to throw me a wave and a dashing, strengthening smile before turning away again and pressing on.

"Sorry if my asking ain't polite. Just wondering. If I's you, I'd sure feel lonesome." I hear the wistfulness in her voice and can't help but smile. I remember when I was a bit older than she, and I had the first tugging of romantic fancifulness upon my heartstrings.

"I'm glad you asked, actually. I miss Owen, but I think speaking of him and the past might help me to feel as if he were nearer."

"You sure be different than your mama," she whispers, her eyes fixed on the fire. She doesn't elaborate, but she doesn't need to.

"Yes, I suppose I am. But she's not the same as she used to be. Many things have happened to change how she deals with the challenges of life."

I sit in silence for a moment. Then, I begin to stitch once more while quietly pouring out my story. "I grew up at Great Point Light—that is, in a keeper's house near the tower. I received my education at home from my mother. When a fire destroyed our cottage eight years ago, we had to move further down the beach, south toward Siasconset, and my father had to walk seven miles each way to reach the tower, to tend the light. Local leaders promised us a new cottage eventually—a promise my parents are still waiting to see fulfilled.

"There were only a few neighbor children close to my age, and the boys went off to join whaling crews when they were fourteen. That left a handful of other eligible men in the area to court me when the time came. One of them was a fellow named Ephraim Merritt. He was ten years my senior, but my parents didn't seem to mind that. He occasionally took his small boat out for a catch but spent most of his time as a courier, running catches and supplies back and forth between town and the eastern end of the Island. He also helped the local men repair their boats and tools.

"He seemed nice enough, but when he began to court me a couple of years ago, I grew uncomfortable in his presence. His behavior turned forward and unseemly—that is, when my parents were not nearby. A couple of times, he brought me to town with him, and I noticed how he watched some of the younger ladies when he thought I wasn't looking.

"One morning, I walked down to Jonathan Marshall's house and came across Ephraim forcefully kissing Jonathan's daughter behind their shed. He was very embarrassed—at being caught. She blushed and ran away crying. He stumbled after me, saying it was nothing, that he loved me and wanted to marry me. To my horror, he followed me all the way home and directly asked my father—who had just come back from the Point—for his blessing upon our marriage.

"Later that day, my parents asked me if I would accept Ephraim's hand. I could see by the look on their faces that they fully expected me to. I don't know if they were unaware of his desires, or if they were simply so eager to keep me near that they would have me accept him anyway, with hope that he would change his ways once he was a married man.

"But I could not agree to it. I told them quietly, but firmly, that I would not accept him. I could tell that my mother was especially hurt and angry.

"Soon after that, my father started to take me with him when he made his monthly trips to town. Each time he would introduce me to the eligible son of a merchant or farmer he knew. He kept me clear of the wharves, not wanting me to draw the attention of any sailors. I didn't understand it then, but now I realize how much he, too, wanted me to marry a man who did not join in the whale hunt directly.

"It's strange in a way. There are many women in town who are proud to have their daughters marry an ambitious mate or captain. But my parents are land-rooted folk, and I think they wanted my family to remain land-rooted too.

"A year ago, on our first town-trip of the spring, my father left me to look at dress materials for my mother and me, saying he'd go to see to his business and be back for me in a couple of hours. I finished with my purchases well before he was to return, so I lingered outside to take in the view across the harbor. The sights and sounds of town were still quite fascinating to me—though the smells left *much* to be desired.

"As I was walking along, paying less attention to the path before me than I should, I suddenly collided with something solid—a man who had just stepped from a shop. My packages scattered, and I bent hastily to gather them. I felt so clumsy and tried to compose myself. But when I looked up to apologize, my head tipped back. He towered over me.

"His face was tanned and a bit wind-burnt but very handsome and framed with dark curly hair that matched his deep brown eyes. He was even more handsome when he smiled. It was not a calculating smile or a forced one, but comfortable and sure. I realized I was staring and quickly lowered my eyes and shut my mouth. That's when my gaze snagged on the chock-pin attached to his lapel. You see, it was a sign that he was already a boatsteerer, a very dangerous job which only the strongest and bravest do well.

"I stumbled through some rambling apology. Remaining completely at ease, he introduced himself as 'Owen Chase, arrived this morning on the *Essex* with a full load,' and he quipped some witty remark that made me smile and relax enough to state my own name calmly.

"He asked if we might sit nearby and talk awhile. We passed an hour discussing a variety of things. Though I'd had little experience speaking with men, I found him to be charming. Father walked up and was clearly surprised to discover us there, smiling like two old friends at some observation I'd made.

"The young men he'd introduced me to were fine, but none of them upon first acquaintance both put me at ease and lifted my heart the way Owen did. The Light was guiding me to him. My father could see that I appeared happy. I made introductions. Father seemed slightly chagrined by Owen's profession while Owen was genuinely respectful of my father's critical work.

"Owen wasted no time and said, 'George Gardner, thy daughter is a beautiful, affable woman. My ship next sails in Eighth Month. With thy permission, I'd like to know her better.' And my father asked, 'To what end?' To which Owen replied, 'To marry her, if she will have me. I've been wanting to take a wife.'

"My father turned to me, his eyes issuing a silent question. I nodded. And Owen was given permission to court me. He borrowed a calash and drove out to spend the better part of every day with me. After a week, I agreed to marry him. Then he spent about two weeks arranging this house and plot for us. At the end of the month, he brought me into town and we were married. And a little over three months later, he was out to sea again."

Silence descends upon the room.

I look up and over to see Annie sleeping soundly while tears drip from Sadie's chin onto the blanket. She stares off into space.

Finally, she comments low and simply. "Yes, ma'am. I'd *sure* feel lonesome."

The next two days with Sadie provide deep fellowship. Hour by hour, I regain physical strength and stamina. Between tending to chores and caring for Annie, we manage a couple of short reading lessons, and I help her compose a somewhat crudely-written but still perfectly legible letter to her Uncle Richard.

Day by day, I've watched her guard come down a little more. Deep inside I believe this can only be an answer to my late-night prayer.

Very early on the fifth morning, Sadie answers a knock to receive a young man, one who is quite like her in appearance.

"Joshua," I guess, stepping across the kitchen and offering a smile while silently giving thanks that I'm already up and fully dressed.

"Yes, ma'am." Like Sadie that first day, he stares downward when addressing me. "I come to get Sadie. Got a birthing back in town. Miz Martha be needing her."

"Well, I've certainly been blessed by her presence and assistance. Please thank your father for allowing her to take part in this important work."

Joshua sends Sadie a startled look.

Sadie smiles broadly. "I know what you thinking. She be the most truly kind white lady I ever met. And she gonna help me read and write better. Look here." She waves her handiwork as she gathers her belongings. "She helped me write this letter to Uncle Richard and told me how to mail it. You gonna take it to the post office for me if the house where we going ain't on the way?"

"Surely. We got to go, though. I told Daddy I'd be back at the mill real soon. Gonna have to work double time when I get there, as it is."

Clutching her bundle, Sadie softly kisses Annie's sleep-covered face. Then she looks at me fully and offers a shy smile.

My heart turns over at this small but precious gift. "Come back soon," I whisper while reaching out to touch her hand. "Annie and I will be here waiting for you, our friend."

* * *

Three days later, Judah Chase pulls his calash to a stop near the gate and steps slowly up to the open front door, knocking on the frame before he passes inside. He must stoop upon entering to keep from hitting his head—just like his son.

I've watched his entrance after securing Annie's diaper. At the sight of him, I simultaneously tense and hope. It's the first time he's made an effort to come here since Owen's departure. In all those months, I've only seen him and the other members of their family at some First Day Meetings. While his wife follows all plain speech conventions both in and outside the Meeting House, Judah and his children generally speak with me in the same way Owen would.

Before he left, Owen told me something of their family's history. Of his mother dying from a horrible fever when Owen was only nine. Of his oldest brother drowning a few months later and his older sister always feeling that loss most keenly. Of Judah marrying a proud and often unpredictable woman in the middle of it all—a woman who bore Owen's half-sister four years later, shortly before he went to sea for the first time. And of Judah's initial anger at Owen for abandoning farming for the ways of the sea, and how the tension between them only grew as Owen's example caused his four brothers—one older and three younger—to follow him. Even Alexander, the youngest, finally shipped out this past year—leaving Judah to tend his crops on his own, apart from those times when one of his sons might be home on leave.

Those things flash through my mind now as Judah and I gaze at each other, my expression speaking respect and compassion. I lift Annie into my arms and step around the bed to the entryway where he has stopped, nervously shifting his hat in his hands. *Make me an instrument of reconciliation.* I draw as near as I dare and turn so that he has a full view of Annie's face. Her arms jerk toward his still-handsome profile.

"Welcome, Judah. We are glad to see you. Meet your granddaughter."

"She's lovely," his deep voice declares. "What's her name?"

"Phebe Ann."

He keeps his eyes fixed on her and swallows. He tries to speak but fails and clears his throat twice. Finally, "You chose her name?" I see the love for his first wife flit across his eyes like a cloud sweeping over the moon.

"I did. Owen doesn't yet know about her. So I took the liberty of naming her. I very much hope you are pleased with my choice. I have no doubt that Owen will be."

Still he does not look at me, but his expression softens. "Yes," he sighs. "I am pleased. I know my Phebe would have loved to greet this child." Finally, his eyes meet mine again. "And her daughter-in-law. I wish you could have known her."

"And I."

He clears his throat again. "I came by to invite you to supper at our house. Will you come tomorrow? I can return to collect you. It's too far to walk, especially for someone so recently delivered of a child."

I choose my words carefully. "Thank you. It's kind of you. But is Ruth also extending the invitation?" Judah's second wife tends to treat me like I'm invisible.

"She will—once I tell her about it." He winks at me and a corner of his mouth turns up—the first hint of humor he's ever displayed in my presence. Then, serious again, "I know Maria will be eager to meet her niece. And there's Joseph still home for a while yet. He and I will strive to make you feel as comfortable as we can. Please say you'll come."

When I pause, Annie gurgles a happy sound. I smile up at him. "We accept."

He bids me good day and runs a rough finger hesitantly over Annie's smooth arm before he turns to leave. While I watch him drive away, I find myself praying again. *I don't know what's to come for us in the days ahead. But please use this baby to help restore broken relationships. If not in both our families, then at least in his.*

CHAPTER
TWO

AUGUST 1820

When I was much younger, Mother often called Eighth Month the "heavenly month." It was the month in which I—her only surviving child—arrived. She told me once the birthing was incredibly long and arduous in the intense late-summer heat.

On this, my twenty-second birthday, we are wading through another heat wave. There is much weeding and picking to be done in the garden, so I decide to start early, before the air turns too thick for working. Checking to see that Annie is still safe and content lying on the quilt in the middle of the kitchen floor, I carry out the needed tools and baskets. I quickly return and scoop her up, kissing her before carrying her outside. The fresh air and muted sunshine will certainly do us both good.

She is strong enough to sit up now, with support, so I set her in a blanket-lined, sturdy rectangular basket. The basket fits between two rows of squash plants, near the edge of the corn stalks. I gaze down at her and observe her movements, marveling at how much she has grown these past months. Her hair, which was already dark and plentiful at birth, is now long enough to begin to curl—like his. Her mouth is like his too: lips from a sculptor's hand surrounding a smile which lights the entire face. And her darkening eyes remind me increasingly of his warm gaze. It seems the only traits she's inherited from me are slender fingers, a petite frame, and a dimple in her left cheek.

Annie looks up into my face, wobbles a bit, and works to regain her balance. Then she reaches out to vigorously pat the rag doll at her side. I turn to my work among the plants, humming a happy tune and smiling at her occasional squeal or grunt.

The better part of an hour passes with me working steadily all the while. One large basket is full of weeds, another is full of produce. My blouse is covered in sweat and my skirt in dirt. Through it all, she has sat and chattered and nudged at her doll. I turn to check on her more closely and laugh aloud at how adorable she appears with smudges of dirt on her nose and right cheek.

"I didn't mean to throw dirt at you. Let me take these weeds to the goats. Mama will be right back." I send her a reassuring smile and heft the basket before stepping over the tools.

Blessedly, a breeze has sprung up, and it brings the slightest measure of relief. I scatter the weeds about the edge of the pen where our goats can reach them while listening for any sound or cry from Annie. How silly of me—the breeze would drown such sounds before they reached my ears.

I rush back, the empty basket swinging against my hip in double time. I spot her sitting motionless with her face turned away, intently studying something to the side. It is certainly a bird hopping by. She's seemed fascinated by them every time she's seen one the past few days. I continue down the row toward her. "Let me store the tools and then I'll give you a bath—"

Stepping past the last cornstalk, my eyes seek that little bird—and my heart halts. A large dog stands near Annie's basket. It is familiar, belonging at the house two plots down the road. But today it looks different. Its eyes are glassy, its mouth drips with thick, excess liquid, and its legs jut at unusual angles. It stands still while growling low in its throat, staring at my baby.

"God," I breathe through tense lips. We are equal distance from Annie. He crouches down and growls deeper.

My heartbeats—perhaps half a dozen of them—slow and stretch outside time's bounds. Then instinct smashes down fear, and both my heart and mind slam back to the present.

The gun!

My body swings low. My hand grasps the handle of the tower pistol resting by the spade. I cock the hammer while taking aim at its chest. Another heartbeat pounds under the clap of fire. The beast crashes into the dirt inches from Annie's basket.

Through my baby's startled wailing and the echo and smoke from the shot, I toss aside the gun and lunge forward to collect her. I stare at the animal, clutch Annie to my chest, and back away down the row, ready to turn and run if need be. Though I see that it no longer seems to be a threat, I turn and run anyway.

Annie shrieks when I stumble in the clumpy soil. I manage to keep us upright and press her wet face to my shoulder while increasing my pace, her shaking mirroring my own.

I rush through the door, shutting and latching it behind us. I fall into our rocking chair haven and try desperately to catch my breath and calm us both. The steady motion works its magic, and after several minutes of shuddering, she breathes normally again though her eyes still release giant, shiny tears. With all the dirt involved, she is quite a messy, precious sight.

My chest constricts at the thought of what I accomplished and what might have been. I close my eyes and center myself, waiting for peace to flow to my limbs, for the Light to melt away the icy claws of fear.

"Well. And what about that bath," I whisper against her hair. "To wash away all those worries and cares?"

Her answering gaze is sober and wide.

I smile with more assurance than I feel. "It's all right now. I will go out again—when I can bear it—and clean things up. But first, I'll clean *you* up." I reach down to gently brush the most ticklish spot on her neck, and she tilts her head and giggles.

Her laughter serves to drive the dark away. I smile and tickle her again. The balm of her delight spreads over my soul.

I lay Annie down on her blanket and talk in a happy tone, keeping her at ease while I warm a bit of water and pour it in a basin. "When I next write to your papa, I must thank him for teaching me to shoot. When he insisted on teaching me, all my mother's early instruction tempted me to refuse his plan."

I set her in the basin and begin to wash her face, neck, and hair. "But he knew how crucial it might be and persuaded me. He is a good man. One day you will know him, when he comes back to us. And I will know him better."

Annie starts to chatter again. I lift her from the water and wrap her in a soft piece of flannel toweling. The water has chased away the dirt and the tear trails while my calm voice has chased away the trauma.

I thank Providence that He guided the bullet to its mark so that I might hold my sweet mite safe in my arms.

Once Annie has been fed and tucked in for an afternoon nap, I bolster my courage and head out under the blazing sun to clean up what's left. With my spade I prod the carcass to the edge of the garden where I set it ablaze and watch it burn. I use the sturdy basket as kindling, destroying it as well, to be safe.

KAYLENE POWELL

Through the haze of smoke and weighty stench, a man's form emerges near me. I jump and clutch at my heart. When his identity becomes clear, however, I relax for a moment before my stomach cinches again. "Abel Williams," I greet the dog's owner with trepidation.

His sober eyes scan the ground before returning to my face. "Mrs. Chase." He studies the fire again. "I've been in town since noon. Upon my return, Susanna told me she thought she'd heard gunfire from this direction a bit ago and insisted I come to check on you." His gaze and graying eyebrows lift.

"She was not mistaken." I force myself not to look away. "This fire is being fueled by your dog, sir. For I have shot it."

When he does not reply, more words tumble from my lips, explaining the circumstances with nervous choppiness. I end with, "Please, tell me what you ask as recompense. You have been deprived of a good guard dog and hunter, if I'm not mistaken."

His gaze remains steady. "You owe me nothing. Whether or not he was threatening a babe, his madness was a terrible thing—a thing to be stopped. You sparred me hardship of killing an animal I raised from a pup and knew like a friend." He scratches the back of his neck. "It is I who owe you something, ma'am, for the terror caused you and the child. Your husband would be troubled at the thought, I'm sure. I don't have much to offer, but perhaps you can come and collect some peat from my marshland when it suits you, should you ever have the need for extra fuel."

The wave of his kindness washes over my heart. I have been afraid to know him better after Owen learned that he has declared a denial of God's existence. Yet here he is, facing my act of murder with a gift of provision and mercy. I study his lined face and stooped shoulders, thinking how I might well believe the same if I had a spouse at home who was made an invalid by the same fire that claimed the lives of all our children.

I wipe away a tear. "Please thank Susanna for her thoughtfulness. And accept my sincerest gratitude for your understanding and your offer. It is very good of you, but I will simply accept the fact that you are not angry. Besides," I offer a small smile, "in this heat, I can barely tolerate a blaze on the hearth."

Humor touches his expression. "It won't stay so hot forever. Don't forget when the weather cools." He looks at the gun still laying in the dirt. "May I assist you in any other way?"

"No, I thank you." I send him a look harboring much more confidence than I feel until he finally nods, turns, and walks back down the way.

After scrubbing the spade, I lock it in the shed with the other tools and use fresh water and a lye cake to thoroughly clean my hands. Though my skin tingles, I want to make sure I don't carry any trace of the animal's madness into the house. I look down and worry that washing my hands may not be enough.

I stop just inside the house, setting down the empty pistol before I strip off my clothes and toss them on the front step for later destruction and shut the door again. I wash with care and put on a clean blouse and skirt, both of lighter cotton. The heat builds while I go about my housework, and Annie tosses in her sleep each time I check on her. I don't like the thought of any more threats, but I finally decide to open the door again.

I peer out cautiously. The coast is clear. I prop it open and sigh with a self-conscious shake of my head. Yet, I can't avoid the nagging sensation that all is not right.

After scanning the yard, I step around the bed and open the lid of his wooden chest. I take out extra munitions and clean and reload the pistol before I set it under a towel on the kitchen table. Now the open door leaves me feeling a little less exposed.

* * *

Annie wakes a little while later, and I sing to her while she lies on her blanket and I sew. Along early evening, fading light leads me to set the work aside. I carry her once more to the rocker by the kitchen table, turning it so I can watch for any trouble while allowing the maximum amount of fresh air to blow in on us.

When she finishes nursing, I lift her away to close my blouse. I settle her drowsy form on my shoulder and feel the hair on my neck rise. I shiver and look up to see a man's form filling the doorway.

An off-Islander. It's clear by the cut of his clothes and his bearing. He looks like a green hand who's still not found a ship—and who's had something strong to drink while seeking one. As tall as my husband and nearly as broad, he looks down upon us with a gleam in his piercing blue eyes.

From the edge of my gaze, I can see Annie is still awake—and staring at him.

No words pass his lips, but his look communicates a message which rattles me. Until I remember the gun.

"Leave us, sir," I say with surprising firmness.

He sneers in reply.

While pressing Annie close, I use my other hand to whip off the towel and level the gun, aiming at his shoulder. *I know I'm not to kill, but surely Thou would forgive me for wounding to defend?* "I will not ask you again." My thumb moves to the hammer.

His dominating expression falters, his eyes widen, and his hands lift.

I force my hand to hold steady and refuse to break eye contact. After several seconds, he steps back from the doorway and turns to stagger away in the fading light. When he is several steps down the path, I set the gun down and step over to shut, latch, and bolt the door.

Annie has remained blessedly still, snuggled against me. I go back to the rocker and sit, swaying forward and back, absorbing the calmness of the house. Only the creaking of the floorboards and the sound of our breathing distract me from thoughts of the stranger lingering.

I continue to rock until long after she has fallen asleep. The air grows stuffy again, and I must peel her away from me when I finally abandon the chair. There will be no sleeping box for her tonight. I want her near me, to know she is safe. There will surely be little sleep for me tonight with this pressure building in my chest and behind my eyes.

When Annie is settled in the middle of our bed, I turn once more to his chest, lifting the lid to remove one of his old linen shirts. I undress and slip it on, swimming in the fabric. I lift a sleeve and inhale his scent.

I curl up on the mattress, close enough to touch Annie without smothering her. On the big bed in his large shirt, the events of the day sweep through my mind again, coming on high tide. And I am acutely aware of our vulnerability, of my singular smallness.

I bring the sleeves to my face once more, this time to stifle my sobs. *I'm tired of being brave. I miss your presence and strength. Providence has surely protected us today. But how I wish it had been your form filling the doorframe tonight, standing guard, watching over us. Please come home soon.*

Though I was so sure I would lie awake, I am too exhausted— for now—to keep any more threats from our door. Tears lead me to slumber deeply until Annie's hungry whimpers wake me shortly before dawn.

* * *

19th of the Eleventh Month, 1820

To my Dear Husband,

I write this to be sent out on the Cleveland, bound to depart two days hence. I wonder if you have received the other missives sent these past months. Your last letter was quickly memorized. I have stored it in your chest with the other two. I pull them out and hold them, reciting them aloud to Phebe Ann when I feel your absence most keenly.

She is growing healthy, vibrant. In many ways, she is the picture of you. Now she has begun to crawl. She is very vocal and can already say "mama" and "sea" and "bir-ee" (birds are her favorite creature among those she has seen). I am amazed at how observant she is. Two nights ago, she noticed your spare harpoon hanging above the door and seemed drawn to it. After I told her what it was called and how you had used it in your work, she pursed her little lips and puffed out: "Poon, poon, poon!" It made me laugh.

"Yes," I said, "That poon belongs to your Papa, God bless him." She turned to me and patted my mouth lightly with her hand and said, for the first time, "Papa." It made me cry.

I eagerly await the day when you will hold her for the first time. If I had any talent at drawing, I should sketch her likeness week by week, to show you how quickly she develops. But since I have none, I will continue to describe that development in words, whenever I have the chance to write again.

Rest assured, we are all well. Your father sent Joseph by with a crate of salt pork and a few other provisions to add to the larder. Joseph reports that they are fine—and that he has recently set his eye on a young lady named Winifred. He believes she will make him a suitable wife one day. She is too young yet, but he wants to marry her after returning from his next voyage. He has had a nice, long leave and will set sail next month. Your brother is a good man—almost as good as you—and I felt free to share his joy.

My parents are also faring tolerably. I hope to see them once more before winter temperatures make the trip unwise. Father's rheumatism has been worse recently, so Mother helps him to complete the more trying tasks on those hard days.

The cow, goats, chickens, and rabbits are healthy and providing us with milk, eggs, and meat. The garden gave a goodly harvest this autumn. I have plenty of vegetables preserved already, and I recently gathered the last of the pumpkins and parsnips.

I must close now and feed our daughter. Though the words have not been many, they are sent with all the love in my heart. May God bless you in body, mind, and soul. And may His Light guide you in your work—and then safely home.

Faithfully yours,
Peggy

The next day, I bundle Annie against the heavy chill and put on my woolen cloak and gloves before I lift her swaddled form and step outside, securing the door behind us. When we start down the path to town, her exposed eyes alternate between taking in the now-sepia landscape and my chin. I hum a calming song of the sea.

We stop first at the post office where I deposit my freshly written letter to join so many others bound for outgoing ships. Then we make our way to the Macy's store—the best place in town to read the latest postings from the *Farmer's Almanac* and the most recent news from vessels currently at sea. I glance down over the notes on the large slate board by the large stove before turning to leave.

I come upon Obed Macy conversing with another of the Friends from our meeting, Thomas Crowell, where they stand outside the door.

"What's it to be for the winter, then?" asks Thomas.

"According to both the *Almanac* and my most reliable Wampanoag sources, we're bound for a fierce and miserable time. Already thou can feel the nip in the air."

"Thou always knows, Obed Macy. Thou hasn't missed a major prediction these past twenty years."

"I'm simply happy to help our community."

Thomas turns back toward the store entrance. "I should purchase another portion of peat, then, and two extra bottles of lamp oil. Perhaps more tea and coffee as well."

"Thou shalt certainly be grateful for those investments, Thomas Crowell."

A sharp gust of wind hits Annie and me when I step away. I shiver despite my warm dress. The thought of such a cold winter to come makes me cringe. Our larder is fairly full, but our fuel store is not nearly full enough. I press my worries to the back of my mind.

We arrive at Gardner Coffin's store, the place where I prefer to purchase our goods whenever possible. Both Gardner and Mary look up from their work to acknowledge us. Their seven-year-old, named for his father, offers a shy smile from where he stands near the window. I feel a pinch in my heart when I look over to see where their daughter, a lovely woman near my own age who died last month after a dreadful illness, should be sitting among the cloth and notions. Though they aren't Friends, they are a dear family, and I feel a measure of peace in their presence.

Mary steps forward and takes Annie so I can lift the satchel from my shoulder and remove its contents.

"I finished the work you asked me to do on these shirts." I unfold them to show my completed stitches.

"Exquisitely done, dear! You certainly have a gift," she says.

"I…" I blush. "Thank you for the compliment."

Mary leans close and pats my hand. "And it must give you some distraction as the lonely evenings get longer," she whispers.

I release a breath and nod. It does help to remain busy, making the days pass a little faster.

"Well, then. How shall we pay her, my love?" she calls to Gardner at the opposite counter. "Same as last time?"

"I'd say that's fair. What's it to be, Peggy?"

I step near to list our most immediate needs. "Candles and another jar of oil. We're also low on flour, sugar, and oats." The younger Gardner helps his father, and soon they have my order prepared—the small bags of dry goods and candles packed in my satchel and the jar bound with a thick twine handle for easy transport.

KAYLENE POWELL

"Can you tell me," I ask Mary while I take Annie back into my arms, "if you'll be needing any extra assistance in the weeks ahead? I could use the distraction." And the income. I pick up the jar's handle with my free hand.

She nods. "Things have lightened a bit, but I have no doubt that business will pick up again. Check back in a week or two." She embraces us from the side before seeing us to the door. "Take care, my friend—and you too, little angel."

Annie answers for us with a muffled squeal cast over my shoulder.

What to do about the extra fuel? Owen left some money for us when he departed, but I've already used a portion of it and must certainly make the rest stretch another year at least, until he returns. I can't spend all of it on one winter's kindling. I drift, praying, down the shop-lined street.

Oh, Great Provider, please give us a way to stay warm—if this winter is to really be as terrible as Obed Macy says.

"Miz Peggy," I hear a familiar voice speak low behind me. I turn back to see Sadie's father, Solomon, stepping close as he dares, glancing about. Young Isaiah stands at his side.

I'm struck, once again, by the lighter shade of Isaiah's hair and the mesmerizing green tone of his eyes. But my heart can't dwell long on where those traits came from. Sadie has mentioned the wonder of Isaiah successfully escaping with them. And I've meditated on the wonder of how tenderly Solomon treats him.

"Hello, ma'am," Solomon says. "And how the babe doing this fine, cool day?" I turn Annie so that she can see them.

Isaiah makes a funny face, and she giggles with delight.

"Yes, your princess be her usual, dazzling self." Solomon's smile fades and a seriousness enters the ebony eyes looking off over my shoulder.

"Is something troubling you?" I coax.

"Work been mighty slow for me and Joshua. And we was wondering, you got anything need doing out at your place?" He rubs the back of his neck. "We'd work for food, goods, whatever you got to pay us with." A note of desperation seeps into his voice. "I hate to ask, ma'am, but we need to lay up some sort of store for the winter. Heard it gonna to be a bad one."

"Yes. If only I had something to offer you…" Then I remember my conversation with Abel Williams at summer's end. "Wait. A neighbor of ours has a larger plot, and he told me some months past that I was welcome to come and collect peat from his marshland. I could never manage to dig up what we need on my own before the ground freezes completely—not while keeping an eye on Annie. But perhaps you and Joshua could come out and gather it for us? I'd pay you with a third of what you harvest, as well as a hearty meal each working day."

"That be too generous, ma'am."

"You should be paid fairly, and you'll be doing Annie and me a tremendous service. We are very low on fuel," I confide.

His voice drops. "Our family would be much obliged to you." He squeezes Isaiah's shoulder while the boy looks up at him.

"Not at all. We all must stay warm and fed in the months to come."

"Yes, ma'am. Tomorrow bein' the Lord's Day, we'll come first thing day after."

I smile. "Wonderful. You are welcome to use any of our tools. And, thank you. You were an answer to my prayers, almost this very moment."

His eyes glow. "No need to thank me, Miz Peggy. We tasting the Lord's goodness."

I offer them both a farewell and turn toward home, walking on air and whispering thanks.

JANUARY 1821

Obed Macy was correct once again. By the end of First Month, I've already gone through nearly half of the peat Solomon and Joshua so efficiently collected for me. I have made two new shirts and a pair of trousers for my husband's future use and completed several more sewing orders to return when I can—which may be some time for all the snow we've been having. We have lost two chickens to the cold, but I'm doing my best to keep the other animals alive in the snug barn. Every time I go to collect water, I must use the old harpoon to break through a layer of ice.

But inside, Annie and I are warm and well. I make her corn mush, applesauce, and pumpkin custard. She eats heartily and plays with her doll, blocks, and scraps of cloth. I sing to her and read aloud from the Bible or one of the other few volumes on the bookshelf. The days are short and gray, and the nights are long and dark, but I find myself at ease. The more I read, the more I realize my husband is dear to me—but he was never meant to be God to me.

It's as Solomon Peterson said: we have tasted God's sweet mercy.

This evening, I ensconce Annie and myself in a double layer of quilts and rock near the blazing fire. She snuggles close and listens as I read those words from David, "'O taste and see that the Lord is good: blessed is the man that trusteth in Him.'" I continue to skim through the Psalter, even after she drops completely off to sleep. "'A father of the fatherless, and a judge of the widows, is God in His holy habitation. God setteth the solitary in families: He bringeth out those which are bound with chains: but the rebellious dwell in a dry land.'"

God is my sustainer and protector. He is my shepherd. With His light in me, I shall want for nothing. He is protecting my beloved. And He is teaching me to trust Him more.

I flip the pages again. My eyes fall on some lines Owen must have underlined, for this is his copy. "'If I take the wings of the morning, and dwell in the uttermost parts of the sea; even there shall thy hand lead me, and thy right hand shall hold me...'"

A bitter wind slams against the catslide. I set the book aside, lay Annie on the bed, and stoke the fire before curling up with her under a pile of blankets. I keep her close all through the night. And when I doze, I dream. The first time, I see us held securely by a giant hand where the mattress should be. The next time, I see Owen floating on the far side of the sea, steadily carried in the matching palm.

CHAPTER
THREE

MID-FEBRUARY 1821

Obed Macy has declared this winter the coldest in our history, or so I hear from a couple of Friends I meet while venturing to town's center for the first time since the middle of Twelfth Month.

The worst of the cold and snow seem to have passed, and we must only contend with rain. Over Annie's bundled shoulders and head, I see the long, muddy street stretched before me while the mud sucks at my boots and cakes the lower portions of my over- and underskirts.

I'd rather not come out and deal with all the messiness. But we are in great need of supplies, and I've waited long enough to return my most recent batch of stitchery. The same Friends informed me that shipments of mail and other supplies have *finally* come through to relieve our severe need and our hunger for news. I thank Providence, therefore, while simultaneously vowing to scrub my skirts and boots as soon as we return home, while the grime is still fresh.

I greet several other Friends when Annie and I enter the comparable warmth of the small post office. We wait in line, me bouncing her gently on my hip while hoping fervently for at least one letter after the months of silence, her teething on her small fist and watching those in line behind us. Finally, I reach the clerk's counter.

"Good day to you, Peggy," Elias Coffin says.

I nod and smile.

"And how is your little one?" he inquires. I've never had an unpleasant dealing with him. He treats every customer with undivided attention and absolute kindness.

"She's well and growing by the day." I briefly turn so he can see her face amid the wrappings. "Are there any letters for us? I heard that a large shipment arrived."

"Yes, very large! We've been working hard to sort the pieces. I think I *did* see something. Please wait while I look."

My heart jumps when I see him coming back a moment later with a single, battered envelope in his hand. My eyes remain fixed on it, spotting my name in Owen's distinctive handwriting. I relish the sight. *He's alive.*

I beam at Elias while thanking him warmly. I tuck the precious missive in my skirt pocket, shift Annie to my other side, and fairly jog out of the post office, setting off in the direction of the store.

* * *

"Ah, yes. These shirts are your best yet. Several customers have been asking for more of the same." Mary looks up, studies me, and sets a hand on my arm. "Something on your mind?"

In a low voice, I confide, "A letter."

Her eyes widen and light with merriment. "One you've already read or one you've yet to read?"

"We've come directly from the post. It's in my pocket. The first in months." I am shocked by the sudden wobble in my voice, the moisture in my eyes.

"Well, why are we standing here discussing business?" she laughs. "Step into the back room. Sit down and enjoy your letter, and I'll make you a cup of tea. We can continue discussing the orders when you've finished."

I offer my own small smile, feeling as though I've been awarded some great luxury. Then I protest, "But, Annie—"

"Is fine where she is," Mary finishes with calm assurance. We turn our gazes to take in Gardner sitting with Annie on the floor in a corner where he entertains her with his favorite wooden top. "He's taken a shine to her—and he's enjoying the excuse to step away from the tedious tasks his father gave him this afternoon. And to put off doing his school work."

"Well, then. I'm much indebted to you both." My smile widens.

Stepping behind the dividing curtain, I settle on a wooden chair near the window. By the foggy afternoon light, I read the words written on mist-wrinkled paper:

18th of the Tenth Month, 1820
Galapagos Islands

Peggy,

> *How have you fared? Are you in good health? Is all well on the plot? I've often recalled the memory of your face, the sound of your voice. And the taste of your cooking. We've collected for ourselves a good number of large tortoises here, and their plentiful meat will supplement our fare in a most welcome manner, reducing our number of banyan days. Months in the Pacific have left us with little fresh food. Though the steward does what he can with what he has, and we officers get the best of what's here, it's*

still a sorry offering compared to the delicious dishes you can prepare.

I've only received one letter from you, telling about your mother's illness and the torrential rains, with the birth of another goat besides. (I'm glad you could sell the goat. You did right to purchase extra feed for the cow and chickens with the income.) I wonder if you've sent any more letters. I've often longed for additional news from home.

We are pressing far to the west, as far as we dare go in the offshore grounds. We've heard from another ship's crew that the waters there are ripe for harvesting. And even as we've come along, we've already reaped a considerable number of barrels. I have hope, then, of returning to you sooner than we originally expected. If all goes well, perhaps by the summer. But I have prayed that it could be even earlier.

The Captain and I often disagree, but the Second Mate is a good and amenable man. Our green hands have all got their sea legs and are handling the ship as well as I'd expect from any on their early voyages. After another year, they'll be thoroughly broken in. One crewman, a black man named DeWitt, deserted us in South America, but the rest are hard-working and loyal, complaining but rarely.

Have no fear for me, I'm well. Yet—I always cherish your prayers.

Truly Yours,
Owen

His words blur when my happy tears overflow. Peace fills my heart. I close my eyes and sigh. He was safe and well when he wrote these words. Surely it is still so. Holding proof in my hands solidifies my belief. I sit for a few moments longer, sipping the tea Mary silently set on the table at my elbow and reveling in the joy of good news.

After composing myself and stowing the letter, I return to Mary's side and find everyone as I left them with two additional patrons in the aisles besides.

"All's well?" Mary inquires without looking up from the cloth she is cutting.

"Yes."

She lifts her head when I say no more. "From the look in your eyes, I'd say your heart is near to bursting. Leave the baby a short spell longer and take a quick stroll with me." We don our cloaks and step out to walk along the street. "Anything you'd care to tell me?"

The words pour out of me, a summary of the news and the echo of my heart's response. Mary has become like a second mother to me, or the older sister I never had. She is so kind and sensible that I feel as if I can share anything with her. "Thank you for listening," I sigh. We've walked all the way to the livery. "I'm sure we should be getting back."

We turn and find Joshua stepping near. "Pardon me, ma'am, but we was wondering if you got any news from the *Essex* these past weeks?"

"As a matter of fact," I smile, "I received a letter today." I address Mary. "Do you mind if I tell him about it? I won't be long."

"No, my dear. I'll walk on. You come when you've finished. Annie will be safe with us."

I touch her hand in appreciation before I turn back to Joshua. "The letter was written in the Pacific, in Tenth Month—that is, October."

"Any word from Uncle Richard, ma'am?"

"I'm sorry. It appears as if my husband has not yet received my other letters, so he does not know of our acquaintance and your desire for more specific news. But he did send a general update concerning the crew."

His face dims and then brightens again. "What'd he say?"

"It seems one deserted in South America—a black sailor, but not your uncle. And all the other crewmen are well and working together competently now. He said they were planning to explore the waters further out. If they are very successful there, they will be home sooner than first estimated."

"That's good. We praying for their safe and speedy return."

My reply catches on my lips when another face catches my eye. Walking toward us is one of my younger brothers-in-law, George. I've only interacted with him a handful of times since he was out to sea when I joined the Chase family and returned this past autumn with plans to depart again on the *Rachel* in early June.

Joshua looks over his shoulder in time to catch George's cool assessment of him. Joshua's gaze swings back to me, and he quickly bids me good day before he jogs away to share our news with his family.

"Hello," I lift a greeting and my eyes to take in George's sober expression. He is nearly as tall as Owen and also has curly hair—but there the resemblance ends. Owen told me once that he and Joseph took after their mother while George, William, Eliza, Susan, and Alexander all favor their father—something I've been able to confirm from recent observations.

"Peggy." He explores my face. Then his eyes slip over my body.

I glance away, searching for words to cover the sudden awkwardness. "I have received a letter from my husband. Please tell your father and Ruth when you see them. He is well, and they seem to be having a productive voyage."

"I will tell them, and I'm sure they'll be thankful to hear it." Something sharp lines his reply.

"And you are not?"

"He's always been the headstrong one, the *right* one... The lucky one." His voice lowers and he studies the ground. "I will not be ungrateful for his safety nor wish him harm. I would only, for once in my life, have a measure of his good fortune and his potential for success."

I am unsure of how to reply. Finally, feebly, "I do not think he would want to overshadow you. He told me once he believes you will one day be a great man in your own right."

"One day," he grunts with a hint of bitterness. "Am I not already a man? And with two long voyages under my belt by the age he only had one? Yes, I will be a great man, and it will be according to my own standard of greatness—not his."

I want to cower in the wake of his fierce expression, but I hold my back straight. "That you shall. If you'll excuse me, I must collect Annie and get home before dark."

He surprises me by clasping my arm, his expression now softening a bit when he asks, "How is she? Has she grown much since the autumn?"

"Yes, thank you. She has a strong constitution." I am alarmed that he has not removed his staying hand, and I tug my arm away. "My warm greetings to your family."

I know not if he will say more. I turn and make my way up the muddy street—feeling his bold gaze upon my back. My insides churn and tense. *I miss you. Come home soon.*

Mary has Annie bundled and ready by the time I return. She's also refilled my satchel with a dozen more shirts to finish. "Come back when you can. I'll have more work for you now that folks are getting out again."

"I'll do my best, but with Annie being more active now, it may take me two or three weeks to complete these."

"Certainly, sweetheart. But, even if you aren't finished with the orders, don't be a stranger. Besides attending weekly Meetings when the weather permits, you have so little companionship."

"I have Sadie's occasional visits and lessons. I have my daughter, my Bible, and the Light within me. And now I have proof that he is well. So I will be well."

She eyes me sharply.

"But I won't stay away too long," I concede with a grin.

She smiles in return before shooing us out the door.

* * *

The weeks pass more quickly than I expect while I care for Annie and complete more orders. Soon, the winter rains give way to warmer winds and signs of spring. Every First Day, we gather for fellowship among Friends, and nearly every Fourth Day, Sadie comes to help me with chores in exchange for more tutoring, delighting me with her steady progress.

The time for preparing and planting the garden also arrives. The intense labor of breaking the cold soil makes my back ache, yet I feel a great sense of satisfaction while planting the seeds. The turned earth stares back at me, but it will be full of green shoots before I know it.

The green shoot within my daughter also sprouts. Already, I see the battle within her, the wrestling against the world's propensities. Already, I see her listening to my instruction and learning how to be good. She is a sweet, mostly obedient mite.

Though still very small, she can stand on her own. Her hair now curls in short, wild ringlets which I can rarely tame.

On her birthday, I bake her a small cake and give her two dresses and a bonnet which I've lovingly made. I also present her with a new blanket: small, soft, and pink. She clutches it with delight and then falls asleep holding it while sucking on her first two fingers. It is a habit I'm trying to break, but tonight—the night when I quietly buck our traditions and celebrate her special day—I indulge her, leaving the fingers where they are.

While rocking her sleeping form, I sing her favorite song, a lullaby of my own creation.

Once there was the wave to take thee from my arms.
Once there was the wave to threaten thee with harm.
Once there was the wave to gather us in dreams.
Once there was the wave to bring thee home to me.
Look, here is the child, the babe held in my arms.
Dost thou see this child I'm sheltering from harm?
Hast thou met this child in dreams upon the sea?
Thou must meet thy child when thou comes home to me.

* * *

MAY 1, 1821

I knead dough on the kitchen table while Annie plays with her doll on the floor. Footsteps strike the front stoop, and a loud rap on the door makes me jump. I recognize Sadie's voice and rush to let her in.

She bursts past me and collapses in a chair, bending to catch her breath. "There's word being passed through town," she gasps. "Somebody done sent a letter with news about our ship, and they say that news's real important. I heard Mister Coffin's gonna read it for everybody soon. So I come to get you." She looks up, concern plain on her face.

I shake off sudden foreboding and fly into action. "It was thoughtful of you to run all the way out here and inform me." I secure my cloak and cover the bread dough. Sadie snuffs out the lamp as I wrap Annie in a sweater and light blanket to ward off the day's slight chill.

Picking her up, I agree that we must make haste. We alternately walk, jog, and run, passing the load of Annie between us, until we reach town's center and join a large crowd that's already formed.

A voice is calling out over the noise of the street. It is indeed Elias who has stepped out of the post office with some papers in hand. "Friends, Islanders: I have urgent and distressing news to share," he calls. All who are within earshot give him their full attention. Sadie and I, with Annie in my arms, press in as close as we can. At the look on his face, my mouth goes dry.

"It is news concerning the *Essex*, in a letter just arrived on a merchant fleet ship from New Bedford. A Captain Wood received a copy of the letter written by another officer, a Captain Paddack. It has indeed come to us with great speed, being written only about two weeks ago. I will read it to you now."

My breath hitches, and I catch Sadie's eye. Then I clutch the letter I have transferred from pocket to pocket ever since its arrival. I try to relax. I hold evidence of their well-being.

I look about the crowd and notice Mary Pollard, wife of the ship's captain. Her face has paled considerably. I also spot my brother-in-law on the far side. George watches me intently with an expression of concern. I glance away when Solomon and Joshua slip up to join us. A few people near me cast them distrustful looks, but I ignore them, returning my full attention to Elias.

He clears his throat. "'...On board the Ship Dauphin I heard the most distressing narrative, that ever came to my knowledge. Captain Coffin had that morning taken up a whale-boat, in which was Captain George Pollard and Charles Ramsdell, who are believed to be the only survivors of the crew of Ship *Essex* of Nantucket. That ship on the 20th November was in Latitude 40 miles South and Long. 120 degrees West of Greenwich, and while two boats were at a distance from the vessel at work on whales, the ship was attacked in a most deliberated manner by a large spermacetia whale which made two such violent onsets with his head that the whole bow was stoven and the ship sunk to the water's edge immediately.'" Elias must pause for a moment as a wave of disbelieving sounds rush from our lips. Who has ever heard of such a thing?

When we quiet down, he begins to read again, telling of how the crew was all saved along with a few supplies in the whaleboats and how they were tossed about at the mercy of the seas for a month before they came upon a spot called Ducies Island. We seem to breathe a collective sigh of relief, until he goes on to share how they could only stay for several days before they were forced to press on, though three of the crew—left unnamed by that writer—decided to remain on the island while the others set out again to take their chances upon the water.

"'On January 10th, Matthew P. Joy the second officer, died and his corpse was committed to the ocean. The 12th, the first officer's Boat was separated from the others at night.'" Air flees my lungs. "'The 14th the provisions of the second officer's boat was entirely expended. The 20th one of their crew—a black man—died & became food for the remainder.'" Many of us shudder audibly. "'21st the provisions being all gone in the Captain's Boat, they were glad to pertake of the wretched fare with the other crew. The 23rd another colored man died in the third boat and was disposed of in the same way. 27th another died in the same boat, and the 28th one died, also black, in the Captain's Boat and in the night following, the 3rd boat was separated from the other. The 6th of February, having entirely consumed the last morsel of sustenance, the Captain and three others that remained with him were reduced to the deplorable necessity of casting lots to see who would be sacrificed to prolong the existence of the others.'"

Once again he must stop. A tide of emotion swells in our chests and we groan, anguished at the thought of hearing more. His voice cracks when he continues to read. "'The lot fell to Owen Coffin, who with composure and resignation submitted to his fate. The 11th Brazillai Ray died being entirely exhausted. By his death the Captain and Ramsdell were kept alive till taken up as before stated.'"

Mary Pollard gives a strangled cry and swoons. All around me, people are gasping, crying, clinging to each other. I clutch Annie to me and try to cover her ears, to protect her from this thunderclap of shock which rocks my own soul and causes me to sway. Sadie grabs my elbow, and holds me upright. Solomon and Joshua hold onto each other, a terrible look on each of their faces.

Above the low din, the reading continues—something about the condition of the Captain and Ramsdell in their initial recovery and how they will sail back home on the *Eagle* to, God willing, reach us in June. I listen attentively, praying for some further word of Owen, Richard, or the others.

By the time Elias finishes reading and looks up at us bleakly, the only sounds to fill the silence are the collective, subdued sobs of nearly every man, woman, and child present. Elias folds the letter and wipes his cheeks.

I realize there is no more to read, to hear. That is all, and my hope is snuffed out.

I don't realize my face is wet until I begin to sob so hard I can barely breathe. I let out a low wail. Around me, others who have known *Essex* crew members do the same. Annie is silent and wide-eyed, unaccustomed to such an unusual display.

An arm encircles my waist. Mary is here beside us, helping to hold me up, her own eyes moist. "Dear friend," she says in a voice full of compassion, "won't you come and stay with us this night?"

I squeeze my eyes shut to cease the flow of tears, but I am only mildly successful. "I thank you for your kindness, but we must return home. I have fresh bread to bake and the cow needs milking. And Annie will want her pink blanket when we go to bed later—" Another sob rises. I whirl away to press through the slowly dispersing crowd. I hear Mary and Solomon speaking urgently behind me, but my desire to escape to the privacy of my own space propels me forward.

When Annie and I emerge from the crowd, Sadie comes alongside, matching my clipped pace. "I's going with you."

I can't bear to look at her. I stare straight ahead, barely seeing the street through my watery vision. "Go home! We don't want to be with anyone. Leave Annie and me in peace!" She stops dead in her tracks while I march on. She's never heard a cross word or a raised tone from me. I berate myself with each determined step I take. Grief is choking me—but certainly I am not the only one. And will my harshness now crush the trust that has grown between us?

Then, suddenly, she dashes around and plants herself in front of me. I have no choice but to stop and search her face.

Her eyes are red and puffy, and her chocolate-rose cheeks are shiny and slick.

The pieces of my freshly-broken heart melt into a puddle.

This time, she whispers it fiercely. "I said, I's going with you."

I nod my apology.

She nods her acceptance.

Overcome with mutual sorrow, we wrap our arms around Annie and each other and shuffle down the road.

Sadie stays with us through the evening and the long, dark night. I lie upon the bed, and she curls up on a blanket by the fire. I gaze toward the ceiling and the stars shining down through the high window and listen to her as she begins to sing softly, soulfully.

> *Never been to Heaven, but I been told the streets up there be made of gold,*
> *Keep your hand on the plow and ya hold right on.*
> *Got my hand on the gospel plow, I won't take nothin' for my journey now,*
> *Keep your hand on the plow and ya hold right on.*
> *Hold on, hold on, keep your hand on the plow and ya hold right on.*

Annie dreams while wrapped securely in a small quilt in her sleeping box, her pink blanket tucked to the side. And Sadie and I fill the darkness with our quiet weeping and fragmented prayers.

My heart claims that Owen must surely have stayed behind on that small island—that he is still there now, waiting. But my mind refuses to listen.

* * *

The next days blur between numbness and pain. Sadie leaves, but we are rarely alone. Mother arrives the next afternoon, insisting she will stay through the night—a thought that gives me little comfort.

"Thou may come and stay with us. We will care for thee again, and the child." Her tone is laced with ice and obligation.

I remember the pledge I made to Annie on the morning after her birth. "We will do very well as we are."

"Did I not tell thee this would happen?" She stares at Annie and frowns.

"Aye—" I bite my lip and dash from the room before fresh tears can spill forth.

Several Friends from the Meeting bring us food and sit with me or care for Annie while I work out my grief on the plot. Mary sends extra supplies and refuses any payment.

On First Day, I enter the Meeting House under the sorrow-tinged gazes of many. Two elders approach to suggest we have the funeral this week, even though there is no body to be laid in our small, plain cemetery. I refuse their offer, saying that I don't want to do anything until after Captain Pollard has returned and I hear the details of Owen's death from the captain's lips. They nod and step away.

I keep Annie with me this morning, feeling the acute need to have her close, and take a seat among the other ladies. When the period of silence begins, I close my eyes and listen for some message flowing from the Light in me. Yet, how can anything bright spring from such a dim shell of sadness? Annie sits quietly on my lap, clutching her doll.

An unfamiliar woman hands her young child over to a neighbor and stands from her nearby seat. We wait for her to speak. Her voice rings out—simple, clear, strong: "To what shall we liken the virgin daughter of Zion? Her breach is great like the sea. Who can heal her? Many hearts are grieving but they are not alone. God is carrying the hurting ones in His arms, and He will bring them through the parted sea to the far side, where they will find healing, peace, and rest." She sits and bows her head.

To the far side of the parted sea. Oh, God. The sea that swallowed their remains—his remains—is threatening to swallow me too. I cannot see through to the dry land on the far side. My vision is too weak, the darkness is too great. How will I go on with any joy in my heart? How will I provide fully for my daughter? How will I find that healing and peace?

I have cried enough tears to cover a hundred sorrows. I have no more to cry now. But my heart still squeezes with anguish, and there is a horrible ache deep in my throat.

Yet, in a sudden flash, I feel a sensation of warmth, like a pair of strong hands have settled a blanket around my shoulders on a frigid day. Then the hands press my shoulders and that warmth, like firelight, crowns my head. They are his hands on my shoulders. I can feel his spirit as if he were standing right behind me. And then I sense his spirit stepping away from me—while the presence of a strong, steady hand remains.

I realize they are God's hands. His hands are upon me, upon Annie. He is guiding us in the storm, and He will see us safely through it. We are not alone.

I open my eyes to find Annie watching me. She is smiling ever so slightly—enough to reveal a hint of her dimple. *Thank Thee for not leaving us alone.*

* * *

There are plenty of chores and tasks to keep me occupied while I await the *Eagle*'s arrival. A rare smile touches my lips when I witness Annie taking her first line of tripping steps. I declare her a big, strong girl and kneel to embrace her. I have paused often to hold her, especially in the evenings, to savor my remaining connection to Owen.

At the very end of Fifth Month, I bring Annie out into the garden and tend the tender young plants. She digs a small hole and plays in the dirt. I have not forgotten that day many months ago, when she was smaller and he was still alive and well, and I've again brought the loaded pistol out, tucking it in the edge of my work basket. On such a lovely, sunny day, it feels foolish to think anything malicious lurks near, but I've learned not to take my chances. I will do everything in my power to protect my daughter—and everything possible to keep her from being orphaned.

Thoughts of that pistol fill my mind when I hear a noise behind me and feel a human presence. Straining against the urge to jerk around, I smoothly twist my neck and peer askance over my shoulder.

Breath leaves me in a soft rush. It is only George.

He has come around the plot two or three times a week since we heard the news, usually to deliver some food or other supplies from Judah. I'd prefer if Joseph were here to bring the provisions. He is much easier to interact with.

George is another story. He always comes to the door to deliver the goods and then asks what he can do to help us, seeming to hope I'll ask him in for tea or supper. I think of some item he can repair—outside or in the barn or shed—or something heavy he can carry. Then I shut Annie and myself in the house while he goes about the given assignment.

Today, however, he has caught us out of doors. And he has come empty-handed.

"George." I nod a greeting while turning to face him more fully.

"Peggy." He nods in return.

Silence. He stares at me.

I bend down to collect Annie.

He smiles at her and caresses her cheek with his fingertips, wiping at some of the dirt now caked there. He keeps his hand and gaze on her while addressing me. "Annie will certainly grow to be as beautiful as her mother."

My eyes slip to the ground. I feel only discomfort at the compliment.

I sense his gaze shifting back to my face. "How will you provide for her now? How will you make it through the coming winter? Can you afford the mortgage on this plot? Will you be forced to take her out to the Point—or take drastic measures to earn a living?"

My face flushes, and my eyes widen.

"I mean no offense," he adds hastily. "I only come with an offer—one that might do us all good. Phebe Ann needs a father's protection and provision. You, too, need the name and support of a good husband, and I've reached the age to take my own wife."

"But how could you provide anything for us when you are to set sail again so soon?"

"That's why I've come today. You agree to marry me. Then I go to the owners of the *Rachel* and ask for a loan on my lay in advance, to leave behind with you. As first mate on this voyage, I'm already set to earn a substantial amount if we are successful. While it is unusual for such an amount to be given beforehand, when I explain the circumstances, I feel assured the owners will grant my request. From all accounts, they are the most generous owners on the Island, and Captain Macy's previous rate of success will only serve to help persuade them."

I cast him a doubtful glare. "Marry you now, a week before you sail?"

His smile returns. "Yes. Though the time would be short, certainly seven days—and nights—would give me sufficient time to provide you with some husbandly comfort."

Clutching Annie in my arms, I whisper, "You are presumptuous. We have been taught, 'Thou shalt not covet thy neighbor's wife.' Does that not also include a brother's wife?"

"Ah," he whispers, "but you are no longer my brother's wife."

"And you, *Brother*, do not know me. I have not fully mourned my husband, and I will not now find comfort in the arms of another. It is too soon!"

I back away and then turn to run, but draw up short when he calls, "Will you wait for me then? With any luck, this voyage will only last a year and a half, perhaps two."

Turning slightly to address him again, I keep my eyes downcast and declare, "Do not ask me for a promise. I cannot give you one. The loyalty of my heart belongs to my husband alone—even now if it is only to his memory." My tightening throat cuts off further speech.

"Then you are a foolish, stubborn woman!" he calls to my retreating form. I shut the door of the house to drive him away, but not before I hear his voice, now laced with more genuine concern and anguish, offer, "You know where I am staying. Please reconsider, and if you decide to accept me, send word immediately. Think of Phebe!"

I do think of Phebe—and how she is *Owen's* child.

I avoid town's center for the next few days, until Sadie informs me that they've finished outfitting the *Rachel* and will be loading the crew on the morrow. A hint of regret tugs on the strings of my tender heart, and I send a neighbor boy with a hastily-penned message, to be delivered to the Chase farm.

I cannot marry you. But I do not wish you any ill health or disaster. God will take care of me and Phebe Ann. Do not worry about us. May He also take care of you and bring your crew success.

When the boy stops by on his way back home, he brings no reply.

And I oddly feel like a game bird which has escaped a snare.

* * *

JUNE 11, 1821

A few days later, Solomon brings news that the *Eagle* has been cited off the coast and should dock by mid-afternoon. I feel a strange sense of calm at the news, a resignation that I will now see the captain with my own eyes and have some finality to my husband's story. I thank Solomon, and he goes on his way. Then I set to work bathing Annie and arranging her hair, dressing her in one of her birthday dresses. I also take time to clean my face, brush my hair, and change into my best clothes. If I should have the opportunity to address Captain Pollard today, I want us looking our most presentable.

An hour later, we press as close to the wharf as we can, given the substantial crowd which has gathered. Though we make some progress, we get stuck near the back and, short as I am, I can see very little beyond the top of the *Eagle* as it approaches and comes to a standstill. I strain to catch a glimpse of the captain or any other people on deck but can only make out a few familiar faces in the crowd near us. There's Mary Pollard in front of me, and off to my right is Judah, standing tall above the rest. He turns to speak to someone at his side. I assume it's Ruth.

Though the crowd is large, those gathered are incredibly quiet. Each of us strives to hold a stoic mask in place while we listen to the sounds of riggings being fastened and the gangway settling against the boardwalk. I set Annie down and take her hand firmly in my own.

A ripple of murmurs starts at the front of the crowd, lapping toward those of us in the back like the tide upon the beach. I catch fragments of words but cannot clearly make out what any one person is saying. The murmurs grow in volume, even as the captain's wife begins to cry and several other people in front of me look at each other in awe. What is happening?

Before I can attempt to press forward and gain answers, I glance to the right. Air rushes from my chest.

There, standing near his father, is Owen.

He's alive? Am I dreaming?

I pinch my arm. At the glorious pain, I gasp and cry out.

He turns and searches the faces in the crowd. So many are staring back at him, but he easily spots me. He moves away from Judah and presses through the throng until he stands before me. When he whispers my name, I sway. His hand shoots out to grab my arm and steady me. He looks down upon my face like one drinking sweet water after hours of working on a summer's day.

I stand frozen, trying but failing to speak.

"Mama," Annie whimpers at my side, squeezing my hand.

Owen hears and looks around me to catch his first glimpse of her. His eyes fly back to mine, and my tongue finally loosens. "You didn't receive my other letters? I wrote to tell you about her."

Shaking his head, he bends his large frame and carefully squats to her level. "What's her name?" he asks as his eyes scan her features.

"Phebe Ann. But I've taken to calling her Annie. I hope you don't mind."

"Annie," he whispers as he slowly lifts one of his large, rough hands toward her and extends his index finger.

"Annie," I say sweetly before I crouch down beside them. "This is your papa. Don't be afraid. He has come home." My voice catches on a sudden knot of emotion. *God in heaven be praised. He is home.*

Annie looks from his face to his hand and back again. Then, while still clinging to me, she reaches out her other hand and wraps it tentatively around his finger.

Moisture gathers in his wonder-filled eyes, and he bows his head to blink it away. We rise while Annie looks up, up, up at her father.

His gaze is focused back on me, however, and he cups my face, moving to kiss me. Having been schooled so long in the evils of publicly displayed affection, I dip my head and press my face against his palm, even as my body begins to recall his long-missed touch. I wrap my fingers around his wrist and sense the glorious reality of his pulse.

I feel his hand tense and lift my head to see Sadie and her family standing nearby.

Sadie presses closer to murmur, "We heard just now that original report was wrong. Is this Mister Owen?"

Owen sends me a puzzled look and drops his hand to rest on my shoulder.

I offer him a reassuring glance before turning to face them. "Yes," I say, unable to hold back my smile. "This is my husband. Owen, these are some dear friends who have been a great help to Annie and me while you were away. Solomon and his children: Joshua, Sadie, and Isaiah."

"A pleasure to know you," he says with a nod, the hand on my shoulder relaxing.

Solomon speaks quietly but urgently while meeting Owen's eyes once or twice. "We don't mean to disrupt your reunion, but we heard there was several of you come in on this boat. Is the sailor Richard Peterson among you? You see, sir, he's my uncle, and we been frightful worried 'bout him."

Owen looks down at his shoes, swallows hard, and then looks fully at Solomon again. Now his hand grips me harder, but it feels more like he's grasping for support.

"No, I'm sorry. He did not arrive with us today." His voice catches. "He is with God."

The four of them gape at him, and I watch Sadie's heart break again. *God, how can I fully embrace my joy when these friends are still hurting so deeply?*

Isaiah asks in a trembling voice, "You for sure and certain it's so, sir?"

Owen stares at him sorrowfully. "For sure and certain." His gaze lifts to meet Solomon's again. "I watched him pass with my own eyes. I promised him I would send a message to your aunt. And so I shall, if you'll tell me where to direct it. You have my word."

Huddling together and crying softly, their family turns and walks away.

And my husband shudders and turns those sad eyes to the sea.

CHAPTER
FOUR

The place we call home bears the name "far away place" in an ancient native tongue. When Owen turns his face and sets his gaze in the direction of the waves again, I see a touch of something nearly indescribable cloud his eyes. He feels for my hand, and when I place mine in his, he clings to it as if I were bound to pull away and abandon him. I gently squeeze palm to palm, and he turns back toward me once more. But now he looks past me, through me. His feet are standing on our Island, but his mind is not near me. It is *Nantucket*.

I tremble all the way down to my soul. Has Providence returned him to me as one on the brink of madness? We have seen it happen to many a good man. I cannot bear the thought that I should see it happen to mine.

Then, as if the Light is driving out some malicious spirit, I feel a sudden rush of breeze swirl over me, and he is seeing me. His eyes are clear once more, his gaze quietly sure—though still full of sorrow. And those fears of mine sit down in silence.

"Come, my son." Judah draws near, issuing a strained, broken invitation.

When he tries to speak further, Ruth interrupts him and voices the offer more surely. "Wilt thou come back to the farm with us to sup at our table once more? And thou can stay the night, even several days, as long as necessary. Eliza will be so happy to see thee. Maria can sleep with us, and thou can use her bed." Only here does she falter. Her eyes skitter to Annie and me, then away. Maria stands close to her mother's side and looks up at each adult in turn.

Annie, who has been quiet until this moment, senses my discomfort and begins to fuss. I lift her and press my check against her curls to hide my rising tide of emotions. I'm tired of feeling worthless in Ruth's eyes.

Ruth rushes awkwardly on. "We'll prepare plenty of hearty food, whatever thou should like. And thou must tell us all about the adventures on thy great journey and the lovely, distant places thou saw." She ends a bit too cheerily: "Maria would love to hear it. She is forever asking for the telling of a good story." Maria continues to gaze upward, a gleam of expectation creeping into her eyes.

There are a few beats of silence. I see in Judah's face this tactless issuance for what it is—the olive leaf I've been praying for. *But, God, must it come like this? My husband, the beloved one I was certain I'd lost, has come home to me. To Annie. Would he seek peace and comfort in their house out of a sense of obligation while I sit waiting for him and longing to comfort him in our tiny home?* I squeeze my eyes shut and stroke Annie's curls while holding my breath.

"I'm afraid, ma'am, that my story is not good, nor is it one for Maria's tender ears." Owen's voice is hushed, grave, tenderly dismissive. Then, his arm is around me. "I thank you for your consideration, Father. But home with my wife is the place I've been longing for these many trying months." I release my breath slowly and look up to find him focused astutely on me. "And now to know my own child." He reaches for her, and Annie settles readily into the crook of his arm. She leans her head against his chest, and they look at me with their matching eyes, thick as thieves, as if they've been well-acquainted forever.

My heart turns over.

He peers at Judah over Annie's head. "Perhaps when I'm more fully myself again, we might all join you for a meal?" Each man stands up in his own quiet pride, and they nod in turn, in silent agreement.

The olive branch has not been crushed.

My joy is complete.

Without another word, he gathers me closer to his side and turns me away, in the direction of our home. I can feel his thinner frame through the outer coat he wears, can feel the tremble of his hand. A weariness radiates from his body. I sense that he draws me close more for walking support than out of physical desire.

I mind it not.

We step through the watching crowd. I slip my arm around his waist and do all I can to help him walk straight and tall. Annie is content on his one side. I am equally content on the other.

* * *

After stopping twice for him to rest briefly, we finally reach home under a descending sun. I take Annie from him and set her on the floor with her wooden blocks. Then I help him ease into the wing chair.

"What's it to be, love?" I drape a small blanket over his legs. "A drink? A hot meal? A bath?"

"Yes," comes the whispered reply. His eyes are already closed.

I lean over to brush the hair back from his brow and press a soft kiss to his temple. I fetch a cup of fresh water and rouse him long enough to see that he drinks it. Then I set about my work in the kitchen though I must stop every so often to check on Annie—and to make sure that Owen is truly here.

By the time our meal of stew, biscuits, and cobbler is ready, Annie is chattering to herself in her carefree way, and the sweet noise lifts him from his nap. He stands stiffly and inhales. "It smells like paradise."

"Well, step out to wash your hands so you can dine with the angels."

We bow our heads to give thanks. Then he sets into the food like I've never seen him do before. Annie sits on my lap, taking the bits of bread and soft vegetables I offer. I watch him scrape his large bowl clean with the end of a third biscuit. Finally, he sits up straighter and looks back at me with silent gratitude. "Even better than I remembered."

My face warms with pleasure at the compliment. "I think next on our list was that hot bath. I took out your extra clothes while the stew was simmering. There's a clean sleeping shirt on the bed. I'll heat water and fill the tub if you'll watch Annie for me."

"Don't wear yourself out caring for me like I'm some kind of invalid," he protests. "Surely I can draw water for my own bath."

"Nonsense," I say lightly. Then, more soberly, "Allow me to show my gratitude to God by serving you, at least until you have regained more strength. Besides," my tone swings up once more, "this little one loves stories and songs, and she's heard enough of them from me. Now it's time she heard some from her papa."

I pass her to him and go on with the preparations, catching snatches of his monologue. Annie sits on his lap and watches his animated face with rapt attention while he tells her the old tale of Ichabod Paddock meeting the green-eyed, flaxen-haired mermaid in the belly of old Crook-Jaw.

At one point near the story's end, he catches my eye and whispers an aside before resuming the conclusion. "I didn't need to find such a beauty in the belly of a whale. There was already one waiting at home for me." I turn away, smiling and blushing furiously.

By the time the tub is full and ready, Annie has fallen asleep with her forehead pressed against his neck. He absently runs a hand over her back and hums a sad sailing ballad. I'd forgotten the rich timbre of his voice—how one can almost float in it.

I lift Annie's limp form and nod him in the direction of the steaming water. Once I have swaddled Annie and placed her in her sleeping box, giving him a moment of privacy to settle in the tub, I step back toward the fireplace and add a bit of fuel to ward off the evening's chill.

When I turn back to face him, I gasp.

The parts of his arms, shoulders, and upper chest not submerged are covered with old scabs and remnants of cuts and burns. His bones show in places where muscle once covered them more fully. Pain sweeps over his face, and I lower my eyes in consternation. I wait and breathe slowly while the faintness passes.

"Come."

I kneel beside the tub, at a loss for what to say or do, and focus on his chest. Finally, when he does not speak again, I reach out to carefully brush the wet cloth over a particularly angry-looking scar.

He inhales sharply.

I seek his face and freeze.

He keeps his eyes fixed on my hand and the water beneath it. "Pray, continue. These wounds need to heal and these scars need to fade."

He lifts a shaky hand to cover my smaller one. Together we bathe those places which have longed for much tender care. I lay a towel in his hand and stoke the blaze on the hearth.

"Make yourself dry, and I'll fetch some of Martha's comfrey salve. There's nothing like it for skin ailments."

When I return with the small crock, he waits on the bed's edge, his gaze on the fire. I gently apply the light brown cream to every needy spot I can find. The crock is too small or there are a great many application sites. I must ask Martha for more, next I see her.

I help him put on the shirt, and he sighs at the comfort of soft linen falling over his clean skin. I smile slightly. "I told you you would feel better after a bath."

He creeps under the bed covers and looks over at me while his head sinks back against his old down pillow. "Pray for me, beloved. I don't know that I'll ever truly feel better again."

My heart clenches at the line of emotions parading through his voice. "I have been praying since the day you left me," I whisper fiercely while gripping his hand, "and I will not cease it now that you've returned. Rest peacefully, love. You'll come 'round again, by the by."

As I finish speaking, he's already asleep.

* * *

In the middle of the night, I'm awakened by Annie's restlessness. I start to sit up, but a big hand presses me back against the mattress.

"Let me." He slowly rises and steps over to the sleeping box where she is now crying. He carries her to the wing chair, his deep, groggy voice soothing along the way. "What's the matter? A bad dream?"

She begins to calm. I watch their faint, joint outline where he sits back and covers them both with the blanket earlier draped over the arm. "I know all about those, Annie. Never fear, Papa is with you, and Mama is very near." She stills completely. Soon

I hear them both breathing evenly—her lighter and quicker and him with a rattle deep in his chest.

I must make him some thyme tea in the morning.

When I awaken at dawn, I pad silently across the room to find the two of them still lost in sleep, embracing one another.

I collect water and set the full kettle over the rekindled fire.

* * *

In the days which follow, a pattern forms. He takes a short walk around the plot and helps me by completing light tasks while he has energy. When the energy runs out, he settles in the wing chair, and Annie eagerly climbs into his arms for a story or a shared nap.

And I feed him—God knows how I feed him. Porridge, soup, vegetables, fruit, eggs, chicken, biscuits, pudding. At every meal, he eats so heartily. I can see it in his eyes, a fear of hunger, though he never speaks of it. I keep his faith afloat by preparing all I can. Yet I know the supplies in our larder are limited. I must go to town to get more. But where will I get the money to pay for them?

I hope Mary has some extra work for me. At least the garden is producing well again this year. The Almighty has shown us great mercy.

There are moments when I step from the house and walk about the plot to quiet my mind and breathe. My heart is so full of simple joys tinged with nagging fears, and deep inside there is a longing to stop being strong and brave so I can release the tears that have pressed within me since I looked up and saw his ghost materialize into a man there near the wharf.

But there's no time for that. There's another meal to prepare.

Another pattern forms—this one in the nights. Time after time, the crying comes. But it is not Annie's. It is his. Blessedly, she has slept through it every time. It's as if he took her nightmare into himself that first night and can't escape it now. Something perpetually haunts him. I know not what. He has yet to tell me any more specifics of his experience.

He cries out and grips his head in his hands. I wake up and turn to him, shaking him until he starts violently and gazes at me with recognition under the starlight raining through the high window. He pulls me against him and buries his face in my hair, crying further over that nameless pain. I hold him until he falls asleep again. Then I lie awake in the darkness and recall the long-missed embrace of a husband who needs more than emotional comforting.

Tonight, he again cries out. I awaken him. But instead of his typical response, he remains completely still.

"What is it?" I whisper into the silence.

I am aware, suddenly, of a tense energy. I reach out to lay my hand over his heart. He rolls onto his side. The glow of moonlight falls on his face.

"I'm hungry," he whispers. But from the look in his eyes, I know he's not wanting my stew. His lips touch my ear, and my heart thrums with a rhythm it has nearly forgotten.

Hours later, I stir under the first breath of dawn. I lift my head from his chest to gaze at his sleeping profile. There is a genuine smile resting lightly on his lips, and his face is full of peace for the first time since he's returned to us.

I move gently so as not to wake him, slipping from the bed and dropping to my knees beside it. I pour out my overflowing prayers of gratitude, using the covers to muffle my sobs and finding the release I have so desperately sought.

My faith and hope have outridden the storm and found a rock to stand upon.

CHAPTER
FIVE

MID-JULY 1821

"Do you know the younger William Coffin?"

"I don't believe so." I hand Owen a cup of cool water. After his walk back from town on this Seventh-Month day, he is clearly warm and weary. "Sit down and rest. Tell me about your trip."

He complies, and I return to my noodle making.

"I picked up the things you needed and delivered your work and message to Mary. She says she'll talk to you soon about several new orders. She sends you warm greetings."

I push a strand of hair from my face. "How are they?"

"Well, as far as I could see. They were doing a great deal of business today, so we didn't have much time to exchange news."

"I'm glad to hear it. I imagine the cold winter and limited supplies were hard on many merchant families, though I've never heard Mary complain. They are the best of people." I've already told him of how much kindness they showed Annie and me while he was at sea. "I hope we might have them here for tea sometime."

"A fine suggestion." His brow furrows. "I've been tempted to view some merchants as lesser men, but Gardner displays great strength and determined character. I have enjoyed our recent conversations."

"He shared the same thought with me when we saw each other last week. But what was that you asked me earlier? This William—he's not the son of *the* William Coffin?"

"The very one. That tells me how truly widespread his reputation is, if you are thoroughly familiar with it after growing up all the way out at the Point."

I smile at his wry tone.

"I walked over to the post office to see what recent shipping news had been delivered, and I ran into the younger William there. We knew each other as boys, you see—both attended the same school in our final three years and sometimes shared a bench."

I roll out the dough to uniform thinness. "They are devout Congregationalists, aren't they?"

"Yes. My teacher accepted both Friends and others. William turned out to be very clever with a great head for details and a natural talent for communicating. He's been away at Harvard College until quite recently, furthering his education in hopes of pursuing a medical career. But now he's got it in his head that he might make a fine writer."

I raise my head and brows in surprise.

"Indeed. I, too, was impressed when I renewed our acquaintance today and learned of his life these past few years. He returned about a week ago and plans to stay on-Island for now, gathering ideas for an initial manuscript."

I lift and separate the thin pieces of dough I've scored, transferring them to the drying rods propped across two chair backs in the corner. Somehow, I feel he has more to say, and I've found my silence is often better for allowing the thoughts to flow out of him.

He surprises me by getting up and moving to the bedroom. Has he misunderstood me? Then I hear him rummaging deep in his chest. He returns a moment later carrying a small cloth sack. Pulling the contents out, he spreads them on the clear end of the table. There are numerous sheets of battered-looking paper, each filled with unsteady writing, as well as a pencil that's been whittled down to little more than a nub. He stands staring down at the items with a slightly lost expression. I reach out and place my flour-covered hand in his larger one.

"Tell me."

"When we were in the whaleboats, after the ship was stove, I tried my best to keep a log on what little paper I had in my small chest. This is it. My record of our journey."

"Was the writing helpful for you?"

"Yes. It gave me something to do, kept my mind alive, gave me a sense of order."

"Then I thank Providence for it."

"Peggy, many have questions about what happened to us. I know there will be a hearing with the officials, but I want to answer the questions, to provide an account which anyone might read and explain our situation to the world. But I cannot do it by myself. You know I can write only tolerably well. My strength is of a physical nature, not an academic one."

My thoughts follow his. "You would seek William's help to record such an account in a more well-written fashion."

"Precisely. You have a very nice way with words, and I would happily seek your assistance. But you already have so much to do. And we have no connections among the publishing houses."

"You mean to publish it for a wide audience, then?"

He lowers his head and his voice. "I'm honestly not certain how well it would sell. But, yes. I hope to sell as many copies as possible."

"But you don't need to. You can rest your body and mind, can stay snug and safe here with us. You can let the memories which have brought you pain go down and remain buried in a watery grave. We will go on, we will get by—"

"That's exactly the point. You have simply been getting by, Peggy!" He grips my hand and then reaches to capture the other one to face me more fully. I sense no anger or censure in his reply, only frustration.

Again I pause and wait in silence. I allow his gaze to run over my face, and in his eyes I catch a glimpse of an emotion I've never seen him display. Helplessness.

"If I could do this, and successfully sell at least a modest number of copies, I would be leaving you and Annie with something, some means of support, when I sign on again. As it is, I have nothing to leave you with. And I will not beg my father for anything."

My chest tightens. "But my sewing work provides many basic necessities."

"Yes—but not all. I spoke with Gardner and Mary."

"I—" He cuts off my protest with a firm kiss. When he pulls away, he keeps my face cradled in his hands.

"Forgive my hastiness and hear me out. You are a woman born and bred on this Island. You are strong and intelligent and extremely industrious. These are things I love about you. But there are other things I love—things which make you different, special. You are not so forthright as many of our businesswomen. You are gentler in a good way. You are content with the constant, the simple. You see good and beauty in so many things. You *bring* beauty to so many things. Hearing you sing again these past days has been a balm for my pain. I'd forgotten how sweet and peaceful your voice is."

My heart drinks in his uncommonly direct affirmation, but my mind continues to object. "You are trying to distract me from the material point. Will my positive traits not help to provide for us? Is my work not enough then?"

"Not if I'm to be gone for another full voyage. I've watched you. You work fastidiously. Serving, doing, sacrificing so the plot will be maintained and Annie will be content—and now, also, so that I will be well. Since I've returned, I can see the toll it has taken on you. I want to spare you further strain. You did well managing the money I left with you the last time, but it could only go so far. You have respected me as a man and as your husband." He glances away and swallows. "Now, as a man and as your husband, understand why I want to do this. I hope to spare my own pride and show you my love by helping to provide for you and Annie until I bring home a larger lay."

I ponder this for a moment, staring away over his shoulder. "I will accept your idea and support you in the endeavor. If it gives you peace of mind to do it as a way of providing for us, so be it." Then, looking fully up at him, "But I love you. Most of all, I will support you in the hope that speaking of these things and laying out your account might do your soul some good."

"But—" This time my kiss silences him.

When I pull away, I continue. "I have felt something radiate from your being. Something unwell. I said earlier you should bury it all in the depths of the sea. But now I'm thinking if you give it wings, it may fly off upon the wide horizon, where it can be swallowed in Light and cease to hold your heart captive."

He lets out a chuckle-laced sigh. "What is it about your discerning spirit that leaves me feeling as exposed—and yet as safe—as Annie where she naps in the other room?"

"It's your knowledge, deep down, that I will never stop loving you nor will I abandon you, no matter what your tale may tell."

He inhales deeply and bends down to speak low near my ear. "Were Providence to give me a thousand gifts, you would be chief among them. One can never endeavor to earn a priceless gift. But I will daily, thankfully and humbly, receive it."

* * *

Owen and William meet in town at first, in the private room of an inn or the library of the Coffin home, to decipher the log and piece together all that happened. Owen always comes home in time for supper, before the mists roll in and finding the way back after twilight becomes perilous.

This evening he greets me with a tired but satisfied grin. Then he picks up Annie and swings her around in circles and alternating arcs. She giggles and squeals with delight. It has become their favorite activity, though the first time he tried it she was somewhat apprehensive. I am simply thankful that the ceilings in our rooms stand much higher than the doorways.

I smile at their antics and dish chicken and vegetables onto our plates. He sets Annie down gently in the highchair he built for her soon after his return. I spread out some food pieces on a smaller plate near her, and she greedily reaches out to grasp carrots in both hands.

"Not too much at once," I softly remind her, reaching out to keep her from gobbling two fistfuls simultaneously. "She's hungrier than I expected," I observe.

He steps around the table to take his seat. "Sorry I was later returning today. We wanted to finish going over some pivotal events. I lost track of time."

"Perfectly understandable. But I'm happy to have you home." I shoot him a look of quiet longing across the table before lowering my eyes to my food.

We eat in silence until I finally bring up what's been on my mind all day. "Are you paying William something to help with this task?"

"I offered, tried to insist on paying him up front, but he maintained that he would only take my thanks and this experience as his reward."

There is a pinch inside—the stinging of my pride. "That is very good of him. But I wonder, would he accept the hospitality of our table to show our joint gratitude? If he were willing to come out here, you could help me with the plot in the mornings and work with him through the afternoons. Then, he could sup with us before he needed to head back. It would be no trouble for me to prepare a bit extra. And think of the rest it could afford you while gaining back your strength."

"It's good of you to suggest it. I have felt badly about leaving you here all day when there's much to be done. And I am eager to be near you and Annie. But you could likewise be a distraction to me. And…" He casts his glance down then meets my eyes again. "I would spare you some of our conversational topics."

"I know our house is small, but I will gladly take some work outside or keep Annie in the other room for a time in order to provide you with space to think and speak unhindered." I hold his gaze. "Simply let me know your need if I do not perceive it. Having you away for many hours a day has chaffed at my heart."

"Very well. I'll ask William about it tomorrow morning. If I can persuade him, we'll return here in the afternoon. Either way, I'll be home for supper as usual. But I do hope, for our family's sake, that he will agree to your suggestion." He says the final words while searching my face, drinking me in from across the table.

When he continues his bold assessment, I feel a flush spread up my cheeks, and I start to busy myself with clearing the dishes.

"Come, Annie." I hear him get up from his chair and lift her from hers. When I turn back toward the table, I find him facing me, watching my every move. Annie clings to his neck and rests her cheek against his collar.

I smile faintly. "She does love her papa."

He presses her closer while continuing to study me. "The feeling is mutual."

The flush burns again, returning with greater speed. I turn away, stare down at the plates, and draw a breath at the depth of emotion gripping me.

I jump when I feel their presence directly behind me. He hovers close without touching me. "I'll bathe Annie and sing her to sleep."

"Thank you, love." I tremble slightly before I resume my cleaning.

* * *

Shortly after noon the next day, Owen comes up the path with another man at his side.

"You must be Peggy," our guest greets me in an amiable tone when the two of them enter the house. Of medium height with light brown hair and keen blue eyes, he looks like he'd never hurt another soul.

I return his smile and allow him to shake my hand. "And you must be William. I have heard the highest compliments of you this past week."

"It seems Owen may be excessive in his praise." He laughs before earnestly studying my face. "But not in every case. Each good word he used to describe you is true—and perhaps was even insufficient. He is truly blessed to have such a warm and beautiful wife."

I cannot keep from blushing. No man besides Owen has ever told me I was beautiful, though many have let their eyes linger on my face and form. Yet, I sense no leering in William's assessment.

William turns to Owen and good-naturedly pats his back. "Even her modesty becomes her. I did not think it was possible for her to be lovelier, but the pink bloom upon her cheeks makes her appear like a woodland fairy I once saw in a famous painting."

My eyes swing to Owen, and I find him watching me with a small smile. "Yes, and she is just as enchanting. She flits about, works her magic, brings life and wellness to all that she touches." His voice has tapered to nearly a whisper, and his smile disappears with it.

I cannot look away.

"I declare," William says softly, "if my Elizabeth and I develop half the fire between us the two of you have, we won't have to light a blaze upon our hearth for most of the year."

My blush deepens and even Owen's face reddens a little. But he still holds my gaze. His smile returns. "William and Elizabeth have recently announced their engagement. They will be married by autumn's end. Otherwise—" he finally looks away to send a half-hearted glare in William's direction, "I would never allow him to come around here and shower you with his charm."

I lift an eyebrow and quietly quip, "I'm so glad you deem him safe and acceptable company." Then I turn to William and offer a most genuine smile. "I know Owen is grateful for your assistance. You are most welcome in our home, at our table. And you are welcome to bring your Elizabeth too. I hope to meet her soon, and I wish you every imaginable happiness. May Providence bless you both."

He reaches out to clasp my hand again and warmly thanks me for all I've expressed. I glance over to see Owen's eyes yet upon me, his face filled with quiet pride and love.

Owen looks down and notices Annie playing in the corner. He calls her name. She jabbers at him when he steps over to pick her up. "And this is the other lady in my life. Annie, meet William. He is a good and trustworthy friend. William, this is Phebe Ann, our treasure."

"Hello." William offers a small wave.

Annie eyes him shyly from the side of her face not hidden against Owen's shirt.

"Is that a friendly greeting?" William asks with a grimace. "At least I didn't make her cry!"

"She cries but rarely," I assure him. "She is, all in all, a good and easy child. I believe she'll come around to like you before long."

The men sit at the table to work. I take Annie outside to stay near me while I care for the animals and weed the garden.

The afternoon passes quickly, and soon it is time to return to the kitchen to prepare our supper. I go about my business while Owen holds Annie and answers William's extensive questions. Owen seems to have slipped into another world and stares at the wall. William listens and takes notes with impressive speed.

Around the sounds of the scratching quill and my peeling and slicing, I hear snatches of the tale—a boy named Thomas warning Owen of a giant whale's approach, the terrible shock of watching the ship sink, the long days in the boat when Thomas and the other men asked him many questions—questions he often had no answers to.

When the shepherd's pie is ready, I gently interrupt and ask them to clear the table and wash. Annie watches me set the table with dishes, bread, butter, and applesauce. I place the pie in the center of the arrangement when the men return.

After tasting the food, William sighs. "Peggy, to your many virtues we should add 'outstanding cook.' I'll say it again. Your husband is a fortunate man. You must certainly be helping to put the meat back on his bones."

I set down my spoon and look across the table. He *has* started to fill out again, bit by bit, regaining some of his former strength. "Yes," I murmur.

Owen looks up from his own plate and stares back at me while William tucks into his food with relish, seemingly oblivious to us, and Annie mashes her peas with her fingers. My husband makes no noise, but his eyes speak words of pain and gratitude.

* * *

Our after-supper conversation is pleasant but brief. Owen warns William that he dare not linger on the way back and must reach the edge of town by twilight. He sees our guest off and milks the cow while I bathe Annie. When he returns, he takes her from me and sits down to tell her a story and rock her to sleep.

I move to the kitchen and wash the dishes. As I set the last clean plate on the shelf, he comes up behind me, wraps his arm around my waist, and presses his face against my hair. He kisses the top of my head and then bends toward my neck.

"Owen?"

"Hmmm?"

"It was good to have you home today."

"It was—good—to be home."

His free hand comes up to work the pins and combs from my hair. Since that night weeks ago, there's hardly been a night when he hasn't reached out to love me—sometimes in the early morning hours and sometimes just after Annie is sleeping soundly. Though he may give me a chaste kiss while she's awake and watching, he holds nothing back when her tender eyes are closed. And I am surprised at how readily I respond.

This evening, however, my heart carries the burden of a question I've long wanted to voice. When he turns me in his arms and caresses my cheek, with great effort, I ask it now. "Love, please tell me honestly—was it hard for you?"

He pulls back slightly and then presses his lips to my ear. "Was what hard for me?" His fingers return to my hair.

"Being away for so long with none of—this—between us." The words come out unevenly, and I blush. Mother would be appalled if she heard me speaking directly about such things.

He freezes. Then, his fingers guide my head back so that I'm looking up into his face. He closes his eyes for a moment before focusing on me intently again. "Yes, it was hard." His hands grip mine, and he leads me into the other room. He settles in the wing chair and pulls me gently onto his lap.

Pressing my head against his shoulder and stroking my hair, he speaks again. "You know I made a vow when I married you, that I would cleave to you and be faithful unto death. You may have heard stories and rumors of the warm welcome many a sailor receives at the ports along our common routes."

"Yes," I murmur with trepidation.

"Before I met and married you, on my earlier voyages, I confess that I was drawn in by those enticements. I saw no reason not to be. Now that I know you—have known you—I regret that I ever did so. It's true that many of those women are exotic beauties, and after months at sea even the most homely woman can look like a goddess to a tired sailor. But it doesn't excuse the fact that we are woefully lacking in self-control. That *I* was so lacking. I vowed again, in my own heart, that I would remain true to you no matter how long we were gone.

"My resolve was tried, even at the first port. Several women were waiting on the dock, offering their company and more for a small fee—or nothing at all. One squeezed up beside me and kissed me. But when I looked at her face, all I could think of was your face and the smell of your hair. She was nothing like you, my emerald-eyed mermaid. I walked away and ran down the beach as fast as I could. By the time my energy was spent, my passion had also calmed. I collapsed on the sand and fell asleep, dreaming of your soft skin.

"And that was the way I dealt with each port after that. Therefore, I kept my vow." He swallows hard. "Aye. It was incredibly hard. But I kept my vow."

His neck and the top of his shirt have become wet with my tears by the time he finishes. I lift my head to kiss his neck, my mouth tasting salt as I whisper, "Thank you." It is both an outpouring of love and a prayer of gratitude. I settle back against him and wait for my tears to slow.

"It will be easier on the next voyage, I pray, when I recall all these moments of loving, and I know how much my vow means to you."

"Your next voyage," I sigh.

"Was it very hard for you?" he asks with slight hesitation.

"Yes."

He kisses my forehead. "Tell me."

I recount the appearance of the man who filled the front doorway nearly a year ago, and I shiver.

He grips me more snuggly against him. "You did exactly right. Thank God you were kept well and safe. And Annie, too. I can only imagine how the gun's firing would have scared her should you have needed to shoot."

"At that time, I missed you so keenly," I whisper.

"Only that time?"

"No, there were other times—attention from another man."

He tenses, and his arms loosen. "Another coof?"

I hesitate. I shouldn't have mentioned it—he'll be so angry.

He pushes me back and clutches my shoulders.

"Your brother," I mouth.

"Joseph?"

I close my eyes to block out the confusion on his face.

"George." He growls it with certainty. He shakes me and my eyes fly open. "Did he lay a hand on you?"

"Only once. And just on my arm. At first, I thought I imagined his attraction. But then, after we'd heard the initial report of your passing, before he went to sea again, he came here to ask me to be his wife."

Owen's grip on my shoulders loosens while my explanation stumbles on.

"I refused and, I confess, I held Annie like a shield between us. He insisted that I must be practical and provide for her. But I wasn't ready to face that need. Not so soon."

His hands fall away and collect mine where they rest under my intent stare.

The gentling of his touch fills my final admission with tender fervency. "As I fled his presence, all I could think of was how I needed you—and not your brother."

I finally dare to meet his eyes and see them also filled with tears. "So often, it was thoughts of you that kept me alive and sane in that small boat. Your faithful love was my lifeline then and is my comfort now." His obvious anger at his brother channels into passion, and he kisses me soundly. I gasp for breath while he pulls back long enough to whisper, "Let's make the most of this time and always be content with one another."

* * *

The weeks pass quicker than I imagine they would. Annie begins to walk with greater confidence. Her curls grow so long I can attempt to tame them with pins—when she will sit still long enough to let me. Her favorite place in the world is Owen's lap of an evening, and she always jumps to join him when he declares it time for "Papa love."

He makes time for her and for me, though working with William to finish the manuscript and assisting with several repairs and improvements on the plot keep him quite busy.

We take a day to go into town when the *Two Brothers* comes to dock. Captain Pollard steps down into a literal sea of silent people, all of us watching solemnly when his wife draws near to take his proffered arm. Then they walk home together, as if they were on some sedate First Day stroll.

Owen returns to town two days afterward to give his part of an official account to local authorities. "Pollard has been offered command of the very ship he sailed home on," he reports somberly when he comes home hours later.

There is an old hint of longing for the chase in his voice. I am reminded that I cannot keep him with me forever.

Sadie comes for a lesson at least once a week, often staying a while to play with Annie so I might catch up on sewing orders and other challenging tasks. Sadie is learning a great deal from Martha. That's good, for Martha does not move as lively as she used to. I have come to cherish my honest and warm conversations with Sadie, and though she is much younger than I, her maturity leads me to feel a sweet connection of heart only rivaled by my affection for Mary.

One day Sadie brings a letter from her Auntie Grace. "I waited to open it. I wanted to read it with you," she says with barely contained excitement.

"What does she say?" I smile with pride while watching her slowly decipher the words on her own.

"Says here she's gonna accept Daddy's offer and come live with us. Just as soon as she gets things in order and finds a boat to come 'cross in." She beams at the thought.

I come around the table and hug her. "How lovely for all of you. I look forward to meeting her."

When I have finished harvesting our last vegetables and preserved what I can for the winter, Owen comes home one day to declare that he's decided to rent a house in town, along the lower end of Union Street.

"I'm going to move our belongings there over the next few days," he says with a grin. "I've borrowed William's calash and horse for the purpose."

I am surprised, to say the least. "Town? Is it true?"

"Yes." He gives me a quick kiss and stoops to collect Annie for a homecoming hug. "Are you not pleased?"

"I am—but it is so sudden."

"I've been thinking of it for a time, but I didn't want to say anything until I knew I could find a suitable, affordable place."

"And you've found one?" I clutch the dusting cloth in my hand and study his face.

"Aye. I feel much better about signing on with another ship if I know that you and Annie will be closer to town's center, nearer to our friends—should you need anything. The new place is very small, like this house, but it's also snug and well-built. There is a bit of yard in front and room in back for a small garden. There's also a shed and pin, so we will take the cow and a few chickens. I'll sell the other chickens and the goats. And I'll build a chicken coop as soon as we've settled in."

"And you say the payment is moderate?"

"The same as here, surprisingly. We can manage it."

"You could have asked me to see it before agreeing to anything, since I'll be the one living there." My voice is quiet, but he hears me clearly and immediately stills where he has been holding Annie astride his leg for a bumpy sleigh ride.

"You've been busy here."

"But I would have found time to listen to you, to go with you."

"Don't you trust me when I do something to take care of you?"

I swallow and turn to stare out the window.

He sets Annie down and stands beside me at the counter. Copying my gaze, he makes no attempt to touch me. "Forgive me. In my attempt to provide, I seem to have hurt you."

His simple apology, delivered in such a genuine tone, immediately cools my ire. *Forgive, just as you have been forgiven.* "I do forgive you."

"And yet?"

Forgive completely. Hold no grudges. "I have to remind myself that when you go away again, I will be supporting us. As you are supporting us. Though you are not here. And we will miss you terribly. I confess that it's hard to trust you when I know that—before long—you will be so far away." I tremble. "I suppose I should also seek your forgiveness for having to wrestle with this time and time again."

He pulls me close. "Never apologize for loving and longing and feeling. I want more for you and Annie than this. As I've said before, that is why I must leave—to provide you with more. Can you understand?"

"Yes. You love us."

"I do."

I pull away and reach down to stroke Annie's head where she stands watchfully beside us. I squat to join her in peering up at Owen's face. "And we love you. May the next journey, whenever it starts, be speedy, profitable, and safe."

I find the little town house just as sound and snug as he assessed it to be. When he carries in the last load, I catch his eye and send him a smile that reaffirms my faith in his judgment. I step across the room to touch his arm and murmur, "Thank you for finding us a nice new home."

"One day," he answers with a smile before turning to set down his burden in the corner, "when I captain my own ship, I'll buy you a fine, big house on Orange Street. And I'll retire there to grow old with you and bounce Annie's children on my knee."

"One day..."

It is a lovely dream. But, try as I may, today I cannot envision it.

* * *

Being in town makes many things more convenient. Only needing to pass several streets—instead of walking a mile and a half each way—to deliver orders to Mary, attend First Day gatherings, and take part in special activities makes me feel almost sophisticated. The autumn weeks slip by, and our circle of in-town acquaintances grows. But I still enjoy spending time with the Petersons and Coffins as often as possible.

Winifred comes around for supper every now and again, and I am delighted to know her better. She is a sweet girl, perfectly matched to Joseph in disposition. One night, she confides that Joseph promised to marry her upon returning from his current voyage. We readily encourage this plan, offering our own suggestions for the best living locations.

William and Elizabeth also come by to visit occasionally, and one day early in Eleventh Month, we experience great joy in attending their wedding celebration. William and Owen worked quite hard to finish their manuscript in the weeks leading up to the grand event, so it seems fitting when we learn the following week that the first copies of the published work were released for sale on the mainland that very day. The publishers send word that many copies will soon be shipped to the Island and released for sale to our neighbors and friends.

There is good news and a jovial atmosphere all around us. We are blessed, for a little while at least, with a deep sense of safety and happiness.

* * *

Living in town also has its disadvantages. Out on the plot, we had some measure of privacy. Here, however, surrounded by many houses so much closer in proximity, we find that everyone seems to know our business. And that brings trouble I certainly haven't been expecting.

It materializes in the form of Deborah Starbuck, Elanor Macy, and Bethany Mitchell—three of the leading Friends in our Meeting. One morning, after Owen has gone to post a letter, I answer a knock upon the door to find their trio crowded on the stoop. "Hello, Peggy Chase. We've come visiting," says Elanor. "May we enter?"

"Yes, certainly." How can I refuse? I step back quickly so they can escape the frosty air. Annie looks up from where she is playing with her doll on the floor by our bed and then ducks her head. *Good. Don't make a sound, little one.*

"Please gather round the table," I direct them politely. "We don't have many chairs, but I hope these will be comfortable enough for you."

They sit and remove their gloves before folding their hands primly on the table. They watch me keenly, expressions otherwise unreadable.

"I'll brew some tea." I start to add water to the kettle.

"No need," Bethany's voice stops me, and I turn back to see them all continuing to stare. I'm not sure what they are expecting from me.

With a pained smile, Elanor speaks again. "We've come to sit in silence with thee for a time."

"Yes," Deborah softly joins in. "Where are thy husband and daughter? They can sit with us too."

"Owen has gone out for a time. Annie is still so small, but she is very active now. The silence is not always easy for her to bear. I will participate, but I think she will be happier if she can play and move about freely," I add with a weak smile and sink into the remaining chair.

They do not return my smile, and a slight frown flits across each face in turn. "Very well," Elanor sighs. "Let us join together, then, in blessed silence, to listen for the Light."

We do just that, though I cannot listen to anything but emerging questions and doubts. Somewhere, in a far corner of my mind, an alarm bell seems to be ringing, warning me to proceed cautiously.

I'm not sure how much time passes. Thankfully, Annie remains in the other room and makes nary a sound except to toddle across the floor so she can stand by the doorframe and peer around it to spy on our actions. I notice her movements when I dare to peek in her direction.

Finally, Bethany breaks the silence. "We've come to speak with thee about thine actions. The Friends have become aware that some of thy choices are not behaviors which reflect what we have been taught to be the better way."

Deborah adds, "We don't believe these things must mean disownment, but we do feel they are the preludes to sliding down the slippery slope to grave sin. We want to encourage thee to change thy behaviors and remain on the straight and narrow path."

"And which choices and behaviors are those?" I keep my voice calm.

"It has been brought to our attention that thy family recently attended a Congregationalist wedding ceremony, after which there was dancing, and some in attendance were said to imbibe," Bethany utters in hushed tones, her eyes widening.

"Thou and thy husband keep company far more often throughout the week with those from the Congregational Church than with members of our own Meeting—and do much business with them too. Thy family also keeps very friendly company with blacks," Deborah adds while sending me a distrustful look.

I cannot keep from scowling at this. "Are we not to treat all people with love? Are we not also taught that in Christ both the sexes and all types of people are equal?"

"Oh, we agree that they should be free, and we are indeed commanded to show others kindness. But that does not mean we are to mingle with and become too close to the world's people, whether they be of a different color or creed," Bethany says with a sniff.

"We've also heard," Elanor asserts, "that thy husband has been writing an account of his last voyage. And we need to know what he intends by this. We want to assure ourselves that he will not write anything slanderous nor anything that goes against Scripture and all the things we know to be true."

"Aye, he has written something to be published. I cannot answer for him, for I have not read his writings." I glance down and take a deep breath. "But I believe in him completely. I trust that he would not include anything which would cause others to turn from the path leading to God."

"We will see for ourselves, I suppose," Bethany says with a doubtful shrug. "And then there is the matter of thy daughter."

My fists form within the folds of my apron, and I struggle once more to keep my voice neutral. "What matter is that?"

"We have heard with our own ears how talkative she is becoming and seen with our own eyes how little is done to curb her enthusiasm. In fact, it seems to us that thy daughter is encouraged to express herself in all manner of noise and activity."

Now I cannot keep a note of defensiveness from seeping in. "Why should that not be so?"

"If thou will not train up a child in the ways of prudence, quietness, self-control, and obedience from the very beginning and guide the child with a tight rein, thou will have to deal with more troublesome attitudes and sin patterns in the years to come—and not only thou, but all of us at the Meeting. We are all responsible for the cultivation of her inner growth." Deborah explains all this as if I were the child.

"But that is her natural personality. She is a happy, expressive little girl. We punish her if she disobeys, but we will not force her to be something other than what she is."

Bethany eyes me coolly. "Then thou will reap what thou sows. We shudder to think what the results will be."

"And," Elanor continues, "we have heard of thy frequent singing. Both religious songs and…others. Is that not true? Art thou teaching thy daughter to sing as well? Wilt thou also lead her down a path of worldly behaviors? Where will it end? Wilt thou dress her frivolously, with gaudy ribbons in her hair and bright flowers on her frocks?"

Tears prick my eyes. I bite the inside of my lip to keep them at bay. I see in their expressions the coldness of my mother's cutting gaze. I feel her flat hand on my cheek. The line I've tried so hard to walk has not been straight enough. These women, deep down, are just like her. "What is wrong with singing praises to God? Does not Scripture tell us to do so? Are we not told—"

My strangled words of defense are cut off by the door's sudden opening. Owen steps into the entry and turns to secure the latch before spinning back around to remove his hat and lift his head. "Hello—" The greeting and smile on his lips both abruptly cease when his eyes take in our unexpected company and the pleading look on my face.

"Elanor. Bethany. Deborah." He acknowledges each with a polite nod.

"Owen Chase," they reply in stiff unison.

Owen throws me another glance, steps to the inner doorway, and bends to pick up Annie where she is apparently still hiding. He carries her across the kitchen and comes to stand behind me, placing his hand on my shoulder, applying a steady, reassuring pressure.

"We were discussing some matters of concern with thy wife," Deborah says.

"A discussion which, no doubt, is important to our whole family," Owen supplies, "as what affects one of us will deeply affect us all."

"That's what we told Peggy," Elanor says hastily. "What each of us does can affect everyone in the Meeting. We have to think of all the Friends and rein in our impulses to do anything that would dampen the Light within us."

Bethany rises. "Therefore, we will leave thee and let Peggy summarize the concerns we've outlined. If thou will not address them, Owen Chase, be duly warned—the men will bring this up for formal discussion at our next Business Meeting, and thou will have to give an account for thy family's behavior. We pray that thou will come to thy senses and change thy ways, having the spirit of humility to remain together with us in one body, mind, and spirit." She nods curtly at the other women, and they also stand.

Owen bends to deposit Annie in my arms before stepping over to the door and opening it. He turns back and bids the women farewell in a tone that rivals the outside temperature for frostiness. They march out, and he closes the door behind them.

He approaches me slowly and draws up a chair before sitting and claiming my hand. "Tell me."

"They arrived unexpectedly and insisted we sit in silence. Then they began to lay all sorts of charges at my feet—things we have done, or have failed to do, which they say are leading us away from the truth." The tremble in my voice is beyond my control while I recount the things they said and clutch his fingers.

When I finish, he says nothing for a moment but only stares off into the distance. Finally he whispers, "Perhaps it is time for another move."

"What do you mean?" I turn to face him more fully.

"You and I were both raised, to varying degrees, as Friends, though you've gathered how the premature ending of my mother's influence greatly affected the spiritual atmosphere in our house. Your mother was very strict with you, and my faith was left to struggle upward while surrounded by weeds of doubt. I don't think we want our home to run to either of those extremes, do we? Don't we want to believe and do what we know to be true without being afraid of the rigors of religion that would tie us down in fear?"

I nod absently, struggling to accept that such a separation is permissible, is even possible. "Not all the Friends are like that, but sometimes the lines drawn for us are impossibly difficult to toe," I quietly observe.

"I've been talking to William and Elizabeth, to Gardner and Mary. There are some expected behaviors in their church, but there is more freedom. They say that they always encourage each other to do good, but they try not to judge others so harshly. Though you and I have experienced faith in unique ways, we both believe it is important. Would it not be better to nurture the faith of our family in a different environment?"

I nod again, this time with a bit more certainty. "Yes. I still want to teach Annie from the Bible, but I don't want her to be chastised for naturally spreading her sweetness to those around her. I don't want her to grow up to be exclusive and avoid other types of people. She should be free to choose the truth because she wants it and not because she's terrified of what others will think of her if she doesn't." My shoulders begin to relax.

"Very well." He squeezes my hand and reaches out to stroke Annie's hair. "They won't have to worry about us, nor will they have to wait till the next Business Meeting to deal further with our unacceptable ways. I'll talk with Gardner about what we must do to join the Congregationalists."

"I'm afraid." I shudder. "What will my parents say when they hear this news? What will my mother do?"

He leans over to softly kiss my temple. "She stopped approving of you some time ago, even as you still tried to please her. Quit trying, beloved. Live to love your family, to love your neighbor, to love your God. All else matters little."

After being silent for so long, Annie looks up at us and declares, "Mama love, Papa love. Annie love!"

A laugh springs from my lips. "I'll trust you in this too. I will follow your lead and try to join them in worship."

His smile is full of peace and assurance. "Won't it be wonderful to sing without feeling like a criminal, to tie some small red ribbons in Annie's curls, and to join our good friends on the first day of the week as well as all the other days?"

"Yes. I do believe it will."

* * *

We are on the threshold of Twelfth Month—December. Owen has left early to attend to some business, so I bundle Annie in her warmest dress, leggings, shoes, and wool cloak to take her with me while I see to my own tasks. I have stayed at home for the past few days, often feeling unwell. I think I know why, so I stop at Martha's house first, hoping that she's both home and awake. I'm relieved to find it just so.

"Hello, dear girls," she greets from her chair across the room while I shut the door behind us. "What a nice surprise."

Annie wriggles to be set down and turns toward Martha's waiting embrace before singing out her name sweetly.

"I'm sorry we haven't been by in a while. It's taken all my extra time and energy to get fully settled over these past weeks. You must come for tea sometime, Martha, when you feel up to it." I sit down in the facing chair.

"Thank you, but I am often weary. I'm grateful for the girls and how they are already able to handle the easier cases without me. Sadie is quickly gaining a trustworthy reputation in New Guinea. Felicity and Hannah have grown in confidence with each passing week." She eyes me over Annie's head. "Speaking of weary, you don't seem quite yourself. Have you been ailing?"

"I don't think I am myself. I think, perhaps, I carry an addition. But I am not sure and wanted to ask for your assistance in confirming it."

She asks me several questions while rocking Annie gently, and my girl—as always—soaks up any form of love like our sandy soil receives rain. Finally, Martha's face lights with a familiar smile. "Well, I should think your little one will be coming to meet us by midsummer."

"Then it's true?"

"After all these years, I'm almost never wrong. Are you not happy?"

"Yes, but…" My gaze drops.

"Your husband is thinking of shipping out again, isn't he?"

"How did you know?"

Martha strokes Annie's hair. "It was bound to happen eventually. Men tied to whaling are much like the tide. They come and they go, all in due time. They feel the pull of it, and there is nothing their wives and children can do to change what will be."

"He's told me it is his double-edged sword. He loves me and misses me when he's away, but it's both for the passion of the hunt and the desire to provide a better life for me—and for our children—that he must not stay at home forever."

"So it has become. Living in town, you are now surrounded by others who acutely know such tension. Will you give Owen the news before he departs?"

"Yes, I think so. The trick will be in the timing. He's already spoken of leaving for some time. I don't want to make him feel any worse for going, but I wasn't able to inform him about Annie before his previous homecoming, so I want him to know from the start that there will likely be a second child waiting for him at his next return."

She offers some helpful reminders about caring for myself in the weeks ahead before I declare it's time to be moving on.

"Come again in a month or two. I'll check on your progress."

"Thank you, Martha." I take a small package of her favorite spice cookies from my satchel and set them on the edge of the table. "I left them extra soft this time." I've noticed how she's starting to lose her teeth.

KAYLENE POWELL

"You are a dear, thoughtful friend. God be with you," she calls after me in a drowsy voice as Annie and I see ourselves out.

The confirmation of a coming child swirls around in my belly, mind, and heart. I feel I must tell someone or I will burst. *Mary.* Skipping the next planned stop, I head directly for the store.

We move slowly along the street—my pace sedate while Annie's little legs work to keep up—and cross paths with several acquaintances. Normally, they would return my quiet greetings with a smile, a nod, or a good word of their own. Today, however, every single one either looks away in passing or sends me a pointedly cautious look. After this happens half a dozen times inside of a hundred feet, I feel completely bewildered.

Coming closer to the store, I overhear two women who are having an animated conversation while they work to hang a banner above a shop entrance.

"…Yes, that's exactly what it said. Can you believe he would have the audacity to write such things for his own gain and profit without a care of how the world will label us?"

"Why, that's terrible! We all know what men are sometimes reduced to, but no one needs to be parading it around so off-Islanders call us uncivilized and unchristian."

"I should say so. And let me tell you what else my husband read to me last night…"

By the time we are out of earshot, we have nearly reached our destination. When I open the door, Annie lets go of my hand and toddles over to the corner where Gardner's old toys always await her when he's attending school. I cross to the sewing counter and grasp the edge of it with shaking fingers.

Mary's greeting is much more reserved than usual, but when she sees that I look unwell, her expression softens slightly. "What is it?"

"I'm not sure. On our way here, a number of acquaintances treated me so coldly when we came upon each other. Has something changed since last I saw you? Have I offended someone without knowing it?"

She pulls me to her side. "Did Owen inform you that his book finally arrived last week? Our shop and two others put it out for sale. At first, few people noticed it. But word has spread and more folks have bought a copy with each passing day. Wanting to support your family whenever we can, Gardner and I bought a copy and have been reading it aloud these past two evenings." Her eyes widen and her brows lift slightly. "Has he not told you his whole story? Did you not read the manuscript?"

"No. He's shared some memories, and I overheard bits and pieces of what he included during the writing process, but I have not read all the particulars. I often wait for him to tell me about personal matters. He doesn't respond well to pestering." The look on her face is disconcerting. "What is it?"

"The things he speaks of..." Her voice takes on added strain. "I don't think anyone would judge him and the others for some of what they were surely forced to do. But no one wants to think of outsiders from across the country—and even perhaps around the world—abhorring the kind of people we are or thinking that one of our own would seek to make a living by sensationalizing it."

"Sensationalizing it?" I whisper back. I think of mentioning William's assistance before recalling Owen's request I never do so. "Owen is a fine storyteller, as you know, but I don't think he's prone to exaggeration. And I don't think he did this with any hint of maliciousness."

"You love him, my dear, and love can shade our vision. I'm not necessarily saying that he exaggerated. I only gather that most readers believe some parts of the tale would have been better kept secretly among our own people. Many feel betrayed, exposed—things which you know are serious offenses within the close confines of our world."

"I had no idea people would respond like this." I press a hand against my stomach. "What shall I do?"

"Hold your head up, precious girl." She slips her arm around my shoulders. "We won't stop loving you, and anyone who knows you well sees what a genuine and beautiful spirit resides in you. No matter what they may think of Owen, they will surely accept you again, even if it takes some time."

"But Owen is a part of me. To reject him is to reject me."

"Yet he is not you. Hold on while the storm blows over. When the calm comes, you will be standing on your own two feet."

I try to draw strength from her counsel, but I know only numbness as I mechanically exchange orders and close the conversation.

I collect Annie and walk home like a dreamer, now even more aware of every look sent and every shunning action shown. Annie trips along, trying to keep up when I've quickened my pace unaware. Finally, she stumbles and cries out in alarm. I pick her up and press her close, keeping my eyes downcast while nearly running the rest of the way home.

It is not until I shut the door firmly behind us and lean back against it, struggling to catch my breath, that I realize I never told Mary my news.

Somehow, at this moment, it doesn't matter.

* * *

I sit in the waning hours of light at afternoon's end, shielded by the wing chair, adrift on a sea of thoughts. Pea porridge simmers and round loaves bake while Annie sits at my feet, picking up blocks in a haphazard attempt to stack them. The house is warm and filled with pleasant aromas, and my little one is completely content. Why am I so downcast?

Alone. I feel all alone.

My thoughts echo in my head and stir a memory. I reach out to the small side table and pick up the Bible I've given much less attention to while Owen's been home again. I search through the Psalms and immediately begin to read out softly when I locate the intended passage. "'My God, my God, why hast thou forsaken me? Why art thou so far from helping me, and from the words of my roaring? ...I am a worm, and no man; a reproach of men, and despised of the people. All they that see me laugh me to scorn: they shoot out the lip, they shake the head.'"

My people do not openly mock me. They quietly exclude and rebuff me. Do not both of these cause the heart equal injury? How am I to hold my head up when I go outside or attend church? How am I to weather this storm and stand strong as Mary advised when I feel forsaken, small, and weak?

Distracted, I do not hear the door open and close. I jump when I feel his lips at my temple as he murmurs, "Hello, beloved."

Beloved.

He moves around so he can see my face, studying me with a furrowed brow. "You seem far way, in another world. I return bearing good news. Would you care to hear it?"

"Papa!" Annie gets to her feet and stretches her arms upward. "Play, Papa! Play!"

My emotions are all tangled, like a large net cast out only to come up empty. "Stay with Annie while I set on the supper," I say, rising and leaning away. "Then you can tell me."

His gaze lingers on my face for a moment before he nods and focuses his attention completely on her. I set the Bible on the table and walk into the kitchen. Annie can say more words with each passing week, and their stilted conversation floating in through the doorway does something to center my heart. Yet, I feel great unease deep inside.

Owen and I sit silently through the first moments of dinner while Annie attempts to feed herself with her small spoon. I reach over to wipe her chin after every third or fourth sloppy bite.

Owen sets his fork on the table. "While I was near the North Wharf this afternoon, I met an off-Islander named Phinehas Brown. He was here recruiting men to sail on the *Florida* from New Bedford. When I gave him my name, he was quite pleased to meet me. He says the book has been sold in New Bedford for about two weeks, that Captain Simeon Price had already read it, and that Brown was specifically ordered by Price to look for 'that Chase fellow and offer him the position of first mate on my ship should you locate him.'" His eyes shine with pride.

"A whaling ship?"

"Yes. A good ship with a good commander, so Brown assures me. He's sailed twice before with Captain Price. They leave New Bedford in eight days' time. Apparently the captain was so impressed by my account that he's offering me the position with a very generous lay—even though he has yet to personally meet me."

I chew my bread more slowly when my stomach begins to churn.

"Do you not think it good news? It is the first offer I've had since I returned—and it is a very good offer at that. Of course, I'd rather advance directly to captain—think I'm certainly capable of it now—but this is still worth pursuing—"

"You can run away." My interruption is little more than a whisper, but he hears.

"What do you mean?"

"You don't have to stay here. You've written your story and set it on display for all to see. And now, when our friends and neighbors are embarrassed by it, would even shun us for it, you can so conveniently sign on with a ship and sail away for years, leaving us to face the storm of silent wrath on our own." I exhale heavily, and my shoulders slump.

"What are you talking about?"

"Has no one been treating you differently?"

"Well, I suppose I've met a few people this past week who have seemed a bit out of sorts." He sighs a chuckle while rubbing the back of his neck. But his crooked smile quickly fades when he looks up again to take in my expression.

"When I went out today, I felt their glares, their snubs, their barbs. Mary says it's because of what you've written."

"Don't be concerned with the simple slights of a few overly-sensitive souls. It will pass quickly enough and all will be well."

"It was not just the words of those I didn't know. It was the coldness and suppressed anger radiating from those I did. Those were my friends, our friends."

"Fair-weather friends," he grunts as he picks up his glass and drains its contents. He sets it back on the table but continues to grip it firmly. The gaze he levels at me is hard, his eyes darkening like freshly-watered soil. "I'll say it again. What those people think doesn't matter. Hold your head up and show them that you won't be beaten down by their petty attitudes about our fine reputation. Are we not common folk, prone to the weaknesses and limitations of every human on earth? Why should we be troubled by the admission of it?"

"It is easy for you to tell me to be strong when you won't be here to stand beside me. You may be strong enough to not care what others think, Owen Chase, but I need others. I need the strength of community. And when most would shut me out because of your need and your choice, this Island may well cease to be my home and become my prison!" I clench my jaw and then plow forward, trying to make him understand. "I have nowhere to turn. I will not move back to the Point and subject myself to life with Mother again, raising Annie in that strain and isolation. And I cannot tuck my tail between my legs and run away to the far-off seas as some means of cowardly escape."

He shakes his head while keeping his eyes fixed on mine. "I am no coward—"

"But everyone will think you are if you leave now!"

"I am *no coward*. And I don't care what those fools think!" He curses like the sailor he is as he raises the glass he's been gripping with whitened knuckles and hurls it between Annie and me. It strikes the wall with a crash, sending down a shower of jagged pieces.

Since I've known him, he's never spoken such vile words in my presence, nor displayed such violence so that I would feel uneasy. For a moment, we all sit frozen—Annie and me staring at him and him staring at me.

Annie's frantic wail breaks the silence, and when she gasps for breath, she begins to shake with great, wracking sobs. She stretches her trembling arms toward me after tossing him a terrified look. I gather her close. Without a backward glance, I carry her into the other room and step near to the fire, stroking her back and head, trying in vain to still the quaking that pulses through us both. My queasiness suddenly increases, and I close my eyes to concentrate on breathing deeply, willing my supper to remain where it is.

After a few minutes, Annie's form relaxes slightly, and her tears slow. In the relative quiet, I hear slight noises in the kitchen followed by Owen's muttering in a pain-laced tone.

Annie hears it too and lifts her head from my shoulder. "Annie down," she whispers in a crackling voice, wriggling until I set her on the floor. She walks toward and then through the doorway. I follow several steps behind and hold my breath, praying he will not harm her if his anger still simmers.

"Papa! Ow!"

My heart stutters, and I dash around the doorframe. At the scene before me, I pull up short and exhale sharply.

Annie is squatting next to Owen where he kneels on the floor. He holds several pieces of glass in one hand, and there is a trail of blood running over the edge of the opposite palm, toward his wrist.

When he looks up at me, his eyes hold a mixture of physical pain and regret. "I'll finish cleaning this up. And I'll replace the glass. I promise."

"Never mind," I reply. "Let's see to your hand."

But at the closer sight of the blood, my stomach finally wins the battle. I spin to heave my supper into the slop bucket on the counter. Now I, too, feel awkward and afraid to lift my eyes. When I have nothing more to put out, I turn to the water bucket and pour a measure with which to rinse my mouth and wipe my face.

I turn back to find Owen sitting in one of the kitchen chairs with a handkerchief pressed against his hand, the cotton turning red as Annie looks on. "Papa bad ow. Papa sad." She turns beseeching eyes to me. "Mama, Papa sad. Mama help!"

"Yes, sweetheart. Mama can look at it now." I approach them slowly.

He lays his hand in mine, and I pull the cloth back. "It's deep," I observe. "It would surely do better with a few stitches. Let me clean my sharpest needle and collect a few hairs from the cow's tail. I'll be back directly."

By the time I've returned and am ready, he has washed his hand and is reseated in the chair with Annie tucked securely against his side. Her love for her papa certainly runs deep. Thank God she isn't petrified of him after that display.

He glances up uneasily. "Are you sure you want to do this? If seeing the blood makes you ill, I can do my best to stitch it myself."

"My stitching is my pride and joy—just as yours is in your skill with a harpoon. You would make a mess of this job, but I'll sew the stitches so small you should barely have a scar." My needle pierces the skin. He sucks in a breath. "Besides, it was not really the sight of your blood that made me retch. I have not felt well for several days."

"I hope it's nothing serious."

"It will pass. Eventually."

At my strange tone, he looks up quickly. "You are rarely ill."

"I am with child."

Silence. Then, "How long have you known?"

"Martha confirmed it today." I pause to concentrate, tying off the final stitch and then picking up a wet cloth to wipe the wound gently. "I'm sorry to be so emotional this evening. I was reckless with my words and seem to be lacking in self-control."

"No more than I!" He grabs my free hand with his uninjured one. "It is I who need to apologize. I let my anger and frustration get the better of me. I scared Annie, and I declared your fears and struggles to be meaningless. I do not regret publishing my tale, but I do regret any unforeseen burden it would now place on your shoulders. Or the aftermath which might spread out to affect our children."

I stand and step closer to him, allowing him to slip his arm around my waist and draw me near so he can press his cheek against my middle and turn his face to kiss the cloth covering my womb. I feel the fear and anger seep from my being, and I run a hand through his hair.

He sighs. "You know I'm not running away. *You* know I am not a coward."

"I know." A tear slips down my cheek.

"I am sorry I cannot stay and greet this little one when it comes into the world. You will write and tell me about it?"

"Yes."

"Mary and Gardner are your true friends. William and Elizabeth will, of course, stand by you. And Solomon's family all love you and Annie to distraction. Martha's long loved you as well. I trust that the others worth holding onto will come around in time."

"Yes."

His hold tightens. "You are still unsettled about something."

"Mary asked me today if I knew your whole story. I realized then that I didn't. In these months at home, you've never shared it with me the way you did with William." I swallow. "There is much I don't know. But I would know it. If you would share it with me."

"There are things I never told you because I didn't want you to have to bear hearing them. Things I did not even tell William—things omitted from the book."

"I am not afraid, love. Will you allow me to support you? Will you trust me enough to share your heart's burden with me?"

He tips his head back and raises his eyes to meet mine. "I'll put Annie to bed while you clear the table. I'll meet you at the wing chair when you've finished."

A short while later, he pulls me down onto his lap. I cradle his injured hand, and he uses his good hand to press my head against his shoulder. We both stare into the blaze on the hearth while he tells me of choices and regrets. I feel his tears rain down and listen in reverent silence.

"I could have spared all the men, Peggy. Spared them so much hardship and—" he chokes on a shudder. "The white devil lay right before me, as good a shot as ever a mate has surely had! Between the blows he rested, floating there like so much flotsam, feigning harmlessness. Why did I not obey the scream of the lance in my hand?" He shakes his head. "Why did I consider possible damage to the rudder as more of a threat than facing the mighty Pacific apart from any ship at all?"

He finishes his confession and, without lifting my head, I raise a hand to cup his cheek and use my thumb to gently brush at his trail of sorrow.

"Peggy?" His voice remains raw, vulnerable.

"Hmmm?"

"When I came in before supper, what were you reading?"

I reach across to the little table and pick up the Bible once more. It is still open to the place where I left off. "Words of understanding for ones who are weak and limited. Shall I share them with you?"

"Aye."

I settle back against him, the book now balanced on our joined hands. My shaky voice gains quiet strength.

"'My God, my God, why hast thou forsaken me? Why art thou so far from helping me, and from the words of my roaring? O my God, I cry in the day time, but thou hearest not; and in the night season, and am not silent. But thou art holy, O thou that inhabitest the praises of Israel. Our fathers trusted in thee: they trusted, and thou didst deliver them. They cried unto thee, and were delivered: they trusted in thee, and were not confounded.

"'But I am a worm, and no man; a reproach of men, and despised of the people. All they that see me laugh me to scorn: they shoot out the lip, they shake the head, saying, he trusted on the Lord that he would deliver him: let him deliver him, seeing he delighted in him…'" My voice catches. Owen squeezes me tenderly, giving me strength to read on. "But be not thou far from me, O Lord: O my strength, haste thee to help me…

"'I will declare thy name unto my brethren: in the midst of the congregation will I praise thee… For he hath not despised nor abhorred the affliction of the afflicted; neither hath he hid his face from him; but when he cried unto him, he heard…

"'All they that be fat upon earth shall eat and worship: all they that go down to the dust shall bow before him: and none can keep alive his own soul.'" I pause again at his small gasp and watch a tear hit the page. "A seed shall serve him; it shall be accounted to the Lord for a generation. They shall come, and shall declare his righteousness unto a people that shall be born, that he hath done this.'"

When I finish, we are quiet for a time. Then he whispers a mixture of prayer and promise against my hair. "You may not feel strong enough to weather this storm, but God is, beloved. God is."

CHAPTER
SIX

DECEMBER 1821

Owen secures passage to New Bedford on a vessel called the *Mist Queen*. The following days blur with busyness. I help him gather supplies, and he sets several matters in order for our family. We both want to soften the impact of his departure on Annie, so we begin to speak frequently about how Papa must go away to use his harpoon for a little while, but he'll come back again when she's a bigger girl.

Today is the final one before his leaving. He goes to order an extra load of peat to be stored in the shed, lest this winter should prove to be as bitter as the last, while I keep Annie at home and work to prepare food for his initial journey. He surprises us by returning earlier than expected.

He shuts the door and leans back against it.

I look up from my work to see him clutching his head with both hands. "What is it?"

When he doesn't reply beyond a soft groan, I put down my knife and cross the room. I can see the grimace behind his hands and notice how he trembles.

"Owen?"

"My head," he mumbles. He tries to stand upright and step away from the door but then staggers.

I jump to his side and put my arms around his waist to keep him from toppling. He leans heavily upon me, and I steer him into the bedroom. Somehow I get him to the bed, out of his coat, and lying upon the covers in a fairly natural position. I remove his boots and loosen his collar before covering him with a quilt. All the while, he remains tense and silent.

Sitting beside him on the edge of the bed, I trail my fingers across his forehead. "What can I do to help you?" I whisper.

"I don't rightly know," he grinds out as he gropes for and then grasps my hand, hanging on to it like a lifeline. "The pain is horrible. Like a dozen knives, one from every direction."

It must be horrible indeed if he is brought so low by it. I've never heard him complain of pain before.

"You need rest, water, tea. I think I still have a little feverfew. Martha gave me some shortly before your return, when I was having headaches of my own. I'll prepare it for you now. And I'll make a lavender compress. That's always soothing."

Urging Annie to let Papa rest by being a good, quiet girl, I gather the needed items. For the better part of an hour, I gently wipe his brow and massage his head while pausing periodically to pour herbal tea and water between his lips. All the while, I pray.

Finally, I dare to ask, "Is it any better?"

"Yes," he says in a slightly heartened tone, "a little. Will you sing for me?"

"If you like." Pausing for a moment to think, I adjust the compress and begin to intone a song Sadie once taught me, keeping my voice low:

Come, ye sinners, poor and needy, weak and wounded, sick and sore;
Jesus ready stands to save you, full of pity, love and power.

Come, ye weary, heavy-laden, lost and ruined by the fall;
If you tarry till you're better, you will never come at all.
View him prostrate in the garden, on the ground your
Maker lies:
On the bloody tree behold Him; sinner, will this not suffice?
Lo! The incarnate God ascended, pleads the merit of His
blood
Venture on Him, venture wholly, let no other trust intrude.
I will arise and go to Jesus, He will embrace me in
His arms;
In the arms of my dear Savior, oh, there are ten
thousand charms.

When I finish, I note the slowness of his breathing and guess he has finally drifted into a deeper sleep. I kiss his cheek and turn to find Annie staring at us from the doorway. I pick her up.

"Papa not good?"

"Papa's head hurts very badly."

She considers this. "Papa head ow? Mama help." She smiles sweetly at me and pats my cheeks with her small palms.

"Yes, little angel. Mama helps Papa. We must both help Papa now by continuing to be very, very quiet. Can you do that?" I carry her into the kitchen and set her down near the table. "We will work and play as quietly as we can. It will be a game. Which one of us can be quieter, do you think?"

Her smile widens. She loves games. "Me be quiet!" she whispers loudly.

If I weren't so tired, I would laugh. "Yes. You will surely win."

After a little while, she grows drowsy where she sits, and I set aside my own work to hold her in the rocking chair until she drifts to sleep. I lay her on the small settee along the wall near the hearth and cover her with a thick blanket. Now I can go about uninterrupted in finishing the packing tasks Owen has not the strength to complete.

A knock sounds at the door while I close the lid of the second small chest. I answer it and allow Joshua and Solomon to step in out of the cold.

"Miz Peggy," they greet in unison, their strong, deep voices resounding like shouts in the face of the recent quiet.

"Please," I whisper. "Annie is sleeping, and Owen has a terrible headache. What brings you by?"

Joshua cringes and lowers his voice. "We told Mister Owen we'd be around to help him carry his supplies down to the wharf. Since the ship sails with the dawn, they be wanting to load the main supplies and baggage early."

"Perhaps we can do all the carrying without disturbing him," Solomon says.

"That's kind of you." I peek around the corner and check on Owen in the dim light. "I know he would want to help you, but he is resting so deeply. I think that's what he needs."

"How much there be, ma'am?"

"These two chests," I point, "and those bundles."

"We can surely take it all in two trips, don't you reckon?" Joshua estimates.

Solomon nods confidently.

I lead them across the room. "All right. But promise me you'll return and stay awhile after the second trip, to have some tea and scones and warm up on your way home."

Solomon smiles. "Thank you, ma'am. It's a mighty cold and gloomy day."

They make one trip while I prepare the scones. When they have left the second time, Annie awakens to a house filled with the smell of cinnamon. She wriggles from underneath the blanket, slips to the floor, and comes to latch onto my skirt.

"Mama. Thirsty." She speaks in a gravelly voice while pointing to her cup.

"So am I," comes an equally rough voice from the bedroom doorway.

Turning quickly, I nearly send Annie tumbling. She holds tightly to my skirt and rights herself before she looks at him too. "Papa head ow?"

"Not anymore," he replies while keeping his tired eyes and smile on me. "Your mama made the pain go away." Though his expression is slightly haggard, he seems mostly himself again.

"Mama help. Annie help. Me quiet!"

"Well, yes. You were." I smile at her darling squeal of self-satisfaction.

"Thank you." Owen pats her head. "Thank you," he says again, pulling me into a tender embrace.

"Thank God," I whisper. I cannot bear the thought of sending him off on his journey in a state of weakness.

He pulls away and then looks about in confusion. "Where are my things?"

"Solomon and Joshua came around to collect them. I'm surprised the necessary commotion did not wake you. You must have been sleeping very deeply indeed."

"I was going to help them."

"We knew you needed the rest. Don't fret. They promised to come back after the second trip and take some refreshment to chase away the chill."

"It smells good."

"I'm baking scones. I hope you can eat with us."

"Aye. My stomach is feeling stronger now."

"You still look a bit weak. Sit and rock by the fire while I make the tea." I see him settled with a cup of water and also give Annie her requested drink before I fill the kettle.

Perhaps ten minutes later, the men knock and let themselves in again before brushing a light layer of snow from their coats.

"Welcome back," I greet them.

Solomon nods a silent response and then notices Owen across the way. "How you be now? Good to see you up and moving."

"The sleep and Peggy's herbal treatment seem to be exactly what I needed." Owen stands, finds his balance, and steps forward to offer his hand to each man for a firm shake. "I didn't mean for you to do all that alone. I'm indebted to you."

"No, sir," Solomon says. "Rev'run Johnson always be telling us: 'Let no debt remain, except the debt of love.' And that's how we aim to live. We really repaying a debt to you. After we first come here, your wife showed us more kindness and friendship than almost anybody else."

Owen's eyes stray to me. "The same friendly lady has made us scones and tea. Come and share the hospitality of our table." He turns to sit and, with some assistance, Annie climbs up onto his lap. She clutches her doll and smiles shyly at Joshua and Solomon when they step over to take a seat. I serve the tea and set a crock of butter on the table before I pull up my chair to join them.

The scones are perfect. Soon Solomon and Joshua appear to be thoroughly warmed. Yet, there is something uneasy lingering in their expressions. I had thought they were growing more comfortable in Owen's presence, but now I begin to doubt my instincts.

Finally, in a moment of silence, Solomon clears his throat and stares hard at Owen. "We got something we'd like to say, if you'd hear us."

"I would," Owen assures them. "Speak freely."

"Our Rev'run Johnson be one of the only educated men among us. He bought a copy of your book and said he'd read it aloud to interested folks. Our family all wanted to know more, specially about Uncle Richard. So we went to meetings with the others these three nights past, to hear the telling of it. Last night, he read us the end, with the part about Uncle's passing. We can't tell you what relief we felt when he told how you ministered to Uncle in the final days and how you..." his voice wobbles, "how you set his body in the sea, whole as could be, after his soul done flew away."

The room is silent for a moment before he can continue. "Thank you, sir. It broke our hearts to hear about Mister Cole, but we understand why you done that. Still, it brought us some peace in knowing Uncle's remains didn't meet the same fate."

"Yes. Thank you for what you done," Joshua echoes quietly.

Owen pulls Annie close and strokes her curls while staring down at the table. "I am no saint." He clears his throat and looks up. "But I am glad I could show Richard that kindness, after he did so much to strengthen our spirits and keep our hopes alive. To speak plainly: because of his words and prayers, I am here with you today."

All three blink back tears. I do nothing to check several of my own.

"It's getting dark. We best get home to Sadie and Isaiah."

"I thank you again. For the assistance you gave today and your friendship to our family," Owen says, standing with them.

"Surely, and we wish you a real safe journey. We'll do our best to help watch over Miz Peggy and your little one, too."

"It means a great deal to me. More than I can say."

They shake hands with Owen once more and turn to offer me a polite nod before buttoning their coats and heading out into the gently falling snow.

In the bitter chill of early morning, I awaken to the sound of Owen washing his face. I sit up and quickly pull on a dressing gown and an extra pair of stockings and step away from the warm covers. Without words, he prepares for the walk to the wharf. Equally silent, I make him a cup of tea and some buttery toast. He partakes of the simple breakfast while I sit and watch him.

Finally, he stands and steps back into the bedroom. In the dim candlelight, I watch him reach down to softly stroke Annie's hair. He kisses her tiny mouth and then her forehead with the utmost care, so as not to wake her.

He meets me where I stand in the doorway, holding his heavy coat, scarf, and gloves. He dons the coat and fastens the buttons while speaking softly. "Do you remember our conversation and the vow I told you about? Please pray for me, that I will have the strength to keep it again."

"I will. And I will be waiting faithfully here for you. I will never turn to another."

"But, Peggy—you must make me another promise."

"What is that?"

He surrounds my waist with his hands. "Promise me that if, one day, something does happen to me—and my death is confirmed—you will remarry, that you will find a good man to take care of the children and help provide for you all. Don't do anything desperate. Don't go up on the Hill to sell yourself. Promise me you'll marry another."

I shudder and throw my arms around his neck. I have told myself I will not cry, that I will be strong to ease the parting. I bite my lip to hold back the tears and press my face against him until I am composed before stepping back.

"I promise. But I'll not need to worry about any of that. For I know you'll come back to us. I feel it deep inside."

His eyes glisten, and he bends down to kiss me fervently.

I respond with all the love—and every prayer for his safety—held in my heart.

Then he shoulders his pack, opens the door, steps out into the gray and ghostly morning mist, and is swallowed from my sight.

* * *

MAY 1822

Annie's second birthday has come and gone, and each day I grow heavier with child. Martha says we have misjudged the timing, and the baby will likely come earlier than she first guessed. This fine, warm Sunday morning, Annie and I walk to church. Now that I must lumber along, it is not difficult for Annie to keep up with me. I leave her in the back room for the children's lesson and squeeze myself down onto one of the wooden pews—now almost unbearably firm against my aching back and hips.

After a long and tiring week, I find today's service soothing and uplifting for my soul. We sing songs about grace and sacrifice, and the pastor speaks a stirring message about the command to encourage one another in the truth of the Gospel. When the service ends and many start to file from their pews, I look up and notice a unique profile two rows in front of me. I'm certain I've seen that tall, willowy figure with the face-frame of auburn hair before, though I can't say where.

She turns where she stands to look fully at me, and I realize that I've been caught staring. I blush.

Yet she does not seem to mind. She steps around the end of her pew and comes to sit next to me. "Good day to you," she quietly greets me.

"And to you. Are you new to this congregation? I've only been attending a few months, and I am sure I have not met all the members."

"This is my first time here. I used to attend Meetings with the Friends, but I recently chose to separate. Truth be told, I rarely come into town now. Last time I was here on a day of worship was over a year ago."

I think back for a moment. Then I suddenly remember. "That time, at the Meeting House, were you given a word to speak, about God comforting grieving hearts?"

"Yes, I was. And I spoke it. My first time—and now my only time—to ever speak publicly in a Meeting."

"You had a child with you, didn't you?"

Her gaze drops. "My son, Gabriel."

"I remember," I whisper, spontaneously reaching out to take her hands in my own. "I cannot describe how much your words meant to me, how much comfort they brought in very dark days."

"Aye, and to me as well." She squeezes my hands in return. "Sometimes I have felt that the words were given only for my sake. But I'm thankful to hear now that they blessed another soul."

"What burden were you carrying?" I ask—before I think better of it.

"My husband went to sea and never returned, though I had prayed often that he would." She swallows. "Several weeks after I received news of his fate—after I spoke at the Meeting— Gabriel wandered away when I was distracted. By the time I found him, he had drowned in a nearby pond."

I don't know what to say, so I say nothing at all.

Her sad blue eyes stare off into the distance. "My husband's name was Matthew, and he was second mate on the *Essex*. I imagine you've heard of what befell her crew."

A rock of emotion slams against my chest making breathing nearly impossible. This woman, whose husband's final story I know all too well, has suffered so much while my own misery was abated and my husband was returned to me.

"What is it?" she asks in alarm as she pulls a hand away and places it on my shoulder, steadying me when I sway.

I gasp for air and hold tightly to her other hand. After a moment, the shock passes and I can breathe deeply and speak again. "Forgive me for alarming you. I will be well."

"Allow me to linger for a moment, to be sure. My name is Nancy, by the way, and I'm pleased to make a new acquaintance. I hope we shall be friends." She offers a gentle, guileless smile.

"My name is Peggy," I whisper. "I'm the wife of Owen Chase."

To her credit, she gazes at me steadily, her smile only faltering a little. "Then, I think you, Peggy Chase, will be a special and empathetic kind of friend. Though I am rarely in town, as I have returned to my father's home out on the road to Eel Point, I hope I may meet you again when next I return?"

"Oh, yes," I assure her. "We live in a small white house on Union Street. My husband is away for some time yet, but you are always welcome for tea or a meal."

She embraces me from the side before she stands to take her leave. "I thank you and greatly look forward to accepting your offer. Farewell."

* * *

Late the next afternoon, Annie and I walk to the store to pick up a few necessities. Passing the mouth of the alley which runs around behind, we hear a terrible commotion of barking, yelping, and cursing. I grip Annie's hand and try to pick up our pace as much as my added load will allow. *God, please protect us. And protect Owen this day from any threats he may face.*

Once inside, I ask Mary about the noise.

"That's the doing of Mr. Ambrose and his partners. They come over from the Cape and bring those big dogs of theirs, boarding in the rooms behind Macy's smaller storehouse and keeping their animals outside in makeshift pens. This is the second time they've come in the past year, and we've learned to take the long way around while they're here."

"Why do they bring such fearsome sounding dogs along?"

"They are in the breeding business. Some Islanders like the heartiness of their stock for raising better guard dogs."

Mary packs my purchases in a small burlap sack, uses the drawstrings at the top to form a sort of handle, and tells me about a challenging dress order she's working on. "The way she prefers the hem is particularly difficult. You know my eyes grow weary more easily these days, and the tiny stitches she demands have become nearly impossible."

"I'd be happy to finish it for you once I complete the two pairs of trousers I'm working on now."

"I hate to ask it. I can see how tired you are."

"Sewing is one of the few things I can do while sitting in the wing chair—the only comfortable seat in the house for me at present."

"Well then, I accept your offer. I'll send it back with you the next time you're in. You have enough to carry today."

"That sounds fine." I slip the handle of the bag over my shoulder, and we move toward the front entry. Through the large windows to the right of the door, I see Annie with young Gardner. He is arranging fruit for sale in some open crates and is allowing Annie to help him. He lifts a single apple from the bag and hands it to her. She cradles it in her little hands and transfers it to the pile mounding at the top of the crate's edge, stacking it carefully while he guides her. The next apple she stacks wobbles and slips. Gardner's hand shoots forward and catches it. He looks down to give Annie a reassuring smile and sets it on the pile himself before turning to arrange a small post with a board attached, no doubt showing the price on the other side. "You have a fine son. I can even see how he's grown since we moved to town."

"He'll take after my father, I think," she muses while watching him with affection. "Papa was a very tall man and quite strong." She glances at me. "You know, I can't thank God enough for your family." We watch Gardner crouch down to tickle Annie. "Especially after Mary's passing—you have been a friend to me but also like another daughter to us, and Annie has been like the sister Gardner was missing."

"You are also a tremendous blessing in our lives," I say with a smile before I step through the entry and into the sunshine to the sound of Annie's trailing giggles.

Suddenly, from the alley comes a terrible crash, a loud bark, and the startled cries of several people. One of what must surely be Mr. Ambrose's finest specimens comes barreling around the corner and directly toward us, down the street along the shop fronts. People scramble out if its way left and right.

Before I know what is happening, Gardner has pushed Annie down and thrown himself over her, forming a kind of protective dome with his body against the display crates just as the dog comes upon them. I watch in horror as it opens its terrible mouth and sinks its teeth into Gardner's curled form, bottom jaw across the base of his throat, top jaw over the side of his neck into the top of his back and shoulder. Monstrous noises come from its throat, and it shakes its huge black head back and forth with tiny jerks.

I must help him and get to Annie. Dropping my small bundle, I fall forward to grab the price sign from the apple crate and turn to beat the dog's shoulders with all my might. Again and again, I strike it and scream for it to let go.

The dog releases its hold so suddenly that I freeze, shocked. It lifts its powerful head to stare at me—my hands and my extended middle, which now must seem an attractive target. Gardner's blood drips from its teeth. The crowd buzzes nervously around us while Gardner still clutches Annie somewhere near my feet.

God, have mercy.

I gasp and move the sign to become my feeble shield right before a giant man steps forward and grabs the dog's collar. Behind him, a very fancily-dressed gentleman emerges from the crowd and commands in an icy voice, "Michael, get Brutus back to the alley and chain him more securely until you can rebuild his pen. And this time, build it *well.*" Michael drags the resistant, growling Brutus backward.

Gardner and Mary press past me. They are both crying and talking at once. Mary turns back to cling to me, and we watch Gardner attempt to move their son. He has gone limp and must be rolled off of Annie's balled form. Blood runs down his neck and back. Some of it has spilled onto her hair, face, and dress. She stands, trembling violently. At the sight of him, she begins to wail.

"Francis, Charles," Gardner cries out above Annie's reaction to two older men standing nearby. "Help me get him inside. Someone fetch Dr. Bartlett!"

"I'll go," a girl calls before turning to race away.

Mary dashes back into the store ahead of the men with their motionless burden.

Throwing down the sign, I move to my knees and open my arms to Annie. For a moment, she stands there by the crates continuing to shake and cry so hard that she is not aware of me.

Then she opens her eyes and releases an anguished, "Mama!" She jumps into my arms and hugs me fiercely, draping herself over her unborn sibling and pressing her cheek against my chest. I rock her gently back and forth until the worst of her hysteria has passed.

I slowly pull away and brace myself against the crates so I can struggle to my feet. I notice that I, too, am now marked with blood. But Annie seems uninjured, so I pay it no mind. I bend over to stroke her hair and retrieve the bundle I dropped. Then I softly command, "Let's go inside, love."

She clings to my hand, and tears continue to slip from her eyes. Boards creak over our heads. They must have taken him to one of the extra rooms they keep above stairs for brutal winter nights. In all the earlier commotion, the store emptied of customers. While people continue to mill about outside and speak of what's to be done, it remains blessedly empty. I shut the door and turn the sign so *CLOSED* faces the window. Annie and I stand quietly for several minutes, waiting for some sign of the doctor. Finally, he comes behind the young messenger.

We let him in, and I thank the girl before shutting the door again and then locking it for good measure. I point the doctor in the direction of the stairs which he takes two at a time. Annie and I follow at our slower pace.

By the time we reach the top of the tall, narrow case, I am winded and weary, and the door to the main bedroom is shut. Under the dim light of a dormer window, I spy a padded bench. I sink gratefully down upon it while Annie crawls up next to me and tucks herself under my comforting arm.

We wait for an indiscernible amount of time, her alternately dozing and crying for "Gadna," and me staring at nothing and shaking myself occasionally with the renewed burden to pray.

The shadows in the hallway have lengthened considerably when the door opens and the doctor steps out. He confers quietly with Gardner, and they proceed down the stairs together with the aid of a tall candle.

Soft light spills from the bedroom doorway. I do not wish to intrude, but I feel it call to us in a silent invitation. After helping Annie off the bench, I pause and peer around the frame to take in the scene before me. Mary sits in a chair by the head of the bed, crying while she strokes Gardner's forehead with a wet cloth. His face is so pale and his prone form small upon the huge bed frame, I am reminded of how young he still is. At the base of his throat, a clean cloth loosely covers the front wound.

"Mary?"

She starts, turns toward us, and sighs out a sob.

"Is there anything I can do?"

"Come," she whispers.

I step further in and pull my somber daughter along with me.

"Gadna?" she asks in a high, tentative tone.

Mary sets the cloth aside and lifts Annie up so she can see Gardner's face clearly. "He's resting. Blessedly—" her voice catches, "he has slept through the whole of the doctor's ministrations."

When Annie turns in Mary's arms to receive a full embrace, I move forward to, ever so gently, lift the edge of the shielding cloth. The mass of stitches that greets me is a grizzly sight. The doctor did an admirable job given the situation, but Gardner will surely have a horrible scar to deal with. If he survives this.

No, I mustn't think like that. I must cling to hope. "Is it as bad as it appears?"

"Dr. Bartlett is quite concerned. He said Gardner lost a great deal of blood because part of the bite struck a vital point. We don't think the dog is mad, so that is *something*. But the doctor has no idea if Gardner will live through the shock of it, nor if he will be normal and healthy should he survive." All of this is shared in a hushed tone, but I hear every word hit my heart and echo with notes of dread. "Oh, how I wish Mr. Ambrose had never brought his dogs here!" She bends to press her face into Annie's hair.

"I am very sorry. If he had not been protecting Annie, he might have tried to dash to the side like the others and been spared."

She turns reddened eyes upon me that are both fierce and tender. "You are not to blame yourself, do you hear? Just as we will not blame Annie. We could not have foreseen this. We will only be grateful to Providence that He provided her with some protection. And proud of this boy for doing exactly what we've been raising him to do—sacrifice for those around him, especially for those he loves." She pauses to gaze at him again while still pressing Annie close. "And you were very brave. You jumped to defend them when no one else knew how to respond. We told the doctor of your actions. He said it was a good thing. If the dog had kept on jerking its head, Dr. Bartlett fears it would have done even more damage."

I sink onto the edge of the bed and reach out to place a hand tenderly over Gardner's still, cool one. "Gardner, if you can hear me, thank you for protecting my girl—" Emotion swells in my throat to cut off my words.

We lay Annie down to sleep on the far side of the bed, and I keep Mary and Gardner company through the long, dark hours of the night as we take turns nursing their son. In the morning, when Annie wakes, we kiss Mary good-bye and quietly see ourselves out. Both my steps and my heart thud all the way home. He has shown no sign of regaining color or waking. I cannot bear the thought of Gardner and Mary losing their only remaining child.

* * *

July 6, 1822

My dearest Husband,

I am safely delivered of our child, nearly these four
weeks. Between her constant care, keeping up with
her lively sister, and caring for the house, I have had
little time to write and post this letter. I apologize for
the delay.

Yes, it is another girl. She also has your dark hair but
she has my nose and chin. I believe she will take after
you in size. She was at least two pounds heavier than
Annie at her birth! I named her Lydia Gardner Chase.
Elizabeth has been a dear, staying with me for a spell
after the birth, when all of Martha's assistants were in
high demand elsewhere. I chose Gardner for the second
name, and everyone thinks it is to honor my family.
But I really wanted to name her for Gardner and
Mary's son who protected our Annie from a horrible
fate. I will say no more about the incident now but
would wait to tell you in person. (Be not alarmed.
Annie is well.) I feel sure, however, that once you know
the whole story, you will be very pleased with my
decision to give our daughter his name.

Annie is growing steadily. She already shows Lydia
much affection, often asking to hold and rock her. Annie
has started to help me with simple tasks in the kitchen,
displaying great enthusiasm when she does something
well. You would be proud of how smart, attentive, and
obedient she is. I certainly am. She misses you and often

asks when you will come home. She enjoys watching me sew. I hope to help her make her first stitches before long.

My father stopped by to visit us while he was in town for supplies two weeks ago. They are getting by and still longing for the day when their promised replacement cottage at the Point is constructed. He seemed pleased with little Lydia and hopes I'll bring both girls east before summer's end. He discreetly admitted that it should likely be a short visit, as Mother remains none too warm toward me due to our decision to part from the Friends, added to our other collective transgressions. Yet I do want to give her a chance to further accept the children, so I will do my best to be brave and go when both Lydia and I are stronger. William said to inform him of when we are ready, and he will gladly escort us in his calash. He believes some time at the Island's northeast end will be just the fresh inspiration his writer's soul needs.

I write this as proof to you that we continue to remain in good hands and you have no need to be anxious about us. We try not to be anxious for you but turn our troubled thoughts into prayers as we eagerly await your return.

Incidentally, in case the news has not reached you before this missive arrives, Captain Macy of the Rachel took ill and died suddenly, and George has taken over as captain scarcely one year into their long journey. "He is certainly young to be commanding a ship," everyone has declared upon hearing the news. When you hear it, please do not let it gall you. Let us pray the circumstances will cause him to mature further and serve to temper his abundant ambition.

I believe your time as captain will come soon enough, and I pray it will not come primarily due to the misfortune of another.

I have kept my vow and my heart remains—yours,

Peggy

* * *

NOVEMBER 26, 1823

"Mama, why Lyddie sad? Papa coming *home* today!"

We stand at the near end of the wharf on this early afternoon, the brilliant sunshine in a cloudless sky matching our excited mood and chasing away the morning's chill. We're freshly bathed and dressed in our best clothes. I even found time to tame Annie's curls with ribbons and shine our shoes.

"She's not sad, love. You must remember that she does not yet know Papa, so she cannot completely share our excitement." In the distance, we can see a passenger ship coming to dock. I can barely make out the name *Raven* boldly painted on the side. That's it: the ship he said he'd be on in the note he sent a week ago. I turn and kneel so I can look both girls in the eye. This is not hard to do since Lydia's recent growth has made them nearly equal in height. "Both of you look lovely. Your papa's heart will certainly melt at the sight of you." Annie returns my smile with shy hopefulness while Lydia's eyes are wide and touched with apprehension. I pull her close in a quick embrace. "He already loves you, Lydia, even before he's seen you. I know it."

Annie pats her back. "Lyddie, Papa so big and strong and good. Us not afraid." I've often spoken of Owen, so I'm pleased that his memory seems to have remained firmly held in Annie's young mind. But I know that the truest test will come when she sees him face-to-face.

When I stand and turn, the ship docks and two waiting men secure the lines. Then the gangway is put down with a thud, and the passengers begin their short descent to the wharf's weathered walkway in a slow, orderly fashion. There he is, at the end. And how different this feels compared to the last time Annie and I were standing near this very spot. We remain apart from the wharf's commotion and wait for him to come to us.

Then he stands here, in the flesh. Flesh that looks a bit more seasoned but just as tall and proud and handsome as I remember. He has a small pack strapped to his back.

"Welcome home—" I begin my prepared speech.

I can say no more when he kisses me unabashedly. Temporarily throwing modesty to the wind, I eagerly return the gesture before pulling away and looking down to school my features. He reaches out to take my hand.

"I can't tell you how good it is to be here," he whispers near my ear.

"Papa?" Annie calls timidly.

He squats and envelopes her shoulders in his big hands. "Who do we have here? A fairy born out of the sea?" His mouth only holds a hint of a smile, but his eyes twinkle.

"No, Papa! Annie!"

"Aye," he says with a mock scowl. "I believe I met you upon these docks once before, long ago, when you were a mere mite of a girl. Now look at how big and beautiful you are becoming."

"Papa!" she giggles before she steps closer and lifts her arms. He pulls her close and breathes in her sweet scent while running a hand over her silky hair. He opens his eyes, and they settle on Lydia. Gently setting Annie back, he asks her, "And who is this?"

"Lyddie," she answers simply.

"Lydia Gardner Chase, meet your papa," I say in my most formal tone. "Captain Chase, your daughter."

Owen's face fills with tenderness and a small smile. Then he gently extends a finger in her direction and offers a quiet, "I'm pleased to meet such a little lady."

Lydia looks at his hand, then his face before swinging her green, solemn eyes up to seek mine. I bend to pat her shoulder. "We told you, dearest, he is very good."

I see a bit of understanding ripple across her face, and she turns back to him again. Slowly she reaches out her pudgy hand and wraps it around his finger, watching him cautiously all the while.

His smile grows. "There now. I trust we'll learn to get along well."

When he stands once more, Annie eagerly asks, "Papa, you carry us?"

"I would be honored," he declares before scooping her up and settling her on his arm. He shoots me a worried look. "Has your mama been feeding you scraps? You are as light as a feather."

"She's fine," I assure him. "Has the appetite of a horse. Eats well at nearly every meal. She's simply bound to be small, I think."

"And lovely, like you." His eyes run over my face and form before he looks at Lydia. "I have a second, very able arm. Would you care to ride with your sister?"

I hold my breath. She is the careful, timid one. Will she reject the offer?

To my surprise, after only the slightest pause, she releases her hold on my hand and reaches up both arms to him.

He bends over to collect her, the dip making Annie squeal with delight while she clings to his other side. Once righted, they stand like a pillar before me, a collection of all I love most in the world. *God, it is wonderful to have him returning to us looking well and whole.* So different than the last time, he walks confidently, carrying both girls with ease. I work to match his pace, and my heart overflows with thanksgiving.

He sends me a shameless grin. "I hope you've been saving up those kisses. Your offering moments ago reminded me of how truly delightful they are."

I blush with pleasure yet cannot keep from teasing him in return. "There's a whole barrel full, just for you. At home."

"Papa, at home!" Annie pats his tan cheek.

"Papa," Lydia chimes in softly with a hint of a smile.

I laugh. "Well, that's the first she's spoken all day, I do believe. She is our quiet one. How delightful she should spend her words on you."

A tear appears in the corner of his eye. He clears his throat, and we walk on in companionable silence. I let us in the front door, and he sets his armloads down tenderly and somewhat reluctantly before removing the burden from his back.

"Would you care to bathe and rest before supper?"

"I'd rather spend time with the children while they are awake."

"That's fine. Girls, play with your papa while I bake the chicken pie."

I listen to Annie's happy chatter as she and Lydia drag out their small collection of toys and introduce him to their rag dolls. Then he pulls them up onto his lap in the wing chair near the stoked fire and begins to tell them of Ichabod and the mermaid and then about the fantastic sea creatures he saw on this journey. They sit with rapt attention until I declare it's time to eat.

We all have hearty appetites this evening but are also easily distracted. The girls and I often watch him. He looks at each of us in turn while letting his eyes linger on me. When the meal is over and the table cleared, I assist him in heating water and filling the tub. While he bathes, I help the girls change into their nightgowns and hold them close in the rocker, singing Annie's cherished lullaby until they are asleep.

I remain there, rocking and humming, lost in contentment. I start slightly when he appears at the side of the rocker in his clean nightshirt and lays a hand on Lydia's drooping head.

"Let me help you." He slowly picks her up and carries her into the bedroom. I rise and follow with Annie. We lay them next to each other in their smaller bed and tuck them securely under several quilts.

He turns to face me, cupping his hands snuggly around my shoulders. "Are you well?"

"Yes. And you, love?"

"The voyage was not an easy one. I had a number of headaches like the one before my departure. You recall?"

"I do." I reach up to touch his temple and cheek. "And now?"

"Like I said before, words cannot describe my joy at seeing you again." He kisses me deeply. "You are my best medicine." He looks down. "And these two angels. You've done well with them. I already see the proof."

I bask in his praise and slip my arms around his waist. We stand together, watching them from our embrace until he whispers, "Come," and leads me gently back into the kitchen. Stopping beside his pack, he reaches deep and brings out a small, full pouch. When he sets it in my hand, my eyes grow wide. It is heavy with money.

He grins. "That is one bag of several. The ship's owners were indeed generous. And we had a fruitful journey, bringing back a packed ship."

My eyes rise from the pouch to him and then fall back again. I dare to hope, and my hand trembles when I slide the pouch back in its hiding place.

Lifting my face to his again, I see that his smile has vanished and his face is all solemn earnestness. "We have enough now to last a good while. And after seeing the girls, seeing you again…" He presses a line of kisses across my forehead. "I would like to stay for a longer spell. If you would have me." He cups my face with his hands. "Will you have me?"

Tears seep from my eyes. He bends to kiss them away.

"Yes, love. For however long you can stay."

CHAPTER
SEVEN

SEPTEMBER 26, 1824

"We says we going over Jordan, but many folks got other names for it. Mostly it's just called heaven." From where I lie upon the bed, buried under a stack of covers, I listen to Sadie's reassuring, one-sided conversation with Lydia from where they sit together near the door.

"Even if you got another name for it, it all means the same. Being with Jesus forever. And, glory hallelujah, how sweet that gonna be. So you see, angel, your mama's heading to a lovely place where she ain't gonna hurt nor cry no more. She gonna be happy and strong again, and she'll be waiting for you."

Until today, no one has spoken of this. In the days following William Henry's birth, I have progressively weakened, but all my visitors have come to pray and have held out hope that I would recover. As well I wish I could. Three young children with no mother and a whaleman for a father face a possibly perilous—and certainly challenging—future.

This morning, after another visit from Dr. Bartlett, I lifted my weary eyelids to see Owen's face filled with both resignation and sadness. Still, it is Sadie, bless her soul, who is the first to speak plainly of my passing and try to explain it to my daughters in terms they might understand. Annie, who's lying near me on top of the blankets, listens with eyes wide open.

"Sadie," I whisper when she's paused in speaking, "thank you."

She lifts her head to look squarely at me and blinks as two fat tears slip down her cheeks. "We'll be doing our best to keep all these little ones on the straight and narrow so they really gonna be there with you one day."

I close my eyes in exhaustion, and salty drops slip from the far corners and trail toward my ears. "Thank you" is still all I can manage. It seems completely inadequate to reflect my gratitude for all she's done these past days, first guiding me through the arduous day and night of labor, and then returning nearly every day since to help Elizabeth and Mary take care of the house and children while Owen has faithfully stayed by me.

All of them serving quietly and steadfastly, loving me and the children. A deep throbbing swells within. My body longs for the pain to end, but my heart is torn between aching for heaven and wishing I could stay with my precious family and friends.

The room has grown silent. I turn my head slightly and open my eyes again, searching for Owen's face. I trust he will be there. He has barely left my side for quite some time.

"Beloved? Tell me what you need."

"Thirsty," I whisper in a cracking voice.

He presses a cup of cool water to my mouth. My trembling lips can only catch half the liquid. He sets the cup down to tenderly wipe my mouth before trying again.

When he settles my head back on the pillow, I whisper again, a bit more steadily, "Read to me. About heaven."

He strokes my cheek and grimaces. "You know I am no great reader. I'm afraid my performance would provide little comfort."

"*Please.*" I sink to the nearly foreign behavior of begging.

Sadie hears. "I'll read, Miz Peggy, if you like."

"Yes."

She opens the Bible and then flips through the pages until she finds the passage she seeks. When she begins to read, my heart thuds with quiet pride at all the progress she's made through lessons and practice since those days following Annie's birth. Sadie's voice flows through the room with the warm, slow steadiness of evening waves lapping the shore.

"'For we know that if our earthly house of this tabernacle were dissolved, we have a building of God, an house not made with hands, eternal in the heavens. For in this we groan, earnestly desiring to be clothed upon with our house which is from heaven…

"'Therefore we are always confident, knowing that, whilst we are at home in the body, we are absent from the Lord: For we walk by faith, not by sight. We are confident, I say, and willing rather to be absent from the body, and to be present with the Lord. Wherefore we labour, that, whether present or absent, we may be accepted of him. For we must all appear before the judgment seat of Christ; that every one may receive the things done in his body, according to that he hath done, whether it be good or bad…'"

I look over again to see a stream of tears cascading, unchecked, down Owen's face. Now I am certain that he could have read aloud in a very satisfactory manner but he didn't trust himself to read the words without breaking down. Still, breaking down he is, and in a way I've never seen, save for those nights directly following his miracle return.

Annie sits up and notices his distress. She slips down over the side of the bed and walks around to stand before him. When she puts her small hand on his knee, he opens his eyes to take in what must be a very blurry impression of her sweet face. He pulls her into his embrace and presses his face against her hair while she clings to him.

"'…For he hath made him to be sin for us, who knew no sin; that we might be made the righteousness of God in him. We then, as workers together with him, beseech you also that ye receive not the grace of God in vain. For he saith, I have heard thee in a time accepted, and in the day of salvation have I succored thee: behold, now is the accepted time; behold, now is the day of salvation…'"

His shoulders shake with silent sobs. My heart shakes with him. I long to comfort him though the words and promises tug at my soul, calling me away. I am so weary.

"'…But in all things approving ourselves as the ministers of God, in much patience, in afflictions, in necessities, in distresses, in stripes, in imprisonments, in tumults…yet always rejoicing; as poor, yet making many rich; as having nothing, and yet possessing all things…'"

He stops trembling and heaves a mighty sigh before finally containing himself again and raising his gaze to the room. His eyes are red, his cheeks blotchy—yet a kind of new peace has entered his expression.

"Want me to stop reading?"

"For a time," he rasps. He clears his throat. "The words are good. But I need to speak with Peggy, to settle some things. Would you mind taking the girls for a short walk?"

"Surely." She sets Lydia on the floor. Owen does the same with Annie. The children take Sadie's offered hands and reluctantly leave the room.

Owen comes around to the far side of the bed where Annie so recently lay. Removing his shoes, he climbs upon the mattress and settles himself with his back against the headboard. Then he carefully lifts and turns me, placing my shoulder against his chest and my head against his shoulder. I see his intention in arranging me thus. When I manage to lift my eyes in one direction, I can catch a glimpse of his profile above me. In the other direction, I behold the tiny face of our sweet son where he lies in the old sleeping box, snuggly swaddled and content.

"He is perfect," I whisper. "Worth every bit of pain and bloodshed."

Owen's initial reply is a soft kiss on my forehead. Finally, he speaks, his deep voice reaching me both through the rumble of his chest and upon the cool September air. "I am glad you feel it so. I would be plagued with guilt otherwise. You have given me a wonderful son. But my heart breaks to see you sacrificed in the process."

"You know I would give my life for Annie, Lydia, William, and you."

"I know." His mouth shifts to clinch in a familiar way.

"Your head?"

"Aye. It matters not," he grunts. "I will be strong because I must be. For the children."

"Are you at peace? With God and with yourself? I cannot leave you thinking that you will become a slave to grief, anger, or bitterness." At my urgent need to convince him on this matter, I feel my energy draining further, faster. I must hold on a little longer. There are things yet unsaid.

He seems to sense it too. His strong hands squeeze mine where he's covered them, and he whispers against my ear, "Save your words and your strength. I'm coming to accept it. With the help of the Almighty, I shall come through this squall."

I feel the evenness of his breathing and sense the anchor of his faith holding steady. *Thank You.* "Please—if you can, try to make peace with George too, when next you see him. And continue to deal respectfully with your father. You need each other. We must do what we can to heal our family's broken places, while we draw breath…" My own breathing has become more labored, my lungs heavier.

He pauses. "What you say is good. I will do what I can to further span the divide with each of them. And your parents, if possible."

"Nearly a year ago you returned to us," I whisper again into the silence. "These have been the happiest, most precious months of my entire life."

"And mine, I think. What a wonderful garland of memories we've woven—memories I will keep alive for the children. I won't let them forget you." He swallows. "But you know the time will come when I must go to sea again. It is my calling, what I am gifted at and designed to do."

"But would they not benefit more from having you near? Please, love, don't leave them alone." The last words come out in a tiny gasp of anguish when I'm seized with panic.

He presses me closer and lifts his fingers to my lips. "Peggy, I swear to you that I will not abandon them. I will provide for them. Somehow."

Calmness washes over me while my heart calls out a solution. His hand lowers back to mine, and I simply say, "Promise me."

"What?"

"What I promised you one early morning. Do you recall?"

He swallows hard and nods slightly.

"Promise me you will marry again. If you find someone you can love, who can bring you comfort—all the better for you and for her. But if you can at least find a woman with an honest heart, who would love our children and treat them well, that is enough." A wave of chills sweeps across my body, and my head slips back in complete exhaustion. "Promise me," I repeat in a voice barely audible.

His voice is sure and clear. "Rest easy. I promise you."

His words fill my heart with peace. I fall asleep to the sound of his heartbeat.

* * *

I'm not sure how long I've slept, but when I open my eyes again, with some monumental effort, the room is dim and a few candles have been lit in addition to a bright blaze crowning the hearth.

Dear faces are crowded around the bed. Judah stands beside William and Elizabeth. Sadie, Solomon, Joshua, and Isaiah are all here, tears on each of their faces. And though they stand a bit apart, it does my heart good to know that every other person in the room counts them as dear friends. Mary holds William Henry tenderly while Lydia clings to Joseph as he stands beside Winifred, his new bride of a few weeks.

I try to smile at Lydia in reassurance. "Owen. Annie." My sluggish tongue barely cooperates.

"We are here," Owen assures me, and I shift my eyes to the side where I hear his voice. I'm too weak to turn my head so he gently turns it for me until I can see them both. He sits near me again with Annie enfolded in his steady arms. They watch me solemnly.

"Annie," I whisper, "I can't take care of Papa anymore. Will you be a big girl and take care of him for me?" My voice is pathetically weak, like the mews of a newborn kitten I once nursed. But her sensitive ears capture the words.

She nods. "Yes, Mama. I will help Papa."

"That's my sweet girl. Owen, I love you."

"And I, you. You don't have to linger. I am—we all are—in good hands."

"I know." My heartbeat stutters. "I have seen them." My throat closes.

I watch the two of them with all the love left in me. Their faces are the last thing I see before my eyelids fall and my chest cannot expand again.

I float in a mixture of warm air and liquid, in the darkness of unearthly sleep. Then I am bathed in a golden light, a light somehow brighter than the sun but one which does not blind me. I have never felt so free, so complete, so accepted.

I move farther on toward what seems to be the source of the light, and I hear an unknown yet strangely familiar voice.

It's calling me by a new, more fitting name.

PART 2
PHEBE

SEPTEMBER 27, 1824

"I am not afraid of storms for I am learning how to sail my ship."

~ LOUISA MAY ALCOTT
AMERICAN NOVELIST, 1832–1888

CHAPTER
EIGHT

Sadie called it something like going over. But how can someone go anywhere when we put them in a box under the ground? I don't understand.

"Mama." I whisper her name because Papa said I must be good and quiet. I hold onto his fingers tightly. His other arm is holding Lyddie. She looks down at the wooden box in the hole and then at me. Papa looks straight ahead.

A man reads from a small Bible. He talks about some things I've never heard before. Sadie and Mama told us about living with God. But the man says that first she must turn into dust. Mama's beautiful face turn into dust? I start to cry. I pinch my mouth closed, but I can't keep the tears in, no matter how many times I blink.

I close my eyes.

Papa's hand squeezes mine.

I look up again. He looks down at me. His mouth is a flat line, but his eyes are warm and shiny. I turn my face and press it against his leg.

I have wanted to cry ever since Mama went to sleep and didn't wake up again. But I promised her I would help take care of Papa. So I have tried to be good and help him with Lyddie.

I'm tired of helping. I miss Mama. I want Mama to come back. Now I need Papa to take care of me. *I'm sorry if you're unhappy with me, Mama.* I cry harder. Papa pulls away and stoops to pick me up in his other arm. He lets me cry against his coat.

A lady from church starts to sing a pretty song. It reminds me of Mama's voice. I feel calmer and cry less. I lift my face and whisper, "Papa, I tried to be quiet and good. Did I do all right?"

He kisses my cheek. But he doesn't say anything.

My stomach starts to hurt.

* * *

A lady named Alice starts coming to our house every afternoon. She is very old. Papa says she wants to help us. That's good. I can't do many things that Mama did. And Papa can't do some of them either.

But I still try to help. I keep Lyddie happy and out of trouble. I change my clothes and help Lyddie change hers. I pull up our bed covers every morning, and I feed the chickens. I put bread and milk on the table for breakfast, and I try to sweep the floor. But the broom is so heavy.

Alice calls me her good helper, almost the same way Mama used to. She is teaching me how to thread a needle, boil water, add fuel to the fire, and milk the cow. But I am still a little scared of the cow. She is *big*.

I miss William Henry. He's gone to stay with Uncle William and Aunt Elizabeth. Papa looked sad when he told us about that. He said we can't feed William Henry the way Aunt Elizabeth can. Why? We have plenty of food. But Aunt Elizabeth brings him around almost every day so we can see him. He's getting fat—just like her baby, Frances. They must have really good food at their house.

***

Papa stays home with us most of the time, but when Alice comes, he goes out to do some work. Unless his head hurts. Then he stays in a dark room and cries and sleeps.

Days get colder and storms come. Papa never leaves us if there is a storm. And when the snow is deep and Alice can't come, he tries to cook for us. I love Papa, but he can't cook. We eat the food anyway because we are so hungry. He holds us and tells us wonderful stories while the wind blows hard outside.

There is a very terrible storm, and William Henry cannot come for a few days.

On the third day, Papa looks outside. He says, "It looks clear enough. And we're out of nearly everything. Let's go see Aunt Mary."

"And Uncle Gardner?" I do up my coat buttons.

"Yes." He fastens Lyddie's coat.

"And Gardner?" I try to tie my bonnet but it's hard.

"Aye, if he's not at school." He reaches down to help me. "I imagine they've had a few days off too, with this weather."

I jump up and down and run in a circle. I'm so excited! Lyddie watches me and starts squealing.

Papa puts on his hat and looks at the ceiling. "I think we've all got cabin fever."

I don't know what that is. I don't feel sick. But it is nice to go out in the fresh air and see other people again.

The store is warm when we go in. I run to Aunt Mary for a hug. Then to Uncle Gardner and hug his leg. Then I run to where Gardner is stacking bags in long rows. I throw my arms around his long, skinny legs and giggle. He looks down at me and smiles and pats my head. Aunt Mary told Papa once that Gardner only smiles for me.

KAYLENE POWELL

He stops his stacking, kneels down, and takes a penny from his pocket.

I open my hand to collect it. "Thank you."

He smiles again. I touch the edge of the scars on his neck. I am very gentle. But he doesn't smile anymore. He looks sad.

"Don't be sad, Gardner." I pat his cheek. Then I run back to Uncle Gardner and ask him for some candy sticks. "One for Gardner and one for Lyddie. And one for me!"

"And have you any money, my dear? Or is a beautiful young lady such as yourself expecting to pay with only a smile?"

I smile and give him the penny. "Is it enough?"

"For three sticks? Certainly. Now, what flavors will you have?"

"Peppermint, orange, and lemon." Like always.

He wraps up the first two and slips them into my pocket. Then he gives me the last one to carry back to Gardner.

"Delicious," he says in his whisper voice. I hug his legs one more time.

Papa comes up beside us. "Has the candy fairy visited?" Gardner nods. Aunt Mary says he only speaks to me too. Papa turns to me. "Why don't you ever get a stick of candy for me? Don't you love me?"

"Oh yes, Papa." I jump over to hug his leg. I turn around and skip toward the glass jars again. But I stop and run back to Papa quick as can be. "I don't know which one you like best. And I only have a smile to pay with now."

He laughs and runs his fingers across my forehead. "I'm only having a little fun. I don't need any candy. I'd much rather have your kisses." He bends low and I stretch high till our faces are close.

"Papa?"

"Hmmm."

"You laughed. You haven't laughed for a long time. I miss your laugh." I kiss one side of his face and then the other.

He straightens. "I've missed it too." He sets a hand on Gardner's shoulder. "Peggy told me about what you did for Annie. But I've never fully expressed my gratitude. I cannot imagine going through these past months without her bright smile and sweet chatter to be my guiding light. Thank you for protecting her."

I turn and spot Lyddie. She is getting very close to the stove. "No, Lyddie!" I call, running over to pull her back. "Are you cold?" She nods. I lead her to Aunt Mary. "Lyddie's cold."

"Well, come here, my love." Aunt Mary wraps Lyddie in the edge of her shawl. Lyddie sighs and snuggles. Aunt Mary winks at me. "You are a good sister, Annie."

"Phebe Ann?" I've heard that voice somewhere before. I turn toward the speaker. She has a kind but serious face. "Do you remember me?"

"A little." I feel shy. "Are you Mama's friend?"

"Yes. I came to have tea at your house, a long time ago. My, how you've grown."

"Annie?" Papa comes near us, watching the woman.

"This is Mama's friend."

She turns to Papa. "Good day to you. I'm Nancy Joy."

The look on Papa's face changes very quickly. "Matthew's wife?"

She nods and swallows.

Papa looks down at the floor. "I guess you know who I am. And I can only wonder what you think of me."

"From all the gossip, my opinion should be low. From all I heard from your wife and read in your own account, however, my opinion has taken a decidedly different direction."

Papa's head comes up. "You do not think me a traitor to the Island?" His voice grows softer. "Or a failure to the crew?"

"I think you a person with weaknesses, like any other—and with strengths all your own."

He clears his throat. "Annie says you knew Peggy?"

"Yes, we met at church one Sunday. I came for tea on a few different occasions. We received news of her passing only recently. I'm sorry for your loss. It is a unique kind of pain, isn't it?"

Papa nods. "Perhaps…" He looks at me and then back at her. "Perhaps you would like to come to tea again? I cannot make her scones, but I can boil water." They both smile.

"Fear not. My muffins are famous among all who have tasted them. Truth be told, they are one of my only triumphs in the kitchen—but, oh, what a triumph. I will accept your invitation on the condition that I am allowed to bring some."

"I concede. Come tomorrow, at midday, if that will suit."

"Yes, thank you." She looks at me again before stepping away.

"Papa?"

She's gone out the door. But he still stands like she's in front of him.

"Hmmm?"

"Can I sit with you when she comes tomorrow?"

"Yes, if you promise to be quiet so we can talk."

"Like I was just now?"

"Like you were just now."

* * *

Nancy's muffins are more delicious than stick candy. She returns to visit us often after the first time. She talks with Papa about many things. I only understand some of what they say. But she also talks with me and Lyddie about the things we like. And when William Henry comes to stay in the spring—Papa says we can feed him some now—Nancy holds him and plays with him. She looks a little sad when she holds him. He likes her very much. But I watch her closely. And Lyddie is so shy around her.

One day, after Nancy goes home, I ask, "Papa, you love me and Lyddie, right?"

"Yes."

"And you love William Henry?"

"Yes, I do."

"Do you love Nancy?"

He stops fixing the broken chair in front of him and looks up at me. "What?"

"Do you love Nancy?"

"I…" He looks over my head at someplace far away. "I suppose I do—in a way. Not like I loved your mama. But I enjoy Nancy's company."

"Will she come to live with us?"

"Would you like that?"

"You smile when she comes. I want you to be happy."

He swallows and goes back to his fixing.

* * *

JUNE 15, 1825

Papa marries Nancy on a sunny day in June. All our friends come to the church to watch. I stand with Uncle William and Aunt Elizabeth, holding Lyddie's hand. After they are done saying a lot of words with the pastor, Papa kisses both of us and tells us to be good girls for Aunt Elizabeth. Uncle William carries William Henry and leads us away to his calash.

"Why is Papa sending us to stay with you?" I ask the question I see in Lyddie's eyes.

"Don't worry, my fairies. He wants to get to know Nancy."

"But he already knows her."

He grins and lifts me onto the seat.

* * *

We stay away forever. Well, we stay away two weeks, but how I miss Papa. "When will we go home, Aunt Elizabeth?"

She looks up from her sweeping. "Tomorrow, I think. We received word from your papa this morning. He has bought a house from your Grandpa Judah. Your papa is to be a captain. Isn't that exciting?"

I clutch my doll. "A captain? Is that good?"

"Yes, sweetheart. He's achieving his dream."

* * *

The new house is so much bigger than our old one. It is closer to the wharves, the church, the store. Lyddie and I run through the rooms, exploring everything. There is even a full above-stairs floor!

When I come back to Papa, I jump to give him a hug. "There are many rooms!"

"Yes," he smiles, "and there's an attic. And a roof-walk. We'll go up tonight after dark, and I will give you your first lesson in reading the stars."

I hug his neck and squeal with happiness.

Later, after William Henry is safely tucked in his sleeping box, we stand on the roof-walk and look up at the blanket of sparkles across the sky. Lyddie won't let Nancy hold her, so Papa lifts Lyddie. He gives me a serious look and a nod. I swallow and let Nancy lift me. Up, up, back, back—my head falls and rolls, trying to take in everything at once.

Papa points to one star after another, telling us the names and pausing so I can try to repeat them. Some are really hard to say. Papa is clever to remember so many names. When he stops naming and stares upward, I say, "Aunt Elizabeth said you are a captain now, and it is your dream."

He sighs and looks at me. "Aye. That means I will be the leader of all the men on one ship. I'm going to sail from New Bedford on the *Winslow* next month."

"You mean you're going away? With your harpoon?"

"Aye."

"For a long time?"

"Aye."

"Papa, no go!" Lyddie throws her arms around his neck.

His eyes grow wide. Then they close. He hugs her back. "I must. Don't fear. Nancy will stay with you and care for you. You will make a new home in this big, wonderful house."

I turn to study Nancy. "You won't go away? And you won't sleep like Mama did?"

"No, dear. If God wills it. I'll do all in my power to stay with you and keep you safe while your papa is gone."

I frown. "All of us? William Henry too?"

She looks at Papa. "All of you. I promise."

He takes her hand. "You have been my good girls. I need you to continue to be good and brave. Listen to Nancy, do as she says, go to church, eat your food all up, drink your milk, and say your prayers."

"We will pray for you every night, when we look at the stars," I offer.

"Thank you, Treasure. As I will for you."

* * *

AUGUST 1825

We go down to the wharf with Papa. The day is warm, and so is the wind. He kisses William Henry's head where he is tied in a sling to Nancy's front. He kisses Nancy's cheek and whispers "thank you" in her ear. He hugs and kisses Lyddie. And then he turns to me.

"One more kiss? It has to be sweet enough to last me all the way to the far side of the world and back." He smiles, but his eyes are very sad.

He lifts me high in the air and brings me down so I can kiss him. Then he wraps me in a bear hug.

We watch him walk down to the boat that will carry him to the other town, the one where he said the big ship is waiting. When he gets on board, he waves one more time and then the boat pulls away from the dock.

We walk home together, Lyddie and me each holding one of Nancy's hands. "Do we need to call you 'Mama' now?" I ask.

"You don't need to. But you can, if you like. When you're ready."

I think about that as we go on silently. I don't want to call her Mama. But I will be good and brave, like I promised Papa.

CHAPTER
NINE

JULY 23, 1827

"Why did Papa name me Phebe and not a better name like Marian or Guinevere?" I carry some dirty dishes to the washbasin.

Nancy cannot hide her smile. "And what makes you think those names so superior?" She adds some hot water while I make another trip to the table.

"Aunt Mary read us the stories of Robin Hood and King Arthur last week. Their ladies were great and lovely and beautiful. But with a name like Phebe, I'm going to grow up to be plain and boring and small. No hero will love me."

"You're too young to be worrying about such things. Besides," she sighs, "your papa loves you, and he is a hero."

"But that's not the same! I can't marry Papa. He's already married to you."

Her smile flashes wide but then fades. "Yes, he is." Her eyes fill with sadness. "Though he has not yet returned to us, so I barely feel the truth of it." She shakes her head and studies me. "You will grow up to be beautiful, I have no doubt of that. And you will find a hero all your own."

"Like King Arthur or Robin Hood?"

"I think I need to speak to Mary about her choice of reading material," she says in a low voice. Then, "I can't say that he'll be like those men. But hopefully he will be well-suited to complement you."

"You mean he will tell me lots of nice things?"

"Well, yes, I hope he will. But he will be a good match for you in the way you think and in the things you value."

I set down the last of the dishes and frown. "I don't understand."

"One day you will. And when that day comes, you'll know you're ready to find your hero. Until then, try to be a good girl."

I pick up a towel. "But, Nancy, what about my name?"

She starts to wash the dishes, handing them to me for drying. "I asked your mama about that once, when I came to visit her and you were very small. You see, your papa was at sea when you were born, and he didn't know about you for some time, so your mama had to name you herself. She named you for his mother, your grandmother. She died when your papa was a couple of years older than you are now."

I frown and try to follow. "You mean Grandma Ruth isn't Papa's real mama?"

"No. Grandpa Judah married again after his first wife died."

"Like Papa married you?"

"Yes."

"Does Papa…" I stare at the counter and swallow. "Does he love Grandma Ruth?"

She hesitates. "I don't know. But boys—and men—are different. They don't always discuss their affections openly."

"Did Papa love Grandma Phebe?"

"Yes, I believe so. He didn't speak of her often while he was home, but it was always with tenderness."

"Then I'm glad Mama gave me her name."

"It's a fine thing to be content with what you cannot change. Always remember that. It will help you through a lot of difficult things in life."

A quick knock sounds at the front door.

Nancy dries her hands and moves to answer it, me coming close behind. Standing in the bright summer sunshine is a boy I've seen running up and down the streets. He has hair straight and gold like hay, and his face is covered in freckles.

"Hello there," Nancy greets him. "What can we do for you?"

"This the house of Cap'n Chase?" the boy mumbles low and fast.

"It is." There's something odd in her tone.

"Got a message for you, sent from Mr. Coffin." He pulls an envelope from his pocket. Nancy takes it, thanks him, and takes a penny from her apron pocket to drop in his waiting hand. He dashes away.

Nancy turns while shutting the door and looking down at the letter. She glances at me. "It's in your papa's handwriting." Then her smile flashes, and she looks up again. "It was sent from New Bedford two days ago."

"Is he coming home?"

She begins to read the now-open letter with shaking hands. "Yes, he writes that he is lately arrived from a very successful voyage, and he will be home on the twenty-fourth. Why— that's tomorrow."

"Papa!" I jump and spin in a circle, my dish towel waving like a wind-whipped flag.

Lyddie and Will come running from the parlor, their eyes wide. "Papa?" Lyddie asks softly.

"He's back in New Bedford," Nancy explains in her warmest tone. "He's to arrive home tomorrow. Oh, it's the most wonderful news. But there is so much to prepare. Annie, we need to clean everything well. And I want to plan a special supper. I'll try my best not to burn everything." She paces back and forth, squeezing the edge of her apron in her fist and looking at something far away, her voice growing lower and quicker. "And I'll wash the clothes he left behind…" She keeps on walking, right out of the room, still talking to herself.

I turn from the doorway and look back at Will and Lyddie. My smile falls. Lyddie looks nervous, and Will looks confused. Far back in my mind, I hear Mama's voice speaking to me when Papa came home the last time. I try to remember what she said.

I walk over and take their hands. I lead them into the parlor where we can all sit on our small wooden chairs. "Papa's coming back to us. Don't worry. He will be happy to see us again."

"What Papa like?" Will asks.

"Big and strong!" Lyddie tells him with wide eyes.

"Yes," I agree. "And he gives the best hugs and tells the best stories. I think I remember that his head hurts sometimes. But all the other times he is nice and good."

"Will Papa stay forever now?" Lyddie asks. She's started learning about forever at church, but I don't think she really understands it.

"I don't know." Will he go away and leave us alone with Nancy again? My stomach drops at the thought. "Maybe, if we ask nicely, he will stay forever, or at least for a long time—"

"Papa stay my birt-day!" Will shouts.

"Will, remember to speak softly inside. And we just told you this morning it's two more months before your birthday—"

"I be twee!" He speaks a little quieter and holds up his chubby fingers.

"Yes, we know. But please don't interrupt. It's not polite and—"

"So Papa stay see me twee." He sits back on his chair and swings his legs wildly.

"I hope so," I sigh. "But you had better behave like a big boy, or Papa will think you're a baby." I manage to say it all before he can cut me off again.

Will stares at me with angry eyes. "I no baby!"

"Then show us, and stop acting like one," I say.

He sits up straight on his chair and holds his whole body— even his face—very still. He looks so serious and unnatural that I almost start to laugh. But then I see that Lyddie still looks worried.

"What's the matter?" I ask her.

"Will Papa stop loving us if we do something wrong?"

"Oh, no. He will always love us. No matter if we do good or bad things. We don't have to worry about that." At least, I hope that's true.

"How do you know?"

"That's what Mama always said. And because Papa is Papa. And, because I *know*." It strikes me funny, and I giggle. I can't stop. And pretty soon, Will and Lyddie are giggling with me.

Nancy sticks her head through the doorway. "What's going on in here?" she asks with a raised eyebrow. We freeze, silencing immediately.

Then Lyddie and I look at each other, and we start giggling all over again. We can't help it. Nancy shakes her head with a smile. But her voice is serious. "Now, Annie, stop being silly. Come upstairs."

I slip from my chair and jump to Lyddie's side. If Mama were here, she would hug us to make us feel better. I hug Lyddie, and then I hug Will. I move toward the stairs then turn back. "We should be good because that makes Papa and Mama and

Nancy proud. And makes God happy. Lyddie, take care of Will. Will, mind Lyddie."

Will relaxes in his seat. Lyddie looks more at ease.

Nancy's voice rings out. "Phebe Ann Chase. I told you to come. And I meant it. Don't dawdle and force me to paddle you. I need your help."

I bite my lip and run up the steps. That big paddle hurts so much. Besides, doesn't she see that I am helping?

* * *

"I see him, Nancy, I see him!" I stand beside her and Will and Lyddie at the bottom of the hill near the wharf. Papa is walking toward us through the crowd of crewmen, dock workers, green hands, and passengers. I only remember his face a little, but I know it's him. I can't wait any longer. I dash into the crowd, running around long legs, crates, animals, and cart wheels.

"Annie! Come back!" Her voice sounds both angry and afraid.

I turn back but don't see her. The things and people around me are too tall. I can't get my bearings. And I can't see Papa. I clutch my dress and spin in a circle, jumping out of the way when a horse almost steps on me. I run into a big, dirty man. He glares at me, and I back away. Another man shouts suddenly up to a boat docked nearby. I jump and get in the way of a woman carrying a large load stacked under her chin. She yells and knocks me to the side with her wide, swaying hips.

Which way can I go? How can I get back to Nancy? How can I find Papa? I look down at my shoes—the ones Nancy made me work hard to clean this morning—covered in muck. Oh, Nancy will be so unhappy. I press myself against some crates and try to become invisible.

But then I remember that Papa will always love us, no matter what we do. Nancy may be angry, but Papa will love me. Papa is home. I have to find him!

I step back into the flow of people and look around again. I start to cry. "Papa!" I yell it as loud as I can in the middle of all the noise, but my voice is swallowed up. "Papa!" My tears make everything blurry. I close my eyes and cry and yell. "Papa, Papa!"

I sob so hard I can't say his name anymore. And then strong hands lift me up and carry me a little way before setting me down on what feels like a crate. I open my eyes and swipe at the tears. I thought it was Papa who picked me up, but it's not. A young man stands there looking at me.

"What's wrong, girl?" His voice carries a jagged edge. "What are you doing down here?"

"I saw Papa, but now I can't find him. I want to go home with Papa!"

"You're too small to be running around on the wharf."

Tears fill my eyes again.

"There now." He pats me awkwardly on the shoulder and tries to smile. "Let's find that father of yours. Did you, by chance, come down here with anyone else?"

"Yes. Nancy and Will and Lyddie. They're over there somewhere, I think. Can you see them?"

The man turns around and strains on his toes. "I don't know what they look like. We can walk to wharf's end and look for them there." He reaches to pull me off the crate.

"Annie." Papa's voice. A big hand lands on the man's shoulder. "Don't touch her!" The big hand pulls the man around. I look up to see Papa staring at the man while stretching his other hand toward me.

It was Papa I saw. But, oh, how angry he looks now. I grip his hand and squeeze it. "He was helping me." Papa pulls me up in his strong arms and holds me near. I hug his neck. "Please don't be angry."

The man looks at Papa with recognition. "Hello, Mr. Chase. It's been a long time, sir."

"Thomas," Papa says with a nod, all his anger gone.

"Sorry if I acted wrongly, sir. Came upon her crying. Wanted to get her off the wharf again is all."

"I thank you for your assistance. And I apologize for responding so hastily."

"Not at all, sir. If it were my sister or daughter, I reckon I'd feel and do the same."

"How long before you sail again? Can you come to the house for supper some evening? I'd like to hear your news and know how you've fared."

"I depart in two weeks. We've much to prepare, but I think I should be free tomorrow night."

"Very well. We live at the corner of Orange Street and Maiden Lane. We'll be expecting you."

They exchange farewells, and Papa carries me until we reach the base of the hill. He sets me down and kneels beside me.

I hug him again.

He hugs me back, firmly, and then pulls away. "You scared Nancy very badly. She couldn't see you. When I came up, she sent me back to try and locate you."

At the same moment, Nancy comes bustling along, bringing Lyddie and Will by the hand. "Phebe Ann!" She struggles to catch her breath. "I told you—to come back—and stay with us!"

"I couldn't see you. I didn't know which way to go."

Papa's voice is calm. "It's all right. Thomas Nickerson happened upon her and kept her safe."

"Thank the Lord. But look how filthy and disheveled you are. After all the work I put in to helping you be extra presentable."

She shakes her head. "This should have been a happy time for us, and you've gone and made a mess of it."

My face feels hot, and my bottom lip slides forward. "I'm sorry!"

"Never mind it," Papa replies with a small smile. "You meant no harm, and while you scared us, I know you were eager to see me. As I have been to see you. Whether you meet me nicely groomed or looking like a homeless urchin, I will soak up your love."

He turns to Lyddie and says, "And here we are, Lydia. How is my other big girl?"

Lyddie glances at me. I nod and smile. She steps forward and lets him hug and kiss her.

He turns to Will. "Hello, William Henry. You've grown a great deal."

"Papa," Will breathes in deep to look bigger and stronger. "Next birt-day, I be twee!" he declares.

"Yes, my boy. I remember." He grabs Will in a bear hug and rubs his hair. "It's your turn, I believe, for a ride from Papa. Unless you are too big for such things?"

"Will ride! Will ride!" he hollers with a grin.

"Very well." Papa stands and sets Will atop his shoulders. Will grabs Papa's hat to keep his balance.

Papa stops in front of Nancy. "In the excitement, we didn't get to greet each other. Perhaps we can start afresh? Hello." He leans down and kisses her cheek.

"Welcome home." She touches his arm. "We've missed you."

"You miss us, Papa?" Will asks, tapping the hat like a drum.

Papa's eyes fly upward. "Every day." We all turn and begin the walk home. He squeezes my hand and sends me a wink before answering Will's next question.

It is good to have Papa back again. We are all happy at supper, even if Nancy is not good at cooking. The roast is charred, but Papa is home. The beans are too mushy, but Papa is home. The cake is gooey in the middle. But Papa is home! I sit through the meal, moving the food around on my plate while I watch him. He talks a little and eats a lot as Nancy tells him some of the local news. Every so often, he glances over at me.

When we are all finished eating, Lyddie softly asks, "May we hear a story tonight, Papa? Annie said you tell the best stories."

"Story. Papa, please!" Will agrees to the grand suggestion.

"I think I can muster up a good one," he says with a glance at Nancy. "Thank you for preparing the meal. It was fine. If you'll excuse us." He stands and turns to me. "Perhaps you'd like to join us?"

I grin and place my hand in his, but Nancy's voice stops further movement. "There will be no story for you tonight. Your shoes and dress need cleaning. Since your foolish spontaneity led to their messiness, you will be the one to clean them. After you help me clear the table, wash the dishes, and milk the cow."

I bow my head and tremble all over. Papa's still holding my hand. He squeezes it. I peek up to the side, unsure of what I'll see. He is looking at Nancy with his mouth set in a thin line. Dropping my head once more, I whisper, "Yes, Nancy," and pull my hand away. I can feel Nancy and Papa watching me while I reach out to stack the plates.

I glance over as Papa leads Lyddie and Will from the room. He gazes back at me. His mouth is still set, but his eyes are warm. "Don't worry," he murmurs when I walk past. "I'll save your favorite tales for another night."

The next morning, while we are eating breakfast, Papa clears his throat. "Nancy and I talked last night, and now I have some things to tell you." We all look at him and wait. Even Will is quiet. "Annie, it's time for you to have more formal schooling. Nancy tells me you're very bright, and it would be better for you to learn from a qualified teacher."

I bite my lip and send him a pleading look. He nods. "Papa, if I go away to school all day, I cannot stay here with Lyddie and Will. And you. And Nancy."

"It will be a great opportunity for you. And you'll only be gone for several hours. You'll still be here in the late afternoons and evenings."

"Annie," Nancy speaks firmly, "you should be grateful to your papa for agreeing to this and paying your tuition. You are a big girl. You mustn't whine."

"I don't mean to whine," I reply. "But what if I don't know anyone else there?"

"I think that can be easily remedied," Papa says as he butters his toast. "I'll talk to Gardner and Mary. I reckon young Gardner is still in school here?" He lifts a brow toward Nancy and she nods. "Though he must be reaching the end of his basic education. I'll ask them about the school he attends and see if I can't enroll you there. Then, you would know at least one person."

"Oh, thank you," I sigh. If Gardner is there, I know I will be all right. "And then I can spend time with you in the evenings, can't I?"

"Aye, you can. That is, while I'm here."

"Why wouldn't you be here? You just came home."

"I must go away again before long."

Lyddie asks, "But Papa, won't you stay forever?"

"No, Lydia, I cannot. They are already preparing my ship, all the supplies, and necessary additions to the crew. The ship owners expect me to sail again quite soon."

"When?" I ask while putting a hand on Lyddie's arm.

"My ship leaves New Bedford in three weeks."

"Papa home my birt-day?" Will asks, his voice high and hopeful.

"No, son," Papa looks at him and then down at the table. "I must go before then."

"Papa stay. Please!" Will bursts into tears.

"William Henry," Nancy calls above his sobbing, "this is difficult for all of us. Be a big boy now, and be still."

But he only cries harder. Papa gets up from his chair, steps around the table, and picks Will up. But Papa doesn't know Will doesn't like anybody to touch him when he's angry.

"Papa—" I start to warn him but then stop when Nancy gives me The Look.

Will struggles against Papa, hitting and kicking. Papa keeps his big arms wrapped around Will and listens to him crying. Finally, after a couple of minutes, Will stops fighting, puts his arms around Papa's neck, and releases a shuddering sigh. Papa sits down again and holds Will close. Papa's eyes are clenched shut, and he looks tired.

"I must go away again, William. I am sorry to miss your birthday. But think of how much bigger you will be the next time I return." He tries to smile but can't quite do it.

Papa looks at Lyddie and then me. His jaw tenses when he sees the tears on both our faces. "All of you will be bigger. And I will love you then, like I do now—and in all the many days between. But, let's not be sad. We have these days together, and I want to spend time with you. Perhaps after church on Sunday we can have a squantum?"

All three of us smile through our tears. "Oh yes, Papa. And can we stay at the beach," I request, "and make sand shapes after we eat?"

"And look for shells?" Lyddie adds.

"And pway tase-tase?" Will mumbles with the side of his mouth still against Papa's shirt.

"Aye, we can do all those things." He turns to me again. "And I'll make the arrangements, but Annie doesn't have to start school until after I leave. That way, we'll have more time together."

I smile my thanks to him but then look back to see Nancy's face. She also looks sad about Papa leaving. But then she nods her agreement, and I sigh my relief.

Papa will go away again. And I will go to school. And everything will change. But today Papa is here and I am here, and days are full of goodness. So I will hold on to that.

* * *

The days fly by as fast as a red-breasted merganser. The next night, the man from the wharf comes to supper. He and Papa sit by the fire and are still talking when I go to bed. We go on the squantum Papa promised—and then have three more on other days when the weather is fine. The freshly baked clams taste so good!

Uncles, aunts, and friends visit or join us for supper. Grandpa Judah comes to see us, and I'm glad. I like him so much—especially when he holds me in his arm-trap and won't let me go until I say the magic words. That always makes me giggle until I cry. Then he laughs too. And his laugh is deep like thunder on a hot night. After he goes home, Papa says I'm a special girl because he hasn't heard Grandpa Judah laugh for many years. Maybe that's why his laugh is so gritty sounding.

Nancy keeps me busy. Cooking, cleaning, washing. She's already taught me how to sew basic stitches, and now she makes me sit with her for hours, patching Papa's clothes, mending holes and replacing buttons. I wish I didn't have so many chores to do. I try to slip nearer to Papa while I'm sewing or cleaning, but Nancy calls me away again before long. I wish I could refuse to obey. Why does she scowl at me so?

One night, about a week before he's to depart again, Papa takes Will up to bed and then reads to Lyddie until she, too, is sleeping, and he must carry her away to tuck her in. I stand in the corner of the kitchen, churning butter. I'm nearly done, reaching the part where I can't continue. My arms are not strong enough. I step away to find Nancy and ask for her help as usual.

When I come to the parlor doorway, I hear her voice. "You spoil and coddle them. When you leave, they will expect such treatment from me, and I will not be able to give it to them. What with keeping this house and my activities at the church and in the community, as well as trying to train up the children—especially Phebe Ann—I don't have time for it."

I hold my breath and peek around the doorframe. Is this why Nancy is often short with us?

"To own the truth, Nancy, they are hungry for affection. Well, now that Annie will go to school, you'll have more time for Lydia and William."

"On the contrary, I'll have my hands even fuller. Annie has often kept an eye on them for me, especially over the past year."

"But you were the one who insisted that Annie should start formal schooling."

"As well she should. I'm simply asking you to help me reestablish a firmer sense of order and discipline before you leave again. Otherwise, how am I to manage after you are no longer here to carry them to and fro and listen to them as if you have all the time in the world?"

Papa gives a weary sigh. "I will do my best to remind them that they must be obedient and well-behaved. But would you begrudge me the love and attention while I'm able to give and receive it? The time is so short—"

"That is your doing. Not ours."

"It is not my doing. Not completely. You know I would like to stay longer. But I must bend to the owners' wishes."

"If only you owned the ship."

"Perhaps one day I shall. But for now, it is what it is." Papa stands and reaches out to touch her shoulder.

"We are both tired," she says, drawing back. "It has been a long day. I'll finish in the kitchen—" She has turned away to find me watching. "What are you doing? Why aren't you finishing your work so you can go on to bed?"

"I was, but it got too hard, and I need your help." My gaze lowers, and my chin trembles. If I could do more things on my own, would Nancy be pleased with me?

"You should know better than to stand there, eavesdropping on our discussion. You should have spoken up and made us aware of your presence."

"But you always say it's rude to interrupt."

"Indeed. But sometimes you must choose the lesser of two evils."

I offer a puzzled look.

"In this case it would have been better to interrupt and ask for my assistance rather than standing there and listening in on a personal conversation."

I bite my lip again.

She plants a fist on her hip. "Learn from your mistakes and do better next time. I'll finish the butter. Tell your papa good night. Quickly now, then to bed with you."

I creep forward to where Papa is standing by the low fire while Nancy sweeps from the room. "I'm sorry if I did wrong."

He turns to look down at me. From the kitchen comes the sound of Nancy wrestling with the churn. Papa offers one hand to me while raising the other hand and lifting a finger to his lips. His tired eyes dance a little.

I look at his face, then his hand. I take it while holding back a giggle. Together, we sneak up the stairs on tiptoe while Nancy is still distracted. I didn't know Papa could move so quietly.

We steal along all the way up to the roof-walk. There, Papa picks me up and holds me, and we look up together to find Hercules and Scorpius and Ursa Minor.

"I should not linger with you," Papa murmurs when I turn back to hug him and kiss his cheek.

"I wish I could stay by your side every moment you are here."

"That would be a delightful thing. But Nancy does require your assistance. And you must learn how to keep house. I simply wish you didn't have to grow up, that you could remain young and innocent forever."

"Maybe we could come up here for a few minutes every night? That could be our special time?"

"That is a splendid suggestion. Nancy can hardly object to that. And if she does, perhaps we can slip away again somehow."

I giggle but then grow still when I see that Papa does not look well.

He sets me down and walks me to the room I share with Lyddie. I open the door a crack but then turn back. Hugging his leg, I whisper, "I love you, Papa. I won't ever grow up too much and stop loving you. I promise."

When I step away and look up, he is pressing a hand to his head. He bends to kiss my forehead. Then, he slowly straightens and turns and, still holding his head, walks toward his bedroom.

* * *

The next morning, Papa is not at breakfast. "Nancy, did Papa leave early on business?"

"No. He is unwell and resting. I've done what I can for him. Now, I think he needs peace and quiet. So I want you all to stay downstairs this morning and make as little noise as possible. Is that understood?"

Now I see that Nancy's face is also very tired. I don't want her to be cross with us. "Yes," I answer for Will and Lyddie, sending them both a serious look. They look back, wide-eyed, and nod.

I help Nancy make dozens of apple muffins for tomorrow's community tea while Lyddie and Will play in the parlor. Papa never comes downstairs. I don't hear any noise above my head. I worry about him.

Finally, at noon, Nancy says, "I need to go to the store and post office. I'll take Lydia and William with me."

"Shall I come too?"

"No. You stay here and weed the garden for me. Remember to watch carefully so you only pull up weeds and not the actual plants this time."

"Yes, Nancy."

"I will stop by Elsa Coffin's house to see how she and the baby are faring. If you finish with the weeding, feed the chickens and then snap the beans in the basket by the back door. We'll have them with supper."

I stare at the wall. "Yes, Nancy."

I am wiping down the cleared-off table when she stops on her way out the door moments later, bringing Will along by one hand and Lyddie by the other. "And, Annie?"

I look up.

"Remember what I said. Be quiet and don't disturb your father." Her tone leaves no room for argument.

I nod and study the table before I go back to wiping.

But as soon as they are out of doors and a little way down the street, I hang up the rag and creep up the stairs.

I pause at Papa's bedroom door and turn the handle so it doesn't make any noise. Then I push the door open and peek around the edge. The room is dim because Nancy left the curtains mostly closed. Papa is buried under the covers, with only his head and one arm sticking out. Slipping near, I can see that his eyes are closed, but his face is all tensed up. The edges of his eyes are red, and the underneath sides are dark. His cheeks hold little color, and his breathing is shallow.

Nancy will be so unhappy if she finds me here. But I don't care. Papa needs help, and I want to help him.

"Papa?" I whisper into the stillness as I lay my hand against his cheek.

He opens his eyes a tiny bit and moves his lips slightly. He tries to speak, but the words sound like rustling leaves.

I look around for water but don't see any. "Don't worry. I'll be back soon." I take care not to spill from the cup or small pitcher while I carry them up. Setting the pitcher on the dresser, I bring the cup to the bed.

"Water." I pat his shoulder to rouse him.

He peeks at me again and then lifts a shaky hand. I help him hold the cup steady, and he drinks until it's empty.

"More?"

He nods weakly. He drains the second cup almost as quickly as the first.

"You were so thirsty!"

"Yes," he sighs. "God bless you for coming, Annie."

"What else do you need? Nancy said not to disturb you, but

I came as soon as she went out. I had to make sure you were all right. But you're not. What's the matter?"

"My head," he groans while looking up at the ceiling.

"When your head hurt before, Mama would put something on your face and give you lots to drink. And she would sing too."

"Just so. You have a good memory." He looks at me again.

"What did Mama put on your face?"

"A cool cloth with something on it. Lavender water, I think." He sucks in a breath, and his face scrunches up. "Mmm…"

Slipping my hand in his—another thing I think Mama would have done—gives him something to hold onto. He squeezes hard, until I almost want to cry that I cannot bear it. Then he relaxes a bit. "I'll try to find the lavender water."

I fly down the stairs and dash to the high shelf where Nancy keeps the medicine box. Climbing on a chair, I'm just able to stretch up and reach it. It is heavier than I expect, and the weight of it almost makes me fall off the chair when I pull it from the shelf. But somehow I am able to set it next to my feet and climb to the floor. When I open the box, I see many different bottles of liquid and powder. Which one is it? Papa said it's water, so it can't be dry like powder. I know what lavender smells like because Nancy puts dried sprigs on the table and in the dresser drawers sometimes.

I open the liquid bottles one by one until I find the one with the right smell. I hope this is it. And I hope there is enough. The bottle is only half full. *Dear God, please let me do the right thing to help him.*

I take a clean rag from the pile and wet in the bucket of cool water sitting by the door. Then I sprinkle the lavender water on it until the rag gives off a strong smell. I close the bottle and slip it in my apron pocket.

"I found it," I call softly when I return to his bedside.

He cannot answer me because he is growling low and squeezing the covers. I reach out with shaking hands and lay the cloth on his forehead, allowing the bottom to come down near his eyes. I hold my breath for a minute and watch him. Very slowly his breathing becomes more regular. The smell fills the room, and he breathes it in deeply. His hands relax, and so does his mouth. "Ah," he sighs. "It's good."

"I prayed that God would help me. He did. But I should go now. If I don't weed the garden and snap the beans and feed the chickens before Nancy returns, she will be very unhappy. And I'm afraid she'll paddle me if she finds me here."

His big hand searches for mine. When I slip mine into his, he squeezes it again, but more gently this time. "She won't paddle you for this. I won't let her—I promise you that."

I wish once more that he could stay longer. Papa may get angry, but I don't think he would ever paddle me. "Why didn't Nancy stay to help you? Why did she leave you alone?"

"She tried to help me when the pain started, but she didn't know the best things to do. She thought that if she talked to me, that would distract me. But she started to talk about things that made my head hurt more."

There is a little room on the edge of the mattress, so I climb up onto the spot at his side and reach out to take his hand again between both of mine.

"Then she asked what else she could do, so I suggested she sing for me." He opens his eyes. "She tried." He looks at me funny. "But that didn't help either."

A giggle slips out before I can stop it. I've always been told that it's not polite to speak poorly of anyone, especially my elders. But I don't have to say anything because I know exactly what Papa means. Nancy's singing is worse than her cooking.

He smiles a little before his face becomes tight again. "So, she decided to leave me alone to try and sleep."

"But you couldn't sleep because it hurts too much."

"Precisely."

"I've learned to sing some songs at church. Can I try singing, to see if it will help you?" I feel shy and nervous.

"Do you like to sing?"

"Yes. When I'm all alone."

"There's only me. Besides that, you're all alone. Please try."

I think for a moment, recalling the first line and taking a deep breath. At first, my voice wobbles. But then I cling to his hand, close my eyes, and sing with all my heart.

Rock of ages, cleft for me, let me hide myself in Thee,
Let the water and the blood from Thy wounded side which
flowed
Be of sin the double cure: save from wrath and make
me pure.

I sing that verse two times because I don't remember the others. Then I hum the music over again, without words, like Mama used to. When I stop and open my eyes, Papa's face is very peaceful, and his breathing is even. He must be asleep.

I move to climb down, but his hand presses mine. "Thank you. That was very good." Some tears slip from the corners of his closed eyes toward the pillow.

"Oh, Papa. Don't cry." I lean across and kiss away the tears on the near side and breathe in the calm of the lavender. "I must go and do my chores," I whisper near his ear, wishing I could stay right here instead. "Is there anything else you need?"

"No." His voice is growing distant, sleepy. "I'll rest…"

I kiss his cheek before I slip down from the bed and through the door. Downstairs, I work to put the medicine box back on the shelf as it was after replacing the bottle.

I pray for Papa while I weed faster than I ever have before. Tossing a heap of feed to the chickens, I dash over to the back door. Then I pray for him some more as I start to snap the beans. Nancy finds me there on the back stoop, snapping and praying.

"Well, you did much better with the weeding this time, I must say. I'm glad to see that you're becoming more mindful in your tasks, Annie. Bring those inside when you're done. I'll start on the potatoes." She turns without waiting for a reply.

My cheeks puff and the curls on my forehead dance when I exhale my relief.

Later, Papa comes down to join us for supper. He looks weak but relaxed. When he leans over to kiss Nancy's cheek where she sits, she murmurs, "Mmm, you smell nice. Are you feeling better?"

"Aye." Papa winks at me over her head before he turns to take his seat.

And I hide my smile by bowing my head extra low for grace.

* * *

MID-AUGUST 1827

Papa is gone again—has been gone these four days. Last night, Nancy said we have waited long enough, and I must indeed go to school. This morning, she wakes me very early and helps me make sure my face is extra clean, my dress is extra fresh, and my hair is extra controlled. She doesn't like my curls. She says they are too wild.

Nancy tugs so hard when securing them at the back of my head that I start to lose my balance and nearly fall off the tall kitchen stool. "I don't want your hair to be a distraction to you or anyone else. So on school days, we will gather it like this. I'll help you at first, until you are able to do it yourself. I don't think it's good for little girls to run around with shorn heads. This, then, will be the solution to our problem."

I didn't know my hair was a problem. Now I look at my reflection in her small looking glass and wonder who's looking back at me. We are sending a stranger to school in my place. And it is too tight. "It hurts my head."

"You will get used to it in time. Later, when you have grown up, you can never let your hair fly away like an untamed bird. You must keep it up."

"Why?"

"Because it's modest and proper and respectable."

"But it's not comfortable."

"You'll get used to it," she repeats, this time in a sharp tone. When she sees my expression, she sighs. "Please trust me. When I tell you something or ask you to do something, I always have a reason. I'm trying my best to raise you well, to be a lady." She turns to face the window and grips the counter's edge.

I climb down from the stool and come to stand beside her. She is blinking, trying not to cry. "You miss him too."

"Hmmm?"

"You miss Papa too, don't you?"

"I..."

"Everything is harder when Papa is away."

She is silent for a long moment. "Yes, it is."

"I'll try to control my hair. And I'll try not to ask so many questions."

She gives me a small smile and turns me around, nudging me toward the table. "Sit down and I'll dish you up some oatmeal with warm apple compote."

Nancy's apple compote is my favorite. It's the one thing besides muffins that she's never messed up. I gobble the bowl's contents while she gives me last minute reminders about all the ways I must behave well.

A knock sounds while I'm setting my bowl in the washbasin. I run to answer it and look up to see Gardner smiling down at me. "Hello, Annie," his quiet greeting descends over me. His whisper is still gritty, but it comes out a little louder than it used to, now that he talks to a few other people besides me.

"Good morning." I return his smile before turning back to the hall table to pick up my new slate and reader.

Nancy steps around the doorframe and hands me some food packed in a small shiny pail. "Thank you for walking Annie to school. It is a great help to me."

He nods in response.

"Remember what I told you. And come straight home after school. I'll need your help with milking and sweeping." She bids us good-bye, and we walk down the street in the heavy morning mist, me skipping at times to keep up with Gardner's long strides.

"Are you nervous?" I can barely hear him past the street noise, but I've grown used to understanding what he means whether or not he uses words.

"Yes. A bit. All right—a lot. I only know how to write the alphabet and read a few words and add a little. Will the other children think I'm stupid?"

"Don't worry about it. You'll catch up."

"I'm so glad Papa is letting me go to your school. I know this is your last year. But it will be nice to spend time with you every day, for a little while at least."

He nods.

"Gardner, promise me that you won't laugh at me if there's something I can't understand."

He looks over at me with a quirked brow. "I will, if you promise to let me know when you have a question instead of stuffing it inside and pretending to understand."

We surprise each other by saying "done" at the same time. He chuckles under his breath, and I giggle.

"Is Mr. Wallace a nice man?"

"He's clever and fair and good."

"Will he paddle us if we make a mistake?"

"No. He only paddles for really bad things like fighting and cursing."

"Oh, I'm so glad. I'd never do such things."

We walk on in silence the rest of the way. When we reach the schoolhouse door, I look up and take a deep breath. Gardner pats my shoulder and nods me inside, following when I step forward.

The big room is nearly full as most of the students have already arrived. They sit on long benches behind narrow tables. With so many seats taken, I'm not sure where I should sit. I can see that shorter students seem to sit in the front and taller students in the back. Does this mean I can't sit by Gardner? My legs start to tremble.

A man sitting behind a big table at the front looks up from the stack of papers beside him. He smiles slightly and waves me forward. I hope this is Mr. Wallace—and that he's as good as Gardner said. I swallow hard and walk up to the table.

"You must be Phebe. Your father said you would likely start this week. I'm Mr. Wallace, and I'm pleased to meet you. Good, you brought your slate and reader." He stands and moves around the table to step up beside me. Then he raises his voice. "Pupils, I want you to meet our newest addition, Phebe Ann Chase." The smaller students study me with wide eyes, but some of the older students start to whisper and snicker.

"Enough." Mr. Wallace doesn't raise his voice any further, but his tone silences them and sends a shiver through me. I find Gardner's face along the next to last row, surrounded by several other big boys. They glare at me, but his expression is steady and comforting, like a lantern on a misty night.

"You may sit here." Mr. Wallace points to an empty seat in the second row. "This is Fanny," he nods to the girl next to me. "Fanny, I trust you'll be a good girl and help Phebe find her way."

She nods and smiles, apparently unafraid of the teacher. She's taller and heavier than me, with plumpness to fill out her beautiful dress. Her hair—the color of golden sand—is tied up in long, loopy braids with blue ribbons, and her eyes—pale like the winter sky—sparkle even with no sunlight shining directly on them. What a pretty girl. I hope she's as nice as she looks.

She is.

I do everything with Fanny as the morning goes on. She helps me when I don't know a word or haven't learned how to work a figure yet. She even asks Mr. Wallace if she can be excused and then takes me by the hand to go with her. I am so glad. I was afraid to ask where the outhouse is and thought I'd burst.

"Thank you for your kindness," I offer while we walk back around the building to the front door.

"I'm glad you came. I miss Maggie."

"Who's she?"

"The girl who used to sit beside me. She got sick and died two months ago. And I haven't had a desk-mate since." Her lovely eyes have filled with sorrow.

I extend a hand to clutch hers. "It's very sad when someone dies. Even if they go to heaven, we miss them."

"Yes." She grips my hand in return. "I hope we can be friends for a long time."

"Me too." I follow her inside and back up the aisle.

We continue to study until it's time for lunch. Though it's a cloudy day, the air is still warm, so we all take our food outside and sit in the yard to eat. Fanny joins me on a dry, grassy patch. I share my bread and butter with her, and she shares her apple pie with me. It tastes so good. *Thank you, God, for my friend.*

She tells me a funny story about her grandmother, and we both start laughing. Then I look up to see three of those big boys from the back of the room standing over me like towers. They don't look happy. My giggles vanish, and my smile shrinks.

"Look, it's the daughter of the mighty Captain Chase," says the tallest one with a smirk.

"'Chasing the wind and tempting fate,' my father always says," his friend joins in. "One day that old whale monster will get him yet, and he'll get his due after selling our folks' misery for profit." All three snicker.

"That's right," jabs the third. "And he leaves his itty-bitty-baby shrimp of a girl to study with us." He scowls at me. "But somebody should have told him that we ain't got no place here for the motherless daughter of a coward."

I feel like I'm drowning under their wave of terrible words. I start to cry and wish I could become invisible.

"Bet she's a coward too. Let's find out—" The leader shuts his mouth. They all back away slowly and then turn to walk off with their heads down.

I feel something behind me and tip my head back. Through blurry vision I make out Mr. Wallace, driving the boys away with his eyes. And standing beside him is Gardner.

I jump to my feet and huddle against Gardner's side. "Thank you," I whisper around my tears. Mr. Wallace bends to look me in the eye. "Thank you," I repeat while gazing into his kind face.

He pats my head. "It was good of Gardner to come and alert me of the situation." He glances up at Gardner before he continues talking to me. "You are welcome to have your lunch in the schoolhouse. And if those boys start to give you more trouble, cry out."

"Yes, Mr. Wallace."

"That's a good girl." He wipes my cheeks with his handkerchief. Then he sticks it back in his pocket and walks away.

I step back and look up. "You were right. He is very good."

"I told you," Gardner grins. But then he peers across the yard. He puts a hand on my shoulder and nods down at Fanny. "Let's go inside." He looks over at me with a frown. "What did you do to your hair anyway? It looks queer."

"Nancy did it up. It doesn't feel nice, but she says I have to be a lady, and I can't let my hair be all wild."

His jaw clenches. "But I like it 'all wild.' It's a part of who you are."

We stop beside Gardner's seat, and he settles down to work on some extra arithmetic.

Now it's my turn to be confused. "It's still lunchtime, isn't it?"

"Yes. But if I get a head start on these problems now, I'll have more time to help at the store after school. Besides," he adds with a funny look, "you'll probably talk about girly things. Who wants to listen to that?"

Fanny and I giggle and turn to find our own seats so we can talk about "girly things"—whatever those are.

Later that afternoon, Gardner walks beside me, but when we reach the store, he doesn't stop. "What are you doing?" My brows scrunch together. "Don't you want to help your parents? I can find the way from here by myself."

"I know you can. But my legs get tired after sitting all day. I need to stretch them a bit more." He looks slowly from side to side as we continue walking. I shrug and smile and let him take my hand. He picks up the pace again, and I jog to keep up. "Annie, promise me you won't tell Nancy about those boys bothering you today. We wouldn't want her to worry and keep you at home, would we?"

"Oh, no. I will, if you promise to let me eat lunch with you every day."

We glance at each other and grin. "Done!" we exclaim in tandem.

"Except for those boys, I like school. I want to go back. But, Gardner, why did they say such terrible words about Papa and me?"

"Mother says that some people are full of venom and fear. Asa, Obed, and Charlie are those kind of people, I guess. They like to see other people hurting. But no matter what they say, your papa's a good man and you are a nice girl." I've never heard him speak so earnestly.

We reach the front door, and he turns to face me. "Remember what I said. See you tomorrow."

I nod.

He turns and runs back up the street.

* * *

September fades into October. Except for a yummy dinner for Will's birthday—when Aunt Mary invites us all over and cooks up a feast—every week is the same. On Sundays, there's church and resting. On weekdays, Gardner walks me to and from school, and I learn lots of new words and all kinds of interesting facts. Charlie and the other boys send me dirty looks, but they generally leave me alone, especially when I stay close to Mr. Wallace. Fanny and I share secrets and happy moments. On Saturdays, I help Nancy do all the extra housework I didn't have time to do during the week.

I'm saving up the words I can write as well as a dropped penny I find every now and then when I'm walking. I dream of writing my very own letter to Papa and sending it to him from the post office all by myself. I don't know how much that costs, but I'm determined to do it. But I really want it to be a surprise, so I don't tell anyone about it—not even Fanny or Gardner.

During the first weeks of October, the weather turns. The rain comes cold and hard, nearly every day, blowing sideways in the wind. It makes the walks to school and back miserable. I have to hold tightly to Gardner's arm so I don't get knocked down. One day, it grows particularly dark by dismissal time, and I am wet to the skin when I slip into the entryway and shove the door shut behind me.

Nancy steps from the kitchen and grasps my shoulders. "Thank goodness you're home safely. I was worried. Why, you're soaked through. Let me take your cloak and bonnet. Take off your shoes right there. Never mind the puddle," she sighs. "I'll clean it up this time. Run up and put on something dry. Then you can sit by the fire and rest for a while."

I'm shivering so that moving is hard and speaking impossible. I do as she says, my shaking legs causing me to stumble up the stairs. I continue to tremble as I change, but the softness of my flannel nightgown helps me relax a little. After putting on dry stockings, I run back down to hand her the wet clothing.

Nancy seats me in the rocker where she's moved it to face a blazing fire in the parlor. She wraps me in a big quilt and puts a cup of warm milk in my hands before she begins to pull the pins from my damp hair. "Oh, you're still shaking. Take care not to spill it. Lydia and William have both been very cross today. I'm going to give them their supper now and put them to bed early. Then you and I can eat something." She pats my shoulder before she turns away.

The hot, delicious liquid makes me drowsy. I drain the cup and set it on the short table. Then I lean back in the chair. As it sways gently, I fall asleep.

Sometime later, a noise wakes me. It sounds like the front door. I feel a gush of cold air spill into the room. I shiver when it comes over my head. Pulling the quilt tighter, I slip off the rocker and creep across the floor. "Nancy?" my voice comes out in a sleepy whisper. Where is she?

The door shuts firmly, and I jump. A gruff voice grumbles around chattering teeth, and a big man, draped in a dripping slicker and leaning on a tall cane, steps into the doorway. He peers into the kitchen, standing with his back to me.

I want to scream, but I can hardly breathe. Then I gasp out, "Nancy!"

The man spins, sending a sheet of water to the floor. The hand not clutching the cane reaches up to pull off a drenched hat.

"Papa."

He falls to his knees with a grunt, throws off the slicker, and gathers me close, quilt and all.

"You aren't a ghost or a dream?" It's hard to talk with my face muffled against his damp vest.

"I'm here." He kisses my hair and my cheeks before pulling back a bit to study me. "It's still early, and you're dressed for bed. Are you ill?"

"No. I got wet and cold coming home from school." I stretch to kiss his face. "You're wet too! You need to dry off."

"Aye." He shudders and sways a little. "Bring me a chair from the kitchen. Quickly."

I let my quilt fall to the floor and run to obey. He uses the chair to lift himself and then sits with a thud. He holds his leg out in front of him and grits his teeth. His fingers shake a bit while he works to unbutton his vest. "Where's Nancy?"

"I don't know. Wait, maybe she's upstairs. She said Will and Lyddie would go to bed early tonight." I turn and run up the stairs, but just as I reach the top, I run into Nancy where she's coming around the corner.

"Annie? Slow down."

"Papa's home!"

"What?" She steps around me and gives a low, startled cry before covering her mouth and running down the steps. "Owen! What are you doing here?" She touches his face and then kisses it.

"You didn't get the missive I sent?"

"No. We've received no news." She sweeps his hair back from his face and looks down. "You should change. What is it? Your leg?"

"I twisted my ankle most severely. It's still healing."

"We'll see to it. Twisted ankles are one thing I know about." She looks up to where I stand watching from the top of the stairs. "Go to the dresser and open the second drawer," she calls softly. "You'll find some of your Papa's clothes there. Bring me a shirt and some trousers and stockings. Hurry now."

I pick up the candle she left burning on the small landing table and run to follow her orders. By the time I come back down, Nancy has helped Papa into the rocker by the fire, has gotten his coat, vest, and shirt off, and is using my abandoned quilt to rub and warm his arms and back.

"Thank you, Annie. Go and heat some water. And set another place for supper."

We sit around the table—me in my nightdress, Papa with his ankle in a pan of hot water, and Nancy serving the food. Nancy and I take less porridge and fish so Papa can have plenty. He eats it all and drinks two large glasses of milk besides. We watch him and wait. Then he tells us about the terrible storms that damaged his ship and left nearly every member of the crew with some injury, forcing them to return to the home port for repairs. "The owners have decided not only to repair the ship but also to enlarge it," he sighs at the end. "They will send orders when she's ready to depart again, but it will be a good long while. Likely the better part of a year."

Nancy and I look at each other. Nearly a year.

Her words come out soft and low. "I'm sorry for your trouble and the injuries. But thank God that you're home safely." She swipes at her eyes.

"Aye." He reaches out to capture and squeeze her hand. Then he peers over at me. "And what do you say? Will you allow me to stay for such a long time?"

I slip from my chair and throw my arms about his waist, squeezing as hard as I can.

"I'll take that as an affirmative response," he says in a rough voice before he presses my curly head close to his heart.

* * *

The second morning after Papa's surprise arrival, I come downstairs with my handful of pins and let Nancy help finish securing my hair. Today is Friday. That means after school I'll have two whole days at home with him. Lyddie and Will are also excited that he's home. They had a wonderful time with him yesterday. This morning, they both woke up extra early and are now sitting at the table having their breakfast—Lyddie watching Will as he jabbers and digs pits in his oatmeal.

"Don't play with your food," Nancy chides. She places a plate in front of me. "Yes, that's a good boy. Annie, eat your fill and go to see your papa. He's working in his study and has something for you."

I inhale my toast and eggs, washing them down with milk. Then I carry my empty plate to the washbasin and slip down the hall to the study at the back of the house. The door is mostly closed, so I rap lightly.

"Come," his warm voice beckons.

I step inside the room I've rarely visited. Nancy keeps it shut up much of the time when he's away. "Good morning. You wanted to see me?"

"Yes. I'd like to walk you to school this morning, but Doctor Nancy says I need to rest my ankle for another couple of days. Your tuition is due, however, so I've written this note to Mr. Wallace and tucked the money inside. Will you take it for me?"

"Yes, Papa." I step forward to receive the square packet he's extending.

"I'm counting on you, Annie. I don't like to be late in paying for anything. You will keep it safe and remember to deliver it?"

"Oh, yes. I promise."

"Good girl."

From down the hall, I hear a knock on the front door and the sound of Nancy opening it. "Annie," she calls.

"Gardner's here. I have to go."

"Nancy told me he's been good to see you safely to school in the mornings and back home again, especially during the heavy rains. I'll have to thank him. It seems I'm further in his debt," he says while I walk around the corner of his desk.

He kisses my cheek, and I turn and run through the doorway. Nancy helps me tie my cloak securely. I place Papa's letter in my right pocket as I follow Gardner down the front path to the street.

I slip my hand in to cover it and feel the solid weight of the money—the weight of Papa's trust in me. I smile. I won't let him down.

The day creeps by. I keep thinking about being at home—keep wondering what Lyddie and Will and Papa and Nancy are doing at this or that moment. When I go to use the outhouse at lunchtime, Asa steps out to block my path. I jump back and freeze under his hard stare.

"Heard your father came home with his tail between his legs," he sneers. "Heard the sea beat him down so he had to limp home, both in body and spirit." His fists form.

I decide to hold it.

Spinning on my heel, I dash back around the building and into the schoolroom. I can ask for permission to go back out after lessons recommence.

When Mr. Wallace dismisses us for the day, Gardner waits for me to bundle up. It has started to drizzle again, and the wind has picked up. I tremble under the force of it. As we cross the schoolyard, I shove my hands in my pockets—and feel Papa's letter still tucked there. *Oh, no.* I stop and turn back, squinting against the stinging moisture whizzing around the edge of my bonnet. Lamplight still burns brightly through the windows. I exhale in relief.

Gardner must have seen that I wasn't beside him anymore. He's come back to stand beside me. "What's the matter?" His voice blends with the wind.

"I have something I must give to Mr. Wallace. I forgot. I'll be quick. But it's cold! Keep on walking, and I'll catch up with you."

"All right." He knows what a fast runner I am. He turns away, and I run back to the schoolhouse. Throwing the door open, I dash inside. Mr. Wallace casts me a startled look from where he sits at his table. "Phebe?"

I scoot up the aisle and pull out the packet. "I'm sorry, I almost forgot. I promised Papa I would bring this to you." I lay the packet on the edge of the table and back away.

"Thank you."

"You're welcome!" I turn and fly from the room, calling out "good night" before I shut the door. While passing through the gate, I look down the street but can't see Gardner. That's strange. I wasn't gone long. Maybe he got tired of waiting for me and decided to run. I plow forward as fast as I can, my lunch pail handle over the crook of my arm, the pail slapping against my side. I stumble once or twice in the gusts of wind, so I change course and aim for the head of an alley. I want to reach it and hide out of the wind for a moment. I know Nancy hates it when I dawdle, but the wind is so cold.

Reaching my target, I hear some noises woven through the wind—grunting and angry yelling. I peek around the side of the building and spy a terrible scene. Even in their coats and hats, I recognize Obed, Charlie, and Asa. They've pinned someone to the ground.

I know that green jacket.

Asa is sitting across Gardner's stomach, punching and slapping his face and his chest while the other boys hold down Gardner's arms. I can see his hands moving. He wants to protect himself, but he can't. And he can't cry for help. Even if there weren't any wind, who would be able to hear him?

Obed is yelling words I've never heard. I'm not sure what they mean, but they sound nasty. Above the wind, I gather snatches of taunts woven in. "And you defend that little Chase…

always doing what's right… teacher's pet… and your scars and voice are so disgusting… call you monster man…"

Asa's fist comes back, and I see that it's slick with bright red blood. Gardner's hands aren't moving anymore. Asa lets out a dreadful laugh. "Right! Let's hit monster man where it hurts!" He pulls his fist higher and strikes Gardner at the scarred point on his throat.

"No!" I scream. Without thinking, I charge into the alley, throw myself against Asa, and knock him over. Now I'm on top of him, and I'm wildly punching and swinging, hitting him with all the fury in my heart.

At first, he is stunned, but then he starts fighting back. Three or four times I feel him strike my face and head, and he manages to yank off my bonnet. But I keep swinging.

Somewhere in the midst of everything, my lunch pail handle is in my hand, and I'm using that to hit him too. Charlie and Obed try to grab me, but I swing at them with all my might. After I whack them both once or twice, they back away. They curse me and then turn to run, disappearing in the mist at the other end of the alley.

Asa has stopped fighting back. He's crying like Will, telling me to stop and get off. I do stop and see his face is all red with cuts on both cheeks and blood coming from his nose and lip. His teeth are red.

Once I let up, he easily pushes me off and drags himself up to stand over me. Now, however, there's fear in his eyes. He looks at Gardner with hatred, and I slide across the mud to shield Gardner's head while glaring up at him. "My father is no coward. And Gardner is not a monster. Leave us alone!"

Asa swallows, wipes at the blood on his face, and backs away until he's vanished like the other two. I feel my body relax a little and pain start to seep across my head. I turn around to find Gardner stirring. His face and neck look terrible. I reach out and shake his shoulder. "Gardner?"

He wakes up. Then he starts to cry. I've never seen him cry before. Now I feel afraid.

"Gardner, can you get up? Please get up! I don't want to leave you here. What if they come back?"

He opens his right eye a little. The other one is swelling shut. His tears slow when he sees my face. "Annie," he mouths.

"Yes. I'll help you. Come on." I lift his arm. He gasps and lifts his other hand to grasp his side. With all my strength, I pull on his arm and help him sit up—a challenge in the thick, slippery mud. Then I bend over and touch my toes and make a triangle so he can press against my back and stand. I straighten and he latches onto my shoulders. Gardner walks and breathes unsteadily, leaning on me as I lead the way, my hands turned back to cover his.

I keep us near the fronts of buildings when the mist becomes thicker and the wind more biting. Finally, I recognize the windows of Aunt Mary's store. We stumble inside and both collapse on the floor.

"What the devil?" It sounds like Uncle Gardner. Then he is there, over me, calling to Aunt Mary.

"Help Gardner. He's much worse." He turns his attention to Gardner when Aunt Mary rushes up to kneel beside me.

"Good heavens!" she cries. "Let's take them in the back room—or upstairs." She helps me stand, and I try to walk. But I feel too tired. And the shelves nearby twist and slant.

I grab my head. It hurts. Oh, no. My bonnet isn't here. It must be out in the mud. And my lunch pail too. I should go back and get them. I try to look for the door, but my vision blurs and my head starts to float.

Then everything goes black.

* * *

Light glows upon my face. I'm wrapped in soft flannel and blankets. Against my side is something solid and very warm. I smell a familiar scent and hear a steady heartbeat. I try to open my eyes—until sudden pain rushes over my head again. I start to cry.

"Easy now," Papa's deep voice resonates against my cheek, his breath spreading a warm fan over my face.

My sobs cut off any reply.

His arms cinch tight, drawing me closer and the blankets snugger. He softly kisses my forehead, right over the center of the pain. "You're safe." His voice is low and calm. I focus hard on it and try my best to relax. My sobs die down and my body goes limp, the tension seeping away.

"Where's Gardner?" My speech sounds strange. Then I realize that my bottom lip is puffy and stiff.

"He's with Mary, resting. The doctor said he will be all right. A few cracked ribs and a lot of bruises."

"But they hit his neck. He couldn't talk to me." I shudder.

"Don't fret. The doctor expects that will heal again, in time."

"How did I get here?"

"Uncle Gardner wrapped you up and carried you home. He's still here, along with the watchman, hoping you can tell us what happened."

A big hand rests against the side of my face. "Annie."

I squint and see his face near Papa's above me. They both look funny. "Uncle Gardner, you're fuzzy." I close my eyes against a wave of dizziness.

"Doctor Bartlett said you might see things strangely for a little while. You've got quite a knot on your head."

I cough hard. Papa rocks back and forth a little until it passes. A cup is placed against my fat lip and warm tea enters my mouth.

"Don't press her." Nancy's tone is quiet but insistent.

My voice comes out rough. "I want to tell it. Uncle Gardner has been waiting."

"All right," she speaks near my ear. "But if you feel too poorly, stop speaking and rest. Do you hear?"

I nod. "We were coming home from school. Gardner went ahead because I had to run back. I forgot to give the letter to Mr. Wallace earlier, Papa. I'm very sorry!"

"It matters not," he whispers.

"I tried to find Gardner, but he wasn't in the street. Then I saw him when I came to the alley. And those big boys from school were holding him down and beating him. He couldn't get away, and he couldn't call for help!" I start to tremble when the scene floods my memory. "They said terrible, horrible things. I got so angry. I had to help him." I start to cough again, and the cup is raised to my lips once more.

"All right. What happened then?" Papa coaxes.

"I jumped on the boy who was hitting him the most. I knocked him over and hit him with my lunch pail again and again. I hit the other boys too when they tried to touch me. Then I sat in front of Gardner so they wouldn't hit him anymore. Then I helped Gardner get up and let him lean on me. I helped him get back to the store. Then I don't remember anything else." I sigh.

There are a few moments of silence, followed by Papa speaking in a strange tone. "I'm humbled. By my own limitations—a setback that allowed me to be on-Island at such a time coupled with an injury that kept me from protecting these children. By how Providence has spared my daughter—and her friend." He sucks in a breath. "By her fearlessness displayed." Two drops land on my forehead. "It seems that Annie has repaid a portion of my debt to your son on her own."

"Yes," Uncle Gardner replies with amazement. "You are a courageous girl, Annie. Mary and I thank you for what you did."

"Thank God they are both safe," Nancy breathes.

"She certainly has your spitfire ways in her, Captain," says another voice. That must be the watchman. "Such a small one but possessing brimstone and fury to be sure. Do you know the names of the boys, child?"

"Yes. Asa and Charlie and Obed."

"I think I know the three. They gave me some trouble earlier this year. If you'll excuse me, Mrs. Chase, Captain Chase, Mr. Coffin. I'll go and track them down."

"I'll see you out," Nancy offers. "And we thank you."

A new thought strikes me, and fear grips my heart. I start to tremble once more. "Papa," I gasp. "Gardner said Mr. Wallace will paddle anyone who fights. Please tell him I'm sorry. Don't let him come and paddle me!" My cough returns.

"I'll tell him all about it. I won't let him paddle you."

"I wouldn't have fought them if they only said bad things. They said a lot of bad things about you, about us. And I didn't fight then. But when they hurt Gardner, I had to do something."

"Hush now. You are my good, brave girl. I'm very proud of you, and I love you."

"You are not a coward," I whisper when I relax again. Sleep rises like the tide.

"Neither are you, Treasure. Neither are you."

I'm aware of him staying with me all through the night, there each time I drift in and out. And starting on Monday, he walks me to and from school himself for the rest of the term.

***

LATE JUNE 1828

On a warm afternoon, we walk from the big house on Orange Street to Solomon's house in New Guinea. I've spent time with his family, out and about or at our house a long time ago. But I've never ventured so deeply into their quarter. It's fascinating. Everywhere around us are blacks, Portuguese, and Pacific island natives. And some of the children who stare back at me look like a mishmash of the different groups. They are beautiful, exotic. My pale skin and brown hair seem boring in comparison.

We arrive at the house and find the rooms and yard overflowing with happy people. There's Solomon and Isaiah with sweet Auntie Grace. And Joshua with Marcie, the girl he's courting. And there's the kind Reverend Johnson. He gives us candy sometimes.

And there's Sadie. Her dress is so pretty, and her hair is specially arranged. I break away from my family and weave through the crowd to draw near and grasp her hand. "Sadie, you look lovely."

"Thank you, precious," she beams down. "So happy y'all come to join the festivities. Even your daddy's here. That's a real treat, ain't it?"

"Yes."

"Come and meet the fellow I just been married to." She leads me to a tall man with skin a little darker than hers and the most captivating eyes I've ever seen. "Eli, meet Miss Phebe Ann Chase. Annie, this be Eli."

I curtsey like Nancy taught me. "Pleased to meet you."

He smiles wide, lifts his eyebrows, and bows to me like one of King Arthur's knights. "You got lovely manners, Miss

Annie," his deep voice pours out. "Your mama must be real proud of you."

I blink and glance at Sadie.

She replies for me with a small, tender smile. "Yes, Eli. She be proud indeed."

We listen to the lively music and eat delicious dishes I've never tasted before. People dance and then stop to drink punch when they grow overwarm. Everywhere there are smiles and laughter.

I move to stand near Papa as the sun sinks low in the sky, pressing close so he can hear me above the instruments. "I'm happy you could be here today. Sadie said it's a real treat, and she's right."

"I'm glad I could be here too, to make this memory with you."

I survey the variety of people all around. "Are they really so different from us, Papa?"

He follows my gaze. "What do you mean?"

"The people from this part of town look and speak different. And they have different music and dancing."

"Yes."

"But they have dreams and families like we do. They work hard and help each other. They want to love and be loved. They want to be happy and know they are valued by somebody. Don't they?"

"That they do."

"That's what we want most of all too, right? So we're not different at the heart of us, are we?"

He watches Sadie and Eli embracing some friends, and his mouth tips up. "Aye. At the heart of us." He smiles more fully before he turns to look at me. "You've grown a great deal—even in these months since I've been home."

"But I'm wearing the same dresses now that I was last summer."

"Not growing so much in body. But in mind and spirit."

"Oh."

"And that makes me prouder than anything." A far-off look enters his eyes.

And suddenly I know. "Are you going away again?"

"Yes. I received word yesterday. I sail from New Bedford in ten days."

I swallow. Then I nod. What can I say? My crying will not help him. So I bury my tears deep inside.

"It will be dark soon. Let's find Nancy, Lydia, and William so we can head home." He stands and reaches for my hand.

"Papa, can we have time on the roof-walk tonight, just you and me?"

"Certainly. I can think of no better ending to this splendid day."

* * *

"Nancy's been sad lately. I think I know why."

"Oh?"

"I saw her holding Mrs. Wilson's baby earlier today, and she looked like she was wishing she could have a baby. There was a strange sadness in her eyes."

Papa looks up into the brilliant night sky and clears his throat. "She has you and Lydia and William. What would she want with a baby?"

"But we aren't hers. We were Mama's before. And now Nancy has to take care of us. I think she'd like to have a baby all her own. So, I was wondering…"

His face swings down, and he gives me a funny look. He clears his throat again.

"When you return from this next voyage and bring us each back a gift, could you bring back a baby for Nancy? I think Will and Lyddie and I are all pretty good. And you brought us back to Mama. I'll bet you can find another nice one since you did so well in picking us."

I stop talking when I see that Papa is shaking—with laughter. At first it is silent. Then he lets his head fall back while he laughs long and deep and loud.

Annoyed, I tug on his trouser leg. "Why are you laughing? Don't you think it's a good idea?"

He grins at me. "Never you mind. I'm simply struck anew by how delightful you are." Then he stoops and lifts me up, holding me close. "You are my greatest treasure. Do you know that?"

I kiss his cheek before I lean away to study his face. "Will you bring her back a baby one day, Papa? I want her to feel happy."

"As do I. But don't hold your breath. I can't promise I'll be able to find a suitable one on this journey. I'll see what I can do after that." He winks at me.

"Thank you."

We turn together and seek the North Star in the canopy above us.

CHAPTER
TEN

MARCH 1830

"What's it called when everything in life changes and nothing seems to remain the same?" I inquire while I take my turn at cleaning the blackboard after school ends for the day.

"A good question," Mr. Wallace replies. He looks up from his marking. "If we're speaking of life moving on and all the changes that come with that, some people say we've entered a new chapter or a new season of life."

I lower my rag and give him a curious look. "You mean like winter turning into spring? Those seasons?"

"Well, yes. And no." He gazes at me. "What season is it now?"

"The *Almanac* says spring has started, but it still feels like winter to me." I smile.

"Yes, this has been a bitter winter, to be sure. But let me ask it this way. When the winter passes into spring, can we make time turn back again so that the grass shrinks into the soil and the flowers and leaves move backward to live inside their stems and branches?"

What a strange thing to imagine. I giggle. "No. Time keeps moving. We can't stop it, and we can't turn it back, even when we want to."

"Precisely," he nods. "So it is with life. Many things change and events happen. Circumstances occur. We can prevent some things but many more we can only respond to—and we must choose how we will respond. Time moves on and so does life, just like the seasons."

I bid him good evening, collect Lyddie where she's been waiting for me in the schoolyard, and walk home while puzzling over my homework, a theme entitled "What my family means to me." I guess our family has started to enter a different season since Papa was last home.

Next month I will turn ten. We received a letter from Papa yesterday, and I can't believe all the things that have changed over the past years. Lyddie has started to attend school with me, and Will has already learned to write all his letters at home. Uncle George has been home for a time, and we got to know him and Aunt Rebecca and little James better. I like Uncle George. He is extremely serious yet so kind to me.

Nancy has taught me more difficult stitching techniques and speaks of sending me to work in a shop one day. She says I have a talent for sewing and will soon surpass her skill level. Mrs. Summers from church, who often sings solos with the choir, heard me singing as she walked past one Sunday, and she told Nancy that she'd like to give me voice lessons. Nancy says we'll ask Papa about it when he returns. She expects that will be within a few months.

I often stop by the store on the way home to talk with Aunt Mary for a little while and help her with small tasks. She and Uncle Gardner have had much to do while Gardner is gone. They sent him away off-Island, to Dartmouth College. He's been there for many months—well over a year now. Aunt Mary says it's a great privilege he can receive more schooling than they've ever had and that they have enough money to send him when he's such a bright boy. But I know she misses him. And I miss him too. She says he hopes to earn a full degree so he may be there quite a while longer.

I miss Gardner. I miss Papa. Those are the two things that have not changed. I pray for them both every night, longing for the time when they'll return to us.

Lyddie's voice draws me back. "What are you thinking about?"

"My assignment from Mr. Wallace. I've got to decide what to write."

"You'll think of something nice. You're good with words."

"That's what Mr. Wallace says. But it's a harder theme this time."

She glances over at me.

"How do I write about *everything* our family means to me in one page?"

She smiles. "Maybe just write about the most important things."

"That's a good idea. Would you do a couple of my chores today? So I can have more time to think and write?"

She nods. "Will you do mine tomorrow so I can go and play with Sara for a little while?"

"All right."

We step into the entryway and put down our school things. I rush through milking the cow and sweeping the floors before I pull a chair up to the parlor table and set to work in earnest.

By the time Nancy calls me to help prepare the table for supper, I've finished and even made a second copy of my work. I leave the ink to finish drying and set out the silverware. Then I dash back to put the papers away. I tuck one copy in my cloak pocket to take tomorrow. And I fold the other one up in thirds and slip it in my apron pocket so I can carry out the rest of my plan after supper.

Later, when Lyddie is finishing with the dishes and Nancy is supervising the end of Will's bath, I slip down the hall and try the door of the study. I'm thrilled to find it unlocked. I step inside and peer around by the light of my stubby candle. Creeping across to the big brown desk, I take the folded theme copy from my pocket and set it on the polished surface. I lay it just so, with the "Papa" label printed neatly on the side facing up.

I hear someone on the stairs and know I'll soon be missed. After closing the door silently, I zip back down the hall to the parlor. Nancy looks in on me a moment later where I am curled on the settee, reading intently.

* * *

"I must say this is very well done," Nancy muses while running her fingers over the finished product.

My heart dances at her rare praise. I have worked hard this past month to make a new shirt for Uncle Gardner, completing each step in the process by myself with only occasional guiding comments from her. On this early June evening, we stand together admiring the result. The soft linen should be comfortable for him to work in during the warm days ahead. "Thank you, Nancy, for answering my questions while I worked. I can't wait to give it to him."

"Well, your timing is perfect. His birthday is tomorrow, isn't it?" When she looks up to see me nod and nearly burst with excitement, she smiles. "I can see that doing anything else before you deliver it is going to be nearly impossible. But it's late. Try to be calm and get some sleep now, and I'll wrap this for you. I'll make sure you're up early enough so you can take it by the store on your way to school. And I'll even walk Lydia to school myself so you don't have to come back for her."

"Oh, thank you." I jump over and throw my arms around her middle.

She lightly returns my embrace and pats my shoulder before pulling away. I look up to see the moisture gathering in her eyes. "On to bed with you," she says with unconvincing sternness. Since we got a letter from Papa saying that he should finally be home again sometime next month, Nancy cries more easily.

It's a wonder I fell asleep, but I must have because Nancy must shake me awake the next morning. I rush to get ready and run out the door and down the front path with the treasured package in one hand and my school things in the other. I can't hide my giant smile. I haven't said anything about his surprise. I should take it around to the back of the store where he often works in the mornings. Then he will truly be the first to see my gift.

I cut through a nearby alley and wind toward the store's back entrance. There's a small wagon off to the side and several crates stacked by the open door. Exactly as I hoped.

Before I can step through the doorway, a man's shape fills it. I draw up short. It is not Uncle Gardner but a stranger. He is a burly man wearing a worn hat and a work-stained shirt and vest. From a foot away, I can easily smell his heavy odors of sweat, fish, and stale tobacco.

"What a lovely and unexpected thing to meet you here this morning, little angel," he says while letting his eyes run over me from my face to my feet. "What's your name?"

I've never had anybody look at me like this before, and it makes me feel queer inside, like I want to dive and hide behind the crates. I have no desire to tell him anything about myself. My smile has vanished, and I stare at him.

My silence does not discourage him, and he makes no move to get out of my way. Instead, he leans his shoulder against the doorframe while sticking out a hand to cup my chin. I want to reach up and push it away but my hands are full. I start to pull back. His other hand shoots out to grip my shoulder. I open my mouth to cry out, but under the horrible look in his eyes, no sound emerges.

"What's the hold up, Mr. Merritt?" Uncle Gardner speaks from somewhere behind the man. "I'm ready for the other crates."

I jump back when the man releases me and steps down toward the waiting stack. Uncle Gardner comes to the door, and his somewhat annoyed look changes to one of happiness when he sees me standing to the side. When he takes in my rattled appearance, though, his gaze darts from me to Mr. Merritt and then back again while his look becomes increasingly serious. "Good morning. Won't you come inside?" He extends an arm to me. I allow myself to be ushered without a backward glance.

We step deeper into the storage room, and I set my things down on top of a small barrel. I turn to look up at Uncle Gardner and see that he is still studying me with concern. He doesn't speak but simply draws me to his side again. And this time, arms free, I can return his embrace. He smells good and his strong arm feels safe wrapped around my shoulders.

After a moment, I pull away and wipe my cheeks. "Thank you, Uncle Gardner," I whisper.

"I'm glad I came to check on things when I did. Are you all right?"

I bite my lip and nod.

"Annie..." He glances at the wall then meets my eyes once more. "I don't know if your father has ever said anything about this. Likely not, as he's been away while you've continued to grow. But many times in life you will meet people—men—who have a variety of motives and intentions. Some of them will be honorable and others dishonorable. And there may be times when you encounter men with dishonorable intentions while you are alone. So you must learn that it is necessary to fight and defend yourself—like you defended Gardner and fought those boys years ago. Other times, you may need to cry out or try and run away. Do whatever you must do to protect yourself if you sense you are in danger. Do you understand?"

"Yes," I give him a small, brave smile. "And I won't forget."

"Well then..." His expression turns puzzled. "I am happy to see you, but what errand brought you around back of the store today?"

"A special delivery," I sing out, some of my joy and excitement returning. "Happy Birthday, Uncle Gardner!" I pick up the package and hand it to him.

He undoes the string and brown paper Nancy used, lifting out the shirt and unfolding it. His face fills with quiet delight.

"I made it myself," I whisper proudly before he can speak.

And then it seems he can't speak. He holds it up against his front, and I can see that it should fit nicely. Suddenly I find I can't say anymore either. He lowers the shirt and pulls me close for one more hug.

When he finally lets go, he clears his throat and says in a soft, gruff voice, "You've made this the happiest birthday I've had in some time. Go out through the store and the front entrance." His voice drops lower while he drapes my gift over the barrel I've cleared my school things from. "You go on. And I'll deal with matters here."

* * *

JULY 7, 1830

He is as big and strong as ever, but I am bigger too. Now I can hug him about his waist. He smells of sea and salt and sandalwood. I breathe in deep. Then I tip my head all the way back to look up into his face. How wonderful he could return during the short summer holiday, so Lyddie and I can be here to meet him too, and so we can have more time with him before he must surely leave again. I swallow hard at the thought.

"Hello, Treasure."

I squeeze my arms once more before letting go and stepping back. We've all had a chance to greet him now. I let the others go first. I'm not sure why. I still love Papa like before, but I feel a little less open about showing it publicly.

He squints down at me. "My, how well you look." He turns to look at each of us once more. "You all look very well. Thank God for that."

Will grabs Papa's hand, and Papa offers his other arm to Nancy. We turn together and walk in the direction of Orange Street. When we reach the house and are all through the front door, Will exclaims, "What did you bring us, Papa? Are there gifts? Do you have new stories?"

We join Papa around the kitchen table while Nancy serves cups of cool water. Papa takes off his pack and reaches inside to pull out a large white object, a flat disk with long narrow holes in it. "Yes, William. This is for you. I found it on the beach when we docked in the Cape Verde Islands. It's called a sand dollar." He pauses and winks. "Perhaps it fell out of a mermaid's coin purse."

Will takes it and turns it over in his hands while the rest of us look on it with interest. His widest grin flashes. "Thank you, Papa!"

Papa smiles and reaches into the pack again. This time he pulls out a lovely comb, perhaps the most beautiful one I've ever seen. It is solid in its coloring, a whitish-gray. And it has some sort of carving across the top. I lean in to look closer. It's a mermaid with long hair flowing out behind her to form the handle. "For you, Lydia. Our second mate was one of the best carvers I've seen, and he crafted this from one of the teeth of the largest bull we caught. You are my little emerald-eyed mermaid, so I thought it should be yours."

"Oh," she whispers. "Thank you very much." She lifts it from his outstretched hand and runs the smooth teeth through the ends of her hair. "I'll keep it forever."

"And for Nancy." Papa keeps his eyes on her while pulling out the next gift. "Tell me what you think of this."

She opens the flat brown parcel to reveal a measure of the softest, most fascinating red material I've ever seen. She gasps with delight and runs it over her cheek before holding it out to let each of us touch it. "Silk."

"Yes. We met a merchant ship in the Pacific, and I traded for it. They were on their way home from China."

"It's exquisite. I've rarely owned silk of this quality and certainly never anything of this shade."

"I chose it because I thought it would complement your hair. It does so most amicably. The man who traded with me explained that a Chinese bride wears red—a sign of great fortune and happiness for the husband and wife."

She blushes and stares hard at the cloth, looking especially pleased. "I thank you for your thoughtfulness, Owen. I will consider how I can best use it. Perhaps a shawl?"

"Oh, yes." I can envision it. "You could wear it with your blue dress to the social."

"When is that to be?" Papa inquires.

"A week from tomorrow." Nancy carefully refolds her gift. "I hope that will give me enough time."

Papa turns to me with a smile tugging at the corner of his mouth. "I saved the best for last," he whispers.

What could be better than silk?

He digs down deep and lifts out a cloth-covered bundle. Unfolding the green linen, he removes a medium-sized cube and holds it out to me. I draw near and pick it up with both hands. It's heavier than I expected.

The sides are white and very smooth like Nancy's china teacups and saucers. The edges are golden. And the top— that's the most beautiful part. There is a picture painted upon it in tremendously fine detail. A large rock juts up out of the sea. On one side of it, a huge wave strikes and sends sea spray up against the terrible, stormy sky. On the other side, protected by the curve in the rock, huddles a man in tattered clothes—one who must have crawled up from the wreckage floating nearby.

I look up. "It's very well done."

"Ah, but that's not all." He reaches out and, while I continue to hold the cube from below, grips something on the back of it and turns it several times. Like magic, music fills the air— delicate notes that remind me of a butterfly's wings. The lilting notes unfurl, revealing the tune. *Let me hide myself in Thee.* Sudden tears prick my eyes.

"I searched for the right gift for you throughout my entire journey," he explains after the music winds down. "But I could never seem to find it. Then, when we landed in New Bedford, as I came up from the wharf, I saw this on display in a shop window. And when the matron showed me the tune that came with it, I knew my search was over."

As tenderly as can be, I set the cube on the table. Then I step forward to hug him.

His hand cups my head, and he speaks low against my ear. "I cannot count how many times on this journey I wish I could have had you near to sing the pain away."

I tip my face up and whisper back. "I will sing for you while you're home, if you need me to. I've never had a gift like this before. Thank you."

* * *

The days slip by, one by one: these glorious days of being together. But I seem to be holding my breath. I am wondering—we are all wondering, I think—when Papa will be leaving us again. This week or the next? One month from now? I soak up the moments and lock every memory away in my heart.

One day, Papa goes out "to attend to some business." Nancy and I exchange a look across the table. We've heard those words before. In just three days, Lyddie and I will have to go back to school. The thought of what news he may share when he returns leaves my stomach in knots throughout the entire afternoon.

We are all in the kitchen when he comes back—Nancy ladling out the soup, me carrying a stack of plates to the table, Lyddie gathering silverware, and Will placing a cup at each place setting.

"Well, and what do you think?" Papa asks with a grin. "They are going to build a new ship right here at Brant Point. I've been asked to help design and oversee the construction of it, and to captain it afterward. I've even been offered an owner's share."

We stare back at him in shocked silence.

"Is it not good news? And it means I should be able to stay with you for the better part of two years, if all goes according to schedule."

All at once, Will lets out a happy yelp, Lydia gasps and lets the forks clatter to the table, Nancy misses the bowl she's holding and sends some soup splattering across the floor, and

I drop the plate I've just lifted. I look down in horror at the shards of china now scattered near my feet.

Silence reigns for a few heartbeats, and then another rush of noise comes—Nancy's bemoaning the mess, Will and Lyddie running to throw themselves at Papa, and me crying and gasping for air. The knots in my stomach have all come undone at once. Their release crashes against my fear of being punished for my clumsiness. I can't see for the wall of water in my eyes nor can I hear for the rushing of sobs in my ears.

The pieces. I must pick up the pieces. I stoop and blindly reach down with shaking hands to where I guess they must be.

A hand suddenly closes over mine. Nancy's voice slips around the sobs. "Careful. You don't want to cut yourself. I'll clean it up." She grasps my elbows and pulls me up only to guide me down again. The solidness of the chair under me helps my heartbeat slow. I take a deep, shuddering breath and blink to see past my drenched lashes.

Papa is untangling himself from where he was likely being smothered with hugs. He studies me with a frown. I look down to see Nancy kneeling near my feet, carefully collecting the sharp pieces up in her apron. "I'm sorry I broke your plate." My voice wavers. "I know you love your dishes." I hiccup.

Nancy pauses to squeeze my hand before turning back to finish her task. "I don't love these dishes. I like them very much. But dishes can be replaced. You and your father cannot."

Papa has crossed to take up a neighboring chair. His steady gaze remains on me.

"I'm sorry to be so careless. I was only surprised. I don't mean to cry like a baby, Papa." But then the tears start to fall again. "Your face is so grave. Please don't be angry. I'll stop crying." I swipe at my eyes.

He reaches out and swallows my hands in his, resting the mound of them on my knee. "I'm not angry, Annie. Only concerned for you. I don't think you a baby. It sobers me to see your response—and saddens me to realize how deeply you've longed for my presence when I have not been able to give it to you."

"But now you shall?" I whisper in a mixed tone of doubt and wonder. "You'll really be able to stay for two whole years?"

"I shall and I will." He leans over and kisses my cheek.

Feeling supremely peaceful, I lean against his shoulder. When he wraps his arm around me, I imagine how perfect these years will be.

* * *

EARLY MARCH 1831

It is a painfully cold day. I tremble in the stinging wind and run home from school. I am returning alone just as I went alone. Lyddie and Will have both had a fever since last night, and Nancy kept them home. She urged me to hurry back instead of stopping at the store, to help her with nursing them and seeing to supper.

When I'm nearly halfway there, I hear a familiar voice calling. "Annie!"

I stop and turn in a circle, squinting when the wind smacks at my eyes. Uncle William is standing on the other side of the street. He signals for me to stay put. I wait, shivering, while he weaves through traffic and puddles to reach me. "Hello, dear girl," he says as he bends to give me a quick kiss on the forehead.

"Hello," I manage around chattering teeth.

"How cold you look!" He takes my hand in his. "Let's get you home. I have news for your father."

I can't reply because my shivering has increased, but his hand over mine is warm and his presence, as always, helps put me at ease.

He tells me about Elizabeth's new interest in lacemaking, and before I know it, we have reached the front path. He pushes the door open and shoos me in ahead of him where a wave of warm air hits us.

Nancy is coming down the stairs with a basin in her hands. A look of surprise sweeps over her face. "William? What brings you all the way over here on such a miserable day?" She reaches the bottom and smiles. "Forgive me. You are always welcome, as you know. Please go and warm yourself by the fire in the parlor. I'll bring you some tea."

"I thank you," he says while glancing at me where I am trying to remove my cloak with shaking hands. "And perhaps something for Annie? She seems to be chilled through."

She turns to me. "Yes. I'll bring you some hot milk. It won't do to have three of you with a fever, though Lydia does seem a little better."

I nod, hang up my cloak and bonnet, and follow Uncle William toward the inviting blaze. We sit side-by-side on the settee, and he draws me close to snuggle under his arm. When Nancy returns with two cups, he asks, "Is Owen at home? I have some news I believe he would wish to hear."

She nods. "He's been working hard in his study since late morning, asking not to be disturbed. But it's not long till supper. And it's you. I don't think he'll mind the interruption. Drink this and I'll inquire."

We sip our drinks and stare into the flames. "Do you want me to leave so you can talk to Papa privately?"

"I don't think that's necessary. You're old enough to hear what I have to say. Besides, we're helping each other get warm again, remember?" He grins down at me.

I smile back and burrow against his side while taking care not to spill what's left of my milk.

Soon Papa strides into the room. "William," he greets with a nod and a handshake. Then he stretches down to touch my forehead. "Nancy said you came home chilled. Are you warm enough now?"

"I think so."

"Stay a bit longer, to be sure. Then you can go and help her with the table. Will you stay to supper, William?" He settles in the wing chair.

"No, I thank you. Elizabeth will be expecting me at home, and it's not getting any warmer. I won't linger but wanted to pass on some news."

"Certainly. A pleasant reprieve, I trust, from the small planning crisis I've had to deal with today."

Uncle William frowns and swallows. "I'm afraid that may not be the case, but I'll let you be the judge."

"Something bad, is it?"

"I've come from 'Sconset. I volunteered to help deliver the first batch of after-winter mail. Though, with the weather last night and today, it doesn't feel like winter will be over anytime soon."

"And what did you hear?"

"News brought from the Point. George Gardner is dead."

"Dead? When?"

"About two weeks ago. Fell on the tower steps and hit his head. Never woke up. There was nothing to be done for him."

"And Judith?"

"It seems she has been numb in her grief, shutting out nearly all of her few visitors, sleeping through parts of the days and continuing to run the light at night. Word reached 'Sconset shortly before I arrived. And I'm sure the officials will be appointing a new keeper as soon as can be. Someone said Caleb Cushman would be a suitable replacement."

"Aye," says Papa while staring blankly at the mantle. "I seem to recall Peggy saying that he helped with the light when he was a boy. What will become of Judith?"

"That's the main reason why I wanted to tell you as soon as possible. She will need to leave the keeper's cottage—a pity when it's, what, only five or six years they've been able to live in the new one, so near the tower again? And she's said to have grown somewhat weaker herself. I thought perhaps you would at least want to try and further investigate her situation."

Papa's voice grows thoughtful. "You did well to come and tell me, my friend. I thank you for the consideration."

My empty cup in hand, I slip off the settee and across the room.

"I pray I did. To own the truth, Owen, you look rather unwell..." Uncle William's voice fades as I enter the kitchen. By the time Papa is seeing Uncle William to the door and lending him a lantern for the walk home in the dusky gloom, Nancy and I have everything in readiness.

After Papa offers the prayer, we all eat in silence for a time. Finally, I dare to voice my question. "The man who died—that's Grandpa George, isn't it?"

Papa pauses in scooping up potatoes and then puts down his spoon to fold his hands. "Yes." When he glances at Nancy's curious expression, he repeats the news. "And I'm not sure what I should do. I promised Peggy that I'd do what I could to help mend and strengthen fragmented relations in both our families. I confess, on her side, I've worked harder at that with George than with Judith. It was easier with him. He was less judgmental."

"Well, you can try at least," Nancy offers. "What are you thinking?"

"To visit her at the Point and make her some sort of offer. To build her a small cottage of her own out that way, to move her to town, or to let her stay with us. Would you be able to bear it if I offered and she accepted?"

"That could indeed prove awkward. But I will support you and do my part, come what may. If you offer and she accepts, I will bear it. After all, are we not her only family?"

"Just so. She has no one else left. Not really." He pauses to smile at her. "You are very good to be willing to do this."

"Only as good as you are in making the offer in the first place." She returns the smile. But, looking back and forth between them, I can see a shared sadness in their eyes.

"I don't want to delay in going to see her. Tomorrow being Saturday, there should be less need of me at the building site, especially with this weather. Yes, I think I shall drive out tomorrow. I'll hire transport from the livery, be off in the morning and back by evening if all goes well."

"Oh?" Nancy asks in surprise. "Wouldn't it be more direct to borrow a small boat and go around by way of the Sound's edge?"

"I considered that," he is quick to reply. "But with the weather we've been having, the going would be more treacherous and uncomfortable. If you please, prepare the spare room, in case I bring her back with me, even if only temporarily."

"I shall do so around tending Lydia and William. In a way, I wish they were well and we could all come with you. I would hope that seeing her grandchildren might help to convince her of her need for others' love."

"With Judith it is hard to say. But perhaps you're right."

I speak up. "May I go with you?"

He eyes me over the rim of his cup. "It will be very cold. Are you sure you want to go?"

"Yes. To be with you and help you if I can. And to see the Point. I barely remember Grandma and the east end of the Island." Truly, what I remember of Grandma is not pleasant. I don't want Papa to face her alone.

Nancy reasons aloud. "We could dress her extra warmly and wrap her in blankets. If she sits close to you or even burrows in the box at your feet, that would help. I don't want to put her in any danger—only to send someone with you on the journey and aid your cause."

Papa looks between us a couple of times and then nods. "We'll try it. In that case, I'm doubly glad I decided to go overland. Annie, I want you to go to bed directly after supper. It will be a long day tomorrow, and we must leave quite early. Is that understood?"

"Yes, Papa." I hastily clean my plate.

* * *

An unexpectedly bright sunrise starts to tap down the morning mist by the time Papa returns with the rented rig, the bottom half-filled with a box and bag of provisions for sharing. Nancy comes out with me and helps to hand me up before passing Papa a couple of old blankets to tuck around me. She has dressed me in thick layers, and in place of my bonnet she's let my thick curls hang free and given Papa a heavy muffler to wrap around my head and face, believing that this combination will be a better shield against the wind.

She declares, "It looks like there should be some sun, and I hope that will help to warm you both." She stretches up once more with a small basket of food and drink, and Papa stows it with the other items near our feet.

He waves good-bye before he encircles me with his arm and uses his other hand to take up the reins while Nancy bids us God's speed. We take off, continuing south to take Lower

Orange Street out of town. Soon we come upon a wide path lined with scrubby bushes on both sides.

Above the strong breeze now pummeling us, I hear his voice. "If you start to feel cold, tell me and I'll go a little slower."

I nod to show my understanding. With my head and mouth snuggly covered, it's all the reply I can manage.

We fly across the land—mile after mile of sandiness. Blackbirds swoop by and voles, and field mice scurry along the ground. It's been so long since I was this far out of town, every sight is fascinating. And here at Papa's side, I feel secure and unafraid. We pass dunes, marshes, fields, grazing sheep, and the occasional plot with a small house.

Then we turn from one road to another, and the woods of Coskata appear in the distance. I stare in wonder at the dense clusters of trees, unrivaled anywhere else on the Island. Papa asks if I need to stretch, and I nod again. He brings the calash to a halt and climbs down before reaching back to lift me out. I step behind a bush to relieve myself and return to find him opening the food basket. "Why don't we have a bit of refreshment before continuing?"

I pull the muffler edge down. "Yes, please. I'm hungry." He helps me back up and hands me a sandwich and a jar of milk, encouraging me to save half of the milk for the journey home. While I eat and drink, he quickly disposes of two sandwiches and a jar of tea.

The sun is a bit warmer now, so when he wraps the muffler more loosely and tucks one blanket around me, I assure him that I feel comfortable. With the muffler down around my chin, I can speak freely. I ask him about Mama, Grandma Judith, and Grandpa George.

He tells me a little about Mama's early years and how he came to take her away.

"I remember a few things about Grandma Judith. But not very much."

"That's natural. You've only seen her a few times." His expression grows harder, determined. "Your grandmother has been through some trials in her life. And she has become unyielding and hard to please. I know how much you like to make others feel happy, comfortable, and satisfied. No matter what Grandma Judith may say or do today, if and when we see her, I want to remind you now: Nancy and I care about you, and you are our good girl. If your grandmother finds fault with you, don't mind it, do you hear? She doesn't know you like we do."

* * *

We reach a point where the landscape becomes so sandy that the horses have a hard time going. Far in the distance—a few miles according to Papa—I can see a speck that must be the lighthouse standing tall as waves crash against the slightly lower shores on either side of it. Papa pulls the calash up in a kind of barn-shelter. "We have to leave the rig here and walk the rest of the way because the ground is too soft for the horses." We get down and look out to see that the field of sand in front of us is mostly dry. The tide must be out. "Would you carry this for me?" he asks, handing over the bundle.

"Yes, Papa." I can manage the weight and feel happy to be of service.

He folds up the blankets and the muffler, guessing aloud that I'll be warm enough without it. Then he takes up the full crate in his arms, and we start out across the sand together. It is harder to walk upon than I expected. By the time we reach the other side, I'm quite warm and glad that Papa left the muffler behind.

When we approach the tower, Papa points me slightly to the right so that we aim for the two-story cottage nearby. Since his hands are full, Papa asks me to knock on the wind-worn door.

I set my bundle on the front step and knock as hard as I can. There's no answer after we wait a moment. I knock again. Still no response.

"Try the door, Annie." It opens easily, and I look up at him, uncertain. He nods me inside, so I snatch up the bundle to comply. "It's all right," he says.

I step forward tentatively, and he follows. We set our burdens down against the entryway wall.

"Hello there. Is anyone home?" Papa calls out.

There is a bustling above stairs, then a creeping on the steps. Papa gazes steadily at an older, slightly familiar-looking woman—one who stares hard at us and then blinks in recognition—making her slow descent.

"Judith. We've come to bring some supplies and see how you fare."

Grandma blinks at him again from where she's now paused on the last step. "Owen Chase."

"Aye. And this is Phebe Ann. It's been a great while since you've seen her, I believe."

"Yes." She nods down and sends me the slightest smile.

"May we come in and sit with you for a time?"

"Yes," she murmurs, seeming to fade in and out of a daze. "Yes, thou may come in. And won't thou stay to tea?" She steps down and shows us into the small sitting room. Papa takes a seat on the settee and I join him, sticking close by his side. She also sits down, holding herself extremely stiffly on the edge of a ladder-back chair. I can feel a kind of tension flowing out of Papa. I need to sit up straighter.

They make stilted small talk, the tone and pace not matching Papa's normal cadence. Finally, he says, "We heard about George and share your sorrow in his passing. We bring sympathy from the family and those in town who knew him."

She nods.

"We came not only to bring you provisions but also to ask what might be done to help you as you adjust to your present circumstances. Is there anything you lack? Anything we might provide for you? Perhaps another place to live?"

She stares at him, her face impassive.

"You could come and live with us in town. We have an extra room, and you would be most welcome. Or I could hire workers to build a snug new cottage for you near Siasconset if you feel you must stay by the sea."

Her expression turns frigid. I don't know how, exactly, as the parts of her face barely move. But I feel a wave of coldness splash against us. Then she smiles at me again—this time a little more but also very tightly. "I should make that tea. Phebe Ann, will thou come and help me?"

Papa nods to me and touches my arm. He loves me. I must be his good girl. Back straight, I follow Grandma into the kitchen.

She shuts the door behind us and goes about setting water to boil. Taking a tin of tea leaves down from a high shelf, she asks me about Lyddie and Will and Nancy. She quizzes me about what I've learned at school and how well I've behaved. I wring my hands behind my back. She asked me to help her, but she's doing all the work. I feel completely out of place.

"I need thee to run outside for a little while so thy father and I can discuss some matters in private."

I start to chew on my lip—then stop myself. Nancy says it's one of my worst habits and very unladylike.

"Go out," she continues, lifting down two teacups and saucers, "to take a look at the sea. But don't go too near the edge of the bluff." She turns and pierces me with her gaze.

"Yes, Grandma." I nod but am otherwise unable to move. I don't want to leave Papa alone with her.

She lifts a brow and scowls. "Phebe Ann, when an older person asks thee to do something, thou should comply. With age comes wisdom. And they will always know better. Thou should not question them or dawdle but do what is required of thee with a ready and willing attitude."

With rock-like feet, I follow her out the kitchen's other door that empties back into the entryway. She helps me secure my cloak and then shoos me out the front entrance, shutting it behind me without another word.

The sea stretches like a never-ending, ever-shifting field. Gulls soar high in the air, crying loudly above the foamy surf. The sun has come out again, and its reflection dances brilliantly, almost blindingly, upon the water. I squint, both against the light and the wind that feel all the more intense here on land's edge. My curls whip about my face, and now I wish we had brought the muffler after all. Wrapping my arms about myself and squeezing tight, I march in place. The scene is full of rugged beauty, but I have no desire to linger in the frigid air.

I want nothing more than to return to Papa's side. But Grandma will be angry if I return too soon. I run back around the tower and then down the path again to keep warm, but still the wind assails me. Maybe, if I go back in quietly, I can stand in the entryway to get warm again. Grandma won't know I'm there, will she?

I shut the front door with great care once I've crept inside. I hold my breath for a moment and then relax when the quiet conversation coming from the sitting room sounds like it is continuing without interruption. In fact, when I stand very still, I can clearly make out Grandma's words while she speaks calmly and yet forcefully.

"I never asked thee for anything, Owen Chase. I seek no assistance from thee now, have asked for nothing these past years. And I certainly never asked thee to take my daughter as thy wife. I think how her life would have likely been spared, would have turned out so differently, if she had married Ephraim Merritt—or any one of those other landsmen her father introduced her to."

I swallow, remembering what Nancy told me before about not listening to other people's private conversations. But thoughts of the nasty wind mixed with curiosity to know more about Mama root me in place.

"Thou who caused her much distress and heartache and encouraged her to leave the Friends, thou who contributed ultimately to her demise, thou who took another wife not long after and gave my husband and I no opportunity to raise our grandchildren."

Through her quiet tirade, I hear no sound from Papa. He must be sitting and absorbing it. Is he is thinking about how much we love him, how Grandma doesn't know him like we do?

"And those grandchildren," she continues with a disappointed note in her voice. "I think also of how much better they would be turning out if they had their true mother and a more constant fatherly presence to guide them strictly in the ways of the Light. Why must thou abandon them again and again? Seeing Phebe Ann today only makes me fear further for how headstrong and prideful she may turn out to be: how very much like thee she could become—"

"You have said quite enough, Judith. As the two of us cause you such obvious distress, we will take our leave and not trouble you further."

I jump at Papa's reply—spoken with as harsh a tone as I've ever heard from him.

Afraid of how they will respond if they know I've been listening, I hastily exit and take several steps toward the tower. A moment later, Papa comes striding out of the house and, seeing me standing there, grabs my hand and charges forward so purposefully that I must run to keep up.

"Let's go," he snaps. We press on until I stumble. He stops and turns to me. At the fear in my eyes, his jaw relaxes a fraction. "I'm taking you home." He breathes hard, staring above me at the stone tower behind us.

We reach the long bed of sand but draw up short when we see how the tide's starting to come in. It's already at least an inch deep. Papa grinds out something under his breath. Then, "I almost wish we'd taken our chances by boat. I'm glad we didn't stay any longer." We gaze across the water, to the faint outline of the barn and higher land on the other side.

The wind hits us hard and throws my trembling form against his legs. The sun still shines brightly, but I can't stop shaking. "Papa?"

"It will not do for you to be soaked. Nancy will be utterly vexed and never let me hear the end of it. Let me carry you."

"But it's so far. And your feet will still be soaked!"

"Aye, and I'll warm them well when we get home. They've been cold and wet before, and I've survived." He bends and scoops me up. "Perhaps I might use one of the blankets we brought to wrap them up if it's very bad." He adjusts me so he has a more secure hold. "Besides, you're light yet. It should be no trouble to see you across."

Wrapping my arms around his neck, I hang on while he begins the increasingly sloshy walk across to the far side. Though his feet sometimes slip, we never fall. He progresses as quickly as possible, but by the time we finish crossing, the water is halfway to his knees, completely soaking his boots and trouser legs. We are both shivering: him from the wet cold and me from the unceasing wind.

He sets me down near the calash before helping me up onto the seat and climbing up beside me. He secures the muffler over my head and the first of the quilts around my body. "I admit that I am quite chilled. Do you mind if I use the other blanket?"

"Please use it. Nancy will be equally vexed if she has to nurse *you*."

He laughs low while he wraps his feet in a dry section of the quilt. "Yes, you are right. And we both want to remain on her good side at every possible opportunity."

The sound of his voice warming helps something inside me relax, and I suddenly feel tears welling up. I nod over at him, and my teeth begin to chatter again.

He frowns back at me. "I thought you said you were all right."

"I think I am. But I feel…" My voice wobbles. "I know Nancy said I shouldn't eavesdrop, but I listened to a little of your conversation with Grandma," I say. "I heard those things she said, and her words hurt my heart. And you were angry. Are you angry with me for listening?"

He sits up straight and turns to take me by the shoulders. For a moment, he silently searches my eyes and face. "You are my good and beautiful girl. I'm not angry with you. I'm very proud of you." He leans to wrap his arm around me and presses my head against his shoulder. Warmth seeps through me, and my trembling lessens. He guides the horses and rig from the barn and sets us on our way before he continues to speak, low near my ear, but still loud enough that I can hear him above the wind. "Do you remember what I told you on the drive out?"

"Yes, Papa."

"We're going home now, and I want you to leave these troubles behind you. What happened today will be today's, and we will step into tomorrow and move forward."

"Will we come back here? I don't want to. But what about Grandma?"

"You've probably guessed she rejected every offer I made her. I'll see if I can help her indirectly. But for now, I've done my part. We will go home and continue on as we were."

I press my cheek against the brushed wool of his coat and rest easy under his sheltering arm.

* * *

We roll up to a halt at the livery entrance as the setting sun and dying winds make way for the mists to settle. Then we limp home—Papa's feet still stiff from their frigid soaking and my whole body stiff from sitting huddled in the same position over the past hours.

Upon our entrance, Nancy gives thanks to God. Seeing our sorry condition, she leads us to the table where she sets Papa's feet in a basin of lukewarm water and wraps me in a flannel sheet. Then she dishes up bowls of pea soup with a cup of warm milk for me and a glass of warm wine for Papa.

She coaxes some details of the day from Papa while we eat. He talks about his offers made in vain and explains how he ended up with wet boots. Nancy bends to add small increments of hot water to the basin, warming his feet gradually. And my eyelids droop like sails being slowly lowered.

"Annie?" Nancy's voice sounds foggy, distant. I awaken with my forehead on the table next to my empty cup and half-eaten soup.

"Mmm?" I murmur, rolling my head around. She looks at me with concern. Papa studies me with a mirroring tiredness.

"Perhaps it wasn't such a good idea to take her," Nancy whispers before she slips around Papa to help me stand. "Come along, sweetheart. Let me get you into bed before I finish tending to your father."

Nancy's face is the last thing I see as my head falls back on my pillow and I fall into a mercifully dreamless sleep.

And it is the first thing I see in the early morning light peeking over my bedroom windowsill. She presses my shoulder and whispers my name. "I need your assistance."

I get up and put on my robe and slippers, taking care not to disturb Lyddie where she dozes in the neighboring bed. Down the hall, Nancy and Papa's bedroom door stands open. I come to the threshold and peer into the dimness. "Is it Papa's head?"

"Yes. He's been in great pain these two hours at least. I've tried to help him, but he cannot sleep. I thought of waking you earlier but wanted you to sleep a little longer."

I creep forward and take in the familiar torture lining his tight face. The scent of lavender hangs heavy in the air, but still his expression is thus. I tenderly fit my hand under his where it rests atop the covers. He starts a little and then wraps his fingers around mine.

"Annie." Anguish fills his tone.

I keep my voice low. "I'm here."

"I'm sorry to interrupt your sleep."

"It's all right. Your pain's very bad?"

"Nearly the worst I've ever felt. Stay and sing, please."

"What do you want to hear?"

"Anything peaceful, hopeful." He squeezes my hand and grits his teeth. Nancy brings a chair and sets it next to me. When his hand and jaw relax a little, I settle myself on the seat and surround his hand with both of mine.

Nancy bends near. "I must get ready for church. After resting yesterday, I believe Lydia and William are well enough to go with me. I have serving duties today, both before and after the service, and must help oversee everything. Will you stay here and nurse your papa? If you can help him get to sleep, you can have more time to rest."

I nod.

"There's extra water there," she points, "and more lavender water should you require it." She turns to press Papa's arm before she picks up her shawl and closes the door most of the way when she slips out.

In the deeper dimness, his hand and face relax a bit further. I begin to hum and then sing a hymn I learned recently, keeping my voice gentle.

> *Oh God, our help in ages past, our hope for years to come,*
> *Our shelter from the stormy blast, and our eternal home.*
> *Under the shadow of Thy throne Thy saints have*
> *dwelt secure;*
> *Sufficient is Thine arm alone, and our defense is sure...*

I'm completing a second song by the time his face relaxes completely and his breathing sinks deep. I slip my hands away and reach up to add more lavender to the compress on his forehead.

I tiptoe around the end of the bed. Crawling up on the bench, I curl up in a ball, rest my cheek against the velvety, padded cover, and listen for any sound of Papa's stirring. Still weary from yesterday, I soon drift off to sleep again and dream of swirling, wet sand around horses' hooves. I awaken sometime later to Papa's deep voice calling through my fog of consciousness.

"Thomas! Pull the helm hard up!" he shouts before he begins to mumble something I cannot understand. He becomes more agitated, and I wake fully. Jumping off the bench and running around the bedpost, I find him thrashing his arms and tossing his head—his face flushed and covered in sweat.

"Papa, wake up!"

He stops speaking but continues to twist and jerk. I'm afraid to touch him—afraid to get in the way of his tense hands and arms. But I'm more worried that he'll hurt himself.

"Please!" I call louder. When his arms still, I take a chance and press forward to grip the one nearest me.

He gasps, and his eyes fly open. Staring at the ceiling, a fog-like sheet over his gaze, his body lies motionless, and it seems he's not breathing at all.

Fear grips my heart. "Papa?" I shake the arm again, harder this time. "It was a dream. You're safe here at home, with me."

He lets out a long sigh, and his arm muscles relax under my grip. He blinks and then turns to look at me, his eyes clearing. He brings his opposite hand across and clings to mine.

I take a shaky breath of my own. "How's your head?"

"It's a little better. The sleep helped. Only the memories at the end…"

I stare back at him, unsure of what to say.

"I would take some water." He accepts the cup I offer and slowly drains it.

"Did you have such bad dreams before? I think I remember you crying in the night, a long time ago."

"Yes." He swallows hard and closes his eyes. "They plague me too, like the pain—though I haven't had dreams that vivid for quite some time."

"Papa, why is there pain? Why do bad things happen to us?"

He opens his eyes and studies me. After a moment he lifts his closer arm and whispers, "Come," inviting me to climb up and curl at his side.

I settle into my favorite place on earth. Sheltered now between the quilts that cover him and his strong arm, with his hand on my shoulder, I wait for him to speak again.

Holding up his other hand near my face, he asks, "See the small white scar there on the palm, to the right?"

There are many rough places, but I can spot it, even in this dim light. "Yes."

"Do you remember how and when I received this?"

"No."

"You were very young. That scar reminds me of a time when I lost my temper and came close to hurting you and your mama because of it. But it is also a reminder of mercy, when your mama came to nurse and forgive me, despite the degree to which I did not deserve those things." He brings that other hand up to let his fingertips trace first the little scar under my bottom lip, then the one on my temple, and the largest one just above my hairline. "But you certainly remember the origin of these?"

"Yes." I close my eyes.

"You rescued your friend, and in the process, you were injured. After your injuries healed, these marks remained. They are a reminder of when you were hurt—but also of your sacrifice."

I nod. The top quilt absorbs the tears rolling down upon it.

"We all have scars, Annie. And the longer we live, the more we often have. Some are on the outside, like these, and some form within."

I ponder this. "Do you mean in my heart?"

"Aye. Heart, mind, and soul."

"Like your bad dreams and memories?"

"Yes."

"And like Grandma's words yesterday?" And the look in Mr. Merritt's eyes at Uncle Gardner's door...

He hesitates, then stretches his hand wider to cradle my head and press me close to his side. "Aye."

"Why does God allow others to hurt us and us to hurt others?"

He sighs. "I believe He lets us make our own choices. That's His way. But your mama always said she knew He had a perfect plan, so I suppose that means He can even use the pain and the scars to somehow fulfill that plan."

I hear the softening in his voice and can picture the gentle smile on his lips.

"Like your mama, we can choose to trust Him. In that way, I believe, the injuries can heal, and the scars will speak of both the overcoming and the mercy that draws us toward the right course time and time again."

My brow furrows. Sometimes trusting is so difficult. "I'm afraid of the scars because the pain must come first."

"Do not fear. Pain is an inescapable part of living in this world. The secret is to rise each morning, step up, and face whatever that day holds with courage and faith, and believe that, in the end, you will be standing on a rock. And if you cannot stand, that a mighty hand will be there to catch you when you fall."

He pauses when the clock on the landing chimes the hour. "God does not want you to live in fear, and neither do I. Be strong, and know that even when the wounds and scars come, you have a shelter, a place to run where you can find safety."

"Papa, are you ever afraid of the dreams and pain?"

"Sometimes," he admits, "they have tormented me. But I must go on. God knows the scars we bear—some through personal choices and others through no fault of our own. And He gives us strength equal to them."

I chew on my lip and consider his words.

"Even at times when I am here, I cannot always shield you from circumstances or people that would harm you, but God is your rock and true protector. He is the one you must cling to, for only He can do the job perfectly."

I press my cheek against his side again.

"Do you understand?"

"I think so. But—if it's all right—when you are with us, can I cling to Him but also cling a little to you?"

He breathes out a chuckle. "As you wish. We all find comfort and strength in clinging to others on this journey, do we not?"

I listen to his breathing and heartbeat until I drift off to sleep for the rest of the morning.

CHAPTER
ELEVEN

LATE MAY 1832

"The owners are a couple named Silas and Dorcas Mitchell. I hadn't been formally introduced to them before, their shop being further north in town than I generally do business. But Mary knows them and suggested I inquire." Nancy passes the bread to Lyddie.

"And they would take an apprentice as young as Annie?" Papa glances in my direction while he reaches for the beans. It's still hard to believe that he's been home for nearly two years.

"Yes. They currently have two girls of thirteen along with their older girls and the ladies who receive full commission. I stopped by yesterday while I was out. When I showed them a sample of her work, they were thoroughly impressed and said they would be happy to consider taking her on—if we are in complete agreement about it. They have room for another, even if she is only twelve, and she could learn much more from Dorcas than I could ever teach her."

Lyddie and I share a look of foreboding across the table. "Nancy, if I go to work there, I can't help you here."

"Don't worry about that. Lydia's old enough to help me with most of the main tasks. And William needs to start taking on more chores."

I look at Papa. "What about school? What will Mr. Wallace say?"

Papa stares at his food and raises his brows a bit higher. "Well, you see—"

"Your father and I recently had an interview with Mr. Wallace. He told us he's already taught you everything in the basic curriculum. You're so bright that he's stretching to find new things with which to challenge you."

"In other words, you're too clever for your own good." Papa offers a wide grin.

"But I love school," I whisper.

"We know it," Papa says. "And you've done very well indeed. Simply think of this as a new kind of schooling. You'll learn a great deal from Mrs. Mitchell and the other workers, skills that you can use in the future in addition to your book-learning."

"And you'll only start out with half-days at the shop," Nancy smiles. "So for the first couple of months, you'll go there in the mornings."

"Then you can spend the afternoons at the schoolhouse, helping Mr. Wallace with the younger children," Papa finishes, grinning again.

I can't keep from smiling too. That is good.

"Then you can come back home in time to help me with supper."

"Yes. Helping Nancy with supper is always greatly appreciated." Papa winks at Nancy. She blows out a frustrated sigh but then chuckles good-naturedly.

I have started gathering cooking advice from Aunt Mary, Sadie, and Elizabeth. My additions have improved things so that our meals are increasingly more appetizing.

"You've arranged everything?" Papa asks Nancy.

"Yes. Tomorrow will be your last full day of school, Annie. Then, on Monday, I'll take you to the shop and see that you're settled."

"You're so lucky," Will grumbles. "You don't have to go to school anymore!"

Lyddie bites her lip to suppress a giggle.

"William Henry!" Nancy scowls. "You are a lucky boy to be able to study with such a good teacher. The new common school, I've heard, is little more than a circus—and education from there must be nearly worthless. Your day to leave school will come soon enough."

Lyddie looks a bit wistful and sad. I know she loves school too, but it has been hard for her to make friends with the other children besides Sara. Perhaps my leaving will help her to be less afraid of opening up and sharing with others.

I fiddle with my spoon. "Nancy?"

"Hmmm?"

"After the two months are over, what will happen then?"

"If they are pleased with you, you will become a full-time apprentice for two years, arriving early each weekday morning and coming home in time to help me here a little. Though I'm sure you'll be tired at first."

I nod and take a bite of dumplings. I like to sew. But when I think of doing it for many hours every day, I frown. Then I think of what Mr. Wallace once taught us, about how we can still choose to look for the good in things even when something doesn't seem easy. He told us that no one can steal the happiness that we choose to hold deep inside our hearts. Papa thinks this is best for me, so I will do my best to embrace the change.

Then another thought springs to mind. "What about my singing lessons?"

Papa looks at Nancy for a moment and says, "We'll see if Mrs. Summers is willing to adjust her schedule. She says you are her best student, so I doubt it will be a problem."

I nod again and smile. If voice lessons continue, holding the happiness deep in my heart will be a lot easier.

* * *

My last regular day at school contains a dozen precious moments, and I try hard to capture them all in my memory, each like a unique shell in my collection. I linger to help clean the board and sweep. Then I weave my way through the congested streets, stepping into the store to share my news with Aunt Mary.

I approach the counter and greet her. "Did you hear that I'm going to work for Mrs. Mitchell next week?"

Her smile blooms till her eyes dance.

"You're very happy."

"I'm always happy to see you, sweet girl. But I'm even happier today. As you will be. Gardner's come home. He returned this morning."

My eyes go wide. "Really? May I see him?"

"Yes, you may. He's upstairs. He's offered to stay above the store so he can open early and stay behind to close at day's end. Then his father can have more time to rest. Gardner's homecoming couldn't have come at a better time."

I nod and shudder, remembering when I witnessed one of Uncle Gardner's heart spells last month.

"Go on up and see him. I know he's eager to see you. Then you can help me fill these orders if you have time. Unless Nancy needs you home sooner."

I creep up the stairs, suddenly feeling a little shy since I haven't seen Gardner in nearly four years. I step forward and reach up to knock on the open door's frame, but my hand freezes in place.

The person unpacking items from the trunk is a stranger. His profile looks a little familiar but he's much taller—and so much stronger. His blonde hair, shoulder-length now, is tied back at the neck. The suit he wears is finely made and fits him well, and it's much more fashionable than his old clothes.

Gone is my brother-friend. How am I to approach him? I start to back away from the door when he turns around.

"Annie!" His face lights with ease. His gravelly whisper voice is a little deeper but still familiar. And his eyes and smile haven't changed at all. When he kneels and opens his arms, I hesitate for only an instant before I step into his embrace.

He pulls back, grips my shoulders, and studies my face. "You've grown."

"Not as much as you!" I giggle.

"Well, perhaps." He stands to his full height, and I must tip my head back all the way to look into his face. Why, he's nearly as tall as Papa. He reaches out to pat the top of my curls like he used to. It is a pleasant sensation, but also somehow different than before.

"I'm so glad you've come home. Will you stay here now, or do you have to go back?" *Please stay.*

"I've finished my courses. I want to help Father, especially with his heart growing weaker. And after he gave me such a great opportunity for further study. He's going to teach me to run the store."

"That will be a lot of responsibility, won't it?"

He turns back to the trunk and starts to lift out small stacks of books, setting them on the table near me. "Yes, I suppose it is. But I think my courses have prepared me well for the work."

"Will you tell me about life in Hanover?" I sit on the edge of the neighboring chair and scan the book titles.

"If you like. What do you want to know?"

"Was it noisy and crowded there?"

"In the town it could be. But on our school grounds, it was quite peaceful, and there were lovely places to walk. All the streets were lined with trees, so green and beautiful in summer, on fire with color in autumn, and full of icicles in winter."

"Like you described in your letters."

"You read them?"

"Aunt Mary always shared them with me, whenever a new one came."

"Sorry that I didn't have time to write more. I should have written directly to you at least once or twice."

"It doesn't matter. I know you must have been very busy. But now you're home."

"Yes." He grins.

"Gardner, you look stronger than before."

He laughs—that old raspy chuckle. "I suppose I am. They required that we be active every day. I often fenced with my classmates, and they all said I was becoming quite good. What about you? You've certainly changed some, though your hair and smile are exactly the same."

"I've grown a little. But Lyddie's taller than me, by far, and Will's nearly my height though he's so much younger."

"They're taking after your father."

I run my hands back and forth over the sides of my skirt. "Yes. He's been home to stay these two years. It's so wonderful to have him here. They're building a ship. He's to be captain and part owner. He's even helped to design it." My heart nearly bursts with pride.

"And he's well?"

I study the floor. "Most of the time. But sometimes his head is very bad. Other times everything is fine. Many things have happened since you went away."

"I'm sure they have." He lifts some clothes from the trunk and sets them on the dresser.

Looking over the books again, I see one volume that's different. I slip it from near the top of the pile and admire the soft leather cover with its tooled details before opening it to reveal page after page of fine handwriting placed in short, neat lines. I read a few of them. "What's this?"

He looks over his shoulder. "A book of verse I copied. I started it during my second-year literature course, when we studied many great poets from the past and present. I copied down some favorites then and have since added others. I've even made a few attempts of my own." He colors slightly before turning away again.

"Mr. Wallace had us read some poems in school. I liked them. They are like songs with no music."

He laughs. "That's one way of putting it. Did you have a favorite?"

"I really liked *The Washerwoman's Complaint*. I thought it was very funny."

"Indeed. We had to study that one too. But I confess, now I much prefer the Romantics. Did he have you read anything by Shelley or Byron?"

I shake my head at the unfamiliar names.

"No. I don't suppose he did. Byron especially. My mother would be scandalized by his personal reputation. But his writing is superb." He takes the book from my hands, flips to a particular page, and turns it back around, pointing to a section of lines.

I study the words before reading them aloud: "'I would I were a careless child, still dwelling in my Highland cave, or roaming through the dusky wild, or bounding o'er the dark blue wave. The cumbrous pomp of Saxon pride accords not with the freeborn soul, which loves the mountain's craggy side, and seeks the rocks where billows roll.' It sounds nice, but what does it mean?"

"I think he is talking about the innocence of a child's life—how things are better and less complicated when one is young. Though what a poet truly means can be known in his own mind and heart only."

"So, you like all of these poems?"

"Yes." He looks at me thoughtfully. "I've got a grand idea. You can come by from time to time, and we can read a few lines together. What do you say? It's always nice to have a short break from work."

"I would like that."

He glances over at the near-empty chest. "I'm sorry. I didn't bring you a gift."

"It doesn't matter." I grin up at him. "Bringing yourself is the best gift for us. We've missed you greatly."

"And I've missed you. It was good to go and learn, but it is better still to return to the Island, to family and friends."

"I should go." I rise from the chair and set down the notebook. "I'll tell Papa and Nancy you're home. Wouldn't it be nice if they would invite you to supper, to celebrate your return?"

"Don't force them to extend an invitation."

"I won't. I'll *suggest* it."

"Besides, my schedule may soon be full," he says while placing one stack of books upright on a shelf above the bed. "It seems that Mother wants me to meet some of the eligible young women in town." He lets out a frustrated sigh.

"But you don't want to spend time with them?"

"I don't see the point. I'm not ready to marry at this time."

"Gardner, you can't get married. That's for grown-ups!"

Even though his back is still to me, I can hear the smile in his voice. "Must I remind you that I'm nineteen? I am a grown-up."

Suddenly, I feel childish, foolish. Blushing, I slink toward the door.

His next words stop me halfway across the room. "But I still enjoy any time spent with you. When will you come by again?"

"Maybe Monday, on my way home," I whisper over my shoulder, my eyes still downcast. Then, when I reach the threshold, I glance up as I try to think of something grand or mature, to seal my departure. I can think of nothing phenomenal, so I blurt out, "Gardner, promise me that you won't stop being my friend even though you're a grown-up and highly educated now."

"I will, if you promise to start buying me stick candy again."

"Done!" We laugh together.

"And, do you still like lemon best?"

He's looking at me fully now, his mouth tipped in a silly grin. "Always."

I grin back before whirling around and running down the stairs.

I find Nancy in the midst of making stew and take up a knife to chop carrots. Lost in a swirl of thought, I nearly cut myself twice. Which of those lovely girls will he marry when the time comes? And will she take good care of him?

While we eat, I share the news. "Gardner's home."

"Oh?" Nancy serves Lyddie a slice of lamb. "His parents must be relieved."

"Yes, they're so happy. Do you think we could have him to supper or tea? He was asking after everyone. I know he's eager to see all of you."

Papa glances at Nancy and declares, "That's very considerate. Why not have all of them? It's been a long time since we extended an invitation to his parents, if I'm not mistaken."

Nancy nods. "Will you help me prepare something special, Annie? Perhaps the rosemary chicken. We had that nearly perfect last Sunday."

"That sounds fine," Papa agrees. "My ladies have made great strides in their cooking skills." He chuckles.

Nancy and I share a smile.

As they discuss and settle on a day and time to suggest, I take and release a deep breath, imagining what a happy evening it will be—and wishing that we could stay content and together like this forever. Gardner can stay. I wish Papa could stay too.

* * *

Early October, 1832

The grand new ship is finished, and they've started fitting her for departure. We visited the building site a few times when the craftsmen began their work, but we have not had a chance to see the assembled vessel. Nancy has requested a day off for all of us—me from work and Lyddie and Will from school—so that we may finally see the results of Papa's labor and have one last family holiday.

How quickly the time has passed. I've grown used to Papa's constant presence and feel bereft at the thought of another parting.

He leaves early to make sure all is in readiness. Upon his return, we bundle ourselves against the damp, brisk air and walk down to the wharf. I stay close to Papa. On his other side, Will does the same. Will is clearly excited about today's adventure and everything sea-worthy.

"Is the ship very big?" Lyddie's voice trembles.

"Aye. The biggest I've ever sailed. A grand ship it is." Papa looks at her with steady tenderness. "Don't worry. It will be quite safe. It has been carefully crafted."

"Rightly so," Nancy says through tight lips. Only then do I notice how pale and drawn her face has become.

"Well, Annie," he peers down with resignation, "will *you* be eager to spend more than one moment on board?"

Poor Papa. The only one showing great enthusiasm is Will. "It will be wonderful to see your ship. I've never been on one before, but when it's securely anchored, it can't be so bad, can it?"

We board a small boat that will carry us to the ship where it has been moved further out in the harbor for full loading. From a distance, it appears impressive. When we finally come alongside, it looms overhead.

Oh, my.

I'm not afraid of the ship sinking while we're aboard. But I do wonder whether I can find my way off if I get lost on its large deck or—worse—down below.

Will jumps for the rope ladder hanging down over the side—causing the whole boat to rock, and Lyddie and Nancy to cry out in fear. Papa's voice halts him. "Wait!"

Obliging, Will pauses until we get closer and then steps on the bottom rungs. Papa allows Lyddie to ride on his back when he follows Will. She glances back over the railing's edge at us and trembles.

I take Nancy's hand when she hesitates. "Papa's right there, and I'll come behind you." She still looks pale and her forehead is a little sweaty, but she nods and squeezes my fingers before grabbing the ladder. "Don't look down. Keep your eyes on Papa." He has stretched over to reach for her. She climbs slowly until he can grasp one of her hands.

When she is safely setting foot on board, I scramble up after her. Papa reaches down and lifts me the rest of the way. Then he starts pointing to and naming the parts of the ship's deck, much to Will's delight.

It is a curious sensation—the choppiness of the water making the solid planking under me wobble up and down a little. Nancy must feel it too. She grabs onto my hand once more, holding it even tighter and standing with her eyes closed.

A man with broad shoulders, a reddish beard, and warm blue eyes steps near and nods. "Captain."

"Mr. Ripley." Papa turns to us. "Augustine Ripley will be first mate on this maiden voyage. This is my wife, Nancy."

"Honored to meet you, ma'am. Welcome aboard the *Charles Carroll.*"

"And here we have Phebe Ann, Lydia, and William Henry."

"A fine lookin' bunch they are. Pleased to know you all." He extends a hand to each of us in turn, as if we were quite grown-up, and we shake politely—though I can see that Lyddie is a little afraid to do so.

Mr. Ripley may have large, rough hands, but he presses mine with care. "What will you do on the ship?" I ask.

"I'll help make sure your father's orders are carried out. And if he's ever indisposed, I'll keep the ship running smoothly until he's well again. That in addition to my duties heading one of the boats, of course."

"He has already helped a great deal with some final details of the building," Papa says. "I believe he'll be a trustworthy and capable mate." We all turn and smile at Mr. Ripley. Even Nancy manages to send him a grateful look. And it makes my heart happy to know he can take care of things if Papa's headaches continue.

"We're very obliged to you for your present and future service," Nancy offers. "Would you care to join our family for worship and dinner on Sunday? We would consider it a benediction upon your sailing."

Mr. Ripley's mouth splits into a grin—revealing a gold tooth! "Aye, ma'am. That would be a most delightful way to spend a day of rest, the last one I'll be havin' for a good long while." His eyes dim. "It's been too long since I was with any sort of family. So I might be a bit rusty at it. But I swear to you that I'll be on my best behavior and wear my good coat. I thank you kindly for the invitation."

Nancy nods in reply, but her smile becomes strained when a hard thud deep in the ship causes us all to sway a bit. She grabs and clings to Papa's arm.

"Nothing's amiss," he says. "They're moving and securing heavy supplies below. Probably dropped something."

I find my balance again and calm at the steadiness in Papa's voice. Nancy and Lyddie, however, are white-lipped with fear. Papa notices and takes up Lyddie's hand in his free one. "Come." He leads them around a big, black square opening in the deck toward a set of ledges built at the base of two giant cauldrons.

Mr. Ripley bows slightly, stepping away to return to his own tasks on the other side of the deck, and Will and I turn to follow the others. Papa settles Nancy and Lyddie on the nearest bench while Will stops by the black hole and bends to peer inside.

"What's this?" he calls.

In his eagerness to explore, he pitches forward. I latch onto the back of his waistband, pulling as hard as I can in an attempt to break his fall. Papa steps up and grabs both of us before we go tumbling in together.

I heave a sigh of relief.

Will laughs from the thrill.

"Take care, William." Papa's voice is grave, just loud enough for us to hear. "That is the main hatch down into the blubber room—and then further down into the hold. Such a fall would be dangerous indeed."

"Yes, Papa." Will sobers. "But, may I go down? If I'm careful?"

Papa studies him. "If you will stay near me and ask permission before touching anything." He turns to me. "Do you want to join us in the mysterious depths of the ship?"

I shiver at his fearsome tone. But then I see his eyes crinkle up at the corners, and I smile. "Thank you. But I'd rather stay up here and look at the sails. They are amazing." I tip my head back to gape at one behind us.

"Very well. Keep an eye on Nancy and Lydia for me. We'll be back in a little while, and I'll show you my cabin, if you'd care to see it." He turns and starts his descent on the nearly invisible steps. When he's almost swallowed by the hole, he lifts a hand to guide Will.

Seeing that Nancy and Lyddie seem to be well, I turn and walk toward the front of the ship, to what Papa called the forecastle area. Three more sails are also receiving some sort of inspection, and I watch the men high above me, working amongst the ropes and cloth flapping back and forth in the breeze. I move further on, nearly as far as I can go, fascinated by the poles sticking out to hold what Papa called the jibs.

Suddenly, an odd sensation washes over me. I turn to find a man a few steps behind me. He's studying me with a great deal of interest.

He is, perhaps, about Gardner's age, of medium height with full, deeply tanned cheeks and hair and eyes nearly black as coal. The cockiness in his gaze makes my stomach clench. "And what have we here?" His voice is filled with mock warmth.

"It appears someone's invited a sea nymph aboard to keep us company and bring us fair winds on our journey. And what a little beauty she is."

I'm done looking at sails. I want to be back beside Nancy or Papa. Then I remember what Uncle Gardner told me before—about running or crying out or fighting. I attempt to slip around him, but he catches me. One fist grabs the front of my cloak, and the other hand clamps hard over my mouth.

"Don't make a sound, and we'll duck behind the windlass."

I can't run, and I can't scream. I must fight. I jerk back my head far enough to grab his thumb between my teeth and bite down hard. At the same time, I bring up my hands and claw at the wrist near my throat.

"Ah!" He cries low and calls down curses while he shoves me back. I'm stunned when I hit the hard deck. He glances at his hand and grits his teeth. I try to figure an angle at which to slip past his legs.

"Clifton." A low, awful voice sounds from behind him. He turns to face the speaker and lowers his head. Scrambling to my feet and inching by, I see Mr. Ripley standing there and let out a shaky breath.

He holds out his meaty hand to me while keeping his eyes locked on Clifton. I draw close to his side. "How shall I describe your behavior to the captain? And what place will you have with this crew when he hears of your actions?"

"Only a bit of harmless fun, sir," Clifton mumbles, clutching his sore thumb with his other hand.

"With the captain's own daughter?"

Clifton's eyes fly upward, and his face fills with color before he curses again.

"Assaulting the lass and using such language in her presence."

"Please, sir. I didn't know."

"No excuse, man. No child, no young lady, should be treated that way. Each should be treated as if she were a captain's daughter. Even if she's fatherless and completely alone in the world. Do I make myself clear?" His voice is a growl and his eyes, blue flames.

"Yes, sir."

"Back to work with you."

"Sir?" Clifton's head snaps up, his expression stunned.

"Do you want to sail with this crew or not?"

"Yes, sir."

"I'll tell you later, away from tender ears, exactly what I think of you. For now, learn your lesson and stop loafing around the deck. Back to work!" I jump at his barking tone and pull back to stand a little behind him.

"Sir!" Clifton spins and swings up on the nearby ropes with great haste.

Mr. Ripley leads me a few steps away. He bends down to look me in the eye. "Were you injured when you fell?"

"It hurt, but I'm all right." I lift my chin.

He searches my face and then squeezes my hand before releasing it and straightening. "I came round the bend of the foremast just as you bit him—and right glad I was to be coming this way. I do admire you, though. You're a slip of a lass, but you have the captain's blood in you. I'll swear to it."

"Uncle Gardner told me to fight if I ever needed to."

"Aye. A pity that it should be so. But he taught you well. I'll tell your father about this—but not now. Your mother seems to be ill at ease on board, and I'd not want to add to her distress in any way."

"Oh, yes. Please don't bring it up now. It's so terrible to see Papa when he's angry."

"He has the right to be in this case."

"Will he punish that man?"

"He's sure to. But I'll ask that Clifton not be dismissed." At my curious expression, he adds—nearly under his breath because we are approaching Nancy and Lyddie—"You see, girl, it's better sometimes to keep threats close. If he comes with us, there'll be no chance of him staying here to trouble you. And perhaps we can make a better man of him yet."

I nod my thanks and paste on a smile before I sit beside Lyddie.

She tugs at her dress sleeves. "Do you think Papa will take us ashore soon?"

I take her hand. "We can ask him when he and Will come back up." I watch Mr. Ripley walk toward the other end of the deck before stopping to help a worker secure ropes around a large crate. "He said we can visit his cabin first though. Wouldn't it be nice to see where he'll stay?"

Nancy and Lyddie say nothing while staring at the railing along the deck's edge. And somewhere behind me, I hear Clifton ask another sailor for assistance.

Perhaps it would be better not to linger after all.

* * *

On Sunday morning, Nancy takes the time to help fix my hair in a different style after I've dressed. "Are you nervous?" She catches my eye in the mirror.

"A little," I admit. Actually, I'm incredibly nervous. Mrs. Summers thought it would be wonderful if I could sing my first solo before Papa's departure. She says I'm ready, and the choir had already planned to sing a familiar number today. But even though I've sang with the choir a few times, I'm not sure if I'm brave enough to stand in front and sing all by myself.

"Your curls are especially cooperative today—thank goodness for that. I know you will do well and make us proud." She secures the last pin and bends to kiss my forehead. "Don't forget your shawl and offering money. We'll see you downstairs in a moment."

As we walk to church, bundled against a bitter wind, Papa lags behind a few steps to talk with me. "It will be a great treat to hear you sing this morning—and to let many others receive enjoyment from it."

"I'm scared." My voice shakes more from nerves than the cold.

"Of what?"

"That I won't do well. And everyone will be disappointed. That you will be disappointed."

"I won't be disappointed. You will do well. I have no doubt."

"How can you be so sure?"

"You are my brave girl. The one who fights off bullies. And the one who stands up and defends herself against ill-behaved sailors." Though he looks straight ahead, he reaches down to squeeze my shoulder. "Besides, when you sing for me, it is always heavenly. How do you do it?"

"I don't know. I simply sing for you and for God with all my heart's love, I guess."

"Then that's what you must do today. Imagine that you are with me, holding my hand. And sing with all your heart."

I take a deep breath and smile wide. "I will." My nervousness melts away.

It hits me with full force again, however, when the fateful moment arrives—our special number directly before the sermon. When I step forward to stand before the rest of the members, a small rush of murmurs fills the reverent silence. Children only perform briefly at the Christmas service, and I am the youngest choir member.

Clenching the sides of my skirt to still my shaking hands, I search the crowd and my eyes land on Aunt Mary. Her smile is ready and warm. On either side of her, Uncle Gardner and Gardner both watch me with anticipation. Across the aisle are William and Elizabeth and Mr. and Mrs. Mitchell.

The pianist has played the introduction, and now the choir sings the first verse. They are in fine form today, their voices washing over me from behind like a soothing wave.

> *Love divine, all loves excelling, joy of heaven to*
> *earth come down;*
> *Fix in us Thy humble dwelling; all Thy faithful*
> *mercies crown!*
> *Jesus, Thou art all compassion, pure unbounded love*
> *Thou art;*
> *Visit us with Thy salvation; enter every*
> *trembling heart.*

I search the crowd again and find my family along with Mr. Ripley sitting beside Papa in the pew. The musical interlude signaling my cue starts and crescendos. My eyes dart to Papa's face—and the complete confidence resting there. His small smile drives the rest of my fear away.

Closing my eyes and imagining my hand in his, I open my mouth. Out tumble the words I know by heart. The first note is like a blind step, and then I'm running up and down the scale's path with complete confidence.

> *Breathe, O breathe Thy loving Spirit, into every*
> *troubled breast!*
> *Let us all in Thee inherit; let us find that second rest.*
> *Take away our bent to sinning; Alpha and Omega be;*
> *End of faith, as its Beginning, set our hearts at liberty.*

We weave the last verse together, me singing an alternate melody Mrs. Summers taught me while the choir intones the main parts.

> *Finish, then, Thy new creation; pure and spotless let us be.*
> *Let us see Thy great salvation perfectly restored in Thee;*
> *Changed from glory into glory, till in heaven we take our place,*
> *Till we cast our crowns before Thee, lost in wonder, love, and praise.*

The pianist stops near the end, and we sing the final bars, my voice lifting to soar like a bird on one of the highest notes I can reach.

The whole sanctuary is utterly hushed.

I sigh and open my eyes. Upturned faces are full of peace, many cheeks shiny with tears. Other heads are bowed low. I've never seen Papa's eyes shine like this.

"Brothers and sisters," says Reverend Emory from the pulpit, "the Gospel of Luke tells us that angels will rejoice whenever a lost soul returns to the family of the Heavenly Father. Surely that was a sample for our ears of how it must sound. Let us pray together and open our hearts to the truth of God's Word."

* * *

When dinner is over, I hear Nancy invite Mr. Ripley to stay for tea and further visiting in the parlor while I start to help Lyddie with the dishes. We work without speaking, and a plan begins to form in my mind. Our task completed, I slip into Papa's study and find a pen and a piece of stationary. I dip the nib in the inkwell and write a brief note in my best penmanship.

Dearest Papa,

I wish I could be there with you. This is for you, when you need it. I know it will help. And you will bring it back to me when God brings you safely home.

Love,
Annie

I let the ink dry and fold the paper carefully. Then I slip up to my room and prepare a small bundle with the note tucked inside. With the bundle secure in my deep apron pocket, I enter the parlor and take up a seat and some sewing on a chair near the fire, listening to the continuing conversation while Will and Lyddie sit reading in the far corner.

"And what of your own family, if I may ask?" Nancy refreshes Mr. Ripley's cup.

"That is a long-ago story, and not a happy one, I'm afraid." He grimaces, his eyes remaining on his tea.

"We did not mean to raise an unpleasant topic," Papa offers.

"'Tis the truth of life. I believe I can tell the story in a way that would both satisfy your curiosity and be acceptable in present company." He glances at me before turning to stare at the fire. "My father, born and bred in New Bedford, was a sailor who became a captain by the time he was just twenty-three. He didn't marry until well into his career, and then, as you all understand, he was gone for long spans of time. We weren't going out quite so far then, and his ship was not so large. But he'd still leave my mother for a year or more on each journey.

"Five years after my arrival, she had my sister Delia—a child who grew to be, in many ways, like your Annie." His eyes dart my way again. "When I was thirteen and Delia eight, we were hard struck by tragedy. Our mother died of spotted fever in midwinter. Thanks to some money left by our father, we were able to stay on in the rooms where we'd been boarding, and a kind neighbor fed us once a day. But several months later, about the time the money was running out, we received word that Father's ship was lost, and the whole crew with it—victims of a terrible squall that brought down at least four vessels.

"We had no one to turn to, nowhere to go. We were without other family, you see. And my parents weren't religious folk. There was a foundling home in town, but they were very crowded and not accepting any new children past the age of three. I did the only thing I could think to do. I left Delia in the care of a family that seemed nice enough with the promise that I'd pay for her care upon my return. Then I went down to the docks and signed on for my first voyage.

"Due to foul weather and other trying circumstances, that trip lasted longer than planned, and I was away for over two years. I was always thinking of her, worried for her. When at last I returned…"

He stops, wipes at the corners of his eyes, and takes a deep breath.

"The family had neglected her and then sold her into a most unfit situation. I found her weakened by sickness—dying, in fact—in squalid conditions. I took what small amount I had earned and moved her to a safe place where she could be warm and comfortable during those final days, me staying by her side nearly every moment. Then I buried her and, heartbroken, signed on for another voyage."

My heart aches. I can't imagine being so strong if I had to watch Lyddie or Will suffer like that.

Papa hands his handkerchief to Nancy, and she wipes her eyes. "And after that?" he gently presses.

"I have lived these past twenty years moving up in the ranks from ship to ship, always searching for peace and living in fear that if I were to marry, the same fate would fall upon my own family. So I have never taken a wife. And I have never accepted the position of captain, though I've been made three different offers. I admire and will support a good captain, but I can't stomach the thought of being one myself. Forgive me, sir."

"There's nothing to forgive, Mr. Ripley. You've faced great hardship. I thank you for telling us your story. It increases my respect for you tenfold. I will not take your attitude nor your experience for granted."

"I thank you, sir. And thank you, ma'am," he adds, turning to Nancy. "Your hospitality to me this day has been a most wonderful gift. I shall not forget it in the long months ahead."

"When God returns you safely to us, by His will, you are welcome to come and visit again, Mr. Ripley."

He scratches the back of his neck. "I confess, I've long struggled to believe that there might be a God and that, if there is, He actually cares a fig about any of us. But after the things I heard this morning, laid out so simply like I'd never heard them before, I'm starting to think that maybe there is—and He does."

He smiles a little self-consciously and clears his throat. "I should take my leave. With so many clouds, it will be getting dark before long, and I've some final preparations to make."

We follow him into the hallway where he dons his coat, hat, and gloves.

"Papa," I finally venture, "may I see Mr. Ripley off? I'd like to walk a bit. I'll come directly back."

He nods. "All right. But you still need to wear your heavy cloak."

I agree, quickly fastening the buttons and ribbons at my neck before lifting the hood. We step out to the tune of kind farewells. As we move past the end of the house, I break the silence. "May I ask a favor of you?"

"If it is within my power, little miss, I would be honored."

"Do you know about Papa's headaches?"

"He did mention them once."

"Sometimes they are very bad, bringing him quite low. He's strong and able the rest of the time, but…" I glance up at Mr. Ripley. "You said you would take care of things."

"Aye. And I aim always to keep my word. A man who breaks his word is worthless."

We've reached the point where I should turn around, so I draw up short and face him. "I'm so glad. Please, the first time he doesn't feel well, give this to him—and until then, keep it safe." I take out the small bundle and hand it over.

His eyes widen. "Such a dense package. Heavier than I expected."

"Yes."

"I confess, I'm curious about its contents."

"It's simply a piece of me, sent along to comfort him. Thank you for doing this."

"My pleasure—truly it is."

I reach out to touch his arm and whisper, "I'm sorry about Delia. And those words I sang today, they were for you. I know that now. God bless you, Mr. Ripley."

"And you, lass." He steps backward, and the growing mist seeps between us.

* * *

JANUARY 1833

On a surprisingly mild Tuesday in January, I step into the shop shortly after seven. My longer days have begun in earnest.

Nancy was right—they wore me out at first. But things have been getting easier week by week.

I greet others who are already hard at their tasks and make my way through the maze of tables, stools, racks, crates, and sacks. Nancy recently insisted it was time for me to begin wearing longer, fuller skirts, and I'm still getting used to them, taking care not to bump an arm or a stack with the extra bulk and width. As I've already discovered in attempting to race through an alley, grown-up apparel will certainly break my habit of running whenever I feel like it.

Reaching the back room without mishap, I part the thick curtain that separates work space from resting space. I pass the bed and three cushioned chairs arranged for our use in case of midday fatigue or sudden illness. Along the far wall runs a shelf with a water basin, and I set my small lunch basket next to several others before removing my cloak and bonnet and stretching to hang them on a peg. I secure a fresh apron and wash my hands.

My seat awaits in the far southwest corner of the workroom. It's a little further from the stove, but I'm so happy to be near a window. The light spares my eyes and strengthens my heart, even on these grayer days. I glance across at the seven other girls and women with heads bent. Allison is absent again—perhaps still ill—but everyone else is present and busy. I'd better get busy too. I know Mrs. Mitchell will expect me to have the hems on every item in this pile of garments finished by the end of the day if I want to receive my full stipend.

"Good morning, Annie," Moriah's whisper reaches me amidst the other soft conversation floating through the air. I look up at my neighbor, the supreme maker of buttonholes and a talented embroiderer. Her work is prized by the women who wear such finery. Though she is seventeen and no longer an apprentice, she is much friendlier to me than Betty and Charity, the two girls closer to me in age. In fact, she has shown me every kindness since my first day here.

"And to you. You look better today."

"My stomach pain abated in the night. I feel quite well." Her usual smile—absent all day yesterday—is firmly back in place, and I think again how it makes her one of the prettiest girls I know. Her hair is fair and straight as pins, her complexion clear and rosy. Some people look at her strangely because she was born without three of her fingers, but her quiet cheerfulness usually helps her to win their favor in no time at all. It has also certainly helped her overcome her limitations. When I watch her work, I believe I can do almost anything if I will try hard enough.

"It looks like Mrs. Mitchell left extra work for both of us."

"Well, we won't be having any trouble with boredom or sadness, will we?"

I thread my needle and knot the end deftly. "No. That is the one advantage of such a big load." She knows how I miss Papa and need to keep my mind and hands busy.

"Will you sing for a while, Annie? That makes the time go by faster than anything." Ever since she heard me humming during my second week here, she has asked me to sing a little nearly every day. The others don't seem to mind, but I know Mrs. Mitchell desires a peaceful environment, so I always sing soft and low.

"I will, after you tell me about Michael's coming to supper Saturday night," I whisper gleefully before bending to concentrate on starting the first stitch perfectly as a true guide. I've been longing to ask her about this for the past two days.

She releases a happy sigh and snips off several loose threads. "I could see he was a little nervous with Papa, but once they started discussing the best fishing spots, he relaxed immediately. And all the dishes turned out perfectly. All in all, it was a happy time."

"So he'll be welcome to return?"

"I think so. My father asked about his intentions toward me, and he said he wants to marry me—if Papa and Mama agree, and I will have him."

"Oh, Moriah, how wonderful."

"Yes. I used to be afraid that I would never find a husband because of my hands. But Michael doesn't mind. He has told me, 'Every person has some uniqueness—but not all of them have to be weaknesses.' It's exactly how I feel. The more I know of him, the more I believe he will be a fine husband."

"When will you marry?"

"Mama says an autumn wedding would be lovely. Perhaps September, before the weather turns."

Moriah turned seventeen last month. To be married at seventeen. Why, that's only a few years away. I suddenly start to wonder who will want to marry me with my wild curls, small frame, dark features, and the scars on my head and face. Is there a man who would treat me with the honorable intentions I was told to watch for? If Michael sees past the outside to Moriah's heart of gold, is there another man who could one day love me from the inside out, the way Mary once said Papa loved Mama?

Moriah laughs. "Your mind has drifted to sea."

"Sorry." I blush. How I wish I could control my propensity to color.

"Do you want to share your thoughts?" She gives me a sly wink. "You know you can avoid doing so by fulfilling my request."

I smile and begin to pour out Papa's favorite sea song, one he often used to sing to us, while my fingers pull forth uniform stitches.

Leave the lantern burning brightly, set the table as before,
Ye know not when I'll be comin', cold and hungry from
the shore.
And I'll need the love and kisses
Of my one and only missus
When ye meet me at the door...

* * *

Our front stoop lantern has not yet been lit when I come up the short path later that afternoon. I shiver a little in the gathering shadows. How odd. Nancy always lights it before the daylight starts to wane. I open the door and step inside to nearly complete darkness—save one small lamp burning on the kitchen table. The fires in both the kitchen and parlor are mere embers. Where is everyone?

Taking up the long lighting stick, I set the end in the lamp's flare and carry it back out, stretching up on my tiptoes to light the outer lamp before extinguishing the transfer flame. When I return to the kitchen, I see I must begin supper preparations even though I'm so tired. Will and Lyddie will be hungry. They've both been growing steadily since the summer. I wish I could grow a bit more too.

I've just finished setting water to boil and scrubbing some potatoes when a loud thud sounds above my head. Was that from Papa and Nancy's room? I feel small and scared. I wish Lyddie or Will—anyone—were here with me.

I bite my lip. Papa would expect me to be brave. I use the lamp to illumine the stairs before me as I creep toward the landing. Another noise comes from down the hall—yes, from their room. "Nancy?"

A strangled cry comes in response.

I shoot down the narrow passage and open the door to peer inside. The room is dark, but by the light of my candle I can detect Nancy lying in a heap on the floor.

"Nancy!" I move toward her but draw up short at the sight of the mess where she must have retched near the washing basin—or retched in it and spilled the contents. It's all down the front of her dress, too. She moans from beneath her mass of disheveled hair.

After lighting the bedside lamp, I turn and bend to touch her head. "What happened?"

Her eyes open, and she tries to focus on my face. "Annie?" she croaks from a raw throat.

"Let me help you. Can you sit up?"

She holds onto my arm, and I pull with all my might, slowly helping her into an upright position. "I'm so dizzy," she whispers, her body swaying while she clings to me.

I try to pull her further up, but my foot slips in the edge of the sour pile near us. *God, please give me strength.* He must hear me because I am able to get her safely up and onto the bed.

Nancy releases a sob and wipes at the drying mess on her face. "Please," she rasps before coughing. "Help me. I feel dreadful."

The realization hits me: Nancy's never been sick a day since she's lived with us. For a moment, I'm frozen with terror. What should I do? *God, don't let Nancy die!*

The front door opens and closes with distant clarity. "Will and Lyddie must be home. Perhaps Mr. Wallace kept them late to help with cleaning duties," I whisper.

"Don't let them see me like this." She shudders. "They'll be afraid."

In the undertow of her words, I hear another plea—that I am to be brave. I must care for Nancy and protect Lyddie and

Will. "It's all right." I run a hand over her sweaty brow. "I'll give them each a task and then come back to help you."

I find them in the kitchen, Will bringing in a bucket of fresh water and Lyddie looking perplexedly between the potatoes and the pot at full boil.

I speak in my calmest tone. "Nancy doesn't feel well. I'm going back to her room to help make her comfortable. Will, please go out to milk the cow and see that she has plenty of feed. Lyddie, I need you to put those potatoes in the pot. And when they're soft, add some milk, butter, salt, and pepper, like I showed you last week." She nods. "Then cut some of the dried beef from the larder and stir it in. Remember to be careful with the knife." She nods again. "And set the table. There's still some bread and butter in the box, I think."

Collecting water and other needed supplies, I return to Nancy's side and set to work. She gratefully accepts a drink, even asking for a second cup. I clean her face and help her rise, trembling, to replace her soiled dress with a nightgown. I brush and loosely braid her long hair while she leans against the headboard before helping her to ease under the covers.

Turning to the floor, I do my best to clean up the mess. Then I take Nancy's bottle of lilac talc from the dresser and sprinkle some over the wet place to cover the stench that remains. After dumping the rags and soiled dress into the dirty basin, I wipe my hands and turn to find her lying still, weariness wreathing her face.

"Nancy," I whisper, taking up her hand, "shall I go for the doctor?"

"No need," she assures me. "I know what has happened."

"Is it serious? Will you be better soon?"

"With time. I'm going to have a baby."

I would drop her hand if she weren't gripping mine so firmly.

"A baby?" Papa didn't forget my request! But why did he wait so long to give it to her?

"I'm guessing it will arrive in midsummer."

"How do you know?"

"There are signs. This retching is one of them. Some women have the sickness earlier, but it was the same for me the last time. You see, I…" She swallows hard and closes her eyes. "I had a baby once before. He would be a little older than you—if he were still alive."

I stare at her, feeling the heat of renewed pain flow from her hand to mine. I don't know what to say.

"I may have some hard days ahead. I'm not as young as I was the last time." She peers at me. "I will do my best to be strong, but I confess I may need to rely much upon your strength, for you to carry out the jobs I've been teaching you. Though I wish I didn't have to place such a burden on your small shoulders."

Now I enfold her hand between both of mine and squeeze it. "You've often been strong for us. It's our turn to try and be strong for you." I raise one hand to wipe at the tears slipping down her face. "Please don't worry." *Thank God you're not dying.*

She shudders and closes her eyes again. "Owen has always seen the strength in you. There have been times when I could not see it. But now I will depend mightily upon it."

I kiss her hand, turn the lamp down to its lowest glow, pick up the smelly basin, and quietly exit the room.

Lyddie and Will have the prepared food set out in bowls around the table, and Lyddie is adding bread and butter to the spread while Will pours water in our three cups. I gaze at them after setting down my load. We can help Nancy get through this—if we cooperate and all do our part.

Lyddie looks up and eyes the basin. "What's that?" Her nose wrinkles.

"Something I'll see to after supper."

They both study me.

"She'll be all right. She's going to have a baby. But right now, she doesn't feel well. So we must be responsible and help take care of everything until she feels stronger." I nod them toward their seats and then say grace. It feels strange to be the one to do it, but somehow also easy and light.

"Does this mean we're going to have a little brother?" Will asks.

"Or sister?" Lyddie adds with sparkling eyes.

I smile, "I guess it will have to be one or the other. And Nancy will get to have a baby all her own. I think she's wanted that for a long time." I blink away sudden tears.

"But will she still want us after that?" Lyddie frets and fiddles with her spoon.

"She promised Papa she would take care of us. And even though she rarely says it, I think she loves us. Maybe she'll love her own baby more, but I don't think she'll stop wanting to be in our family." *God, please don't let her hate us when the new baby comes.*

Lyddie sighs with relief.

"But I don't think we should talk about the baby—tell people about it, I mean—until Nancy says it's time," I say. "Can you both help me keep the secret and do the chores here every evening while I do Nancy's work?"

They both nod. I'm tired, but my heart is content. Nancy said Papa could see strength in me, and now I realize how much of that strength comes from the love, unity, and support of our warm home.

JUNE 1833

The noon sun rains down upon me, relentless without the normal, refreshing sea breeze, and rivers of sweat run down my back and around the small curves of my chest. I reach the humble stoop and knock hard on the worn door.

"Hey, Miss Annie," Eli greets me warmly. At my expression, however, his smile dims. "Something amiss?"

"Nancy," I gasp out, struggling to breathe after walking so quickly the whole way. "I came home during my midday break to check on her. I found her in terrible pain. Can Sadie come?"

"Eli?" Her voice calls from somewhere behind, and he opens the door fully. There she sits at the table with their boys. Carl waves at me, and Samson glances my way before continuing to shove food in his mouth with his chubby fingers. "It's time?"

"I think so. And I don't want her to be alone." My hands clench the folds of my apron.

"Don't be fretting." She reaches to put several items in a bag. "All's gotta be well when the Lord's in charge. And He is— you can trust that across the sea and back." She bends to kiss each boy on the forehead and then kisses Eli soundly on the mouth. "When you gotta get on back, ask Metta to watch 'em," she murmurs. "And tell her I'll be back soon as I can. We got cornmeal in the cupboard, to use for supper if need."

She steps out beside me, and we walk quickly in the direction of Orange Street.

"The others in school?" When I nod, she grunts. "Good. Maybe we get through the worst of it before they get home. Can you stay to help? I can do it all, but having assistance be a grand thing."

"Yes, I think so. I'll ask a neighbor to take a message to Mrs. Mitchell so she won't worry about me. But how can I help?"

"I'll direct. You can fetch things I may be needing, bring fresh water, and encourage Miz Nancy to keep on a-going when she worn through. Maybe do some of that fine singing of yours?" She winks at me and then jerks her head back to stare hard. "Lord above, but you do look bewildered. I gotta prepare you a little more lest you shocked to death by what you see. Surely somebody done told you by now 'bout babies being born?"

I look up, wide-eyed, and shake my head.

"No? What about where they come from in the first place?"

"Well, I don't know the specifics, but I asked Papa to bring back a baby for Nancy during his last trip. So he must've done it. But how it got inside of her, I don't know. Was it some kind of magic?"

"Oh, it sure be magic—of a kind," she laughs under her breath. When she glances at me again, she gasps. "Heaven help these children of prudish mamas." Then, a bit more gently, "Well, and she can't help it, being raised mostly in town with her daddy gone near all the time."

She pulls up short and turns me to face her squarely. "Now," she charges in a low voice, "I gonna tell you something for your own good. It probably ain't like anything you ever heard before, but you'll be thanking me for it later—today and on the day when you get hitched to some nice young man. All right?"

I nod automatically, unsure of what I'm getting myself into.

She faces forward again and draws nearer so she can speak as softly as possible while we continue walking. A few other people on the street glance at us oddly, but I mind it not when I get caught up in Sadie's words. By the time we're in sight of the house, she's told me about the "magic" of how the baby gets inside and grows and comes out of the mother. And how I'll have blood coming out of me every month one day—so that when it happens I'll know not to panic.

Along the way, my face flames and my ears tingle. Yet, when she's done, I feel relieved. But I realize my relief is not over the end of her monologue on a topic I'm sure Nancy or Papa wouldn't bring up in a hundred years. It's over answers to the questions I never knew I had—or knew how to ask.

After we pass my message to a neighbor lady, we pause at the front door, Sadie gazing at the wood before us. "I hope I done right in telling it. Did I shock you?"

"A little," I stammer, dropping my eyes before I can look at her again. "But it was good of you to teach me, especially about the bleeding. Mr. Wallace often said, 'Knowledge of the truth is the best weapon in combating fear-enforced ignorance.' And I don't know when someone else would have told me. With you it's always plain-speaking and truth."

"And with something like this, that make it go down easier." She smiles a little.

I nod and shyly return her smile before I lead us inside.

We hurry upstairs and down the hall to the spare room Nancy had already prepared for the birthing. There we find her writhing on the bed and crying out, her skirt and the quilt wet underneath her.

"I found Sadie," I call above the noise.

Sadie sets a hand on my shoulder. "I'll take a look. I see Miz Nancy already got the soap and towels. You go back down and fetch both cool and hot water."

"Won't be too long now," she says confidently over the end of Nancy's latest groan as I come back into the room and see Nancy positioned in a way that would have made me fall over in shock if Sadie hadn't prepared me. As it is, I avert my eyes, place my supplies on the dresser, and move forward to stand beside Nancy.

"Water," she pants.

"Not too much," Sadie cautions while she opens her bag. "Give her a small drink and then bathe her face." Then, to Nancy, "I know how it hurts you, but the Lord done had mercy. Looks like a short labor. Babe's coming along fine."

"Now that I truly recall the pain, I never want to go through it again!" She screams so loudly that I must drop her hand to cover my ears. I'm shaking when I lower my hands to moisten the cloth that's slipped from her brow and reposition it on her forehead.

"Annie," Sadie coaxes in a calm voice—a still spot in the storm I can immediately focus on. "Speak to her, sing to her. Give her strength."

"What do you want to hear, Nancy?" I try to mimic Sadie's tone.

"Something stirring, to remind me I'm not alone," she whispers before another terrible cry spills forth.

I immediately think of the last song I sang with the choir a few weeks ago. In the midst of the pain-laced sounds and pauses in between, I sing out steadily.

> Guide me, O Thou great Jehovah, pilgrim through this
> barren land.
> I am weak, but Thou are might; hold me with Thy
> powerful hand.
> Bread of heaven, bread of heaven,
> Feed me till I want no more; feed me till I want no more…

When I finish the last verse, she lets out the loudest cry yet, and I open my eyes to see Sadie looking up with a hint of concern in her eyes. Fear laps at my heart. "Babe's little bit stuck, Miz Nancy. Don't you worry—I gonna help it along. This gonna feel bad, but I'll be quick as I can be." She drops to the floor, becoming completely shielded by the blanket over Nancy's legs.

Nancy releases the most terrible sound and squeezes my hand until I nearly scream with her. Then, suddenly, she goes limp.

"Nancy? Nancy? Nancy!" I lift my throbbing hand and pat her cheek. There's a long moment of silence. Then somewhere over my shoulder, a pop, a smack, and a blessed wail.

"Annie," Sadie calls, "I need your help here."

"What about Nancy?"

"I'll see to her. Gotta do a bit of needlework."

Sewing?

"I need you to take the babe and care for her."

Her. I have another sister.

Sadie quickly lays the messy infant on a towel draped over the other side of the bed. She glances my way and then gives me The Look. "Now, you best not be getting squeamish on me, child. I done said there'd be blood. She'll be real sweet-looking after you clean her up." She instructs me on how to wash, rub, and wrap the baby as she waves a threaded needle in the lamp's flame and then sets to work under the blanket, murmuring as she goes, "You keep an eye on Miz Nancy too, and tell me if she goes white as them sheets or starts to stir, hear? I pray the Lord gonna stop this extra bleeding."

"Yes," I manage around the lump lodged in my throat.

Her head pops back up, and she gives me The Look a second time. "None of that fretting. Now sing to drive them fears outta here."

I'm nearly done cleaning off the blood now. She does look better. I start to sing, and I immediately relax as I focus on the baby squirming against my chafing hands.

How sweet the name of Jesus sounds in a believer's ear!
It soothes his sorrows, heals his wounds, and drives away
his fear...

Sadie stands and wipes her hands on a bloody cloth. She steps near and tells me how to carefully lift my sister with my hand under her head. I lay the baby in a padded basket on the bench that's been pushed to the side. Then I climb up on the bed and assist Sadie in the struggle to reposition Nancy higher on the mattress.

"Will she be all right?"

"She lost more blood than normal. But her color—that be good. I hope she wakes before I leave so I can make sure the babe feeds proper. But how she gonna hurt when she wakes!"

I shudder at the thought of more pain. Then I close my eyes and remember that I'm supposed to be strong. I look up resolutely to see Sadie back at the foot of the bed, bunching up a wad of soft cloth and binding it with string. She works for a moment under the blankets and comes out empty-handed. "What should I do now, Sadie?"

"Let me teach you the basics of seeing to 'em both. I gotta leave before too long, but I'll send back one of my friends, either Jenny or Deborah, to come and stay with you. They both good women, got a lot of experience, and will help you taking care of everything."

I let out a deep sigh of relief and try to capture every word of her instructions while we clean up the mess of towels, rags, and blankets that will need a "mighty good soaking."

Thankfully, Nancy does wake up soon after that, and Sadie performs a final check before she picks up her bag. "Lord bless you and that babe of yours, Miz Nancy. Rest well and go easy on yourself."

"God bless you, Sadie." Nancy smiles softly at her. "A million thanks to you—for all you did for us today. I'll pay you the next time I see you."

"No rush. Just be well."

"I'll be back soon," I tell Nancy before slipping through the door to see Sadie out. Downstairs, we pause in the open doorway, the afternoon sun lapping bronze and gold waves upon our skin. I see how disheveled Sadie looks and put a hand to my own hair, self-conscious of how I must certainly appear.

Sadie observes me and smiles. "Yes, we probably a sight to behold. Eli often laughs at me and the mess I be upon returning home from this work." She glances up and down the street and, seeing we're alone, reaches out to embrace me and speak against my hair. "I tough with you when I had to be. But I real proud of you, too. I know your daddy and mama would be just as proud. You done good today—real good. And you gonna keep doing good, Annie. You just do like I shown you. And the Lord—He gonna take care of the rest."

A little while later, Lyddie and Will get home. And when I bring them up to see the new baby, Nancy sleepily announces her lovely name: Adaline Claire.

* * *

I've been back to work these two weeks while Sadie's friends and my aunts have all taken turns helping Nancy. It has given me great peace to know she's not alone. And though I'm weary from completing so much extra work at home in the evenings, I'm happy to know that my assistance is really helpful.

Moriah sighs. Her wedding date grows closer, and now she is often the one miles away in her thoughts. Yet she always comes back to show consideration for me. "You seem a bit distracted today," she observes, glancing up from her work to catch my eye.

"I guess I am. It's Nancy's first day on her own, but she's still been tired. I'll be glad when the summer holiday begins next week and Lyddie and Will can stay with her each day."

"Worrying won't change a thing," she reminds me. "Save up that energy for praying and for working once you get home."

I look outside at the changing angle of the sun. It's not long until closing time. "I heard Mrs. Mitchell say something this morning about Allison leaving the shop for good?"

"Yes. Her health is so poor. Her husband insists she stay at home and rest more."

"I'm glad she can take better care of herself, but that's a pity. She does some of the finest collar and cuff finishing."

Moriah lifts a spool of dark blue thread. "Mrs. Mitchell says so too. But she told me we're not to concern ourselves about the vacancy. She'll start looking for a replacement soon."

"I hope she finds someone who's both skilled and amiable."

At closing time, I feel the urge to get home but also know I must stop by the store and pick up some sugar. I promised Nancy I would.

When I approach the main counter, a lovely young woman in a fine green dress turns away and walks past me with an ugly little pout shadowing her features. Gardner stands behind the counter, staring down at the dark surface with his lips pressed together. I slip up and stand across from him.

"You look sad," I observe.

He starts at the intrusion on his thoughts. "Never mind." He blinks several times while attempting to smile. "Do you have time for a stanza of Keats? I came across a grand one last night."

"I'm sorry. I can't tarry. Nancy's home alone today, and I want to get back and help her with Addie. But we need a small bag of sugar."

"You're a wonderful girl. Nancy's blessed to have you." His smile flashes easily before he turns to pull a bag from a shelf behind him. "I'll add it to your account."

"Thank you. I'll bring money to pay it in full next week."

"That's fine."

I turn to leave but then swing back and lean close. "Gardner?"

His brows lift.

"Don't stay sad. You're also wonderful, no matter how some people may treat you." Before he can respond, I spin around again and scurry out the door, eager to hide the flush spreading across my cheeks.

* * *

I meet Will a short distance from the house. "I'm glad you're back earlier today. Where's Lyddie?"

"She stayed to help Mercy Bradley with her long division. But Lyddie said not to worry—that she wouldn't stay more than half an hour."

"That's fine." Stepping into the entryway, I set my lunch basket and the sugar on the deacon's bench and remove my bonnet to hang it on a peg. Before I can say more, I hear Addie close by, fussing a little. I step around the edge of the parlor doorway to see her tucked in her sleeping basket that's sitting on a chair.

A noise reaches me from the other side of the room. Nancy must have been napping. "Nancy," I call as I walk in that direction. "Addie sounds hungry. Would you like me to try rocking her awhile or do you want to feed—"

Coming around the wing chair, I gasp and freeze.

Nancy is sitting on the floor with her back slouched against the seat of the settee at an odd angle, her head falling to one side. A river of red has spread across folds of her skirt, and a tiny puddle of blood is forming at her feet. Her face is extremely white, and her lips are moving feebly with only a breathy whisper slipping out.

Will watches me from the doorway.

"Get Dr. Bartlett!"

At my expression and tone, he turns and runs.

God, what do I do? I see the small blanket on the back of Papa's chair. I grab it and, gulping a deep breath, lift her skirts back enough to see underneath. So much blood. I press the blanket between her thighs, and she cries faintly. Pulling her skirts back down, I reach to grasp her hands. "I'm sorry if I hurt you, but I want to stop the bleeding. What else should I do?"

"Thirsty," she whispers.

I rush to the kitchen to collect a cup of water, then back to lift it to her lips so she can sip some. "What happened?"

"Feels like something cracked inside."

"I sent Will for the doctor. I think they'll be back soon." *Please let them come back soon.* I give her another sip.

"Annie…"

"I'm here." I set the cup down and sit beside her, propping her up and letting her head rest on my shoulder. Now she can whisper right beside my ear, and I can hear her better over Addie's fussiness. "I won't leave you."

"Annie. Forgive me."

"For what?"

"For times when I was jealous of you. How good, sweet, and talented you are. How much your father loves you, and how much he loved Peggy."

I swallow and press her hand.

"I wanted to love you, to be your mother. For us to be like a real family."

I stroke her hair. "We are a real family. You're our family."

"Then I'm sorry to leave you now. And to leave my baby." She coughs and struggles to breathe. "I wrote a letter last night. To your father. On the dresser. Give it to him when he comes home."

"Nancy?" My voice cracks. I cling to her hand.

"You have been a good daughter to me." She wheezes.

Tears spill down my cheeks. "And you have been my mother." My quivering lips struggle to form the words. "Thank you for all you've done for us."

"Take care of them." Her voice is barely audible now. "Adaline too."

"I will," I manage around a sob. "I promise!"

"Thank you." She exhales and relaxes completely, her full weight on my shoulder nearly pushing me over.

"Nancy? Nancy!" I look down to see a stream of brighter blood running in a thin line across the floor.

Will and the doctor rush in moments later with Lyddie coming close behind to find us thusly: me wailing and trembling under Nancy's heavy form with some of her blood seeping into the edge of my own skirts, and Addie screaming in response as she thrashes hungrily against the sides of her basket.

* * *

A warm breeze flows around the curtains to caress my face. Desperately needing some moments of solitude, I have curled up in Papa's chair—which somehow got pushed to the far corner of the parlor and turned to face out, toward the window. I stare at nothing, my mind floating away from the noise of a dozen quiet conversations in the crowded room behind me.

KAYLENE POWELL

I've jumped between numbness and the need to be strong for Lyddie, Will, and Addie ever since the doctor found me and made me drink something to calm my nerves.

I've barely slept, and now I am tired all the way down to my bones. I burrow in the chair's bend and close my eyes, inhaling deeply. I can smell Papa, and I imagine his strong arms around me.

A hand cups the back of my head. "Sweetheart," Elizabeth speaks near my ear. "We must finalize arrangements. Please come over and join us. You can sit by William and me, if you like."

I nod and rise to follow her through the crowd of relatives and close friends to William's side where he sits on the settee. Under our feet, a lovely new rug covers the terrible memory imprinted on the floor. Lyddie and Will press near for security, as they have done countless times over the past two days. I scan the room and sigh with relief when I see that Addie is sleeping in Aunt Maria's arms.

At a lull in the speaking, Aunt Eliza declares, "We must see to the house and the children." Around the room, a quiet but passionate discussion breaks out. Suggestions are made and considerations offered while Lyddie and Will grasp my hands.

Grandpa Judah finally speaks, his question causing all the grown-ups to freeze. "And what is it the children want?"

Grandma Ruth scowls at him. "They're children. They don't know what they need. And what they want is rarely what's best for them."

"If I know my son," Grandpa growls low, "he loves his children." He turns to study me with sad eyes, and his tone softens. "And he would say what's best for them should also take their happiness into consideration."

"I agree," says William. "We all know Adaline cannot speak for herself, but the others are old enough to have a say." He opens his arms to us, and we crowd inside. "We're sorry that no one has room to take all of you right now. We will need to divide you to stay in separate homes." I rock under the weight of his words, but they are a little easier to accept with his solid arm around my shoulders.

"I want to stay with Annie," Will and Lyddie whisper almost in unison.

I return their sorrowful looks with one of my own. "Others will help to care for you, but I'll still come to see you every day and make sure you're all right."

"Addie too?" Lyddie presses.

"Addie too. I promised, remember?"

She nods and squeezes my hand.

Uncle William is away at sea—like Papa, Uncle Joseph, Uncle George, and Uncle Alexander. But our aunties and the other uncles all send us welcoming expressions.

"Can I come to stay with you, Aunt Lydia?" Will asks with hopeful eyes.

"That would be fine. I'd be happy for your help and your company." She offers him an endearing smile, and he pulls away from us to press against her side.

"Lydia," Aunt Winifred calls. "Won't you come with me? I know Joseph would want you to."

I see both love and sadness in our aunt's eyes. She must certainly be aching to once again hold her own children: baby Joseph who died two years ago and sweet Elizabeth who left us only two months ago. My heart feels the rightness of this.

Lyddie rushes to her and is swallowed in her warm embrace.

"What about Addie?" I ask, turning to look at her with concern.

"Don't worry," Aunt Emeline speaks up. She bounces her own baby against her side. "I'll continue to feed and care for her. She's an easy child."

KAYLENE POWELL

"Thank you," I sigh with relief.

"And you, Annie?" Aunt Rebecca steps closer. "George has always had a special place in his heart for you. Why don't you stay with James and me?"

At her gentle tone, I feel my heart cinch up. "Thank you. But I..." A tear slips out, and I swipe it away in frustration. Right now, all I wish is that Papa was here and I was standing beside him. And I realize in this moment that I want nothing more than to stay with his closest friend. Turning in William's loose embrace, I look between him and Elizabeth. "I want to come and stay with you. I know we aren't related by blood. But would you take me anyway?"

They glance at the aunts, uncles, and grandparents and then at each other. Elizabeth smiles at me. "We would be overjoyed to have you live with us."

"Then I'll be more centrally located between the shop and where everyone else is staying." I look back at Aunt Rebecca with remorse. "You were very kind to offer. May I come and visit you when Uncle George next returns?"

"You are always welcome, dear."

"What about the house?" Aunt Susan asks.

"Eliza and I are happy to help keep it up," Uncle Ariel offers, "since we live closer than anyone else."

There are relieved smiles on several faces and murmurs of various offers to help.

Leaning back against William, I truly relax for the first time since I discovered Nancy at this very spot. I think, too, of Delia Ripley. At this moment, I cannot ask for a greater gift than God's peace flowing from the knowledge that we will all be well cared for.

***

March 30, 1834

Dearest Papa,

I pray that this finds you well and quickly filling your ship's hold. We look daily for a letter from you. Have you received my first missives with the news about Nancy and Adaline? Today I have more sad news. Uncle Gardner died last week. His heart finally stopped. Mary and Gardner are very sad. I am too. I attended the service as a representative of our family. Every time I walk by the store, I hope to see his kind face looking out at me. But I never will again.

We are all well here. I go around every day after work to check on Lydia, William, and Adaline. Lydia and Adaline were both very sick at the beginning of this month, but they are fully recovered and are gaining back the weight they lost. William has grown at least two inches since you left, I believe. I had to give up my singing lessons. I simply did not have time for them after Mrs. Mitchell asked me to work extra hours on Saturdays. And I always try to help Elizabeth with the housework and in caring for Frances and Mary. She and William have shown me a tremendous amount of kindness. I try to repay a small portion of it.

Everyone has been very good to us, Papa. God has given each of us a home until the day when you return. I don't know when that will be, but I know with each

passing month, the day comes closer. So I keep myself
busy to pass the time and do my best to be strong and
make you proud.
*   We often pray for you. God bless you and keep you.*

Love,
Annie

* * *

OCTOBER 10, 1835

The sun pierces the dense clouds to illuminate my work
space and the wall behind me. I glance up to spy the date
on the calendar. Three years ago this day Papa left us on the
Charles Carroll. And more than two we've all been going on as
best we can without Nancy. Only two letters have reached us,
along with a little news from Uncle Joseph when he was home
last, after he and Papa had a gam some months earlier.

I concentrate once more on the fine linen jacket laid out
before me. After finishing my part on this one, I'll be done for
the day. I look up to see Mrs. Mitchell walking around with a
stranger in tow. They stop at every table while Mrs. Mitchell
makes introductions. She draws up beside the space I still
share with Moriah. Though I am no longer an apprentice, we
both fulfill our same roles as before, working side-by-side in
comfortable companionship.

"Ladies, I want you to meet our addition—Eunice Chadwick.
She'll be joining us as the new collar and cuff finisher starting
tomorrow. Eunice, this is Moriah and Phebe Ann."

What a relief. We've all had to do extra work since Allison
left many months ago.

"Hello," she says with a broad smile and a tip of her head.

We nod our greetings. While Mrs. Mitchell explains each of our responsibilities, I take in Eunice's appearance. She is of medium height and full of generous curves. In fact, I don't know when I've seen such a figure. One of the poets I have studied with Gardner would call her voluptuous. Her hair is a light reddish-blonde and pulled back in a loose bun. Her eyes are dark blue and sparkling with energy.

Eunice looks down her pert nose, and her smile curves wide, showing an alluring mouth. There's something about her that makes me uneasy, but I shake it off. What a lovely face and figure she has. I wish I could fill out a dress so well. My glance darts down to take in my own very modest curves. I stifle a sigh.

Later, when I go to the back room to collect my cloak and bonnet, I overhear Alice and Rachel speaking in hushed tones.

"I hope she won't bring us bad luck."

"What makes you say that?"

"I remember my brother talking about her. He works down at the wharves, if you recall, and he had a mate name Wilson Roberts. Well, Mr. Roberts was engaged to Eunice, but he died at sea before they wed. But before her engagement to him, she had at least three other beaux—even two of them at one time. And all of them received—shall we say—very generous treatment from her before they tossed her over and moved on."

I feel a blush creep over my face and glance to the side before fumbling with my cloak fastenings.

"Well, I'm not calling your brother a liar." Rachel removes and folds her apron. "But it could be that the story's not true— at least in part. It may be that she's a decent enough woman after all."

"Could be. But otherwise, how's it that she's nearly twenty-seven and unmarried still? And with such a figure as hers, you know she'll be drawing the attention of every man with eyes to see. Vibrant as a hothouse flower. I have a feeling deep in my bones about that one. It's going to be different for all of us with her here."

Slipping past them and on through the shop, I try to push their gossip from my mind.

* * *

After stopping to check in on Lyddie, Will, and Addie, I head back to William and Elizabeth's. But when I pass near the store, I long to speak with Gardner. He has been my truest friend these past months, more dependable than ever. Because he works so hard in his father's place and I have much additional responsibility, however, our conversations have been few and far between. Yet I cherish each one.

I glance at the growing misty gloom. I shouldn't stay long. Entering the store, I spot Mary in the far corner, surrounded by three open crates. She smiles when she looks up from her work. "Hello, my dear."

"Good evening. How's business been today?"

"A bit chaotic. Many people are gathering further provisions for the winter. But as you can see, things are slowing down now." She lifts small bottles from one of the crates and sets them on the counter.

I glance around the room. "Is Gardner here?"

"No, but I'll certainly let him know you stopped in. He's been working too hard, and I'm concerned about him. So when the Russell family invited him to supper tonight, I urged him to accept and offered to close."

"That was thoughtful of you." I reach down to help her with the unpacking.

"To own the truth, I think Mr. Russell hopes his daughter, Cynthia, will take a shine to Gardner and Gardner will decide to court her."

My eyes widen. "Is that what Gardner wants?"

"I don't know. He rarely talks about it. I try not to pressure him, but I have been eager to see him married and starting a family of his own. And in my few interactions with her, I've found Cynthia to be a nice enough girl. Of course," she laughs, "she's also quite a shapely thing. Which never hurts in catching a man's eye, if you'll pardon my saying so."

I swallow and bite my lip, thinking of my own lack of shapeliness. Why would Gardner want to spend time listening to the troubles of a little shrimp like me when he can have supper with the beautiful Cynthia Russell?

Then I blink away a rush of tears. Why can't I have a figure like Eunice Chadwick so I can capture the attention and heart of some wonderful man? I set a bottle down harder than intended and startle us both.

Mary turns to look at me in surprise.

Drawing a quick breath, I force a smile. "Sorry about that. My, how late it's getting. Elizabeth will be expecting me, and it looks like the mist will be very thick tonight."

I turn and nearly run out the door. As I walk along in the shadows, I let my tears fall freely. When I arrive, I slip in the back way. I should wash my face before we sit down to eat.

Turning away from the narrow dressing table, I spy the Bible lying open by the bed. Papa said this was the copy Mama always read, and he wanted me to have it. I flip back several pages to find the most beautiful pressed flower. Next to it on the page, I note some words at a spot where the paper is water-stained. *For the Lord shall comfort Zion: he will comfort all her waste places; and he will make her wilderness like Eden, and her desert like the garden of the Lord; joy and gladness shall be found therein, thanksgiving, and the voice of melody.*

I sigh and thank God for His promises. I don't know what's going to happen to me, but though my lack of generous curves makes me feel unlovable, God will do what's best. Mama would say He always has a supreme plan.

I haven't sung for a long time. That's what I need: to sing and to count my blessings. Then, when my joy returns, I will be in fine form. Taking a fortifying breath, I snuff out the lamp and head for the supper table.

CHAPTER

TWELVE

EARLY MARCH 1836

"**W**hat ship called? Where Papa?" Addie's pure, lilting voice lifts like birdsong from where she sits on Will's arm. She's petite and Will has continued to grow steadily so that he can hold her easily for long periods of time.

"The *Charles Carroll*. He's out there." Will points across the harbor to the giant ship now dispatching crew members and their personal effects to smaller vessels for the final trip to the wharf.

I smile. Will's of an age where he can become easily annoyed over many things. But he has a tender place in his heart for our little sister, and he never grows cross with her. I thank God for that.

"Papa come, Papa love us?" She looks around to me for confirmation with dark eyes that match my own.

"Yes." I caress her cheek and repeat once more the phrases we've told her several times in the days since we learned of his impending homecoming, as we've all worked hard to freshen up the big house for our reunion. "Papa's returning and we'll all live together. And he loves us and he loves you. I have no doubt he does." And we'll all be home again.

How will Papa be able to keep from loving her? She also has his thick curls, but with Nancy's auburn tints. Her cheeks are ruddy, and her small mouth is so easily given to lop-sided smiles. I've cleaned her up thoroughly and dressed her in one of my own creations, a purple dress trimmed with swirling white stitches. The delicate matching cloak makes her look like a little princess.

We've all cleaned up well and wear our best clothes, each of us eager for the sight of that dear face. Though the morning air is crisp and breezy, I've intentionally left my bonnet at home and let my curls hang loose around my face and down my back. I want Papa to see me the way he's always loved best.

I straighten Will's collar and help Lyddie turn down the edge of her cloak. Then we all look out again to see the first of the boats coming up to dock.

When the crewmen snake their way through the crowd, I spot another familiar face—one which brings me no joy. At the head of the line, a little older and a little more rugged, is Clifton. He draws nearer, and I duck my head to pick at my skirt.

He notices me anyway and steps close. "Good day to you, Miss Chase."

I glance up quickly and then back down, out to the wharf and the sea, anywhere but his face, while bunching my fists against my skirt's folds. "Mr. Clifton." I nod stiffly.

"Well, you remembered my name."

I continue to stare straight ahead and catch sight of the second boat docking.

"Come now. Don't be snobbish. You're growing up. And I've learned a few things about how to treat a lady since last we met. Besides, I was promoted to boatsteerer on this journey. Certainly that's a reason for one who's returned home from a voyage worth a small fortune to hope he might win the hand of a captain's beautiful daughter. Assuming there aren't a dozen men already vying for your devotion?"

There aren't. But he doesn't need to know that. Papa alights at the far end, shouldering his pack before starting in our direction. And I'm keenly aware of my siblings watching us with intense curiosity.

"Perhaps I might come to call on you so we can spend some time together?"

"Sir, I am not yet sixteen," I hiss, daring to look him full in the face.

A hint of the look he gave me last time we interacted flits across his eyes, and my skin prickles. "But you will be."

"I'm here to welcome my father home, Mr. Clifton." I pretend to ignore him, though I still catch a glimpse of his aggravating grin before he turns and continues on his way. My breath rushes out over my relief at his departure—and the fact that Papa is now only yards away.

Displaying her increased boldness, Lyddie jumps forward to throw her arms around him, and he sways a bit under the impact. She's grown taller and now reaches his shoulder. Surprise and joy sweep across his face while he returns the embrace and gazes at the rest of us over her head. "Lydia," his deep voice comes, familiar and comfortable in our ears. He pulls back and cups her chin with his hand. "What a lovely young lady you are growing to be."

She stretches to kiss his cheek. "Welcome home. We missed you terribly."

"And I, you." He steps to the side. "William. As I live and breathe, you're as tall as your sister."

"Yes, Father. And I can lift sixty-pound bags when I help Gardner unload shipments at the store," he says, his slim chest puffing out.

"I'm proud of you." Papa's voice is a little unsteady, and he reaches out to clap Will soundly on the shoulder. "And who do you have here?"

"This is Adaline Claire Chase," Will replies, further pride spilling over in his voice. "Best baby sister in the world."

Papa studies her face, his eyes especially drawn to her hair. He slowly reaches out a hand. When she doesn't shy away, he cups the side and back of her head with it.

She stares up a bit uncertainly but then leans against his palm and gives him a small, darling smile.

"A pleasure to meet you, Adaline Claire. I have looked forward to knowing you."

He pulls his hand away and turns to face me. I see now that though he carries a deep sadness and tiredness in his eyes, he appears otherwise well. We seem to have no words. My gaze confides the hardship of having to be strong for so long combined with the intense joy of having him back again.

He opens wide his arms, and I step into them. His hand presses my head close, and his steady heartbeat sounds faintly through his thick coat. I breathe deep, reveling in the contentment of the moment.

Opening my eyes, I see Mr. Ripley where he's stopped on the path to readjust his pack. When he looks up and I catch his eye, I mouth "thank you" against the scratchy cloth of Papa's coat. Mr. Ripley smiles tenderly and nods before moving on. Papa finally releases me and thumbs away the tears I didn't realize I was crying.

He grins. "Let's go home, shall we?"

After supper, I shoo Lyddie and Will into the parlor, insisting I can clean up alone. I catch snatches of Papa telling them an old tale from the Hawaiian Islands while I prepare hot chocolate to ward off the night's chill. I peek in once to view the captive audience. Lyddie sits on a stool near the fire, Will sprawls on his stomach, stretched over the length of the settee, and Addie sits on Papa's lap, watching his animated face with wonder.

Thank you, God, for bringing him home. How many times has my soul whispered that prayer over the past three hours?

I come in to join them, and we all drink our chocolate—all except for Addie who must have drifted off right after the story was finished. She lies draped against Papa's chest like seaweed washed ashore.

"Your dinner was spectacular, Annie. I can only dream of such delicious food while aboard ship."

"Thank you." I look up from my mending. "I'm more confident after Elizabeth taught me so much."

"I'll reap the benefits of it every day I'm with you. Remind me to thank Elizabeth."

I smile.

"Papa?" Lyddie asks. "Can you, will you, stay home now?"

"For a few months. The timing is uncertain."

Will sits up. "But you just got back, and that man said you earned a fortune."

Papa looks at him and then at me with a raised brow.

"Mr. Clifton. He spoke with me before you came upon us."

He eyes me with concern, but I shake my head and turn my gaze to the fire.

"It's true that we had our share of greasy luck," he admits. "But I must make at least one more voyage before I can comfortably retire. If all goes well on the next journey, I'll be home for good."

"But what if it doesn't?" Will whispers his question—one we've never asked aloud.

"*Will.*" Lyddie frowns.

"It's all right. I've encouraged all of you to speak freely before, and I won't stop now. We may run into trouble. But I feel confident that, with the same ship and most of our returning crew, we can bring in another full load without much difficulty."

"So, must we go and live in separate places again when you leave?" Will leans forward. "I wish we didn't have to. I like being back together."

I look up to find Papa's eyes on me. "Your sister is becoming a capable young housekeeper, but I would hate to see the responsibility of all this rest on her shoulders alone. I fear it would be too much for her to bear."

I reply most earnestly. "I'll do whatever it takes to help you here, to make sure our family is well."

"I know. And I thank you for it. It has given me peace when—" he swallows and clears his throat, "things were difficult. But still..." He lowers his head and kisses Addie's curls. "I'll think on it and see if I can't find a more satisfactory solution. All right?"

We nod.

I note how tired Will and Lyddie look. "We've had a long, exciting day. And since it's back to school for you and back to work for me first thing tomorrow, we should retire."

They get up and lean in so Papa can kiss each of them on the cheek. "Good night," they chorus before heading for the stairs.

Papa stands, carefully shifting Addie. "Where shall I put her?"

"Please carry her to my room. I've prepared a bed for her there. I didn't want to have her disturbing your sleep on these nights when you need it so."

Once we have her tucked in, her favorite doll at her side, I follow Papa back to the threshold.

"How are you getting on at the shop?"

"It's fine. Mrs. Mitchell is always pleased with my work and gives me extra responsibilities on occasion."

"May I come and observe?"

"Yes. If you want to come tomorrow around half past three, you can see the end of our work for the day. We can walk home together and pick Addie up from Aunt Emeline's on the way. How does that sound?"

"Excellent. I'll be happy to care for Adaline sometimes while I'm home, but I do have pressing business to attend to tomorrow."

I nod and start to turn away.

"Did Clifton give you any trouble this afternoon?"

"No." At his doubtful look, I clarify. "He seems to think he can sweep me away, court me, and marry me soon as can be." I release an overly-dramatic sigh.

His eyes darken, as does his scowl.

"Papa." I reach up to touch his cheek. "Don't fret. I won't encourage him. And if he comes around to bother me and you're not present, I'll fend him off with your old harpoon." A grin flashes across my face before I regain a sincerer tone. "I want to wait for someone more worthwhile."

He pulls me close for a long hug and muses above my head. "To think that you're nearly old enough to start courting, to be some man's wife. That may be one of the hardest aspects of leaving again. I won't be here to help you make the right choices."

"You've already helped me. And Mama and Nancy taught me many things too. I know what I'm looking for. And I know I can always ask William, Elizabeth, Aunt Eliza, or Mary if I need any help in the matter while you're gone. But please pray for me—that if I have an offer, I will make the right choice."

He sets me back and looks down with misty eyes. "Oh, I have no doubt you will have an offer—probably several. Take care, Treasure. Guard your heart."

"I will. And for a few weeks longer, I'll simply go on being a girl of fifteen." My smile draws his out. "God grant you deep and peaceful sleep."

* * *

Mrs. Mitchell warmly welcomes Papa at the door when he steps in the next afternoon. At the sound of his deep voice returning her greeting, all other conversation in the room ceases. I glance about to find every pair of eyes fixed on him, all with admiration and a few with dreamy longing.

I dip my head and shake it a little, laughing under my breath. But when the women's silence stretches, I raise my head and attempt to view him objectively. He has a striking figure, confident and exuding power through all his movements. Though he is now about forty, he is still handsome and carries not a single strand of gray in his dark curls. To me he is Papa. But to other women, he must be attractive. My brain wrestles to fully absorb this thought.

Mrs. Mitchell leads him back to my table, and the other women's gazes follow him, turning as one across the room. I fight not to roll my eyes. If he notices—and he surely must—he doesn't let on. He is focused completely on me and smiles when I stand and stretch to kiss his cheek.

"Just as you hoped, a special visitor." Mrs. Mitchell beams at us both, the lovely dimples appearing in her slightly olive complexion. Though she is willowy in form, I always find her face so pleasing—a well-proportioned nose, large hazel eyes, and straight white teeth. For someone of her age, she too is still quite good-looking. Mr. Mitchell must love her deeply.

"Thank you, ma'am." I turn to offer Papa a seat on an extra stool. Moriah is looking over with interest so I quietly introduce them. "This is my good friend, Moriah Pinkham. And this is my father, Captain Owen Chase."

"A pleasure to make your acquaintance, Miss Pinkham." He nods.

"Oh, it's Mrs. Pinkham. And I'm also pleased to know you. Annie often speaks of your admirable traits."

"As you know," he speaks to her while winking at me, "she is extremely generous in her praise of those she loves."

"Yes." She laughs. "You have a wonderful daughter, sir."

"That I do. And what do you do here in the shop?"

She passes across a sampling on a lapel she's just finished.

"I have no talent for sewing, as Annie's mother liked to remind me, but I can perceive fine work when I see it. The Mitchells are fortunate to have you."

She blushes. "I thank you. I like the work and am happy to have it."

"It's a fine thing to be both good at what one does and pleased in doing it." His gaze moves back to me. "And are you satisfied with this work?"

"Yes." I respond with greater ease now that quiet conversations have fully resumed around the room. "My tasks today are less tedious than usual. I am quite content."

"Show me. Or will I make you nervous by watching?"

"Not at all." I go back to the article in hand, explaining the stitches while I make them. He sits watching, listening, asking occasional questions.

Soon everyone is cleaning up for the day.

"Thank you for showing such an interest in what I do," I murmur, placing pins and needles back in their respective tins. "I haven't asked you to share more about your work as often as I should. I'm sure it's extremely challenging but also enjoyable to you because you are so good at it." I bite my lip and look up at him where he now stands. "I must seem selfish and uncaring."

He grasps my hand in a reassuring squeeze and helps me to my feet. "Think nothing of it. You've been a good listener when I needed you to be. And up until now, you've been too young to understand or be exposed to some of the less pleasant details of my work. I have never, for a single moment, thought you selfish."

"I need to collect my things. I'll meet you outside in a moment." We part ways when we reach the front counter.

Before I bundle myself, Mrs. Mitchell detains me to ask about assisting with a special dress order. By the time I exit the shop and approach Papa's side, he has company.

"Hello, Phebe," Eunice greets me sweetly. "I hope you don't mind, but I took the liberty of introducing myself to your guest. I didn't know your father was a captain!"

"Yes," I mumble, feeling awkward at her forward behavior. I adjust my satchel and glance up at Papa. He's watching her with mild interest.

"Have you worked here long?" he continues their conversation.

"About five months. Before that, I worked as a weaver, but I left that job. For I was planning to marry."

His brows lift.

"It was not to be, however," she says with a forlorn expression. "The sea took him."

Papa's eyes dim with deep sadness of his own. "It has taken many a good man." He clears his throat and offers me his arm. "Well, we should be going. Pleased to meet you, Miss Chadwick."

"And you, Captain Chase. Perhaps—I hope we'll meet again." Sorrow has quickly been replaced by her dazzling smile.

"Perhaps," he says solemnly. "Good evening to you." He steers me around, and we head for Orange Street.

* * *

I'm nearing the end of our supper preparation a few evenings later when Papa arrives home. I hear him shake the rain from his hat and coat before hanging them and sticking his head through the doorway.

"Papa!" Addie charges forward in her choppy run, tripping when she reaches him. He catches her and lifts her high.

He crosses the room and asks softly, "Where are the others?"

"Will went out to do the milking, and Lyddie's upstairs sweeping and dusting, I believe. Why?"

"I'd have a word with you, before they join us."

"The stew does need to simmer awhile longer."

"Let's step into the study."

He shuts the door behind us and turns. Addie cuddles against him contentedly. "I've invited company for Sunday dinner. Would you prepare a bit extra?"

"Certainly." I fold my hands in front of me. "How many will be joining us?"

"One. I asked Miss Chadwick to be our guest." When I only gaze steadily at him, he turns to stare at the flame of the lamp I brought in. "I've met with her for tea at the inn near the shop during her midday break the past three days. Each time, I've found our conversations to be pleasant. I'd like her to come and meet your siblings. If all goes well..."

I suddenly find I'm holding my breath.

"I think I will ask her to marry me."

The air leaves with a soft whoosh.

His eyes fly back to my face. "Do you need to be seated?"

I shake my head. "I'm not given to swooning. But, so quickly? Should you not take time to know her better?"

"I don't have time, Annie. The key owners told me yesterday that the ship should be outfitted to sail again by summer's end. I have only a few months to both marry again and see everything settled for you with your new guardian." He kisses the top of Addie's head. "You want to stay together. I want you to stay together. This may be the perfect solution."

"But how would you feel if I came home tomorrow and said, 'Hello, Papa. I met a captain named Ahab five days ago, and we're going to be wed next week'?"

He huffs. But then he sees I'm serious and declares coolly, "This is not the same."

"It isn't?" I try to keep my voice low. "How so?"

"Because I'm a mature man who's been married twice before—not a girl on the high end of fifteen who knows nothing of such relations," he bites out.

The combination of his words and his tone cuts into me. Tears form, but I fight to keep them at bay. "I'm only concerned that she may not be the best choice for you—and for all of us."

"If you're concerned about the age difference," he sighs, relaxing a fraction, "don't be. Thirteen years is a sizable gap, but greater spans are not uncommon."

"Are you sure she's not a hunter of fortunes?"

"Again, you show your ignorance of the world's ways." He begins to pace back and forth. "Providence has indeed been good to us, but if that were her intent, there are other men—widowers and otherwise—on this Island who could provide her with a great deal more in riches. She has not said a word about money. But then, what woman would not seek financial security? Besides," he stops and stares hard at me, "do you not think there are enough other factors to make me reasonably attractive?"

"Yes." I blush and glance away. "But…"

He waits, his tension obviously still running high.

"What about her past?"

"She's told me all about her engagement and broken, grieving heart."

"And before?"

He offers a curious scowl.

"I heard some information." I pause. "About her behavior."

His scowl deepens. "I thought Nancy and I raised you well, not to listen to or take part in idle chatter and slanderous talk."

"You did."

"What's all this then?"

"I generally don't pay attention to any of that. But I overheard some things that, if true, make me believe she would not be a proper wife for you."

"And she told me only today that people have often misunderstood her and spread false reports about her." When his voice rises sharply at the end, Addie begins to whimper. She's completely unfamiliar with his temper and has stiffened to lean away from him.

I, too, am unsettled. Papa has never been angry with me before. This conversation has led us into uncharted waters. I take a steadying breath and swipe at two rebellious tears.

He sighs and also attempts to calm himself while stroking Addie's curls in a gentle rhythm. "Please. Try to withhold judgment, to know her based on her own merits and not the accounts of others. You hold much sway with Lydia and William. I need you to approach Sunday's dinner with an open mind."

I avert my eyes, wishing I could find a way to deny his request.

His tone softens further. "You have always trusted me. Won't you continue to trust me now?"

I swallow hard and swing my gaze back to his.

"I want to do what's good for all of you." His eyes warm and fill with love as Addie exhales and relaxes completely against him once more.

Not so long ago—and my whole life—I was like Addie. Trusting him completely. What's come over me? Finally, I nod. "Yes. I trust you. You have never harmed us. I know you simply want to provide for us." I turn toward the door when I hear the back entrance open and shut. Will's steps echo in the hallway closely followed by Lyddie's on the staircase. "I will do my part to welcome her here. And, if you marry her, I promise to know her for who she is and not for who others claim her to be."

He steps near to kiss my forehead before pulling away with a relieved smile. "Your support means the world to me. And I sincerely believe you won't regret it."

* * *

APRIL 5, 1836

A small band of relatives and friends join to witness the marriage of Papa and Eunice the Tuesday afternoon two weeks after her introductory dinner, one that went exceptionally well for her being a stranger to my brother and sisters. Papa thought that a good omen.

I had thought others of our acquaintance would be equally shocked and reserved over the speed of it all, but more than one has made some comment such as, "'Tis a way of life for the seaman and the woman he loves."

Gardner alone seemed to understand my reservations when I admitted them in passing. But then he sighed and said, "A man must make his choices and live with them, whatever may come. Be at peace."

His words rang true. But they have not touched the apprehension lingering in my soul.

Eunice is radiant in the loveliest dark blue dress, and Papa stands slightly apart from her in his best suit looking sober and somewhat nervous. I truly hope that he will be happy—and he isn't forcing himself to do this simply as a sacrifice for our well-being. Their witnesses stand nearby—William for Papa and Mrs. Mitchell for Eunice. Our dear employer offered her support when she heard that Eunice's father and his second wife rejected the wedding invitation. Eunice did not seem surprised by their refusal, telling us plaintively of her father's extreme devotion to moneymaking and her step-mother's extreme coldness.

The pastor leads them in repetition of the vows while I marvel at the difference between the wedding today compared with the one of a little more than a decade ago. Though I may be present in the same space, I understand much more of what is being promised and expected—and how holy this covenant is.

Lyddie sits beside me, soaking it all up with a wistful expression. Will looks a little bored but still listens respectfully on her other side. They like Eunice well enough, but we've already politely informed Papa that we won't be calling her "Mother" or anything of the kind. He's agreed that "Eunice" is perfectly acceptable. When he declared it so, Addie tickled us all by calling her "Nice" when saying Eunice was plainly a challenge for her. Eunice *has* been nice—amiable every step of the way while they've planned this ceremony and moved her belongings into our house.

The pastor offers a benediction and makes the final pronouncement. They turn to face us, Eunice still smiling wide and Papa looking relieved, and we clap softly to shower them with congratulations.

APRIL 23, 1836

The Saturday following my birthday, I dress in older working clothes and head downstairs to make breakfast. Our new family has developed a unique rhythm over the past weeks. Eunice now only works half-days at the shop so she can stay home and watch Addie. And I've been given Saturdays off for the foreseeable future, to help her keep up with our housework. "This is my gift to your family, in celebration of the marriage," Mrs. Mitchell said with shining eyes. "A new husband and wife need time to bond, and you'll want to know her better too."

I'm surprised to find Eunice already up and hard at work making pancakes and frying eggs. She has slept late many mornings and left the food preparation to me. She's humming cheerfully. It's a little off key but still better than any of Nancy's attempts. And Eunice is much better at cooking—on the days she's willing to do so.

Will and Addie sit at the table, both looking very happy as well. Will sets out the silverware, and Addie plays with her doll.

"Good morning, Eunice. How may I help?" I reach for my apron.

"Hmmm? Oh, never mind. Sit down and wait for a moment. And let me serve you a splendid breakfast!" She sings out the last two words.

I move slowly across the room and study her with suspicion. Has she been imbibing? But she doesn't seem to otherwise be in a drunken state. Only happier than I've ever seen her. Yet, now that I think about it, she's been quite happy and distracted the past couple of days. And so has Papa…

As if thoughts produce people, he steps, smiling, through the doorway, wishes us all a good day, and takes his seat. Eunice turns to set the platter of pancakes on the table and gives him a cheeky smile. I glance back to spy Papa's answering wink. My eyes go wide, and my gaze flies to my lap.

"Everything's ready." Eunice collapses onto her chair.

"Must we wait for Lyddie?" Will ogles the food stacked high in front of us.

"She looked very tired last night," I say. "Maybe she needed some extra rest."

"We'll start. She can join us when she's ready." Papa bows to offer the blessing.

The discussion around the table is light and full of laughter. And I think I've never seen Papa look so peaceful—not for a long time anyway. Will is less moody than he's been in ages, and Addie chatters like a magpie when she's not jamming food in her mouth.

I'm sorry I ever doubted him. Certainly Papa knows best, and all is well. I'm finally relaxing and being drawn into the teasing banter when Lyddie slides into her chair beside me.

My smile fades. I can see evidence of recent tears in her eyes and lines of anxiety across her brow.

"Good morning, Lydia," Papa says. Then he looks up to study her a bit more closely. "It's a beautiful day. Are you well?"

"Yes, I'm fine." She glances up and gives a tight smile. "Only tired."

I reach out under the table and take her hand. She clings to mine as she lifts her other hand to spear a pancake. She pretends to eat it, pushing the pieces across her plate.

The general mood has swung up again, everyone else oblivious to her simmering discomfort. Something's not right. I'll speak with her, first chance.

An hour later, I grab my opportunity to investigate while we sit close on low stools in one row of the small garden, sowing cabbage, onion, tomato, and pea seeds.

I speak calmly. "What troubles you?"

She glances around and then focuses on me with fear-filled eyes while sharing in a frantic whisper. "This morning, when I woke up early, there was blood on my sheets and nightgown. It was coming out of me! How do I stop it? I feel so awful! I put a wad of old fabric against my underthings. Is what happened to Nancy happening to me?"

I exhale sharply and grip her arm. How can this be happening to Lyddie now when I have only been passing blood for three months? Then I recall what Sadie said about different times for different women. "Did Aunt Winifred ever say anything to you about this?"

When she shakes her head and bites her trembling lip, I realize I'm not surprised. If Sadie had not had the gumption to tell me, I would have been equally shocked.

"I'm sorry, Lyddie. I didn't think I needed to tell you yet."

"Tell me what?"

"Something Sadie told me about before Addie's birth." I draw closer and speak lower, starting by assuring her that her condition is not the same thing as what Nancy suffered, and then telling her all I can remember of Sadie's explanation.

Her eyes grow wide, and her cheeks flame.

I suppress a smile when I think of how my face must have looked that day I heard it all. "So it's all right, you see. It's natural."

"It's dreadful," she exclaims under her breath.

"The bleeding is unpleasant. But from what I've read in the Bible, I think the other part is actually a gift from God to us—

maybe to enjoy even—if we treat it with great care." It's taken me a long time to reach this conclusion, and I have a feeling that some people would be appalled at my opinion. But I can't figure it any other way.

"Maybe," she says with a thoughtful look in her eye. "But, I'm glad you told me."

"You'll get used to it. I think we both will. Eventually."

We work for a moment in silence, listening to the breeze and birdsong before Lyddie's head pops up, her eyes searching mine once more.

"What is it?" I ask, suddenly apprehensive again.

"In the middle of the night, before the bleeding started, I was thirsty. So I went downstairs for a drink. Coming down the hallway, I heard a noise. When I passed Papa's door, I heard more noise. I was startled. But now, I'm thinking. You don't suppose…"

We search each other's eyes while her face turns red as a beet. The sight of it tickles me, and my giggling spills forth. When I catch my breath, I whisper, "Well, that would explain why Papa's so cheerful."

We both continue to succumb to my contagious laughter until Will walks by carrying a pail of milk with one hand and leading Addie along with the other. We freeze where we are, our laughter falling flat.

He pauses and eyes us. "What's so funny?"

Lyddie and I glance at each other and burst into riotous giggles again.

He scowls. "Sometimes girls are so weird," he grumbles while rolling his eyes. "Come on, Addie. Let's leave these two loonies alone." He pulls her toward the back door.

My laughter finally calms, but my smile remains. If Papa is happy, then I should be happy for him. Though it may be one of the oddest prayers I've ever prayed, I thank God for the blessings He is giving our family—every single one.

* * *

LATE JANUARY 1837

A nasty wind and swirl of snow chase me inside the front door on a Thursday afternoon. The house is so cold and dark, I shiver anew. I wouldn't expect Will and Lyddie to be home quite yet, but where's Eunice? Did she go out and take Addie with her?

I step to the side table and strike a match to get the lanterns going. When I turn up the flame on the one in the kitchen, I nearly upset the lamp. There, sitting on the floor at my feet, is Addie. She's clutching her blanket and rocking back and forth, staring into the distance.

"Addie?" I breathe. "Sweetheart, what's happened?"

I kneel beside her and feel her face. Her cheeks are pink and cold. Still she stares and makes no sound, almost as if she's gone blind and deaf. I must warm her up.

Moving swiftly, I light a fire and stoke the blaze. I heat some milk from the pail and set a cup of it on the table. After sitting in the nearby rocker, I lift her—blanket and all—to my lap and wrap my arms snuggly around her. "Where's Eunice, baby?" I try to coax her into speaking. "How could she leave you like this?"

She starts to whimper and then fret until she's crying in earnest. Low, mournful sobs like I've never heard. "Papa!" she says every so often.

That breaks my heart more than anything. We've all been missing him keenly, but in the five months since he left, Addie has asked for him less frequently and seemed to grow accustomed to spending the better part of every day solely with Eunice. Eunice only leaves her with one of our aunts to go to the shop for a couple of hours. Something must have shocked Addie deeply indeed. "It's all right, Papa misses you too. One day, he'll come home to us. But I'm here with you now, and I won't leave you."

She calms a bit and accepts a hearty drink of milk before turning to burrow her face against my chest. I dip my head and begin to hum a melody near her ear. It is a tune I don't ever recall studying—but one that feels somehow ingrained in the fiber of my being.

The worsening storm drives Will and Lyddie into the entryway.

"What's for supper?" Will asks, rushing to stand by the fire and searching for a pot or pan with some concoction inside. "I'm hungry."

"Nothing yet," I whisper over Addie's dozing form. Her cheeks are finally flushed with blessed warmth.

Lyddie looks around. "Where's Eunice?"

"I don't know. I last saw her when she left the shop around noon. I came home and found the house frigid and dark, with Addie huddled in a chilled ball on the floor."

They stare at me.

"I wondered about Eunice, but my first thought was seeing to Addie." A new plan now forms in my mind. "Will, hold Addie a while longer, and Lyddie, prepare some corn mush with salt pork. I'll go and search for Eunice. I'll start with the house and shed— to be sure." I transfer Addie to Will's embrace. "And if she's not here, I'll go back out and ask the neighbors if they have seen her." I step around the table to light and take up a candle lamp.

I move about each room of the house silently praying that I won't find her there in some horrendous condition. I look in her room and nearly scream and drop the candle. Eunice is lying prone on the bed. *Dear Lord!*

I creep closer and swiftly exhale when I see her breathing heavily. She's partially covered with a quilt. She must have come up to rest and continued to sleep longer for some reason. Unless she's ill, she will want to get up and eat.

"Eunice." I shake her shoulder. "Wake up."

She moans and tosses her head to the side with a frown.

"Are you unwell?" I shake her again, a little harder.

She stares up at me with glassy eyes. After a moment, she swallows hard and asks coolly, "What do you want?"

"To help you if I can. Will you come down and join us for supper?"

"Go away," she grumbles.

"I found Addie downstairs, chilled and frightened. Is something wrong?"

"That little twit is a thorn in my side. Every day she needs a hundred things from me. She'd better learn to grow up."

I lean back like I've been struck. Eunice has become less patient over the passing months. But I've never heard her talk like this. It's like the storm raging outside has finally broken inside our own walls.

"You're a thorn in my side too." Her speech slurs. "Get out of my room and leave me alone. I want to sleep." She jerks around like a fish in a net before landing back against her pillow and drifting off again almost immediately.

Hurt and bewildered, I pick up the lamp and back out of the room. *God, how in the world do I deal with this?* I smooth my expression and calm my heart while I descend to the ground floor. When I enter the kitchen, Will and Lyddie both look over expectantly.

"I found her." My voice is filled with a strange sense of peace. "She's resting upstairs—tired and overwrought. I think maybe she needs a break from her workload. It has been a big adjustment for her since Papa left."

I go through the motions of setting the table. "I'll take Addie back to Aunt Emeline's tomorrow and ask if they can keep her for a few days. We'll do extra chores here and see if that helps."

They don't question or protest. They simply nod, and I send up a prayer of thanksgiving. I rouse Addie and feed her a bit of supper before laying her tenderly in my own bed where I can later provide a continued sense of security through the night.

In the morning, I leave early, carrying her still-sleeping form covered in a thick quilt to the house up the street before I press on in the slushy snow toward the shop. Though a bit surprised to see us, Aunt Emeline is already awake and accepts my simple explanation without question. She assures me they'll pray that more rest for Eunice will help our situation improve.

* * *

It does not improve.

The following two weeks are a wild ride of unpredictability. Every time we come home we encounter something different. Eunice may be lost in deep sleep or awake but walking around in a fog. She may be alert and extremely snappish. Or she may be something of her old bubbly self. Lyddie and Will are as confused and unsettled as I, though I try my best to be the strong and not let my fear show.

I keep Addie away, not wanting to cause her any more distress. She is safe and happy, especially when Uncle Alexander arrives home for a short leave.

I make excuses for Eunice at every turn. Especially at work, on those days when she decides not to show up at all. Mrs. Mitchell seems a bit flabbergasted, having apparently replaced one frequently ill worker with another. But she often gives all of us the benefit of the doubt, so she hasn't yet spoken of replacing Eunice. That's the one thing that makes me glad. On the days Eunice does come to work, she's not quite as mean.

One evening, she's again shut herself in her room after nastily informing me that she's not to be disturbed.

In the parlor, I sit mending while Will does his homework and Lyddie reads. I glance up and notice, however, that she's not reading—she's staring at the book through silent tears. She *was* unusually listless at supper. I set my work aside to come and sit beside her, putting my arm around her shoulders. "What is it?"

Her sudden outburst of hysterical sobbing nearly unnerves me. She shakes all over and gasps for air.

"Hush now," I say near her ear. "I'm right here. Tell me what's upset you so." I look past her to see Will staring at us over his books and papers set out on the small table. I sigh. "Please go and put the kettle on and make Lyddie a cup of tea." He nods and dashes toward the kitchen, eager to escape.

After a few moments, she is able to speak in a broken voice around shudders and hiccups. She shares her tale of heartbreak: how she was betrayed today at school by her best friend, Sara. I hold her close and stroke her hair, listening and understanding well. I remember a day years ago when Fanny treated me almost exactly the same way. I came home vowing that I would never have another friend. I didn't keep the vow, of course, but the pain was all too real.

Sifting through her words, I see that this normally difficult thing has done a magnified amount of damage because of the additional strain she's recently been feeling at home. It seems like a small volcanic eruption—the kind Papa has described to us.

She is clearly overwrought, her eyes wide and fearful, her hand clinging to my arm. "Annie," she whispers, "I can't go back to school tomorrow."

Well, I certainly don't want you to stay home all day with Eunice. "What you need is a good night's sleep. You'll have more courage in the morning. I know it."

She starts to cry again. "I don't want to sleep. What if I have bad dreams?"

Some part deep inside me starts screaming. *God, how long can I go on being strong for everyone else?* I take a deep breath and release it. "Let me go and find something to help you relax. If you can't sleep immediately, that's all right. But you need to calm down, Lyddie." I gently pull my arm from her grasp and stand, offering her a reassuring smile before I slip into the kitchen.

Taking the box down is not as difficult as it was years ago. I can reach it now without standing on anything, and it's lighter than I remember. To my relief, there's a bit of lavender water left in the bottle. I need to get more before long.

When moving to close the lid, I notice the two laudanum bottles are completely empty—and the vials of opium are not there at all. How strange. Papa and Nancy always told me we were to use those as a last resort, only for the most unbearable pain.

I wonder at it while I use the lavender and the tea Will made to help lull Lyddie to sleep. I kneel beside the settee, humming hymns before covering her with quilts and stoking the fire so she'll be warm through the night.

And, somewhere in my nursing task, I stop wondering at it.

My stomach sinks with what I know.

"I'm sorry, dear. He's gone out." Mary smiles apologetically and sets the full bottle of lavender water on the counter in front of me. "He'll regret having missed you, I'm sure." She notes my charge in the ledger at her elbow.

That's the same thing she's said during my last four visits. And I've been coming in at various times. Is Gardner avoiding me? I shake my head to clear it. Four stops at the store—and nearly four more weeks of extreme ups and downs at home. I long to confide in someone who knows me well but who can still see things objectively.

"How have you been? Any word from your papa?"

"We're all doing as well as we can," I dance around the truth. "And, yes, his first letter arrived last week. It was sent from the Azores. He and the crew were all well, and they'd already taken a sixty-barrel bull not long after leaving the Island. Papa believes it was a good sign of fair winds for their journey."

"That's wonderful news." Her smile widens. "Perhaps Providence will favor them with a trip that is both fully profitable and considerably shorter."

"I hope so. He said he picked up two dogs while they were in port—of mixed breeding—and younger ones at that. He's named them Jacob and Esau. It sounds like they are both good animals and will be most useful to the crew, but he seems to favor Jacob."

"It's nice that he can have the companionship on such a long trip. Is there anything else you need today?"

I hesitate. "Can you tell me when I might speak to Gardner? I know he's been very busy. But even a few minutes of his time would be a great help to me. If I come back in an hour, might he be back by then?"

"I *can* speak to that. I'll be closing the store tonight. I'm afraid he has a previous engagement."

"Oh?" I punch down my intense curiosity.

"Yes." Her voice slips to a confiding whisper, requiring me to lean closer. "You know I've done my best to help him meet other young ladies after things with Cynthia didn't progress like I'd hoped. I keep praying that he'll commit to one of them. Tonight, he's having supper with the Swain family. Maybe Lillian will be the one for him."

"Try not to worry," I whisper back while squeezing her arm. "He'll marry if and when he's ready."

"But will it still be while I'm alive and well and can hold my own grandchildren?" She huffs in frustration. "Forgive me. I don't mean to complain."

"We all carry our own burdens and our own dreams." I stow my purchase in the pocket of my cloak and step away.

"Come back tomorrow at noon, if you can. I'll do my best to see he's here then."

When I return as directed, however, he's "stepped out" again. And Mary doesn't know how long his errand will take.

I guess some burdens are not meant to be shared.

* * *

My one source of personal consolation during these trying weeks comes in the short hours spent at choir practice. There, as we learn new songs and revel in beloved older ones, my mind wanders freely to peaceful places.

Then, I find myself being distracted in a different way. Philip Brock, the only son of one of the Pacific Bank's owners, has recently returned to the Island after studying both finance and law. And he's decided to join the choir.

Perhaps his only shortcoming is his height—or lack of it. He's only a couple of inches taller than me, and he's the shortest man in our group. Yet it quickly becomes clear that he has a much stronger and better voice than any other man among us.

Tonight, by the end of his third practice session, the director is already speaking of how Philip and I should sing a duet in an upcoming service. I turn away to hide my blush at the suggestion. He's a nice-looking man, and well-mannered at that.

He lingers after we finish, introducing himself formally. "Very pleased to meet you, Miss Chase. Your voice is indeed lovely, and I shall greatly enjoy the honor of singing with you." He smiles, and his eyes search my face with open admiration. Yet his perusal doesn't make me uncomfortable.

"Yes. It's nice to have someone to stand beside when performing. God has gifted you with a great deal of talent, sir."

"Kind of you to say so. I hope you won't think me too forward, but I would like to know you better."

"Oh?"

"You strike me as a special young woman. Might I meet your father in church on Sunday or call upon him at home and ask for permission to spend time with you, perhaps even to court you? If you feel comfortable in my company, of course."

I hesitate. "My father is at sea presently." I feel awkward and don't know how to proceed. Eunice is supposed to be our guardian, but I cannot be sure how she will receive him—or if she'll receive him at all—should he come calling at the house.

He studies me carefully, seems to sense my discomfort. "Is there someone else I can ask? Truly, I want to treat you honorably."

I bite my lip and think quickly. "I hope, perhaps this Sunday, I can introduce you to William and Elizabeth. They are our good friends, almost like another set of parents to me. I think if they approve of your designs, Papa will too."

His grin is back in full force, and his brown eyes shine. "Well, then, that will do nicely. And no matter what they may say—though I hope it is affirmative—I look forward to every Tuesday evening in the coming weeks. To every chance of seeing you."

I feel color flood my face, and my stomach does a funny little flip. I bid him good night and walk away with as composed an expression as I can muster. But all the way home, I am grinning too.

* * *

EARLY MAY 1837

Rachel looks up from her work. "I'm glad Mrs. Mitchell is finally doing something about that door. The way it had gone to squeaking was enough to drive a person mad."

I raise my head to find our employer standing beside the open entrance, greasing the hinges with an oil-doused rag. Something about her posture and expression make me uneasy. We've a while yet until closing and I'm already on my next to last piece of the day, so I venture to stand and approach her. While she checks the now noiseless function of the hinges, I quietly say, "It's very good of you to do that, ma'am. I would have been happy to complete the task, especially if you are unwell."

She casts me a look both pained and quizzical. "From where comes your keen sense of perception? You so often seem to know what others are feeling."

"I don't know if that's an inherited trait, but Papa has told me that Mama was the same way. Is there anything I can do to assist you?"

She closes her eyes and releases a tense breath. "To speak truthfully, I have felt progressively worse all afternoon. First my stomach. And now my head is starting to pound."

"Go and rest awhile. Let me store these things for you." I take the rag and bottle of oil.

When I follow her into the back room, she crumples upon the bed and curls onto her side.

"Phebe?" she whispers when I cross back toward the doorway.

"Yes?" I stop and kneel beside her.

"I hate to ask it of you often, but would you mind very much opening everything tomorrow and setting out the next orders in the morning? I know you probably can't linger to do it this afternoon."

"I don't mind at all." Frankly, I'm very tired, but when I see how terrible she must be feeling, my propensity to sacrifice swells within me. Besides, with each of the other three times she's needed my opening assistance since Papa left, my confidence in completing the necessary tasks has grown. True, it will mean getting up at an incredibly early hour, since it takes me longer to complete those tasks than what she requires after so many years of practice. But I would much rather get up early than stay up late.

"Here's my key." She searches in the pocket at her side and removes it, the red string loop trailing behind. "I'll rest here a bit and then go home. I'll send Silas over tomorrow to see if you ladies need anything."

I hang the key around my neck and let it slip under the front of my dress. "That sounds fine. I would appreciate Mr. Mitchell making sure we are all right. But if you have the ledger lists up-to-date and I divide the work correctly, we should be able to operate smoothly."

"You're a godsend, my dear. And I again bless the day I took you on."

I smile. "Rest well, and let us know if you would like an escort home."

At closing time, I clean up my table before extinguishing all the lamps, following the others outside, and locking the door behind us.

This early May afternoon is gorgeous. The sky's as blue as a morning glory with puffy white clouds skimming upon it, sunshine warms my shoulders, and the streets are blessedly dry. In fact, the whole spring has been lovely—with the exception of my seventeenth birthday, when we had a damaging storm.

And it hasn't only been pleasant because of the weather. For the last several weeks, home has again become a place where we wanted to be. After such a rough winter, Eunice is now energetic and kind nearly all the time.

At first I was afraid it wouldn't last, but as one week has given way to the next, we've all started to breathe easier. It's wonderful to have Addie back at home with us, and the last several days I've returned to find Eunice playing with her or preparing her a delicious treat. Addie is so happy, soaking up the affection. Eunice has been back to work without fail as well—still working reduced hours but always coming on time, doing her fair share without complaining.

The only thing I can figure is that she's been missing Papa too much and the winter took a great toll on her. But since the end of March, she's turned over a new leaf.

Thank you, God. I count my blessings during the walk home, thinking about how faithful He has been to sustain me when I've felt like a storm-battered vessel. He has brought me into a safe harbor once more.

"How was your first day in the new position?" I ask Lyddie when I walk around the side of the house and join her in gathering dry laundry.

"It was fine. I don't know why I was nervous. Mr. Wallace has always been kind to us. I think working as his formal assistant will be very fulfilling." She, too, recently reached the end of all the prescribed books and exams, but Mr. Wallace was eager to offer her this work and make good use of her patience with the youngest students.

"I'm thrilled to hear it. And thrilled to see how much you've grown, even since the autumn." I squeeze her shoulder before lifting the second full basket and following her inside. Sara's betrayal was indeed hard on her, but instead of nursing a broken heart, she learned from it and has moved forward to become stronger. I mentioned it in my most recent letter to Papa. I believe it will make him proud.

As we eat our fill of mutton stew and Will tells a funny story about the passage he had to recite at school today, Eunice looks somewhat distracted. She remains silent while pushing the food around in her bowl. I begin clearing the dishes and return to find her staring at the tabletop. "You look very tired tonight. Do you need extra rest?"

"Yes," she sighs. "In fact, I think I'll go to bed now. I haven't been getting the deepest sleep recently."

"Me either." I smile. "But it's often like that in the spring." I pick up the remaining cups.

"Aye," she murmurs. She scatters a general good night to us all from the hallway before climbing the stairs and shutting her bedroom door.

While washing the dishes, I find my mind wandering. What if things don't stay as nice as they have been? I blow out a hefty sigh. Worrying won't help anything. I must set my mind on lovely things.

I walk into the parlor and find Addie giggling while Will tells her one of Papa's funny old stories. Smiling at their antics, my heart relaxes. Yes, that will do very well.

I awaken easily at the necessary hour, my body unusually alert. Feeling my way in the dark, I slip down the stairs to find the cloak, lantern, food bundle, and satchel in the entryway where I set them out last night. I secure my cloak and bag with the food now tucked inside and light the lantern before closing the front door. The unusually thick mist still carries a frosty note in the strange dimness of early morning. I'm glad I've worn my cloak.

The town clock strikes four as I pass within its vicinity. I keep my head up, remaining watchful. It's too early yet for even many of the apprentices to be out. Some of the few people about—besides the watchmen—have less than superior motives for traversing the streets. My stomach relaxes a little when I reach the shop entrance.

My key turns in the lock, and the door opens with blissful smoothness. There's something sacred about the incredible stillness of the shop under the light of night's departure. I gently place my lantern on the front counter. I know I need to light the lamps and set to work, but I want to stand here for a few moments and soak in strength from the quietness.

A soft noise from the back room disrupts my meditation. Ugh. Is that the third mouse this month? I wish Mrs. Mitchell would bring in a cat. Other than Mr. Mitchell, I'm the only one who's not afraid to chase the little beasts. I'd better catch it now, before the workday starts and it causes pandemonium. Wanting to maintain the element of surprise, I leave the lantern behind and step stealthily toward the curtain. Drawing it back, I scan the floor.

Where I'm expecting to glimpse a rodent, I see a heap of clothes. And, when my eyes jump upward, the bed occupied.

My hand flies to my mouth. Even in the dim light from the lantern behind and the high window above, I can distinguish Eunice embraced by the form of Mr. Mitchell. They are dozing peacefully under one of the quilts, a small smile lingering on each face.

I step back and drop the curtain. How mortifying if they wake and find I've been here. Backing across the room on tiptoe, I snuff out the lantern, set it noiselessly on the shelf, let myself out, and lock the door again behind me.

I attempt to run, stumbling against the layers surrounding my legs. I don't pay much attention to where I'm going. I only go. Away. I have to get away. How can I go back there? How can I face either of them? Or Mrs. Mitchell? Tears fill my eyes, and I press on through the misty streets and alleys as the first hints of pinkish light shade the sky's edge. *Oh, God, won't this break Papa's heart? Should I tell him? Where can I go? With whom can I share?*

Rounding a corner, I run into a solid object and am thrown back from the impact. But I'm kept from falling by strong hands which grip my shoulders. I gasp and blink, trying to clear my blurry vision.

"Annie?"

At the sound of that whisper, I sway and began to tremble and sob harder.

Gardner's arms surround me. He presses me close until the worst of the hysteria has passed. Then he pulls back to examine me. "Are you hurt? Has someone been after you? We told you to take extra care if you had to be out this early." He sounds more disturbed than I've ever heard him.

"I'm unharmed. But extremely relieved to see you." I shudder and sniff, lifting a hand to wipe my eyes.

"What on earth has happened?"

My voice low and breaking, I reply, "I went to open the shop for Mrs. Mitchell. She was very ill yesterday afternoon. And when I got there, I discovered something so awful." My tears fall faster.

He slips his arms around me again, this time a little more loosely. "You can tell me."

My face heats where it rests against his lapel. "I saw Eunice. She was with Mr. Mitchell. In a most inappropriate manner."

His arms tighten around my shoulders, and he remains silent for a moment. Finally, he speaks with his chin dipping near my forehead. "Some folks say such things will happen, but I can't abide by it. It doesn't make the heartbreak any less for those who've trusted."

I listen to the sound of his deep breathing and calm a little. *Thank you, God, for hearing my cry.* "I prayed that I wouldn't have to bear this alone, and you were the answer to that prayer." I sniffle. "The past several months at home have been terribly difficult—and now this."

He gently sets me back. "What will you do?"

"I don't know. I can't bear to encounter them again, but I need to go back and prepare the shop. I have a little time, but I can't wait too long. I promised Mrs. Mitchell I'd see to everything."

"Let's walk together then. I'll make sure you get back safely, and I'll go in first." He takes my hand and pulls me forward.

"But what about you? Were you on your way to open the store? Won't Mary be counting on you to do so?"

"I have time. I couldn't sleep well last night. So I walked over earlier than usual. Let me help you."

We walk side-by-side, my hand still wrapped in his. "I've missed talking with you. I came by many times in the past months." My voice catches. "I needed you. But you were never there."

"Annie…" He sighs deeply. "I'm sorry."

"I don't mean to make you feel guilty. I know you've been so busy at the store and with lots of…" I bite my lip. "Engagements. Your friendship is the most important one in my life. But I don't mean to be selfish and should learn to rely on you less. Especially when you'll be starting your own family soon. Mary told me about Miss Russell, Miss Swain, and the others. Have you decided who you're going to marry?"

He pulls up against the side of a warehouse and turns to face me. "I can't marry Miss Russell or Miss Swain—or any of those other young women Mother has arranged for me to meet."

"Why not?" I squint with disbelief. "They're all so pretty and talented. And from well-to-do families."

"But they can't bear me—not really." He stares at his shoes, looking miserable. "When they hear my voice or see my scars, they treat me with cool aloofness or—even worse—gushing pity. I can't go through life with a woman who is revolted or embarrassed by who I am."

"And you shouldn't have to. I'm sorry they hurt you." I squeeze his fingers.

"But there's another reason I can't marry any of them."

"What's that?"

His eyes slide up and pierce mine. "They aren't you."

"Oh." My breath leaves me in a rush. For the first time, I really see my friend as a woman sees a man. He's as kind and intelligent as ever, but also extremely handsome. Much more handsome than Philip. My stomach doesn't simply flip a little—it soars up and drops all the way to my toes.

"This isn't the best time to say this. I don't want to take advantage of how vulnerable you are. And I know we've been friends—like siblings almost—since you were a baby. But in the past year, something's changed—at least for me. I see the beautiful woman you are becoming, and I can't think of anyone else I want to spend my life with. Yet, I want to honor you and treat you properly. You were—are—still young. I won't force you to do anything that might not be best for you. So the waiting has been torture. Especially when I've seen Mr. Brock speaking with you so freely the last few Sundays." His whisper cracks, though I can't tell if it's due to emotion or the strain on his voice from giving such a lengthy, fervent speech.

"Were you avoiding me?"

"I didn't trust myself to behave chastely and be able to hide my feelings. So I thought it would be better if I simply stayed away. But seeing you now, and knowing what's happened—"

"Gardner, you are the most wonderful man in the world. Why would you be attracted to a little shrimp like me?"

He draws me close and breathes, "Never repeat their old names for you again." He tenderly kisses the scar on my temple.

When he leans back, I see part of his own scars exposed at his open collar where he's yet to don his tie. Instinctively, I grip his jacket and pull myself up to press my lips to the spot.

He exhales sharply before he pushes me back.

"Did I do something wrong?" A blush prickles my cheeks.

He turns and starts walking, pulling me along once more. "No. And I fully intend to keep it that way." He glances at me before facing forward again. "Annie, I want to marry you. Will you have me?"

"Yes!"

"I wish I could wait and ask your father for formal permission. But I confess, I can't wait—both for my sake and for yours."

"What do you mean?"

"I won't leave you to live with that woman any longer than necessary."

"But if I go and live with you, who will stay and protect the others?"

"You have carried that weight for a long time, sacrificing much to be strong for your family. Now, for once, take care of yourself. And, let me help you. We'll keep an eye on them, and they can always find a safe place with us."

His words crack open something deep in my heart and pour a balm over wounds I didn't know I had—incredible expectations I've never seen as anything but normal. "What about your mother? Will she object?"

He smiles for the first time since we, quite literally, ran into each other. "I think she will be momentarily shocked. She still sees you as a darling child. But when she overcomes her surprise, I feel certain she'll welcome you as she always has—with open arms."

I return the smile, my assurance feeding from his quiet confidence.

"And it would be horribly awkward for you, continuing to work in the shop for years, waiting for your father to return and knowing what you now know."

"Yes." I shudder.

"You can come to work in the store when the time is right, helping me and fulfilling sewing orders there. I know Mother will greatly appreciate the assistance."

He looks past me and draws us both up short, slipping his arm around my waist and setting his fingers against my lips. In the strengthening light and slightly diminished mist, we see Eunice slip out of the shop carrying a tight bundle of sheets under her arm. Head down, she walks quickly in the direction of Orange Street. And a moment later, Mr. Mitchell ducks out to lock the door before strolling away in the opposite direction. When he passes near us, Gardner pulls me back and presses us against the neighboring building.

He glances around and waits until they are both out of sight before he releases me. Taking my hand once more, he leads me to the shop and, after I've unlocked the door, inside. We find the floor cleared and the bed perfectly made. We gaze at each other with sad eyes before turning back toward the entrance.

His hand cradles my cheek, and he inhales deeply. "I'm sorry for the terrible shock of this betrayal, but I'm elated to think of our future joy."

I smile a little. "Think also of today. My heart is already yours."

"Annie, promise me that you'll send word to me—or come away—if being here in the shop becomes more than you can bear as the morning wears on."

"I will, if you promise to pray that God gives me strength whenever it crosses your mind."

Our eyes lock. "Done."

His smile returns. "But no matter what, come and see me on your way home?"

I nod. "Thank you. For helping me."

His expression sobers before he steps backward over the threshold. Then he turns, and his retreating form is swallowed by the first piercing, brilliant splay of sunlight.

* * *

Gardner eyes me skeptically. "You're sure you don't want me to be with you for support?"

"Yes." My resolve is firm. "I think they will be more accepting of your offer if I speak with them alone. Especially Eunice. Will, Addie, and Lyddie all think the world of you, but Eunice—I'm sorry she's treated you with coldness. Let me introduce the topic and try to deal with her in my own way."

It's been nearly two weeks since he proposed, and we have gone on about our lives as normally as possible. The main exception is my visits to the store, often conducted like this one—inside the back entrance with talk of the future and a soft parting kiss to my cheek or forehead. Gardner won't kiss my lips until after our wedding—which feels like an awfully long time from now.

He wants to take a few months to court me properly. We haven't breathed a word of what we witnessed to anyone. We want to spare my siblings and other family members the shock and scandal of it.

We finally told Mary our news yesterday. To my relief, she responded much as Gardner predicted. She is delighted and accepting of this addition. Now we must inform my family before she bursts from the pressure of trying to contain her excitement.

"Then you'll tell Eunice and the children at supper. And I'll arrive by seven to collect you so we can call on William's family and as many of your father's siblings as possible to announce our news. Hopefully, we can make the complete rounds to in-town relatives before curfew."

"And I'll prepare a short message to be carried to Grandpa Judah. I believe they will all accept your suit—though, it may catch them unaware. Gardner, promise me you'll let me do most of talking when we go calling tonight, to help spare your voice."

"I will, if you promise to let me hold your hand on the walk home."

"Done." We laugh.

"May God give you wisdom when you deal with Eunice. Until this evening." He leans down to grasp my elbows, lift me, and kiss my temple before releasing me slowly. I was initially confused at his insistence on such brief contact, but I came to realize it's another way he's protecting both of us. I love him all the more for it.

I step down into the alley and glance up at him. He watches me, concern clouding his features. I toss him my bravest smile before turning and facing the inevitable. I can do this—and I will.

Addie and Lyddie are so talkative when I get home—even through much of supper—that it's hard for me to say anything at all. I sit eating and passing dishes for second helpings, trying to find a way to join the conversation.

"And, Annie, did you know Ruth Macy is going to be married in September?" Lyddie asks.

This is my chance. "Yes, I've heard. And, I'm to be married as well. In November."

Will snorts and nearly spits out his mouthful of potatoes. Then they all look at me and freeze when they see I'm in earnest.

"And who will you be marrying?" Eunice's eyes narrow.

"Gardner. He made me an offer. I accepted him."

"Oh!" Lyddie claps. "How wonderful!"

Eunice lays down her fork. "It's not wonderful. It's foolhardy. What were you thinking, accepting him? He's not nearly good enough for you."

"What do you mean?" Will says before I can form a reply. "Gardner's family has a good business, and he's one of the finest fellows on the Island."

"Yes," Lyddie says. "And he's so intelligent and strong and kind and—"

"Gadna gives me hugs and candy!" Even Addie comes to his defense.

"Be that as it may," Eunice pauses to scan the three of them with a withering look before piercing me with her eyes once more, "he is still a merchant, the son of a merchant—and a maimed one at that. You are the daughter of a captain, Phebe Ann. One who has become quite well-to-do. And you possess a great deal of beauty and talent."

Her tone is far from complimentary. "You must consider carefully how you can use those things to your advantage—and to the advantage of us all. Think of how, should we market your availability to the right families, you could attract a dozen men at once—and could then choose the richest one. Think of Mr. Brock, for example."

"I don't need to marry a wealthy man," I reply evenly, low—beating back my temper.

She scoffs. "How do you intend to be happy if he has no money to provide you with a comfortable living?"

"We'll be comfortable, working together each day and snuggly content in their lovely house."

"With his mother?"

"Mary is very dear to me. It will be a joy to live with her."

"It will be awkward and a detriment to the marriage."

Along with the others, Will is trying to keep up with our fast-flying exchange. "You mean Gardner won't come to live here with us?"

"I certainly hope not." Eunice throws her napkin on the table.

"Oh, yes," Lyddie says, her gaze drifting away, "you'll be leaving…"

Addie drops her spoon and frowns. "Don't go!"

"You see." Eunice serves herself another generous slice of roast. "They don't want you to go. You're needed here."

Lyddie starts to protest. "It's all right. We can—"

"And I would wager you haven't received Owen's permission. If you have, I certainly haven't been notified. As guardian of this family, I'm to speak for him while he's away. Think of how upset he'll be when he learns of such an event long after the fact. What a bull-headed and heartless girl you are."

I pull Addie around and onto my lap, embracing her and stroking her hair to help still her whimpering. When I reply, my voice is completely calm. "He was the one who admonished me to guard my heart and choose wisely. And Nancy and Mama also taught me something about the important traits I should seek. Gardner possesses every one of them. He is a well-mannered, hard-working, Christian man who matches me better than anyone else I know. And considering my present circumstances, I have complete faith that Papa would approve my choice if he were here. As for timing, I refuse to wait. And if that makes me 'bull-headed,' so be it."

Turning to address Will and Lyddie, I add, "I will see each of you—and Addie—often. And you will be as welcome in the store—and in my new home—as ever. This is a part of life. One day you will probably marry, and I will be happy for you. But more than anything, I love you sincerely, and this won't change that at all."

They nod their understanding, and Addie sighs.

The clock on the landing chimes the hour, the last stroke echoing while a rap sounds at the front door. I stand and pass Addie to Will. "Please excuse me. We have news to spread."

* * *

EARLY AUGUST 1837

"I'll miss you when you leave," Lyddie sighs one Saturday afternoon.

I laugh and then reply with mock sternness, "Only because I'll no longer be around to do your dirty work for you." I lift a heavy bucket and pour some of the water into one of the washing basins. At my feet is a bunch of our monthly rags in another bucket where they've been collecting and soaking for the last couple of weeks. It's the one household duty that Lyddie detests above all others. And Eunice hates it too. So it often falls to me. When I reach in to remove some for scrubbing, however, the bucket is not nearly as full as usual. "Ugh," I groan. "I think Eunice forgot to put hers to soak. The last time that happened, they were so awful to deal with. Do you remember?"

"Yes!" Lyddie looks queasy at the thought while stirring the clothes floating in a big pot of soapy water.

"Well, there's nothing for it." I dry my hands, step from the narrow washing room, and turn to march upstairs—the last place I know of Eunice being. I come to her open doorway and see her sitting on the edge of the bed, refolding a letter. "Eunice? I'm washing our monthly cloths, but it seems yours weren't in the bucket again. Please collect them if you want me to clean them too."

She looks up. Then her eyes dim as if she's staring through me. "I don't have any for you today."

"You washed them yourself? That was very good of you."

"No. I haven't used any for the past three months."

Oh, no. All this time I have said nothing, given no hint that I knew of her rendezvous. The shock I now display at the thought of the further ramifications is genuine. There will be no hiding it. "Does this mean…?" I sink down on the dressing stool.

"Yes."

"But Papa's been gone for nearly a year."

"And you're old enough to work these kinds of sums," she murmurs.

Tread carefully. "Who's the father?"

"I don't know," she says with a hollow chuckle.

How can she not know? It's Mr. Mitchell! Unless... I suddenly feel sick to my stomach.

"Well, I suppose others will be able to notice my condition before long." She sighs. "But it's the circle of life, the hand fate has dealt me. At least I'll have the child I've often dreamed of." She gazes somewhere past me.

Anger builds in my heart. "Don't you care? What about Papa and the vows you made to him?"

"It seems," her voice drops to a whisper, "my desires were stronger than my will to keep them. He's human. He'll understand that. He loves me most passionately you know." When she again looks at me, her smile is small, smug, and sure.

How could you do this? Why don't you leave us? Why don't you *die?* The vehemence of my sudden hatred shocks me nearly as much as her attitude. *Lord Jesus Christ, Son of God, have mercy on me. Help me!*

I stand and hasten from the room, down the stairs, out the back door, and into the shed. After retching in the corner, I find some comfort in sobbing against the warm side of our benign old cow. Then, I lift my chin, manage to collect myself, and return to my unpleasant task.

* * *

My next great source of concern is how to tell Papa. I know it will be some time before he hears the news. But I fervently hope that hearing of it before he returns home—and from someone who loves him deeply—might somehow soften the blow.

I ponder it for a few days, asking Gardner for advice on what I am to include in a letter to be dispatched as soon as possible. I stay up late one night, writing and rewriting until I'm satisfied that I've conveyed the most important details with greatest care.

Now how to send it? This is the type of news I cannot leave to chance. All of our sea-faring uncles are supposed to be away for a long time yet. Before I drift off toward a restless sleep, I try in vain to think of how I can find a reliable messenger.

My dilemma is solved the next day, however, when I overhear two ladies talking about their husbands signing on for new voyages during my walk to work. Of course. That would be a good place to inquire about a trustworthy source, someone who might be departing before long, without setting tongues to wagging.

Later that afternoon, I press through the busy streets and enter the active crowd in the main room of the customs office. It's full of all manner of men. In fact, I appear to be the only woman present. I feel many stares when I press forward, but I do my best to ignore them. Looking about, I see extensive lists on large slate boards lining the walls, including one that has impending departures. I weave through the sea of sailors and businessmen. Some tower over me, and I have to get as close as possible to see the whole list.

A name near the bottom strikes a chord in my memory, Captain Reuben Joy to sail out on the *Hero* in five days' time. I remember his presence at Nancy's burial, Aunt Rebecca explaining that he was the brother of Nancy's first husband briefly home between voyages. Papa knows him—Aunt Rebecca mentioned that too. I sigh, my heart feeling the rightness of it.

I've nearly made it back to the entrance when a big hand clamps around my arm and spins me about. An intoxicated sailor leers down at me. "Hello, my lovely."

Before I can react, another arm falls between the two of us, wedging us apart. A low but firm voice from behind me speaks. "Leave the lady be, Wilkes."

Wilkes looks at the speaker and grumbles, "Oh, a fellow can't never have a good time," before huffing and turning to press on toward the clerk's counter.

My savior squeezes around to stand before me, and when I see his face, I sense something familiar in it. Then I remember those long-ago, terrifying moments on the wharf. "Mr. Nickerson?"

"Aye." He blinks and squints. "You're—you can't be Miss Chase?"

I nod and smile at the surprised delight entering his eyes.

"I'll be hanged! And how you've grown to be so becoming, if you'll pardon my frankness."

"How have you fared these last years, sir? Will you be shipping out again soon?"

"Got me a bit of leave. Going to sail again in about eight weeks."

"Oh."

He guides me through the door and away from the building. "And are you and the family all well?"

"We're managing while Papa's away again. I'm to be married in three months."

"Well, congratulations to you! Your man is indeed a lucky chap, though he'd better be both strong and good to serve as son-in-law to your father."

I smile again, wider this time. "He's the strongest. And the best. I thank you for your help in there a few moments ago. You have a knack for getting me out of scrapes."

Now it's his turn to grin. "Don't mention it. And if I come across your father at some port or gam, I'll let him know of my seeing you."

"That's very good of you, Mr. Nickerson. God bless you, sir."

"And you, Miss Chase." He nods cordially before we part ways.

"Where are you going?"Will inquires when he passes through the entryway after supper and spots me fastening my cloak.

"Out for a walk."

"On a night like this? It looks like a storm's about to break."

I lift Papa's old slicker from its peg. "This will do, if I need it. I should be back before long."

"Well, if you get soaked and wake up with a cold tomorrow, it's not my fault." He shuffles into the parlor.

My letter—the one that's remained hidden in my skirt pocket all day—feels much heavier than it actually is. I press through the strong wind blowing along Orange Street, thankful the rain hasn't started. At the house I believe to be the one I seek, I step up and knock on the dark door.

After a moment, it opens slightly to reveal the lined but kind-looking face of an elderly woman. "Yes?"

"Is this the home of Captain Joy?"

"It is." A blast of wind whips up my cloak and skirts. "Oh! Won't you come in?" She eyes me with curiosity once I'm safely inside. "What brings you calling on such an evening?"

"A matter of some urgency. Otherwise, I wouldn't dream of disturbing you. Is the captain at home? I want to ask him to carry a message to my father, Captain Chase."

Her eyes flare with recognition at the mention of Papa's name. "Yes. He is here—attending to some business in his study. Please step into the sitting room. I'll ask him to join you and prepare some tea."

A few minutes later, she returns with a tray, and a moment afterward a somewhat familiar-looking man strides in. I rise from the small sofa and look up into his dark gray eyes.

"Miss Chase, isn't it? Good evening to you."

"And to you, Captain Joy. I thank you for receiving me without an invitation."

"Think nothing of it. It is good to see you again." He directs me to be seated while taking a chair opposite before the housekeeper serves us.

She must see how I glance at her, though I'm trying to hide it. "Is something troubling you, dear?"

"I'm afraid there is. I don't mean to presume, or to spurn your hospitality. But might I speak to the Captain privately?"

"Certainly. I've plenty to do in the kitchen." Smiling at me, she slips away.

He peers at me warmly over the rim of his cup and takes a drink. "What can I do to relieve your present anxiety?"

"Allow me to be brief and direct, sir, if I may?"

He nods, sets his cup on the low table, and leans toward me.

"I am aware that you'll be departing again very soon. Would you take a letter with you and deliver it personally, if at all possible? And perhaps, if you see one of my uncles before you see my father, you might pass the letter and connected information on to them. Somehow it must reach Papa."

"I hear the depth of your distress. Do you need some wine to calm your nerves?"

"No. Thank you. Only, let me tell you a bit about the news you must take to him."

He nods again.

"My father's wife has betrayed his trust. And she is with child." I swallow around the lump rising in my throat. "I don't know how the news will affect him. But I wanted him to hear the truth of the account from one who loves him deeply."

"When is the child to come?" His low tone matches my own.

"Midwinter, by my best guess."

He studies the rug for a moment before meeting my eyes again. "It must have been a hard thing for you when you learned about it."

"Yes." A strangled sob slips out with the reply.

He reaches into his coat pocket and offers me his handkerchief. With great patience, he waits in silence for me to regain some control over my emotions and return the thoroughly moistened cloth to his large, rough hand.

"Thank you, sir."

"You are still quite young to bear this—and all that is certainly to come in the days ahead. Do you have anyone else to support you?"

"I'm to be married, to Gardner Coffin. In late November. Will you also tell Papa that when you see him? For I'll pray every day that you do see him—and quickly."

"Aye, I'll tell him. Something sweet to assuage the bitter."

I stand and he follows. "Captain Joy, I cannot tell you how this comforts my heart. I thank God for your understanding and your dependable assistance."

He reaches out to press the hand I offer and then accepts the letter when I produce it. "You may recall that I am not married. If I were, heaven forbid the same would ever happen to me. But—if it did—I would hope to first receive the news from a trusted friend. It is my honor to do you and your father this service." He glances through the high, narrow window above the door after he escorts me back into the entryway. "Please allow me to walk you at least most of the way home. It's grown incredibly dark."

* * *

NOVEMBER 28, 1837

"There you are, little fairy." William steps up to meet me outside the door of the church beneath two brightly burning lamps. "You look enchanting. I couldn't be prouder of you nor love you more, unless I were Owen of course." We share a smile. "And I think that Gardner is the luckiest man on the Island this evening."

Elizabeth presses near me and squeezes my hand while sending William a stern look. "Then you'd best not stand out here orating for hours on end, my love—keeping him waiting and letting the bride become thoroughly chilled." Her scolding can't continue when he leans down to tenderly kiss her before shooing her toward the door. "But you do look like an angel, Annie," she throws over her shoulder. "See you inside."

If I look like an angel, it has a great deal to do with her planning skills, Mrs. Mitchell's dress design, Moriah's embroidery talent, and Aunt Eliza's gift of the most luminous pearl-tipped pins. My new cloak is loosely tied to shield me from the stinging air while still revealing the dress of dark green silk, the skirt and bodice detailed with trailing vines of flowers beneath soaring birds—all stitched in golden thread. The pins dot my hair where Elizabeth helped me deftly tuck my most errant curls up while leaving the rest of the mass to flow freely.

I know everyone expects the bride to pin them all up and cover them with a veil or bonnet. But everyone is not Gardner, and he's the one I'm longing to impress this evening.

William offers me his arm, and we step inside to walk up the aisle. Though I can barely take my eyes from the groom, I'm aware of each family member and friend present. We didn't want to exclude anyone but had no desire for a large crowd of guests. His gaze meets mine and follows me, eyes overflowing with love despite the rest of his face looking very serious.

Moriah and Mr. Wallace stand to witness our vows. The words wash over me and then flow from my lips. I can't think of a time when I've felt more honored—nor when I've meant a promise more sincerely.

Reverend Emory breaks from traditional wording near the end. "If you don't mind, I'd like to say something personal. It has given me great joy to watch these two grow up. And now it is with greater joy I see them joined together as man and wife. May the love of Christ be the cornerstone of all your days together. And may the peace of Christ guard your hearts whenever trials come. Phebe Ann, Gardner—God bless your life together." We smile at him and then each other at the delight of such a personal benediction.

Afterward, we linger to receive embraces and handshakes—best wishes from all present. "It's a pity Eunice wouldn't come," Aunt Rebecca murmurs after hugging me.

"It was her choice," I whisper. "The coming child gives her an excuse to lounge about day and night. More than that, she's told me multiple times that I'm making a mistake, and this is a terrible waste."

She gazes at me somberly and then pats my cheek. "She is certainly not the best one to give advice on marital relations. I think I speak for all the rest of us when I say you've chosen wisely, sweetheart."

"Thank you." I blink back tears. "Your words mean a great deal to me."

Departing into the frosty night, Gardner and I escort Mary as far as the store and see her safely in the back entrance.

"You're sure about this?" I grasp her elbow.

"Absolutely," she declares with a radiant smile. "Everything is ready for me upstairs. I'll be quite comfortable—even if I remain too excited to get much sleep. I'll be up early to open and see to everything tomorrow. Don't worry for a moment about things here. William Henry already said he would come in the afternoon to bring me some relief and help close." She kisses each of us tenderly on the cheek before speaking to Gardner. "Take her home and love her. Forget about all other responsibilities for now."

I blush and embrace her with all my strength, whispering my love and appreciation before we say good night.

It begins to snow while we walk on, and we are both covered with a dusting by the time we step, shivering, into the entryway of the snug house on New Dollar Lane. "I'll start a fire to curb the bedroom's chill," he whispers after shedding his wet coat and boots.

By the light of the candle lamp he leaves with me, I undo my cloak and brush the snow from both our garments before hanging them up. I wipe our shoes with a nearby rag and set them against the wall. Then I turn in a circle, taking in the dim atmosphere of my new home. Cozy, peaceful, good.

Lost in thought, I start when he embraces me from behind. "Welcome home, Mrs. Coffin."

I turn in his arms and smile up at him. At the intensity in his gaze, however, I go completely still.

"Annie, promise me you'll wear your hair down every day for the rest of our lives." He pulls me closer.

"I will, if you promise to run your fingers through it."

"Done," we mouth in unison before he kisses me.

He leads me up the stairs and knows me fully. And in the early hours of the morning, I awaken to two sounds: his heartbeat in my ear and the voice of melody in my soul.

CHAPTER
THIRTEEN

FEBRUARY 15, 1840

Gardner leans forward to be heard above the strong breeze while they shake hands. "It's good to have you home, Captain Chase."

"I thank you for the welcome. And you might as well call me Owen, son."

At this pronouncement, I'm supremely happy. He received our news. And he's not only accepted it—he fully supports it.

He turns to where I stand huddled by Gardner's side, shivering against the harsh February chill. "You didn't need to come down here and stand out in the cold." His words chide, yet he pulls me forward and embraces me tightly. "I would have come to seek you out, soon as could be."

"It's tradition." I smile unsteadily while I shiver. "Haven't I always been here to greet you? And even the time you surprised us, I saw you first."

He feigns annoyance. "True. But at least your siblings apparently had enough sense to stay at home so they wouldn't freeze to death." We all grin.

"Yes…" Our smiles simultaneously fade.

There are several emotions swirling in his expression, and all of them press down on my heart. I turn to look up at Gardner.

We finish a conversation from earlier this morning—now speaking only with our eyes. "Papa," I begin when the three of us start to walk away from the wharf across the frozen ground, "Gardner needs to get back to the store, and I'll join him there in a little while. But I want to come with you first. I haven't seen everyone for a few days, the weather being so poor."

"As you wish." When he glances down, I see a kind of understanding in his profile and sense his appreciation that I've not openly declared any doubt in his ability to handle this alone.

He turns to Gardner. "Are you sure you won't come and join us for a few minutes at least? Annie wrote about how her siblings adore you. It would be a bright spot in their day, I'm sure."

"I appreciate the invitation," Gardner says. "While they are indeed affectionate toward me, I haven't been completely welcome in your home since you departed."

Papa's jaw tenses. "I'm very sorry to hear it." We reach our parting point, and I release Gardner's arm to take Papa's. "That will change. Along with other things. You're a good man."

"I thank you, Owen." They shake hands once more, and he kisses my cheek before he speaks beside my ear. "Remember, return as soon as you can—and sooner if it becomes unbearable for you."

He pulls back. I blink my understanding. He's given me such admonitions every time I've gone back to the big house for a visit these two years—after I returned from the first instance to suffer uncharacteristic melancholy for a week.

Papa turns us homeward, and I think of something to fill the silence. "You didn't bring Esau home, then?"

"No," he sighs. "After Jacob died, Esau became a good companion. But I could see that he'll be happier at sea. So I gave him to the second mate, to be taken along next they sail. I'd wager, though, that I'll come to regret it. Home does not hold all the love it once did."

"Perhaps not. But I'm not far away, and Lydia and Adaline were thrilled to hear of your impending return. William's not here to welcome you now, but I know he'll be eager to see you again once he's safely completed his first voyage."

"I was indeed proud to hear he'd signed on, and also to receive a report that the captain and crew have already been impressed by such fortitude in one so young."

"I'm pleased to hear it but not surprised. He's so much like his father."

Papa lowers his voice. "And what of Charles Frederick?"

"Oh, he's a delightful little boy. I know he's not yours." I swallow. "But I hope—I believe—that you'll find him as endearing as we do. Truthfully, he's very somber for a child so recently turned two. But, if you'll pardon my saying so, I think that has a great deal to do with how his mother treats him. When Lydia has brought him away to our house, he's shown signs of curiosity and delight. With consistent love and attention—especially from a father—I have great faith that he'll turn out well."

"She doesn't care for him?" His voice carries an edge I recognize but don't fear. It is the beloved protectiveness I heard on more than one childhood occasion.

A good sign. "At first she saw to his every need, even doted on him. But after the first year, he seemed to become one more burden she didn't want to bear." One more thorn in her side.

"Anything else I should know before we arrive?"

"Yes! I'll let her tell you all the details, but Lydia's to be married next month."

He pulls up short and eyes me sharply.

"She's nearly eighteen, Papa. And he's a fine man. We all like him very much." Even Eunice thinks he's a much worthier choice—as she's pointed out to me repeatedly.

"Who is he? Do I know him?"

"William Tice."

"Ah, yes."

"Then you won't be surprised to learn that he's recently returned from another successful voyage and is to be made captain of his next crew, set to sail in July."

"I know him to be an upstanding man. I'll wish them both every happiness. And so Lydia's life will be quite different from yours. Though very familiar."

"Yes."

"There is something I would say to you." His expression turns grave. He slows our pace when we come within sight of the house.

I watch him search for words.

"Thank you. For writing to me. Not only about shameful matters. But about William's unexpected death, about the new pastor's coming, and so many other things—the difficult and the ordinary. Your letters were like manna for my soul. Even when it must have been as painful for you to write as it was for me to read, the carefully chosen words and the speed with which you chose to inform me did make the news somewhat easier to accept."

"Thank God for that. I prayed fervently it would be so. But I confess I also worried for you a great deal."

He nods. "And, Annie, I'm sorry."

"For what, Papa?"

"You were right. You had reservations about Eunice. You sensed things I could not—would not—consider, and you tried to warn me." He blinks back tears. "I spoke harshly to you. In my pride, I refused to listen. And look at the pain it caused you—and all of us."

I stop and face him fully, reaching up to cup his face with my gloved hands. "You are not God. You couldn't see into the future. And you are not Eunice, so you are not responsible for her choices and actions. I forgive you freely, in the hope that this beginning of your retirement will represent a new start."

He closes his eyes and inhales deeply before I lower my hands. "That it will. I plan to visit the legal office first thing next week and request the marriage be ended." At my slightly shocked look, he adds, "Thank you for your forgiveness, Annie. I've done my best to forgive Eunice and restore some peace to my soul. However, I cannot bear to go on living with her as my wife, and I believe that type of process takes a good deal of time to complete. Now that you're married, can you understand?"

"Yes," I murmur. "I think I can." A sudden blast of wind knocks me against him. I shiver violently.

"Come inside and warm yourself." He keeps me close to his side and sweeps me along toward the front door.

We step into the entryway, and he helps me unfasten and hang my cloak before shedding his own coat. "Hello?" A hint of trepidation laces his soft call.

A rush of footsteps is followed by Adaline's head poking through the parlor doorway. She peers up with bright eyes while biting her lip.

Papa exhales sharply and kneels before her. "This can't be the tiny bit of sweetness I left behind."

She searches his eyes and clutches her hands together. "I'd like to start school next month. Mr. Wallace thinks I'm ready. Annie said we should wait to ask your permission. May I?"

He drinks in the sight of her, from her long curls tied back with red ribbons to her rosy cheeks and longer limbs. "I'm happy to hear of your eagerness to begin. By all means, you may."

"Oh, thank you!" She smiles, jumps forward, and throws her arms around his neck. Her eyes sparkle up at me where I stand behind him while he returns her hug. "And welcome home, Papa."

"It's good to be here with you."

"Papa?" another voice comes from the parlor.

He stands and fully enters the room with Adaline and me following close behind. Lydia rises from the settee where she's probably been reading to Charles. Listening to stories is his favorite thing in the world.

She turns and hurries to embrace him. "Thank God you're safely home. For good! We've long dreamed of this day." She pulls away. "Go, sit by the fire. You too, Annie. You look completely chilled. Excuse me while I make you both some tea."

"Come and meet Charles." Adaline takes Papa's big hand and tugs him toward the fire. "He's shy," she whispers. I've slipped my own hand into his other one and now give it a gentle squeeze as we move forward. He swallows hard when we step around and he sees Eunice's son for the first time.

Charles Frederick looks up from the book left open on his little lap, the illustration showing a pastoral scene with a father and son walking together along a winding path. My heart pinches tight. That is the ending of his favorite story, the book he carries from place to place and wants me to read to him every time he sees me. His wavy light brown hair and cowlick remind me of a painting of cherubs I saw in an art book. Spotting me, he offers a tiny smile before his gaze darts to Papa's powerful form and uncertainty fills his large hazel eyes.

I release Papa's hand and sit beside Charles. "Hello, sweetheart. There's someone special who would like to meet you. Like I told you before—he's come home to us. Don't be afraid." I reach out to stroke the fine wisps of hair back from his forehead. "He is strong and good. And he tells the best stories and gives the best hugs. And he will love you." I glance up at Papa, and Charles follows my gaze. "In fact, I know he already does."

I rise and gently nudge Papa to take my place before stepping across to settle myself in the old wing chair and watch them. Papa sits awkwardly, studying the rug. Finally, he points. "What do you have there?"

Charles glances at his book and then over at me. I offer a gentle nod, and he gingerly tugs the book further across his lap before letting it rest against Papa's leg. His eyes lift again, silently begging Papa to continue where Lydia left off.

Papa turns the book so he can see the words better and begins to read. "'They walked along, and the son asked, 'Father, when I grow up, will I be tall like you?' His father patted his shoulder and said, 'I can't say. Yet, I will be proud of you regardless, simply because you are my son.'" Papa's voice catches, and he clears his throat again before reading the final words. "'So they continued on until they reached home where they lived happily together for many years. The son grew tall and strong. And his father was very proud.'"

Lydia enters with the tea tray and pours some for each of us. "How nice of you to finish it for him. Though I think he has the story memorized, he never tires of hearing it." She smiles sadly and passes Papa a cup.

"Will you join us?" Papa still seems at a bit of a loss. "Tell me your news. Annie says congratulations are in order?"

Lydia sits on the other side of Charles and begins her own story. I sip my tea and watch Charles clutching his book and studying Papa intently with wide eyes. Then I turn toward the fire and remember again the night when Charles was born.

There was a sharp rap on our door after supper, and Gardner answered it to find a young neighbor boy from Orange Street there to fetch me. "Your sister's asking for you, Mrs. Coffin. She says to come immediately."

I turned to Gardner. "It must be time."

"I don't care what she thinks. I'm coming with you, even if only to see you safely there and back."

Mary looked up from her sewing. "Shall I come too?"

"Thank you," I replied, "but I know you haven't felt well today. Stay and rest. We'll be fine—I'm sure Lydia must have also sent for one of the midwives."

We bundled against the driving snow and wind, carrying our brightest lantern and following the boy, turning up the front path just after Will and Sadie. We all stepped inside, hit immediately by both the warmth of the house and the terrible sounds coming from upstairs.

"I tried to find the other midwives like Eunice ordered," Will said through chattering teeth as he unfastened his coat, "but they were both away helping other families. So I ran down to New Guinea, praying the whole way I'd find Sadie."

"Good thinking." I took off my cloak. "Go and wrap up in a quilt by the fire. You must be half frozen."

"Annie and Sadie!" Lydia came running down the steps. "I'm *so* glad you're here. Please go up and attend her. I have no idea what to do next."

"Boil some water and get us some clean towels if you got any," Sadie directed calmly. "We'll see to her now."

Gardner gave me a quick hug before stepping into the parlor where he sat and drew a clearly rattled Adaline up next to him.

I climbed the stairs at Sadie's side, and she murmured under her breath as we went. "Ain't too excited 'bout this one, Miz Annie. Every baby be a gift, but I don't like what that woman done to get herself hers. Never mind. We gonna bring it into the world with the strength God be providing us."

But when she followed me into the spare room and Eunice laid eyes on her, raw fury spilled forth. Eunice cursed and raved in between her screams of pain, making it very clear that no black person was going to lay a hand on her or her child. Remaining placid as a pond on a winter's night, Sadie managed to quickly assess how things were progressing. Then she pulled me back downstairs where she could hold a brief conference with Lydia, Gardner, and me.

"I ain't been talked down like that since leaving the master's house," she huffed. "You got to do this yourself. But I gonna stay right outside the door, praying, and you just come on out if you got some question or worry, you hear?"

"Yes." I swallowed hard. "Lydia, will you help me?" She nodded with apprehension in her eyes, and I turned to Gardner.

"I'll be here, fetching and boiling more water, tending the fires. Whatever you need."

"Pray!" I gasped.

"Always." He sent me a fortifying look and reached for a bucket.

Sadie quickly instructed Lydia and me where we huddled together on the landing. Then, holding hands for courage, my sister and I re-entered the makeshift birthing room and the onslaught of groans, screams, and foul cries.

Three hours later, in a rush of fluids, a boy slid into my waiting hands. We worked quickly to care for him and then presented him to his exhausted mother. We cleaned up as best we could and, seeing Eunice sleeping soundly, asked Sadie to check on everything.

When we descended to the first floor, we found Will sleeping peacefully under his quilt on the settee and Gardner quietly but alertly watching for us where he occupied the wing chair with Adaline asleep against his chest. Traces of hot chocolate lined two cups sitting on the side table. He studied my drained face and form with concern.

"A boy. Big and healthy," Sadie announced. "You gals done one spectacular job up there. But you ain't got the stamina for more of this. Go on to bed, Miss Lydia, and I'll wake you if she need something."

Lydia nodded gratefully and kissed her cheek and mine before reaching to take Adaline from Gardner and carry her up to their room.

"I gonna stay till morning. Don't you worry about it."

"Thank you. I couldn't have done it without Gardner's prayers and the knowledge of your presence. I feel awful about the way she spoke to you."

Her soft sigh was laced with resignation. "That just overflow of the heart, all that be. I gonna stay cause the Lord said we gotta treat others way we *want* to be treated—and cause every babe be worth caring for." She turned to Gardner. "You take her on home and see she rest real good. I know it be after curfew, but if you stopped by Watchman Pollard or anybody else, you tell them what you been doing. They usually real understanding."

The continuing gales drove us through our own door a little after one o'clock. Mary kindly left a lantern burning in the hall and a fire lit in our room. Utterly done in, we crawled into bed where Gardner held me and prayed for my family while my silent tears soaked the front of his shirt.

"Annie?"

"Hmmm?"

"What were you thinking about?" Lydia gently asks.

I turn my eyes away from the flames. "That night when—"

My voice fails. Little Charles Frederick has climbed onto Papa's lap and is curled contentedly there, hands clutching Papa's shirt front, giant tears staining his cheeks as he stares straight ahead. And Papa's face holds a mixture of tender sadness and peace with evidence of tears in his own eyes.

I smile. "I told Charles Frederick you give the best hugs. That hasn't changed."

Papa's answering smile is brief. "Where is she?" he asks Lydia.

"She was tired. Said she wanted to sleep a while and that we should wake her when you got home." Lydia tosses me a knowing look. "I apologize if I did wrong, Papa, but I thought it might be best if you met Charles Frederick on your own terms. Without any distractions."

He slowly pulls one arm away from the embrace to capture and press her hand. "Thank you, Lydia. I wouldn't have had it otherwise."

I stand and step forward to kiss each of them in turn. "Gardner will be expecting me. But I'm glad I was here to see this. I've been praying a great deal, and I won't stop. God grant you strength when you finally see her, Papa. And may He bind up our soul-wounds with more of His grace."

* * *

MID-AUGUST 1840

"It was wonderful to have you here tonight. And Susan." I stretch upward as he bends so I can kiss his cheek, a cheek more feathered with lines from the strain of these past months—but still ruggedly handsome.

My father was granted his divorce and the right to adopt Charles when Eunice refused to take him. Now Papa has brought Susan Gwinn along with Adaline and Charles for supper at our house, and we have shared a delightful evening.

"Thank you for welcoming her so warmly," he says with a smile. "I can see you have no reservations this time." He seems to appreciate this bit of private discussion before they extend their farewells and walk home.

"I always enjoyed our interactions when she was in the choir. She stopped singing completely after James died. But she confided in me tonight that now that she's come to know you, she may begin again. I do hope so—both for her sake and for yours."

It's easy to accept the fact that Papa's spoken of marrying the sweet widow a few years his junior. She carries a blend of the traits found in Mama and Nancy—and none of the traits found in Eunice. From their first formal introduction at Sunday services several weeks ago, they have seemed completely at ease with one another. "So, you will marry her?"

"A quiet ceremony, next month. I asked her last night, and she seemed very accepting of the idea. Adaline and Charles both greatly enjoy her company—and her delicious cooking." We laugh softly. "She's a good woman. And I guess that's my one weakness, Annie. I need a good woman in my life to steady me, curb my temper, and comfort me when the pain and regrets roll around again."

"I don't know that that's a weakness. I think it's simply the story of your life. And this is the next chapter. I pray it will lead to a happy ending." I wink up at him and take his hand to lead him out into our small front yard where Gardner is chasing Adaline while Charles looks on, giggling at their antics. Mary and Susan stand to the side, discussing the plentiful late blossoms in our flower boxes.

Papa watches the game with a thoughtful expression. "Gardner would make a good father, I think. Is he interested in such a role?" He glances sideways at me before his eyes dart steadily forward again.

I blush and then sigh out a laugh. "I think you have grandchildren on your mind all the time now—thanks to Lydia."

His chuckle comes deep and easy. "Yes. As the weeks pass and her condition becomes more noticeable, I confess I am eager for the arrival of the New Year—and her child."

I bite my lip. "Actually…"

He turns to look at me with a slight frown and raised brow.

"I wasn't sure when I should tell you—it's still early, and I only told Gardner last week. But, most likely, in the spring…"

I think I've melted two or three years off Papa's age with those few words. When he pulls me around to face him fully, I see a brilliant sparkle in his eyes driving away lines of fatigue, strain, and hardship.

I raise a hand to his cheek. "I spent my whole childhood wishing—living—for your happiness. I live for more than that now, yet I still rejoice at the sight of it."

"I'm not happy, Treasure. I'm *overjoyed.*"

* * *

MAY 1852

I walk along Main Street, pressing through the light rain on an overcast afternoon, eager to return to the store and help Gardner close things up after delivering the lavender water Susan sent word Papa was very much in need of. I look up just in time to keep from colliding with two men standing right in my way: one much older and vaguely familiar-looking with silver-white hair sticking out beneath his hat rim, the other handsome and perhaps my age with a dark, full beard nearly hiding his mouth.

I gasp in surprise and stop short. "Pardon me."

"Not at all," replies the bearded man. "We should be more careful while we get our bearings."

"Are you lost, then?"

"Not exactly. But my father-in-law hasn't been here for several years, and I've not been here at all. We've reservations at the Ocean House. But we're not sure how to get there. Would you be so kind as to direct us?"

"Walk with me, if you like. My destination is not far from there, and it's no trouble for me to take you."

"That's good of you, ma'am," the older man says in a crackling voice while offering me his arm. They walk on either side of me in the direction I indicate. "I'm Lemuel Shaw, and this is Herman Melville."

"Pleased to know you. I'm Phebe Ann Coffin."

"Ah. Coffin's a very common name on the Island as I well recall from previous visits."

"True. But my maiden name is Chase."

"Chase, you say?" Mr. Melville's head jerks around, and his eyes narrow. "You aren't, by any chance, related to a Mr. William Henry Chase?"

"As a matter of fact." I smile. "He's my younger brother, and a dear one."

"Well, I'll be." He chuckles under his breath.

"Do you know him, sir?"

"Yes. We met many years ago at sea."

"Where he is again, as we speak."

"I'm not surprised. He was destined for it. He has your father's blood in him, does he not?"

"He does." I eye him curiously. "Do you also know our father, sir?"

"I have not had the privilege of formally meeting Captain Chase, though I believe I saw him once, also years ago. An amazing man." He clears his throat. "Mrs. Coffin, would you be so kind as to give your brother a message for me, when he returns?"

I nod.

"Thank him again for allowing me to read his copy of the book. It proved to be an invaluable source of inspiration. Truly, how could one not be inspired in the face of such bravery?"

I mull over his words for a moment. "I'll pass on your message. And what do you do for a living now, sir? Or are you still given to the sea and only home on leave?"

"I'm a writer."

"Oh! Are you, by chance, a poet? My husband has dabbled in poetry. He's never had anything published, but I think him quite talented."

"Yes, in fact, I am something of a poet, though more recently I have devoted all my time to fiction."

"I see." I draw up at the intersection where I should turn. "Here we are, gentlemen—the Ocean House is that one there, on the right."

"Stay, if you please, madam." Mr. Melville pulls a small notebook and pencil from his pocket. After scratching out some words, he rips off the sheet and presses it into my hand. "I do so enjoy reading a good poem, Mrs. Coffin. If your husband would care to share his, he is welcome to send them to me. I promise not to be overly critical—and may even be able to introduce him to a publisher I know."

"Why, that's very kind of you, Mr. Melville. I'll tell him." I nod to each of them. "Mr. Shaw. A pleasant evening to you both."

Later, after our daughter Lydia complains of a stomachache and we send her to bed early, I tell Gardner and Mary about my interesting encounter. Gardner pauses to think hard, feeling sure that he read the name Melville somewhere recently. And he's amazed that someone besides me would want to read his drafts.

"But what do you make of the other? The book to which he referred?" I inquire as my own brow furrows.

The two of them exchange a look before Mary crosses the room and removes a shallow box from one of the bookshelves. I recognize it as the one where she keeps some of her husband's old effects. Lifting the lid and shifting the contents, she closes it again before returning to my side with a slim volume. She hands it to me, and I open the plain, old cover to read the front plate.

She sets a hand on my shoulder. "Perhaps it's time you read the tale for yourself." She quietly walks from the room.

I begin to read words I soon recognize as much more William's style than Papa's, almost as if I can hear his warm tenor voice reading the words aloud while he revises his text. And yet—the details of the story, the essence, behaviors, feelings—those are Papa's to be sure. But only Papa's name was on the title page…

Page after page, I read on. I barely notice how Gardner sits nearby through it all. Emotions flow through me—amazement, horror, and overwhelming sadness. I finally close the back cover when the clock on the mantle strikes twelve.

Gardner gently removes the book from my hands and tucks it back in the box. Then he leads me, dazed as I am, up to bed and holds me all through the rest of the night while I remain wide awake, staring into the darkness. The headaches and bad dreams, the worries over provisions and the habit of shoving away his own pain. I can now understand the logic of what I could only sense before.

CHAPTER
FOURTEEN

SEPTEMBER 1856

"Come along, my darling." I help baby Adaline to her feet after I've fastened her little shoes. "I know Grandpa will be especially happy to see our birthday girl." At my joyful tone and animated expression, she squeaks out a giggle.

My hand swallows hers, and I stoop over to help her walk toward the front door. She arrived over a month early and was so small at birth, many did not expect her to live—let alone be walking by now. I simply thank God every day that she is well. Especially this day when we will have a special supper in her honor.

I glance into the kitchen after Adaline loses her balance and plops down on her bottom beside the doorway. Her sister Lydia and Grandma Mary are hard at work, preparing pie and several other delicious dishes. They, too, are excited for the celebration to come.

"Thank you." I smile at them. "I'm hungry just thinking about it. We'll stop at Grandpa's for a little while and then help Papa close the store."

"Will you bring back a bag of flour for the larder?" Mary sighs when she looks at the productive mess. "We'll surely use the rest of what we have."

"Certainly. Anything else we need?"

"Perhaps some sugar as well," Lydia estimates. She has become a supreme baker under Mary's careful guidance. Gazing upon her now, my heart swells with pride. Just as I can't believe how quickly Adaline's first year has passed, I can barely grasp how our older daughter is really a young lady, one who will likely be collecting suitors and marrying within the next two or three years—if she's to follow in the footsteps of her mother and her aunt.

Except for having Gardner's hair, Lydia looks almost exactly like her namesake and has her temperament, too. I only wish the Tices had not moved to Albany so her aunt could see with her own eyes what a fine young lady our Lydia has become.

"Of course. I'll try to remember. You know, it's so much easier to forget things when you get old," I tease her with a wink. She rolls her eyes but then grins wide enough to show all three of her dimples.

"More truthful words were never spoken," Mary cackles lightheartedly.

I make sure Adaline is fine where she's still sitting and step to Mary's side to kiss her petal-soft cheek. "We thank God for your long life. Though your birthday was a few months ago, I think we can consider tonight a celebration of that as well. It's not every year a body turns eighty-three." Mary continues to amaze us with her vibrant zest for living, something that has only started to wane slightly over the summer. Indeed, I cannot imagine my past years of married life and child raising without her wise, dependable presence in our home.

"We'll see you later." I set the baby on her feet again, grasp her hand firmly once more, and step through the open front door into glorious early September sunshine.

We move along at a pace Adaline can manage, my mind fleetingly and somberly recalling our three sons or daughters who were not to be. Finally, I stoop down to collect her in my arms and shake off my sorrow. "Grandpa told me once that scars remind us of both pain and mercy. Thank God for you, little love. Thank God for grace to go on and somehow find joy again," I murmur before kissing her fuzzy blonde head and picking up my pace.

We come upon Papa just as he, too, approaches the big house. Adaline eagerly moves into his embrace—something that always brings the happiest light into his eyes.

I was not consistently awake to witness it, but Gardner told me later how Papa came and stayed through the night and all the next day to help with the doctor's orders, taking his turns at rubbing her little limbs and chest to help her breathe and thrive. And how, when he wasn't gently tending to her, he was kneeling at my bedside, praying.

"One year, Annie," he observes simply.

"Aye." I understand him. One year to the day since Adaline came into the world. Only a couple of months after Uncle Joseph departed it. Papa still seems hearty and strong, though Susan says he's given to sitting in the wing chair and muttering to himself of an evening, more often than not. I'm thankful she's such a suitable companion for him now that Charles has gone to sea and the big house is otherwise empty between our frequent visits. "And how have you been passing this day?"

"Mostly at the bank."

We climb the steps and enter the house.

"Your investments continue to do well, I trust?"

"Yes, and a good thing too." He leads us into the parlor. "We'll have enough to set up a bountiful store for the winter." He sits in his chair and adjusts Adaline on his knee so he can give her a somewhat muted version of his famous sleigh rides. She loves it just as much as the rest of us used to, and Papa's still strong enough to take her on a wild chase. She squeals and giggles with delight.

I smile at Susan when she slips in with a basket of knitting. She gazes back at me serenely and takes up her yarn while Papa takes up his tale—holding Adaline's attention completely as he begins the story of Barnabas McFee. That was one of Will's favorites.

Listening to the first lines, I find my mind wandering. I think of what Papa said moments ago, of his gradually increasing anxiety over having enough money and supplies, even as the number of people living under his roof has decreased. I recall how I felt while reading Papa's book. My thoughts are flooded presently, imagining him with protruding cheek bones, painfully sore limbs, and a body so parched he could not cry even if he wanted to. And certainly he must have wanted to. I want to now, feeling a fresh ache over all he suffered in my body, heart, and soul.

Shuddering and shaking away the painful images, I hear Papa groan out the suspenseful ending of the story to the best audience of all—one who's still too young to remember exactly what happened the last time she heard it.

"And the hungry bear said, 'You think you can fool me and hide the princess from becoming my tasty dinner, Mr. McFee. But I know exactly where she is!'" His voice sinks. Two of his fingers walk up her chubby leg and her darling eyes grow wider. "'She's…there!'" He grabs her belly in a gentle but furious bout of tickling and she, taken completely by surprise, giggles until she is breathless.

Papa has a good, deep laugh, and Susan grins beside me. "It's good for him. He told me, only last week, that you children and now the grandchildren—you are like the North Star, a place where he can root and focus his mind when he starts to fret." She squeezes my hand. "Thank God for that."

Amen.

"What a wonderful party it was," Lydia sighs blissfully before she continues sweeping the kitchen floor. Mid-morning sun from the window behind outlines her graceful figure.

"Thanks to your hard work." I finish nursing Adaline, fasten my blouse, and drape her sleepy form against my shoulder. "You and Grandma truly outdid yourselves."

"Yes." She grins. "She was happier than I've seen her in ages."

"Well, I think after your Grandpa Owen put Adaline in such high spirits with his wild tickling, it was simply contagious. We were all laughing to the point of tears at least once as I recall." I lean to tenderly kiss the sweaty forehead near my chin.

"But it must have worn Grandma out for her to sleep this long," Lydia observes. She concentrates on cobwebs in the far corner.

"You're right. She needs her rest, but you know how she detests sleeping the day away." I rise from my chair. "Will you come and wake her while I put your sister down for a nap?"

She nods, sets her broom aside, and follows me up the stairs. I enter our room and bend to arrange my load in her basket, and Lydia moves on down the hallway.

Satisfied that Adaline is content and securely tucked in, I turn and then jump when I nearly collide with Lydia at the threshold. "My goodness." I put my hand to my chest. "You—"

Her hand shoots out to clutch mine. "You're so warm," she speaks limply, staring vaguely across the room. "Grandma isn't."

I stretch around to pull and quietly shut our door before leading her down the hall. I peer in to see Mary's prostrate form on the narrow bed under the lovely quilts she made some years ago. Lydia won't release her hold, so I try to use my body as a shield when stepping forward to confirm the discovery. Hands indeed cool and stiff, chest still. But on Mary's face, the most lovely, serene expression I've ever seen her wear. Stretching out, I kiss each cheek in turn and murmur, "Farewell, Mother. Taste of the Lord's goodness."

Lydia now looks upon her again and quick, silent tears rain down her face. "Mama," her voice squeaks out, "what happened?"

I say nothing—only lead her back through the hall, down the stairs, to the sofa's soft cushions. I sit beside her, holding her close. "I don't know what happened, sweetheart." I smooth back her hair while she quietly weeps against my shoulder. "She was very old, you know, and she'd had a good, long life. I simply thank God that it appears she didn't suffer."

She pulls back to gape at me. "How can you thank God for anything related to death?"

"I can because I've witnessed it several times—and compared with a few of those instances, hers was likely peaceful. When the body wears out, the soul only longs to be in heaven. And Jesus longs to have each of His brothers and sisters there with him. Death is a terrible thing in a way, but it is not the end and it does not have the final victory." I say every word calmly, tenderly, confidently.

Lydia's rare outbursts of temper have always been short-lived. "How I will miss her." Her hands enfold the one resting in my lap.

"Yes, love. Each of us will grieve the parting in our own way." Tears slip from my own eyes, but I fight to keep my voice steady. "And God will comfort us through every moment of it."

"Oh, Papa!" she shudders against me. "I can't bear the thought of his hearing it. Will you tell him?"

"Of course. I wouldn't ask you to take such news—at least not alone."

"Are you afraid?"

"No. He hasn't had a spell for some time. I'll tell it gently, in an effort to lessen the shock. But I'd appreciate you praying for both of us."

She nods against my shoulder. "I will." Her voice sounds steadier. "You've always been strong, Mama. I want to be like you."

"God is strong, Lydia. Find your strength in Him. That's the only way I know."

"Has Papa's heart always been weak? I can't recall."

"No. Though Grandpa Gardner died because of heart trouble before you were born, your papa didn't show any such signs until the morning after the fire. Can…it have already been ten years now?"

"Yes. A long time ago. But I remember a little of that terrible night."

"Oh? Will you tell me?"

"I remember standing by you and Grandma, watching the whole world hot and dark and full of smoke and flames. It was rolling toward the house—and it felt horrible to try and breathe. Then, something sent it away—did the wind drive it back? Or water from somewhere? I remember Papa leaving us and running down the street, I guess to the store or to help someone. I panicked and I screamed and screamed until I couldn't anymore."

"Yes, you were hysterical, terrified he wouldn't return to us." As was I. "You inhaled so much smoke that you became hoarse and had the most wretched fit of coughing."

"And you and Grandma brought me inside and gave me a drink and tried to calm me down. And then there were explosions. I don't know where they were, but I remember the ground shaking. I must have fallen asleep sometime after that. When I woke up, in the early morning I guess, everything was gray, hazy, and smelly. So smelly! We walked to the store—where it used to be anyway—and found Papa by the ashes. There were still buildings standing farther away. But that area was totally destroyed. You and Grandma helped him home with me walking beside you and holding your skirt. He went to bed for a long time, and I tried to be quiet and good. Later, you let me go in and sleep beside him."

"I had no idea you recalled so much. You were a great comfort to him that afternoon, as every time his mind turned back to battling the fire his heart would race. He told me once, sometime later, how watching your sleeping face gave him the will to live, to rebuild, to not remain defeated. I believe God spoke to his soul through our comforting—and then infused him with mostly stable health over the past years. He's been very blessed to only have rare episodes."

"And you were so good to support him and work hard by his side when the store was being rebuilt and you knew he needed more rest. I remember that too."

I put my hand on Lydia's arm. "Are you all right now—enough for me to leave you alone? You don't need to go back into Grandma's room. I'll go and inform Mr. Halliday on my way to the store, and ask him to send his boys over with a coffin by day's end. Simply check on Adaline from time to time. And when she wakes, if I haven't returned, bring her down here and keep her distracted."

"Yes, I can do that." She sits up straight, and I see a spark of bravery light her eyes. "And I'll pray."

"It's a great help to me, Lydia." I kiss her before standing.

Once my errand is completed, I hasten to the store. Gideon, our young assistant, greets me warmly when I step around the counter.

"Where is Mr. Coffin?"

His brows dip at my tone and expression. "He's in the back, checking some inventory. Are you well, ma'am?"

"Not completely, but I shall be, by the by. I thank you. I need you to close the store today and open it tomorrow. Are you up to the task?"

"Yes, ma'am." He smiles broadly. "I've closed several times before. Opening's simply most things in reverse, isn't it?"

I nod and offer a relieved smile of my own. He's a good, dependable young man. "I can't tell you how blessed we are to have you, Gideon."

He blushes slightly. "Thank you, Mrs. Coffin."

I slip behind the curtain into the back storeroom that's considerably larger than the one we had in the old store, stepping around stacks of crates until I spot my husband. Standing somewhat behind him, I still and watch his peaceful, methodical work for a few moments—praying all the while. Then, so as not to startle him, I lightly click my heels against the floor.

His eyes come up and fill with pleasure at the sight of me. He sets down his notebook and pencil, stepping over with an easy grin. "I wondered when you'd finally arrive. It's been delightful having you here again every day."

I try to return his smile, but I can't. "Let's sit down."

He studies me for a few seconds and then takes my hand, leading us to a chair by one of the windows. He sits and pulls me onto his lap. "What's troubling you?"

I turn to face him squarely. "I must tell you something. You will tell me if it affects your heart?" I should have brought some medicine with me. I hope we still have some under the counter.

"Yes." His eyes search mine.

I hold his face between my hands. "Your mother's gone home, Gardner. Lydia found her a little while ago. I'd wager she passed sometime early this morning."

His eyes slide closed, and he breathes slowly, deeply—like Dr. Mason told him to if his heart ever started racing again. I wait, now holding his hand near my own heart. "Take your time. When you're ready, we'll leave. Gideon's already agreed to see to things here. I trust he'll be able to take care of the store until you're fit to return."

After a few minutes, his eyes open. At the invitation in them, I lean forward to kiss his lips—and then the tears that have started to fall. I slowly pull away, stand, and collect his coat and hat before helping him to his feet. He wraps his arm around my shoulders, and I slip both my arms about his waist. I lead him out the back way, acting as a crutch to steady his wobbly steps, and take us home by streets less commonly used.

We step into her room so he can see her body and kiss her good-bye. Then I help him to bed, give him some medicine, and lie beside him until he falls asleep. All through the afternoon, Lydia sits at his side. And in the evening, I place a drowsy Adaline in the crook of his arm. She sleeps between us through the night as we lie awake, whispering memories and wiping away each other's tears.

In the morning, my husband rises early to light the kitchen fire, his heartbeat steady and the familiar glow once more in his eyes.

And I fall on my knees beside the bed to worship.

CHAPTER
FIFTEEN

EARLY MARCH 1869

O range Street has long since come to be known as Captain's Row, though fewer of those captains are now living. I stride down it, like I have nearly every afternoon throughout the past winter months. An unseasonably warm breeze pushes me along.

I don't bother to knock once I arrive—only quietly step in and make my way upstairs, like I have every day for the past two weeks. I know no one will be downstairs to answer. There's only dear Susan, and she'll be upstairs with him until I come to visit and give her time for her much needed respite. My sister Adaline comes when she can, and Mrs. Wilson drops by daily to help with the house. But Papa's care, that's mostly left to Susan and me.

We were the ones who stumbled upon his hidden stores of food and supplies, packed tightly under one corner of the attic's floorboards. And we are the ones he'll consistently allow to speak to or touch him without lashing out with word or fist.

He has withered and faded in nearly every aspect, just as the years have seen the population around us and the industry of his livelihood dwindle until they are only a shadow of what they were in my infancy. Gold and oil from the earth have drawn our men away, never to return. War has divided our nation and set a people free.

I step into the bedroom through the partially open door in time to hear the end of Psalm twenty-seven read by Susan's steady voice. She looks up and offers her typical smile—one that has never faltered, a reflection of her steadfast love and faith. "Hello, Treasure," she whispers.

Kissing her cheek, I murmur, "Hello, Mother," before she makes a place for me, passes off his gnarled hand, and slips from the room. I study his face for some sense of his current condition. He's quiet—a great relief after three full days of nearly continual crying over the pain. And when he turns to look at me, I see genuine recognition—absent this month at least. His gaze moves over my silver-tinged curls to land on my eyes.

"Annie."

I'm glad I've sat down by the time he says my name. It both threatens to knock me over and refreshes my soul.

"I'm here. How are you today?"

"Tired," he grunts. "The pain is more than my old head can bear."

"I can only imagine. Has Adaline been by?"

"Aye. And she brought Nancy and George. They're beautiful children."

"That they are." I'm glad they could see him in a better state and he was willing to receive them. "What can I do for you today, Papa? Have you had enough to drink?"

"Sing for me, Annie."

I have sung for him every day, but I know that on the recent ones he probably had no real awareness of it. "What would you like to hear?"

"Anything at all. Your voice is as lovely as ever."

"Perhaps one about our Rock?"

He nods slightly and relaxes, his head sinking further back against the pillows while I begin.

My hope is built on nothing less than Jesus' blood
and righteousness.
I dare not trust the sweetest frame, but wholly trust in Jesus'
Name.
When darkness seems to hide His face, I rest on His
unchanging grace.
In every high and stormy gale, my anchor holds within
the veil.
His oath, His covenant, His blood, support me in the
whelming flood.
When all around my soul gives way, He then is all my
Hope and Stay.
On Christ the solid Rock I stand,
All other ground is sinking sand; all other ground is
sinking sand.

When I finish, he asks, "Did I ever thank you for sending the music box with Mr. Ripley?"

I shake my head, my eyes filling at the thought that he remembers such a small, long-ago detail so clearly and brings it up now.

"All that long voyage—and especially after the news of Nancy's passing—I held it near me every night. I rarely wound the key. I could still hear your voice at my side. 'Twas the picture that comforted me most."

"I'm glad." I smile and blink back more tears. I've often missed having the gift in my possession but have never regretted sending it with him, knowing it would likely be broken or lost at sea.

"How is Gardner?"

Delight fills my heart at the inquiry. "He fares well, thank you. If you'd like to see him, I'll send him over this evening."

"Do. I guess I haven't seen him in some time?"

"No," I reply in my lowest tone. "You've been out of sorts recently."

"I'm sorry for that." He reaches up to rub his forehead. "Tell me, what are Lydia and Adaline doing now?"

My happiness begins to fade when I realize, with his next questions, that he's referring to my sisters, imagining them young again, perhaps running through the house or eating muffins in the kitchen. He seems once more completely unaware of my own children he's known and loved so well before he began to change. It was sweet to have him come back for a few moments. A lump forms in my throat.

He grips my hand more firmly and begins to mumble about water and provisions, harpoons and sails. I hum and pray, often reaching out to stroke his brow and cheek. The hours pass, and Susan returns to take up her post once more.

I know I must be going, but somehow my heart can't bear the thought of leaving today. When I stand and lean to kiss him, he stirs and looks at me again, even more lucidly than before.

"Promise me, Annie."

"What, Papa?"

"That you'll bury me beside your mama." Tears spill down his cheeks.

"I promise." I kiss him once more and brush at his tears. "I'll see you tomorrow. Rest well. I love you."

He nods and swallows, watching me back away and turn for the door.

In the morning, Susan sends a young messenger to the store. He repeats her words a bit breathlessly after running the whole way. "Don't rush yourself today. You're welcome to come and help with the preparations. But he's no longer in need of comforting."

Some moments later, my hands clutch the edge of the faded blue curtain hanging over the storage room window while I stare into the sunlight. Gathering tears create tiny rainbows in the corners of my vision.

Gardner slips up behind me and wraps his arms around my waist.

A dam breaks, and my cheeks are soon soaked. I choke out a request. "Recite it again. The end of the piece you penned last month."

His breath tickles my temple, and his words meet my ear, forming a shelter for my soul.

> *Say this of me when e'er I'm gone:*
> *There are no tears where he has flown—*
> *Or only tears of joys yet known*
> *When life slays death in Heaven's dawn.*

* * *

Gardner's sudden movement jolts me awake, and I lift my face to observe him in the gray morning light—his brow deeply furrowed and lips in a pout. I kiss them. "Love, wake up."

He calms, breathes deeper, and opens troubled eyes.

"Tell me."

"A strange dream." His slight voice has worn further with age, but I can still easily make out the words in the complete stillness of the dawn. "I saw your father and mine. They were in a boat, away off shore, calling to me. They were young again, handsome and strong. I was perhaps ten or so. I called back to them, telling them to wait for me, but when I dove into the water, they rowed away. I couldn't keep their pace, and I had to turn back. When I reached land again, right before you woke me, I turned and looked to the sea once more. The boat was gone."

"A dream." I find myself whispering replies to him more frequently, especially when we are alone. "That's all. And a blessing that you could see them as they once were." I kiss him again, this time more deeply. And this time he returns the gesture.

He pulls back to study me after feeling my tears upon his face.

"I wish I could move on." I squeeze my eyes shut and press my forehead against his shoulder. "I trust he's with Jesus now. And he was suffering so greatly. But I miss him dreadfully. It will get easier, won't it?"

"Yes." Experience bleeds from that single word—the only reason I find true comfort in it. "Be patient with yourself, Annie. We only buried him a week ago. Day by day, you're finding the way forward."

"Why is it that you dreamed of him but I haven't?"

"I don't know, but I'm glad. I think you slept more deeply last night than you did in the previous seven combined." He brushes at my slackening tears.

His crooked smile warms my heart. I sit up. "You know, I think you're right. In fact, I feel hungrier than I have in all that time. I'm going to make us an extra hearty breakfast before church. How does that sound?"

"What's it to be?"

"Biscuits and gravy. And poached eggs."

"My favorite." He sighs with glee, rising up and pulling me back for another kiss.

I laugh when he finally releases me. "If you keep me here all day, you'll miss breakfast and supper both."

His grin turns utterly mischievous. "I won't mind."

"Oh, no you don't!" I gasp, wiggling out of his reach.

He sinks back against his pillow and watches me change into my everyday clothes for cooking. My light blue linen dress—his favorite—hangs nearby, ready to be worn to worship.

"When you get up in a little while, would you wake Adaline? She must be growing again. Have you seen how she's been eating lately? I'm sure she won't want to miss the feast."

"I'd be happy to. Waking her is about as fun as waking a hibernating bear." He grimaces before unleashing his raspy chuckle.

I can't help but join him while trying, very much in vain, to reply grimly, "Thirteen-year-old girls and bears share some common traits."

"Lydia wasn't quite this moody, was she?" He studies me again, his smile fading while I gather and tie back the front strands of my hair. "Every day, Annie, you make the second half of life sweeter than the first."

My grin softens. "Gardner, I love you. Have I ever told you?"

"Only every day since I brought you home. And even many days before that."

"It's truer each time, if that's possible."

"Aye. For me as well. You're more beautiful every time I say it too."

His compliments still make me blush. "See you downstairs."

I'm about to cut butter into the flour when I look out through the kitchen window and spy a robin hopping across the ground.

He is a bright, lovely specimen—the first I've seen on this cusp of spring. I let my hands rest and simply watch him for a moment. Standing there, the sun rising before my eyes while I silently cheer his progress in capturing his own breakfast, I am filled with goodness. It's a new morning full of fresh mercies. It will get easier. It must.

The china in the cabinet rattles when a thud sounds above my head. My eyes fly upward. Oh, no. Is Adaline sleepwalking again? She has a tendency to break things or stub her toes, so I turn and rush up the stairs though I'm sure Gardner will reach her first.

But as I pass our room—the door still open—I see the source of the noise. He's lying on the floor near the bed. And he's gripping his chest. I dash to his side and cradle his head in my lap. My hand reaches back for the bottle of medicine we keep on his end table, but it's not there.

"Adaline!" I cry.

Her sleepy but curious face appears in our doorway.

"Get Papa's medicine. I think there's another bottle in the pantry."

I'm vaguely aware of her stumbling footsteps when she runs to obey.

"Annie." His face contorts, and he gasps.

I take his free hand in my own. "Hold on. She'll be back soon."

"No. It's not the same this time." He pants, and his face continues to twist in pain.

"Your—it's not only racing?"

He nods. Sweat beads on his forehead.

"Gardner?" My voice wavers.

"Annie, promise me. When I leave you, you won't be like Susan. You won't stop singing. Promise me you'll keep singing every day for the rest of your life."

The edges of his lips turn blue, tempting me to panic. I swallow hard. "I will. If you promise to use your new voice to sing joyfully until I join you."

We speak with our eyes. *Done.*

Now Adaline is beside us, pushing the bottle into my hand with a trembling one of her own. When he shakes his head slightly, I set it to the side.

"Adaline." His voice is faint. "I love you. Tell your sister I love her."

"Yes, Papa. We love you." She clutches his other hand.

His gaze slides back up to meet mine again. He wheezes a few more breathes. Then I lay our entwined hands on his chest and find it completely still.

The sunlight that was filling the kitchen before now seeps into this room, bathing us. Adaline calls to Gardner and cries. I close my eyes and let my own tears fall. When the light hits my eyelids, I see a fleeting, shadowy image of three young men in a boat, rowing together toward the brilliant horizon.

* * *

I keep my promise. Starting the next day, I continue to sing.

We lay his casket in the ground as a heavy mist rolls in. Gideon, my beloved son-in-law these past ten years, shelters Adaline under one arm and a heavily-expectant Lydia under the other, while three-year-old Judah clings to his mother's skirt.

I stand opposite them, all of us surrounded by a faithful band of relatives, patrons, and church friends. At a cue from the pastor, I begin to sing the words of a newer song Gardner loved so dearly.

Abide with me; fast falls the eventide;
The darkness deepens; Lord with me abide.
When other helpers fail and comforts flee,
Help of the helpless, O abide with me.
I fear no foe, with Thee at hand to bless;

Ills have no weight, and tears no bitterness.
Where is death's sting? Where, grave, thy victory?
I triumph still, if Thou abide with me.
Hold Thou Thy cross before my closing eyes;
Shine through the gloom and point me to the skies.
Heaven's morning breaks, and earth's vain shadows flee;
In life, in death, O Lord, abide with me.

In the singing of it, a strange and wonderful sensation comes over me. A hand rests on my back—warm, strong, sure. I can't say how or where, but it seems I've felt it there before. And I hear Papa's voice behind me and from long ago whispering, "God is your Rock and true Protector. He is the one you must cling to." The voice fades. But the feeling of the mighty hand remains.

* * *

The clock chimes noon a few days later, and I set down my pen and close the ledger I've been balancing. I note the small assortment of midday patrons moving about the shelves, barrels, and bins, and my grandson Judah where he sits playing near my feet. "Will you be all right if I leave now?" I call softly across the way.

Gideon looks up from where he's writing out a list at the other end of the counter. "Certainly. Business has been steady but not overwhelming. If you wouldn't mind taking Judah home, however, that would help me remain more focused on the customers' needs."

"Happy to do so. I have something else to do before I return him to Lydia's care and check in on her. Was she still having much extra discomfort when you left this morning?"

"Yes." His brows lower with anxiety. He steps nearer. "I confess I've tried to stay busy this morning simply to keep from worrying so much."

"Sometimes," I smile sadly, "keeping busy is the only way we can make ourselves function."

He sets a hand on my arm. "You are well?" His kind eyes study my face. "I declare, between your recent grief, Adaline's increased withdrawnness, and Lydia being so near to the birthing, I feel the pull to be anxious at nearly every turn."

I work to bundle first myself and then Judah. "Well, then, let me ease your mind. I will be well. I am finding my way daily, just as Gardner said I would. And so is Adaline. She simply needs time and comforting in the moments she's ready to receive it. It was a great shock for her, you know. It was hard enough for me to have Papa pulled away time and again, never knowing with complete certainty that he would return to us safely. I can only imagine how it would have wounded me if I had lost him at her age."

"And Lydia is surely in good hands whether we are by her side or not." He finishes my pithy remarks like a mind reader.

"God bless you, Gideon—you have come to know me well," I laugh—the first time I've really felt like laughing since Sunday morning.

He grins. "He has blessed me, Mother." His smile falters, and he swallows. "Knowing you and being drawn first into your business and then your family was His way of restoring the ravages of my childhood." He squeezes my shoulder and bends to pat Judah's head. "Be good for Grammie."

"I'll spend as long as I can with Lydia, but then I want to get home. It's been important for me to be there—for the house to be occupied—when Adaline returns."

"I understand. Farewell."

We walk along the street, Judah's hand gripping mine. "Going home, Grammie?"

"First we're going to Grandma Susan's, dearest. She asked me to come today and see to something. Won't it be nice to visit the big old house?"

He nods. He's fascinated with the roof-walk and so many rooms to explore.

"Perhaps she'll have something delicious to eat." She always does.

"Grammie, please sing."

"All right." Every day I'm with Judah helps me keep my promise.

I think to recall all the words and then quietly start in on a melody I know he's fond of. To my delight, he begins to vocalize the tune with me.

I know that my Redeemer lives; what comfort this sweet
sentence gives!
He lives, He lives, who once was dead; He lives, my ever
living Head.
He lives to silence all my fears, He lives to wipe away
my tears,
He lives to calm my troubled heart, He lives all blessings
to impart.
He lives and grants me daily breath; He lives, and I shall
conquer death:
He lives my mansion to prepare; He lives to bring me
safely there.

"You have a wonderful ear for pitches," I sigh with delight when the song is completed. "Maybe one day you'll sing in the choir."

"Like you, Grammie?"

"Yes." We've reach the front door, and I issue a firm knock. Susan's hearing has faded a bit, though I'm not sure she's noticed.

"Hello, my dear." Her face brightens when she sees me—and even more when she looks down to spot Judah. "Oh, what a delight! Two dears when I only expected one."

"We're not deers. We're Judah and Grammie!" He issues a darling scowl.

Susan laughs and shakes her head. Then she bends and Judah jumps forward to eagerly accept her hug.

"Grammie said you have treats."

She straightens and winks at me. "Don't I always?" She leads us into the kitchen and settles Judah at the table with some milk and cookies. "Enjoy those, chew slowly, and stay right there. I'll be back soon." She motions for me to follow her. Curious, I soon discover her intended destination: the study. I haven't been in here for ages.

The furnishings are a bit faded. But she's kept everything clean and comfortable, as if he could return from a voyage tomorrow and sit down to business.

My eyes settle on an old, well-worn box upon the desk. It's about as large as one of our closed ledgers and perhaps eight inches deep. The wood is scratched in places. The hinges and latch are tarnished.

"I hope it's not too soon to bring this to your attention. But I was going through some of Owen's things last week, and I found this at the bottom of his old chest in the spare room. I remember—before his decline—how he sometimes sat in here, removing and then replacing the contents. I haven't opened it. I thought, perhaps, that should be up to you. I hope I've done right?"

"Yes, I'm sure that's fine." I wonder what it contains. "We

already found the main legal effects in his desk or at the bank, didn't we?"

"As far as I know. Perhaps you'd like to sit awhile and go through it. Then you can decide if it's anything you want to take with you. I'll keep Judah busy. Take all the time you need."

I swallow and nod.

She offers a tender smile before stepping out and pulling the door shut.

I circle the desk and pull out his old chair. The wood and leather creak when I sit, worn as it is after many years of bearing his large frame. I stare at the box for a moment before running a hand over the surface. Undoing the latch, I lift the lid and let it swing all the way back to rest on the desktop.

I'm not sure what I was expecting to find, but at the sight of the contents, my eyes well. There is a bundle to the side, the aged cloth still instantly recognizable. I lift it and loosen the material to reveal the gift I thought forever lost. The gold edges have grown dull, one side bears a slight crack, and the picture is somewhat faded. But the details from the brushstrokes are still distinct.

When I turn the key, the old tune floats out. Though slightly tinnier than I recall, it is a testimony to the fine craftsmanship of the piece and how much he must have paid for it in the first place.

"I'm still clinging to that Rock, Papa," I whisper toward the ceiling. "I haven't forgotten."

I return to the task at hand and lift out the two neat stacks of documents that remain. The taller stack reveals a collection of Mama's letters, and a few letters from Nancy including the one I kept safe until his return. The second stack contains copies of court papers legalizing the divorce and Charles' adoption, both signed by a Judge L. Shaw. Further down are several small, faded pieces of paper, the uneven lines scribbled in graphite so faint they are nearly invisible. I study the sheets for a moment, wondering at what notes they originally contained and why he kept them.

And at the bottom, I find some letters of my own, including the most painful one of my life. The last paper in the stack, however, is the one that makes my heart skip.

There is no envelope to enclose it—only his name in my sweet schoolgirl script centered across the back. When I unfold it, the paper falls open almost automatically—the creases gone, the three sections of the page nearly falling apart, the ink smudged and faded in places from frequent handling with evidence of emotion evoked in watermarks at the bottom. He never said a word about it.

I lean back in the chair and read the theme I haven't seen in nearly forty years.

What My Family Means to Me
By Phebe Ann Chase

There are five people in my family. My father is often gone away for a long time. He's married to Nancy. She's not our real mother but she takes good care of Lyddie, Will, and me, just as if she were.

Mr. Wallace taught us about proof and evidence in our science lessons. He said it's very important to show proof if we want to say something is true or real. He said that applies to everything, even things we can't see. Like gravity. I wonder if that applies to God too. Do *we have to prove Him? If we do, I can prove Him. That's what my family is, proof of God.*

God is very creative. He made us all different but we still fit together well. God is faithful and caring. He brought Nancy to join us, when we needed her most. And I think she needed us too. God is a good provider. He makes Papa strong and successful at his work so we have all the things we need. God is a great healer. We pray and I sing hymns for Papa, and those things help him sleep when his head hurts so much. God is love. Papa comes home safely to us and holds me close until my heart is so full the love is spilling all over my insides.

I heard a lot about God in church. But I see Him at home in the eyes and hearts of my family.

I reverently fold the page back on itself and slip it carefully into my pocket. Some moments later, when the other items have been replaced and the lid closed, I wipe my eyes and return to the kitchen. Susan looks up at me over Judah's head where he stands drawing squiggly lines in the fog left by his breath on the bottom corner of a windowpane.

She steps near. "Is everything all right?"

I nod and offer a small smile. "Thank you, Mother. This afternoon I have been supremely blessed." I lower my voice. "I left the box on the desk. I'll come back one day soon and take it home. But for today, I'm only ready to carry one precious piece."

"As you wish, Annie. Whenever you're ready. I won't move it an inch."

I embrace her, murmuring my love. Then I call softly to Judah, "It's time to go home and see Mama."

"Mama!" He jumps up and down.

Susan bundles him while I fasten my cloak.

We walk back up the street again, blanketed in the golden light of a lower sun.

"Grammie, tell a story."

My mind flies back through memories just glimpsed. "Did Grandpa Owen ever tell you about the mighty Crook-Jaw and the enchanting mermaid who lived in his belly?"

He shakes his head and eyes me with anticipation.

"Then I think it's time I carry on the tradition." I wink. "Long, long ago, Ichabod Paddock said good-bye to his beautiful wife and set out with his mates in search of the toughest old whale in these waters…"

* * *

Judah's little sister finally arrives three days later, in the early afternoon, after I've helped Lydia through one of the easiest labors I've ever witnessed. The babe is ruddy, crowned with a swath of her father's dark red hair and staring out at the world with the eyes of both my mother and hers.

I place her swaddled form in Lydia's arms and wash my hands thoroughly in the basin while staring off at nothing in particular.

"What are you thinking about?" comes Lydia's weary voice.

"How I miss Sadie. Like I did the night Judah was born. Wasn't anybody in the world like her." I sigh. "Well, I shall go down and ask Adaline to run to the store and tell Gideon the good news. He must be pacing a hole in the floorboards." We share a smile. "Will you be all right?"

"Yes."

I return a bit later, having dispatched Adaline to speedily obey so she can get back and meet her niece. I lead a suddenly shy Judah by the hand and help him climb up on the edge of the bed so he can get a good look at his sister.

"Here she is, Judah."

"What's her name, Grammie?" His wide blue eyes gaze up expectantly.

"I don't know." Turning, I inquire, "Would you rather wait for Gideon?"

"No, it's fine. We've talked about it a great deal this past week. This is Mary Ann Felicity."

I gasp and then laugh with delight. "What a beautiful name—but quite a mouthful for such a tiny bit of love."

Lydia kisses Mary Ann's rosebud lips and smiles up at me. "We agree. We've already planned to call her something shorter and dearer at home."

POSTLUDE

In March of 1869, the same year the last Nantucket whaling ship sailed from the Island, Owen Chase and Gardner Coffin passed away within ten days of each other.

Susan Coffin Gwinn Chase lived for another twelve years.

Phebe Ann Chase Coffin remained on the Island and passed away in 1904. She never remarried.

NOTE TO THE READER

As I researched background information and began to write *The Voice of Melody*, some of my questions remained unanswered. What were the occupations of Peggy's father and Phebe's father-in-law, husband, and son-in-law? Where on the Island did Peggy grow up? Exactly how and when did Owen meet each of his four wives? Did any relatives of the *Essex* crew members know each other before the related tragedy? And, if they did, how closely were they acquainted? How did Matthew and Nancy's child die? Who was the father of Charles Frederick? What did Peggy and Phebe look like? Gaps in information available to me opened the door for my imaginative responses.

Yet I still wanted to be true to known facts as much as possible. This is why nearly all the names of historical characters have been included in their unaltered form and I generally followed dates and key life events as they have been recorded. There are, however, a few points where I chose to diverge from the facts.

· Peggy was actually the youngest of four sisters, and her third sister (Lydia) married Owen's older brother, William Chase. I made changes to Peggy's family to simplify already complex and extensive family relationships a bit.

· Though I don't know George Gardner's true occupation, I know he was probably never a keeper of the Great Point Light. (The other facts mentioned, including the two fires and light's keeping at that time by a man named Caleb Cushman, are accurate to the best of my knowledge.) I wanted to describe another part of geography and life on the Island, so I chose to diverge thusly.

- Nancy Joy Chase was not a Quaker but a member of the Congregational Church from an early age. Matthew (who had been raised among the Friends) was disowned when he chose to marry Nancy (what the Friends would call leaving on the grounds of "marrying out"). I chose to portray this differently so that I could conjure a special, earlier connection between Peggy and Nancy while including a snapshot of Quaker worship.

- Gardner and Mary Coffin had (as many as) eleven children and more than one of them died young. While I decided to leave out most of the siblings, comments about their daughter Mary dying (not long after she married to a husband who did not long outlive her) are true.

- William and Elizabeth Coffin eventually had five children, the last one being born shortly after William's death. For the sake of simplicity, I decided to only mention their first two daughters.

- Phebe's daughter Lydia was indeed married and had a son and daughter; however, her husband's name was William and her daughter (Anna) was born three years before her son (Francis)—Francis being born more than half a year before the deaths of Owen and Gardner. I opted for Gideon because I already had several Williams to deal with, and I changed the order of the children's genders as well as their names for the sake of plot continuity.

- A final historical divergence: I read information from a variety of sources about the development of music box technology. Though boxes produced in the early 1800's were generally different in terms of size, style, and materials compared with Owen's (fictional) gift to Annie, there still seemed to be a smattering of experimental and creative forms being produced. Therefore, I imagined something different.

Beyond these willful changes, if I unknowingly portrayed some documented detail inaccurately, I meant no offense by it and ask that the reader accept this retelling as a work of fact-based fiction.

On a couple of points, several theories abound. One is about how and when Owen Chase received news of Nancy's death and Eunice's infidelity. We don't know for a fact that it was Captain Joy who delivered news of the second event, but it seemed as likely a possibility as any, so I went with it. Likewise, while scholars are fairly uniform in believing Owen had help in writing his account of the *Essex* tragedy, more than one ghost writer has been suggested. I decided to go with William Coffin, Jr. because that theory seemed reasonable to me—and because I really liked descriptions of the historical figure, especially of his disposition.

In portraying Quakers as I did, I only intended to touch on the ramifications of dogmatism and legalism in any denomination or group while showing how Quakerism was evolving during that period of U.S. history. Members of every denomination and religious group, human as we are, have put forth admirable accomplishments and regrettable actions. I respect my Quaker brothers and sisters and believe that the practices of seeking simplicity and listening more in worship—and in all of life—are great things.

I also wanted to touch on the ethnic diversity of historic Nantucket—and how many Caucasian Islanders supported abolition and equal rights for African Americans while still encouraging a segregated environment. Language used in this story reflects terms used at that time. While I don't know that the Chase family was so open to interactions with members of the New Guinea community, I imagine that they were in an effort to show a variety of attitudes among Islanders. Richard Peterson and his wife were historical characters and many details included about Mr. Peterson are true. Sadie and her family are figments of my imagination, created to show a deeper connection between Owen Chase and one of the men who died in his boat and included to explore the issue of prejudice. As such, while distinguishing between the ethnic groups, I wanted to display my love for people from many different backgrounds. I am not an expert on African-American English, but I did my utmost to create the speech of Sadie's family members according to research and observation. Please accept my attempt as one done with the best intentions.

Above all, I trust that the reader will sense my respect for the real people portrayed in this novel, the people of Nantucket in general, and all the people of the past and present who have had to survive and love each other despite long physical separations and hard life circumstances.

Should the reader care to know more about related details of this story as well as Nantucket, Quakerism, and the whaling industry, I recommend the following resources which aided me in spinning this yarn:

Leviathan: The History of Whaling in America (Eric Jay Dolin)

The Quaker Family in Colonial America (J. William Frost)

The Quakers in America (Thomas D. Hamm)

Stove by a Whale: Owen Chase and the Essex (Thomas Farel Heffernan)

The Loss of the Ship Essex, Sunk by a Whale: First-Person Accounts (Thomas Nickerson, Owen Chase, et al)

Away Off Shore: Nantucket Island and Its People, 1602-1890 (Nathaniel Philbrick)

In the Heart of the Sea (Nathaniel Philbrick)

Likewise, current and back issues of *Historic Nantucket* and other resources available at www.nha.org are insightful. In particular, pictures and rubbings of epitaphs on the tombstones for the following characters on that same website are particularly meaningful to see: Mary J. Coffin, Gardner Coffin (Phebe's husband), Owen Chase, Peggy Chase, Nancy Chase, and Elizabeth B. and Joseph L. Chase (Joseph and Winifred's children).

The archives of the Nantucket Historical Association contain a fascinating array of letters, maps, and other documents. While researching the facts related to this story, I was thrilled to be able to see a copy of pages from the Paddack letter (which really was publicly read to a crowd of shocked townsfolk). Viewing the spidery script of the document nearly 200 years later and thinking of the heartache its incomplete, premature report caused filled me with a sense of both wonder and sadness. Likewise, finding a town map surveyed by Henry

F. Walling in 1858 and spotting the names of several of my characters on the map (with a magnifying glass!) helped me have a better sense of space and direction as I envisioned them all walking from place to place in town. (See map and images of the letter on the following pages).

Many tales have one main hero and one main villain. In this complicated thing called life, however, defining people in such black and white terms is not always so easy—nor so wise. The reader may walk away from this story seeing multiple heroes and villains as well as something of both the hero and the villain in nearly every character, just as the story of every person contains evidence of the life-long struggle between good and evil. In the end, I would say there is only one true Hero in my tale. That, too, is a reflection of life.

KAYLENE POWELL

Map of the Town of Nantucket, 1858

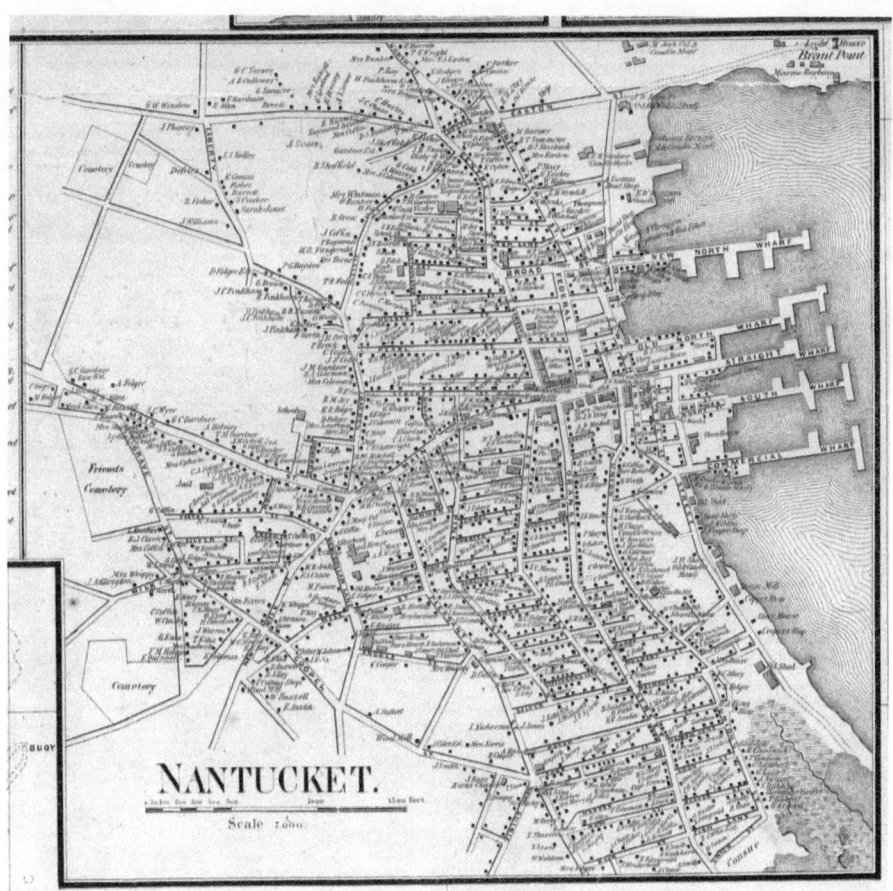

Courtesy of the Nantucket Historical Association, MS1000–rolled30

Early glass plate negative images of Captain Paddack's original letter, penned 15 February 1821

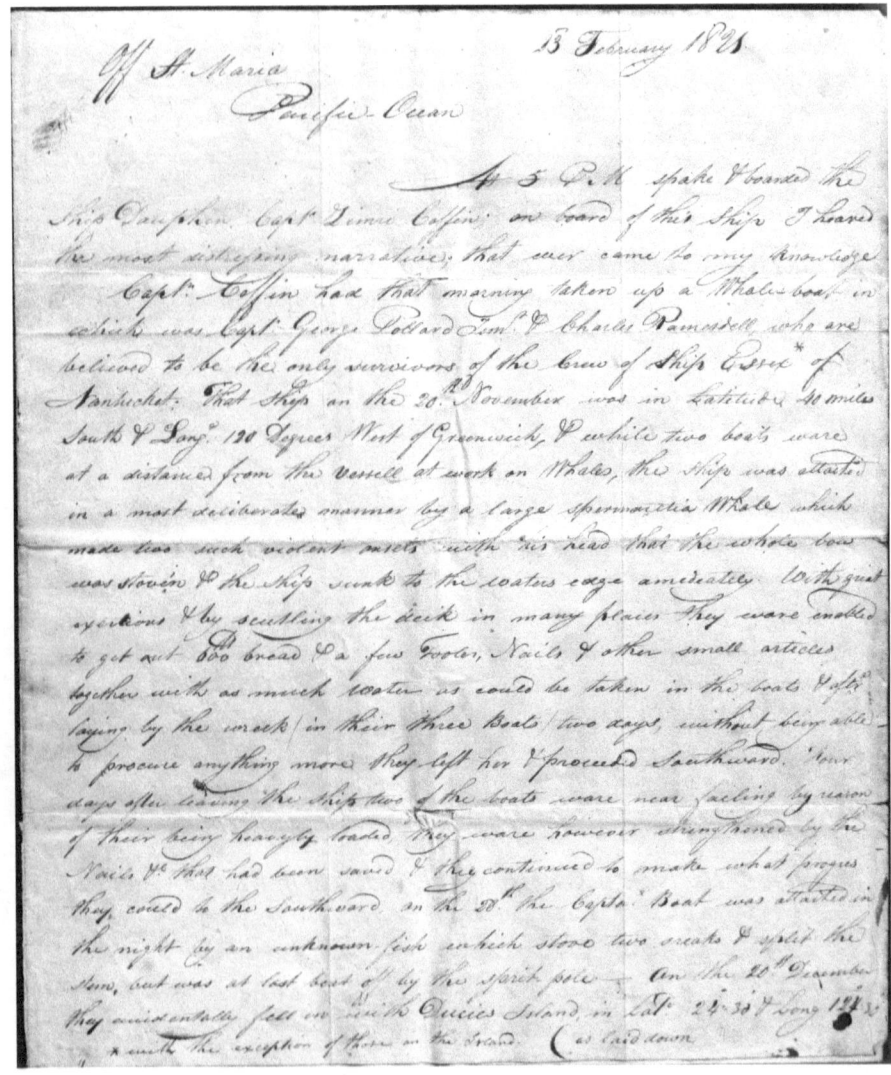

Courtesy of the Nantucket Historical Association, GPN3253

on this Island the whole Ship's company landed, hauled the boats onto the beach & remained there, & remained Six days. The water they obtained at this Island was very brackish & was found to spring up through a rock, at near low water mark. A few fowl & Fish was the only sustinance that could be got & not sufficient to subsist a further part of their number. Three of their number chose to remain on the Island & the others (Seventeen) again took to the Boats with the hopes of being able to reach Easter Island, but by adverse winds & being too much exhausted to make exertions they were drove far South of it.

January 10th 1821. Mathew P Joy (second officer) Died through debility & exertions & his corps was committed to the Ocean. The 12th being in Latitude 31.0 & Longitude about 117.00 the first officer's Boat was separated from the others in the night. The 14th the provisions of the second officers Boat was entirely expended, the 20th one of their crew (a black man) died & became food for the remainder. 28th the provisions being all gone in the Capt's Boat, they were glad to partake of this wretched fare with the other crew. The 23 another (colored man) died in the 3 boat & was disposed of in the same way. 27th another died in the same bo[at] and in the night [...] them in Lat. 35.00 [...] consumed the last [...] remained with her [...] casting Lots to see [...] of the others. the [...] resignation submitt[ed] [...] of God. The 11 [...] neath the boat & [...]

The Officers & Crew at the time of the Shipwreck

George Pollard Senr Master
Owen Chase   1st Officer
Mathew P Joy   2d do
Oard Hendricks   3d & 4th do
Thos Chaplin   }
Benjn Lawrence
Charles Ramsdell
Brizillia Ray
Owen Coffin
Isaac Cole
Thomas Nickerson
Joseph West
Wm Wright
Seth Weeks, & Six Blacks
          In all 20

[...] who it is neccessary to add has administered [...] in the power to their wants

NB Capt Pollard though very low when first taken up has immediately revived I regret to say that young Ramsdell has appeared to fail since taken up

ACKNOWLEDGMENTS

"The Lord and I did it between us."

~JOSEPH SCRIVEN, AFTER COMPOSING THE LYRICS FOR
WHAT A FRIEND WE HAVE IN JESUS

So many people have helped me along this journey.

Sandra Wendel and Lisa Pelto, I could not have asked for better shepherds in this publishing process. You are both wonderful. Thanks for keeping me from the wolves on more than one occasion! Olivia Nixon and Ellie Godwin, thank you for your intense effort in the home stretch to transform my manuscript into a beautifully designed book and help me get off on the right foot in marketing it. You are each uniquely and incredibly gifted in performing your vital roles at Concierge Marketing.

Elizabeth Oldham, the Research Associate in the Nantucket Historical Association's Research Library and a professional copy editor, provided invaluable feedback and helped me catch some critical historical inaccuracies in my early manuscript. If any mistakes great or small remain, apart from the details I knowingly changed as mentioned in my notes, the blame should land on me and not on her. Thank you, Libby, for your invaluable assistance.

The Nantucket Historical Association's archives and resources provided a wealth of useful information. Thanks again to the staff for permission to quote parts of the "Paddack Letter."

Numerous authors and scholars aided my research process with their valuable published materials. I am thankful for all I gleaned from them. I also appreciate the cast and crew of *In the Heart of the Sea*—the cinematic production which first introduced this powerful story to me.

Megan DiMaria shared valuable feedback as a content editor. Thank you, Megan. Additional thanks to Nadine Brandes and Cecil Murphey, and to the countless other authors who have inspired me over the years.

My brothers and sisters in the Wordsowers Writers Group have provided me with a tremendous sense of community. Special thanks to Kat and Jeanie for believing in me and encouraging me in both writing and life. And thanks to Lee and Pebbles for your techie help with my annoying manuscript issues.

To my former supervisor, Dr. Amy Nejezchleb: thanks for being my friend and encouraging me as a writer. And to my CAS colleagues—Tony Jasnowski, Gloria Lessmann, and Dean Clif Mason: thank you for inspiring me and believing in my writing potential.

Thanks to those who were willing to read manuscript drafts including Linda Boelter, Lynette Ingram, Lois Imig, Bai Yingjie, Mia Pan, Mechelle Vestal, Jordan Concannon, Paulette Adjovi, Laurie Cordray, Kathy Wheeldon, and Rick Johnson—thank you all for providing general feedback and cheering me on. I also appreciate the prayers and encouraging words of Jayne Heimer, Carrie Downs, and Allie O'Connor. Judy Kaczor, Eddie Chen, Michelle Hepfner, Carol Baker, and

Fanny Schio: a thousand thanks for helping me catch many typos and more closely analyze my characters and plot.

Tutu, thanks for joining me on this adventure and for the love and support you've provided throughout my life.

My middle school English teacher, Mrs. Robin Chestnut, saw the writer's soul in me and breathed life into it when I felt otherwise talentless. Grad school professors Dr. Alan Seaman and Dr. Cheri Pierson also gave me ample instruction and opportunities in refining my grammar and written communication skills. God bless each of you. Good teachers dream for *and* with us.

I went to see *In the Heart of the Sea* with my friend Becky Arnold on a whim. And soon afterward I told her, "I wonder about the rest of Phebe's story. I think I need to write it." She encouraged me to do so, and she listened to me read each part of my draft aloud so I could catch more mistakes. Thank you, Becky, for using the gifts of support and encouragement God has richly poured into your heart.

Nathan, thanks for being the best brother in the whole world. Jodi, I thank God for you. Emma, Grace, and Elijah, I would not be the storyteller I am without each of you. I love you with all my heart.

Thanks, Mom, for spurring me on toward love and good deeds every day of my life. And to Dad: for always showing me the meaning of humility and trust…and how to appreciate the beauty of well-written words.

My Rock, thank You for filling me with stories of Your goodness, and for teaching me how to cling (Psalm 18:16-19, 28-32).

ABOUT THE AUTHOR

Kaylene Powell is an instructor of English and English as a Second Language at Bellevue University near Omaha, Nebraska. She also writes curriculum, non-fiction, fiction, essays, and poetry, and she uses her love of writing as a primary mode of worship.

A fan of history, old movies, harp music, calligraphy, guinea pigs, sunshine, pomegranates, and dark chocolate, she is a Midwesterner through and through. *The Voice of Melody* is her first novel.

Check out her webpage and blog: www.kaylenepowell.com.